THE
SILVER
CORD

LOST SOULS BOOK TWO

GABRIEL LEA

THE COMMON THREAD

Suffering has many faces, but within the span of a single life, you will know but a few of them. The rest will remain strangers to you. Strangers that drift by you on the street each day, unnoticed, nameless and soon forgotten. But then every so often on life's long journey, you'll see a face that makes you pause, that draws you in. It looks you right in the eye, gives a knowing nod and demands your recognition. In those rare moments, it's as though you're caught in a mirror. You know that face as well as your own because you've already traced the silent words of grief written all over it. And suddenly, there is one less stranger in the world.

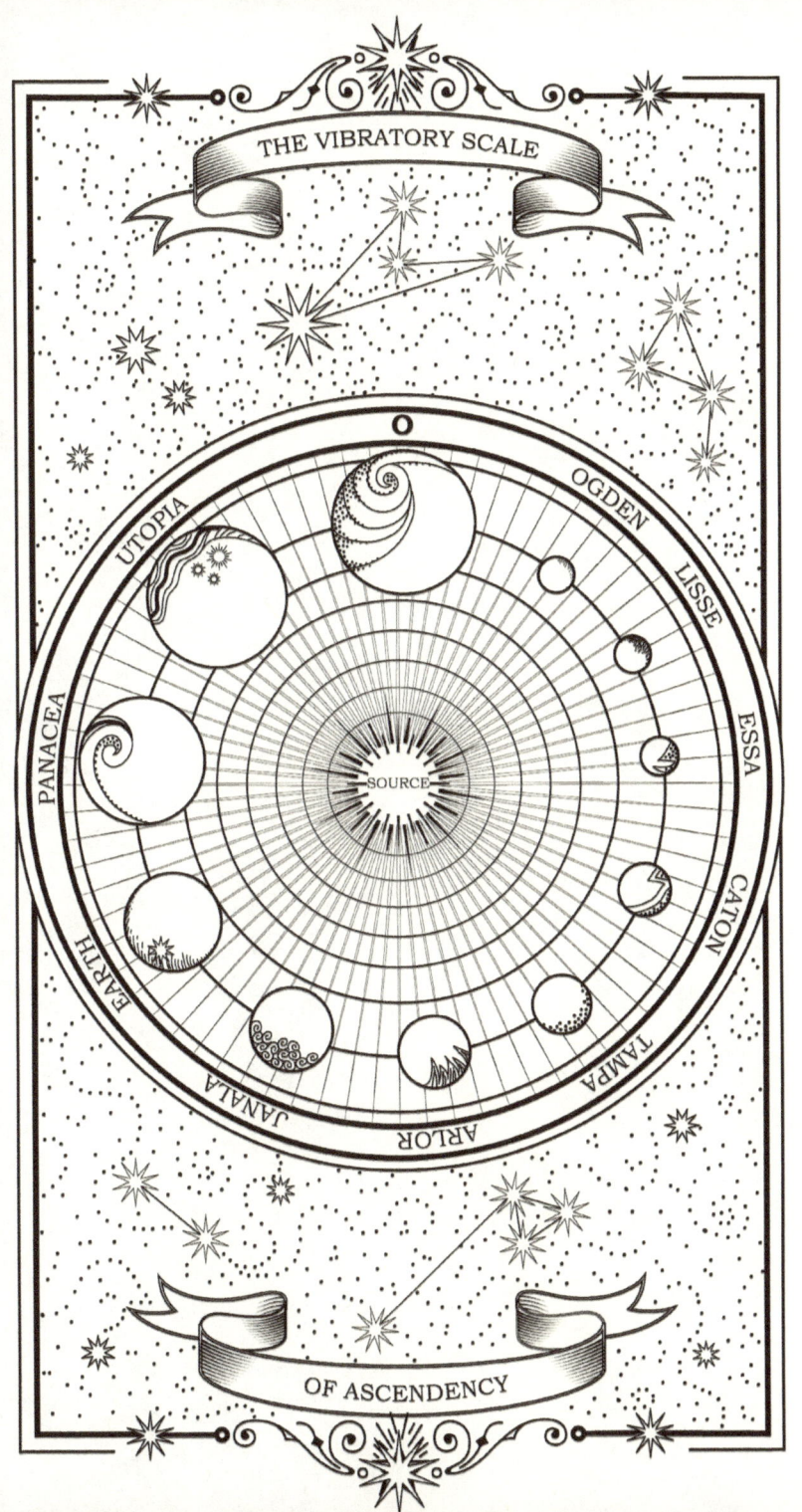

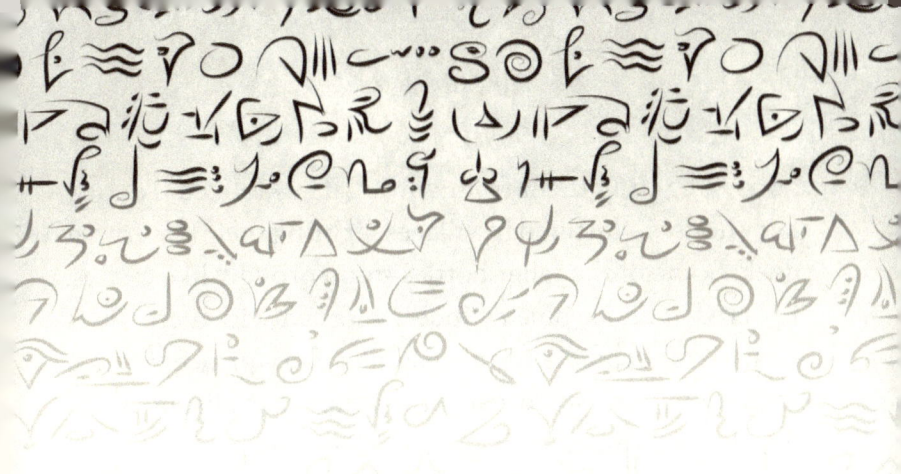

ONE

Lilly

"You look pale."

I shied away from the concerned fingers fluttering at my forehead, unsure why it irritated me in that moment.

What is it about a mother's gaze?

It misses nothing.

Like you're see-through.

Like you're made of glass.

I gave her a dull look. "I'm fine, Mum," I said, turning back to the shelves crowded with hand-blown glass bottles. Smooth spheres of magenta, glistening cubes of lime green and pyramids of fiery red – all with elaborate, sculpted stoppers.

A chime sounded as another customer entered Paget's Perfumers, stirring the air and driving puffs of thick scent from the infusers by the stained glass doors. Sunlight spilled into the dim, candlelit room and hit the rainbow of bottles, lighting them from within. They looked like tiny fairy houses, clustered in villages, lighting their lanterns at dusk. Some of the taller bottles stood proudly like castles. I peered at an ice blue cylinder, adorned with a crown of clear stars. I could almost imagine a fairy princess inside with a gown of spider silk and wings that glistened like dewdrops. I smiled. It might have been my first real smile in days, because in truth, I wasn't fine at all.

I frowned, hanging my head. The black floor of polished stone was dotted with the reflection of a hundred white flames, glowing from a wrought iron chandelier. I felt like I was standing on a slice of blackest night amid a spray of flickering stars. I was near exhausted, and yet I had just told Mum I was fine. I had actually *lied* to my mother about how I was really feeling. If we were human, it wouldn't have been a particularly interesting fact – given that humans seemed to lie so easily – but the go-lite way of life made lying redundant. When you live in a world where people treat one another with acceptance, rather than judgement, there isn't much use for it.

I felt giddy at how easily the words had slipped from my tongue. I stared down at the starry floor, wishing that I was free to tell Mum the truth, but it was impossible. I had inherited a dusty, old manuscript that held a world-altering secret and I was bound by The One Source to keep it.

A group of giggling girls burst through the stained glass doors, their eyes effervescent. Ada Avris, from my crystal healing class at *magistrument,* waved and smiled as she passed. I watched them titter and drift through their uncomplicated lives, my eyes lingering. A few short weeks ago my laughter had been as carefree as theirs, but not anymore. These days, my every waking moment was spent straining and struggling to see the invisible symbols that Great-grandad Flights had hidden in his manuscript, and then struggling some more to decipher them. I kept seeing the snaking green ink dancing in my mind and the promise it was pressing me to keep. My great-grandfather had discovered something truly powerful, a knowledge that must be guarded by decree of The Source. Since I hadn't felt inclined to go against the wishes of the power responsible for all of creation, I was carrying this secret alone. But that wasn't the only thing weighing on me.

I watched my mother as though I was seeing her through a dream. She moved from shelf to shelf, reaching out to lightly caress the glittering bottles like they were prized jewels. I tried to imagine what she would say, if right here, right now, I went against The Source's wishes and blurted out that I'd been running myself ragged trying to decipher magically veiled instructions in an ancient manuscript. And as though that weren't fantastical enough, what if I told her the impossible truth that I was in love with a human? I eyed the delicate amber vial pinched between her thumb and forefinger and imagined her caramel eyes glazed in shock as it shattered to the floor of Paget's Perfumers.

I ran an absent finger along the glass shelf. Each sparkling perfume bottle was fixed with a label of gold ink - *Luck, Grace, Faith, Endurance, Support.* I stared at the last, thinking I could probably use some support right now. I picked up the teardrop shaped bottle, opened it, and waved it under my nose, hoping to feel an immediate effect. I'd stayed up half the night poring over the manuscript. It was hard enough maintaining the focus to see his invisible writing, let alone decipher its meaning. The swirling, green script was still hovering in my mind's eye, distracting me from any semblance of my normal life, and now it seemed, had me telling lies to protect the secrets it held. Great-grandfather Grayson Flights had carried out his work in secret, only confiding in his best friend, and now I was duty-bound to do the same.

"You don't look fine, Lilly." My mother's voice cut through my thoughts. "In fact, you look positively exhausted." There was nothing sharp in her words. Her feelings hadn't been hurt by me flinching away from her concerned fingers. She was too kind for that, and kind people knew how to keep loving someone, even when they were being... what was I being? *Tired, Irritable?*

She had one eye on me, while sniffing the contents of a spiralling indigo bottle, labelled *Charisma.* The wide bells of her linen sleeves fell back to her elbows. Her elegant neck curved, slender as a swan's, as she inhaled the scent. She smiled at me, a smile of honey and starlight, the kind that spreads slowly at first and then sweetly reaches in and lights up your world.

I could already feel the tension draining from my body. As well as being kind, my mother was also wise, so when I didn't respond or offer any explanation for my lacklustre appearance, she embraced me with her smile for a few moments more and directed her focus back to the shelves.

"What about this?" She held up a deep violet, squatted bottle with a blunt, square stopper. The gold ink label read, *Confidence*.

I raised my brows. "Do you think Dad is nervous about the Council election?" I couldn't see why he would be. I felt sure he was the obvious choice to take Elder Sparks' seat. But maybe I was a biased, doting daughter.

Each country of Panacea was led by a High Council of Elders, chosen by merit of good deeds, exemplary use of their Gifts and mastery of the go-lite *Quests*. There was no doubt in my mind that my father fit the bill. If chosen, he would become one of thirty-two Elders in Citrine's High Council, overseen by three Grand Masters. The matter of how a Grand Master was chosen was something else entirely; a magical occurrence that had been repeating through the ages. They were hand-picked by The Source itself, receiving three divinatory signs: a golden feather to show that the Soul is light, a kiss from a child as the peoples' blessing, and a visit from the Great White Owl as a sign of wisdom gained. If an Elder received all three mystical signs within the turning of a moon, they were elevated to Grand Master.

It wouldn't surprise me at all if one day a golden feather was summoned, shimmering on the air, to drift into my father's worthy hand.

"No, I don't think he's nervous," Mum waved the thought away, "but a little extra confidence never goes astray, and besides, I wanted to get him a present. I thought he could wear this as a bit of a pick-me-up on election day." She held the open bottle under my nose.

It flashed deep purple in the warm candlelight. It smelt of allberry, cinnamon and firestorm. I nodded my approval. "Have they named a date yet?"

"Not yet."

"I wish we could go inside with him," I frowned. "It seems like an outdated rule that the decision should happen behind closed doors, without the support of family and friends." Since breaking the biggest rule of all – reaching through the veil and touching a human – I'd started questioning a lot of things. If I'd sounded rebellious, my mother didn't acknowledge it. She grinned at me mischievously and smoothed back her ebony hair which she rarely wore loose. Today it cascaded midway down her back, streaked with silver. In old photos it had been like mine, as dark and glossy as varnish. Everyone said they could scarcely tell us apart, if it weren't for our eyes. Instead of rich, warm caramel, mine were somewhere between blue and green, just like my dad's.

"If he's elected as the new Elder, your father will

be attending a great many meetings behind closed doors at Ophanim Dome."

"I suppose," I shrugged. I trailed behind her as she made her way over to Mr. Paget who was half asleep in a carved rocking chair tucked into a rosy corner. A wall of wooden, glass-doored cabinets rose behind him filled with cruets and vials, housing the base essences of his trade. He startled when my mother cleared her throat, the crocheted rug slipping from his knees.

"Good afternoon," my mother greeted him cheerfully and it wasn't long before the bartering began.

Money did not exist in our world. Needs were met through a system of exchange where the talents, creations and services of others were valued in place of coins or paper notes. After settling on a cooking lesson for his wife in exchange for the scent, Mr Paget carefully sealed the stopper with a dripping of gold wax and wrapped the bottle in black velvet, fastening it with thin, gold twine. We bid him good day and left with a gift of *Confidence* for Dad, although I hardly thought he would need it. Of the three nominees that stood to assume Elder Sparks' role on the Council of Elders, I was certain Jonathan Flights was the forerunner.

We wove our way down Cosmos Street, through crowds of people admiring the creations of the street art festival. Every year we came, just Mum and me, ever since I was small. She said I'd loved to draw when I was young, although I had no memory of it. 'Oh, yes,' she'd said, 'you'd spend hours scribbling away, surrounded by piles of paper and wax crayons.' There was always a hint of sadness behind her eyes whenever she mentioned it. 'If you're lamenting the loss of my budding talent as an Artist, you needn't bother,' I'd once told her, 'have you seen me try to draw a stick figure?' She'd laughed and changed the subject.

We stepped into the flow of the crowd, a jumble of colour and noise that moved like a river between banks of candy coloured buildings. A choir of children were assembled before the frescoed facade of Citrine's Artisan Lyceum. One hundred voices sang the go-lite anthem of unity. The sweet sound painted delight on passing faces while the Artists lining the streets painted theirs on canvas or conjured images in the air. Even the sidewalk had been transformed into a gallery, thanks to clever chalk Artists sketching bright mandalas, lush landscapes, and bringing all manner of creatures to life.

We paused by a woman drawing a lion in a dense jungle. She looked up and gave us a toothy grin and waggled her chalk stained fingers at us in mock claws. As soon as she'd drawn the finishing stroke, the lion leapt to life, roared, and bolted out of sight between the twisted jungle vines, the chalk lines quivering from its rapid departure. She laughed and began drawing a toucan.

Up ahead, a Conjurer was balanced on stilts as he sent hazy mirages of blue sailing ships, red tea cakes and golden suns lilting into the air with just a wave of his silk cloaked arm. They shimmered like glitter and moved like smoke before dissipating into nothingness.

"How is our darling Sky?" Mum asked.

"She's great," I smirked. "She and Gabe are essentially joined at the hip now."

"Really? I bumped into her a few days ago at the grocers. She seemed a little off to me."

There she went with the x-ray eyes again. I guessed being a mother to someone meant you couldn't help being a mother to *everyone*. "She's perfectly fine, Mum. Better than fine."

She said no more about it and I was left to wonder as we walked between the food stalls: *Had Sky been a bit uncomfortable around my mother because she was keeping my secret about Jay?* She was the only person I had told, and even then, she only knew a snippet of the truth. Sky didn't know that Jay and I were in love or that I had spontaneously materialised in his world or he in mine. She had no idea that I'd done what everyone thought to be impossible. Still, it had been such a relief to tell someone that a human had somehow seen me through the veil, *really seen me.*

To Jay, I was more than a whispered voice in his head or a lightness of feeling that brought comfort. I was more than a Soul Guardian doing their duty for a lost human Soul. To him, I was real. He had seen me and touched me, in the flesh. And even more incredibly, we knew that we had known each other in a life long ago. One thing was clear to me: I had to decipher Great-grandad's instructions and get Jay to Panacea, just as he had with Aurora. Beyond that, I was blind. I was placing my faith in The Source to reveal the rest in good time. Maybe Jay was destined to do something remarkable here on Panacea, or maybe this was simply The Source's way of reuniting two people who were meant to be together.

"And Christian?" My mother toppled my thoughts like a set of skittles. "Have you seen much of him since the ball?" There was thinly veiled hope in her voice. Or was it conspiratorial, rather than hopeful?

"I haven't seen a great deal of anyone, Mum," I replied airily, dodging her question as well as a vendor pushing a cart with wobbly wheels. It was piled high with drawing wands. Held inside each wand was enough magic to produce an artistic masterpiece, no matter how talentless the wielder. "I've been quite busy which is why you and I are spending the whole day together. Remember? I've missed you," I smiled.

"I've missed you too, honey." She seemed appeased. "I know your dad misses you too."

We skirted a ring of people surrounding a woman dressed in butterfly wings and a painted face. She held a vibrating crystal wand aloft as it captured and amplified the thoughts of those around her and manifested them into temporary form. A man guffawed as his wife imagined a gigantic bouquet of semaron flowers and they appeared in the air before her. Before she could reach out and catch their stems, they disintegrated into dust leaving a purple smudge in the air.

"Where should we go for lunch?" Mum asked.

My stomach growled at the mention of food. I honestly couldn't remember the last time I'd eaten a decent meal. "Can we go to Gregor's? I feel like grilled holdt fish with some of that amazing brackenberry and cosh nut salad that they do." My tummy growled again. I was guiltily aware that I'd been pushing myself too hard. I hadn't been looking after myself at all because I was so preoccupied with the manuscript. I wanted to find some definite answers before I told Jay about it and what it would mean for us. So, by three o'clock, I was making excuses to Mum and saying goodbye, promising we would catch up again next weekend.

I drove away from the frivolity and giddy lightness of the festival and turned my mind back to pressing matters. I wove through the aesthetic jumble of Citrine's suburban lanes trying to picture what Jay's face would do when I told him that I'd found a way for him to join me on Panacea. That careful line carved between his brows – a symbol of too many hard choices – would it smooth into oblivion, stripped from him in a breathless moment of deliverance? Or would it buckle down, trench-deep, as he weighed yet another hard choice?

I drove on, as the symphony of colour that was my city whizzed by in a blur. A strange feeling stirred in my gut, accompanied by another unwelcome wave of tiredness, then the question solidified in my mind. *What if Jay didn't want to live on Panacea with me?* I had just been assuming that he would. The thought haunted me all the way to my front door.

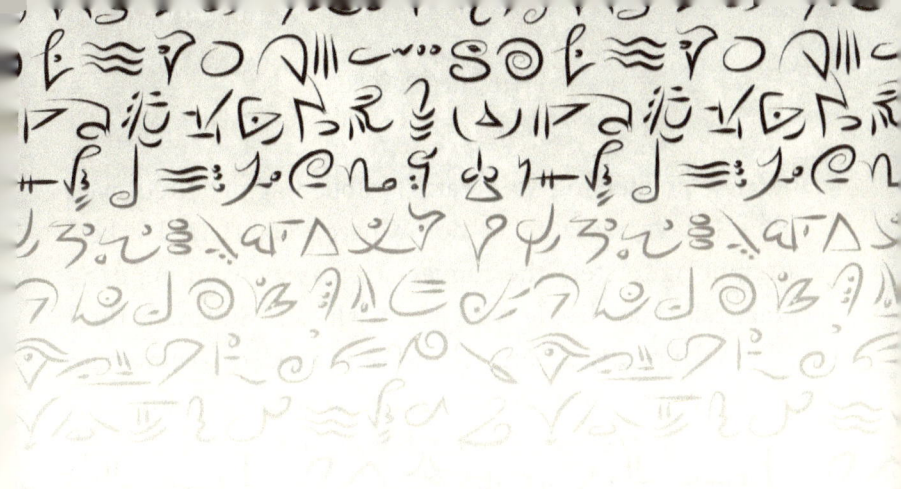

TWO

Lilly

"You're home early." Sky had her eyes trained on a thick volume that was balanced on her lap. She was perched on the edge of the sofa, her spine erect, and a slender, pale finger poised over the page. Incense was thick in the air – *koderoo* – sharp and heavy, the perfect scent for concentration.

The ever-present *Blue Lady of Flowers* (as we had dubbed her) smiled peacefully from the wall behind Sky. The gorgeous mural was a wash of violets and blues and was bursting with blooms. The Lady's dewy skin was powdered with blue pollen and pierced by tender shoots of green growth. In place of hair she grew a crown of unfurling flowers that rained petals at her feet. So in love with nature was she, that the two had become one.

I threw my keys on the hall stand. "I think Mum would have liked to stay at the festival a little longer but I'm not feeling so great," I rubbed at my tired eyes. "Plus I have research to do. Where's Gabriel?" I asked, attempting to steer the conversation away from me. He'd practically been living with us since he and Sky made their relationship official and I'd become used to seeing him potter around our tiny cottage. Sky was one of my dearest friends and the world's best house mate and I couldn't have been happier for her. Gabe was endlessly kind with hair that fell in silken, nutmeg waves; the kind of soft hair you would expect to see on the head of a child. He was smart and unassuming and had a gentle way of perfectly balancing out Sky's boldness. He was more than just a little bit handsome, with long limbs and golden eyes.

"I do have a life beyond Gabe, you know," Sky sniffed, tucking a short lock behind her ear. Her ivory skin glowed against the midnight blue cushions and her jet black hair, catching the sunlight through the window, looked scattered with shards of mauve glass. She was wearing a singlet that bared her china white shoulders and wide, flowing pants of sheer cotton. An amethyst crystal glinted at her throat.

"Really?" I raised a brow, sinking into the tapestry armchair and kicking off my shoes. "I was thinking I'd have to break out the pruning shears before too long to cut away the love vines crushing you two together."

"Very funny." A slight blush rose to her cheeks, almost the same shade as the baby pink roses arranged before her in a vase. There'd be no prize for guessing who had sent them. "He's training so I thought I'd do the same," she glanced down at the heavy book on her lap. I could just make out the title at the head of the page: Elemental Law. There were four water glasses lined up on our up-cycled coffee table, three of them empty and the other, brimming. I never tired of watching Sky use her Elemental Gift to raise the water in an arcing stream that skipped from glass to glass. We were both in our first year at *magistrument* and while Sky worked to manipulate the forces of fire, water, earth and air, my Gift to master, was Healing.

"How was your mum?" Sky quizzed.

"Fine. She asked after you. She said she bumped into you the other day."

"Oh?"

"Yes, she said you seemed a little off and I wanted to ask if you felt uncomfortable around her because I told you about Jay?"

She sat up even straighter and seemed to take my measure before responding. "Well, it's a pretty big secret, Lilly. So, yes, I did feel a bit awkward knowing something so huge when everyone else is totally oblivious."

I paused to see if she had anything else to say but she just stared at me with her glassy blue eyes, calculating. She was right. It *had* been an enormous secret that I'd laid on her. Even the small amount of information that I had shared with Sky was still a huge responsibility. What had happened with my great-grandparents, and now with Jay and me, was unheard of. There was an unwritten rule that the veil between worlds was not to be breached. Soul Guardians took a vow to watch over and guide humans from a distance. To them, we were an invisible presence of strength and calm, or to the rare few that caught a glimpse of us, we appeared as insubstantial as a dream. A go-lite's interactions with humans were necessarily limited. As Soul Guardians, we were supposed to see and hear, but never touch. My job when I'd met Jay had been to listen and offer support from behind the veil between worlds, not push my way through it and fall in love with him! I knew that every go-lite in Panacea would be fearful if they knew I had breached the veil. It was not only supposed to be impossible, but it also went against the way things were, and had always been.

Great-grandfather Grayson Flights had only entrusted his discoveries to one other person because The Source had demanded secrecy around his work. And Grayson, wielding his faith like a sword, obeyed with unwavering devotion. He charged forward, never knowing why The Source was asking him to breach the veil or raise a human to Panacea, or what the future purpose of his discoveries would be. Now, I was being asked to follow the example of his faith and pick up where he had left off. Although why I had been chosen and gifted with the ability to read the invisible symbols, I had no idea. I certainly wasn't a Master Scholar like Great-grandad Flights. In fact, I'd always thought of myself as quite ordinary, especially next to extraordinarily talented friends like Christian and Sky. Perhaps it came down to a simple matter of having the right blood running through my veins – Great-grandad's blood. Maybe only a Flights could read the invisible script. "I'm sorry, Sky. I never wanted my secret to be your burden. Maybe I shouldn't have shared it with you." I felt something like guilt sinking into my bones and tipped my head back to rest against the armchair. Sunlight was kissing the crystal chandelier, casting silvery reflections across the ceiling and dazzling The Blue Lady of Flowers in chips of light.

"It's not that, not exactly," she paused and released a thoughtful sigh, "I'm just not entirely sure you should be pursuing this at all." She inclined her head and watched me in her catlike way, waiting for me to process her words.

I suppressed a small pang of disappointment. Her change in attitude was bewildering to me. "But... but you were excited when I first told you about Jay."

She smoothed an imaginary wrinkle from the sofa cushion next to her. "I know I was, but I've been thinking about it and now I'm not so sure it's a good idea for you to encourage Jay's attentions." She eyed me with apprehension. She knew how important this was to me.

"I don't understand." I felt breathless, knocked askew. I could feel frown lines feathering my brow. I looked away from her and out the window, to the quiet turnings of our street. Mrs Dundast toddled by wearing another of her startling millinery efforts. She appeared to have tentacles dribbling down one side of her head. It looked as though she'd tried to create a sea theme and I could see a tangle of green wool that was meant to be seaweed, some plush orange starfish, and a sad, droopy octopus that I was sure she'd made from old socks. Out for her afternoon stroll, chatting with the neighbours and showing off her latest creation, she was blissfully unaware that the veil between worlds had been breached. Mrs Dundast, my parents, Christian, Sky, and every other person on this planet had no idea that what they'd grown up believing about the veil, simply wasn't true. It wasn't impenetrable at all.

Sky sighed and closed the book on her lap. "I mean, what possible good can come from this, Lilly? Yes, it's thrilling to have been seen through the veil by a human but are you any closer at all to understanding why he can see you and speak to you directly? And have you figured out what your past-life dreams about him mean?"

I tore my eyes away from the *hat*, and blinked at Sky. The dreams were another reason I was so exhausted. I kept seeing my past-life self being swept out to sea while Jay looked on through tortured eyes, firmly rooted to the shore.

"Or resolving the past-life karma between you?" She tapped a perfectly buffed nail against the book's cover.

The answer to all of her questions was *no*, but I had discovered a great deal more than she knew. The situation had become infinitely more mind-bending since I'd last spoken to her about it. Sky sat, waiting for an answer.

"It seems to be a bit more complicated than that,"

I said sheepishly. I didn't know whether to tell her the whole truth or spare her the burden of knowing any more than she already did.

Her eyes narrowed and zeroed in on me with laser focus. "What do you mean, *more* complicated? What happened when you went to see Elder Tunes?"

Atticus Tunes, a well respected member of The Council of Elders, had shown a keen interest in seeing the manuscript and I'd had a strong suspicion that there was much more to the dusty, old tome than met the eye. I'd taken it to his house seeking answers and had come away with my world turned upside down. It was thanks to Elder Tunes that I knew the truth about my Great-grandfather and his human wife, Aurora, and once I deciphered his instructions, I had a potential way for Jay to ascend to Panacea.

Sky's head was cocked to one side and I wondered how long she could stare at me without blinking. She didn't have the motherly x-ray eyes. She had the *I'm your friend and I'm really worried that you're going to hurt yourself* eyes.

She wasn't alone in that. I was worried too, deep down. I was still wondering why The Source had chosen me to be the keeper of this knowledge and I was worried I didn't have enough skill to decode the manuscript. Everything hinged on it. It was the only way Jay and I could truly be together. The thought of sharing a life with him sent me soaring from worried to enraptured in seconds. I was a ridiculous mixture of excited, shocked, hopeful and terrified all at once. And now I was surprised that I could possibly be feeling all those things at the same time. *How strange?*

"Lilly Flights!"

I jumped and sat up straight in the armchair. "Huh? What?" What had she been saying? I had completely spaced out.

Sky was standing now and prowling across the rug toward me. "For The Source's sake! What has gotten in to you?" Her long, porcelain fingers curled around my wrist as she pulled me out of the tapestry armchair, bustled me into the kitchen and through the double glass doors into the back garden. "Sit," she pointed at the centre of the circular lawn. "I'll be back with tea."

Sky's commanding air only revealed itself for two reasons: when she could see that another person was floundering and needed her help, or when she was rallying others to a cause. The rest of the time she was sweet, but never soft. She may have been compassionate and patient but she was nobody's fool. While I had always been a bit too soft-hearted, Sky had very clear boundaries. She knew when to *give* and when to *give up*. She knew how to love and care for another person while remembering to love and care for herself. If someone tested those boundaries, she defended them with the heart of a lion and the cleverness of a minx.

I knew better than to argue with Sky in Commando mode, so I plopped heavily into the thick grass and sank my fingers between the cool, blades. A princess beetle bumbled over my knuckles, buzzed into the air on ruby red wings, and settled again on my knee. I could smell the last of the jasmine flowers turning on the vine. Instead of the heady, white scent of buds just bloomed, there was an over-ripeness that tainted the perfume. I glanced over to check the progress of my new sage heart plant. My last one had died a few weeks ago when we'd had unusual flooding rains. Strangely, it was the only plant in the entire garden that should have appreciated the soaking. Sky had bought me a new one which we'd planted together and it seemed to be happy and thriving.

I was so tired and wound up, my mind was wandering in a dozen different directions at once. *Just like a human,* I thought, and quickly dismissed the troubling comparison. Instead, I breathed and focussed on the air filling my lungs, then leaving again. The sheltered quiet of our garden brought welcome relief after the noise of the crowded festival and the too-close press of bodies. I lay back in the grass with my hands cradling my head and stared at the cerulean sky. The Projectors must have been summoned to training today as well. Streaks of rainbow light flared across the blue backdrop accompanied by deep, muffled booms; each one a bolt of energy amplified and launched from the hands of a Projector. They possessed the Gift of gathering huge amounts of Source energy and directing it at a target in concentrated bursts of pure love.

"Wow! I didn't think we'd be able to see it from

here!" Sky was holding a bamboo tray with two leaf green cups and an ebony teapot.

Commando Sky had gone to fetch tea and Sweet Sky had returned in her place. I smirked. Christian had originally been the one to nickname Sky, *Commando*, after she'd single-handedly inspired and organised the entire student body at magistrument to help the Elders re-catalogue Ophanim Dome's archives; a tedious and arduous task that took months. The name had stuck ever since but she wasn't too fond of it so we tended to avoid its use around her.

She settled the tea tray in the grass between us. "Gabe is out there. The Hands are training with the Projectors today."

"What are they doing together?" I asked.

"He said they were going to be isolating the Projector's energy bursts and stopping time around them. So, effectively freezing the burst mid air, I think."

"Like that?" I pointed up at a glittering streak of light and colour that hung in the sky like frozen fireworks."

Sky squealed and whooped. "Amazing! My boyfriend is soooo clever."

"You don't know if that was Gabe," I ribbed her.

"That may be, but we both know he'll pick it up easily," she gave an assured grin and a haughty lift of her chin.

She was right, of course. Gabe's talent for manipulating time had already been noticed by magistrument's Scholars. He was turning out to be something of a prodigy. "Fine, Gabe is soooo clever," I agreed. She was satisfied with that and her answering smile was a glittering concoction of love, pride and an overdose of glee.

I was already feeling better, more grounded, and somewhat revived just sitting here in the grass. Learning that my relative was some kind of inter-dimensional maverick and that I had the power to read invisible writing in ancient books wasn't exactly a minor discovery. I did, in fact, have every reason to feel tired and overwhelmed.

"So, are you ready to tell me what's going on?" There was no hint of Sky's trademark sass, just genuine concern.

I fidgeted with the hem of my sundress. "Are you sure you really want to know? What I found out was a huge shock, Sky. Elder Tunes knew something about my family that no-one else knows, not even my parents."

She gracefully plucked the teapot from the tray like it was made of air and poured two steaming ribbons into waiting cups. She moved with the poise and purpose of a Geisha I had once observed on Earth pouring ceremonial tea. "I just want to know that you're okay. If that means sharing some massive family secret with me and you're comfortable with that, then I can handle it." She jutted her chin at me. "And Lilly, I'm sorry for being terse before." She was balancing her cup in the centre of her palm and sitting ramrod straight again with her slender legs folded.

The voluminous legs of her white pants fanned out like a lotus blossom. "You've been so tired since all this started and I worry about you."

"Don't apologize, it's fine." I accepted the proffered cup. "I'm sure I'd feel the same way if our situations were reversed."

"Thank you," she smiled, "but there are still things I need to say to you because I care." She touched the crystal at her throat and drew in a steadying breath, "I know you, Lilly, and sometimes... well... you just don't know where to draw the line. Have you even been eating or sleeping lately? Seriously, there's a whole packet of chocolate fudge cookies in my not-so-genius hiding spot that you haven't even found! And they've been there for a week!" She looked genuinely grave, her skin stark white against her black, pixie cut hair.

"Okay, *now* I can see why you're so worried," I laughed.

She refrained from laughing with me. "Look, we're Soul Guardians in training. We do our job and we don't get personally involved with humans and their emotions. If we did, we'd be of no help to them at all. We can't operate if we're caught up in a tsunami of emotions. No good decision or action ever comes from there." She was studying me intently.

"Sky, I'm not caught in a tsunami of emotions," I protested.

"Of course not. Heaven forbid! I mean, because

that would be completely crazy. We're *go-lites* and we don't allow ourselves to be controlled by fleeting emotions. Do we?" Her eyebrow was arched perfectly in challenge.

"Right," I nodded mechanically. She'd been excited and intrigued when I'd first told her about Jay and I'd been so grateful to have someone to share in my excitement. Now she was full of dread and uncertainty and I didn't really understand why.

I was determined to decipher those instructions and any misgivings I had were outweighed by my belief that Jay and I had been thrown together for a reason. I had not asked for this. The Source itself had peeled back the veil between worlds and sent me hurtling to Earth where I'd miraculously landed at Jay's feet; delivered by a divine hand. When you're in the midst of a miracle like that, the greatest of fears seem very small.

"Lilly, I get why this feels personal to you, what with the crazy past-life dreams and thinking that you knew Jay in a previous life on Earth, but I'm worried that you're becoming too involved and I don't think that's going to help him, or you." Her voice was firm but her gestures were soft. Her fingers fluttered in my direction like timid butterflies. "You're not human anymore, Lilly. Maybe this isn't a puzzle that you need to solve. Maybe there's no big mystery. Maybe the next human Soul I'm called to support will be someone I've known in a past life too." She paused and took a thoughtful sip of her tea while she stared at the garden beds overflowing with flowers, all of which had been planted with her china white hands. "I've been thinking about it, and in the thousands of years that go-lites have been serving as Soul Guardians to humans, it's statistically likely that this *has* happened before."

"You could be right about the last bit. Maybe there have been other instances of Soul Guardians being called to help Souls they've known in other lives, but not like this," I shook my head adamantly. "I know for a fact that this is different. If I were to tell you the whole story you'd understand what I mean." I stared into my teacup and followed the slow path of a stray tea leaf circling the rim. "I have to warn you though, I have no idea if this is something that I'll ever be able to tell other people. My great-grandfather carried this secret to his grave and if I tell you, *we* might have to do the same."

She gave me a long, hard look and pursed her lips. "Well, I can't pretend that my curiosity isn't killing me right now, but ultimately, it's your decision whether you want to tell me or not. As I said before, whatever it is, I can handle it." She loosed a sighing breath and planted her palms steadily on her knees. "I love you, Lilly, and I only want what's best for you. If I can help keep you on course, you know that I always will."

A smile of sheer relief flooded my face while my conscience ducked and weaved around the ramifications of telling her. Maybe it was selfish to involve Sky. Since the day I'd met Jay, it had been a battle to maintain my sense of right and wrong while trying to navigate uncharted waters. Now I was considering embroiling one of my dearest friends even further in this complicated situation and sharing a secret that would alter her view of our world forever. On the other hand, I couldn't deny how comforting it would be to have Sky share some of the load and help keep me on course as she'd offered. Grayson had confided in his best friend, Thomas, who must have been a great source of strength and comfort to him. There was no reason I shouldn't be permitted to do the same.

Even though the day was warm and the sun hung golden overhead, Sky hugged her fingers around her teacup, relishing the heat. It had been over four years since she'd fled the ice and snow of Endua and moved to sunny Citrine, yet her romance with the sun, scalding hot baths and anything else that radiated heat, was an ongoing affair. She sat quietly and patiently on the lawn, waiting for me to speak. In the end it was her patience and love that won me over. I must have spent ten minutes in silence, deciding whether to tell, while she placidly sipped her tea and gazed at the frozen rainbows in the sky. "All right," I said finally. "This secret has lay dormant for a hundred years, but if you're sure you want to know..."

"I am."

I drew in a deep breath. "My great-grandfather Grayson Flights was married to a human." She gasped, clutching at her throat. I didn't wait for her to recover, I just barrelled on. Better to do it quickly; like ripping off a poultice that's been left too long and has dried on the skin. "He breached the veil between worlds and brought a human to Panacea... and married her!"

Sky was paler than usual. She had that deer caught in the headlights look again. "Source preserve us!" She put down her teacup and slumped back on her elbows. A stray blossom drifted down from a hanging branch and landed in her hair.

My great-grandmother, Aurora, had been a human, living among go-lites, undetected, but the greatest secret was how Grayson Flights had achieved it – a secret that he'd had gone to great lengths to conceal until The Source chose another to reveal it to.

Sky gawped at me, speechless.

"I know. It's a lot to take in," my voice was flat, almost monotone. "Elder Tunes' father, Thomas, was Grayson's best friend and he was the only one who knew about Aurora. It turns out, Grayson was sent to her as a Soul Guardian. They met when he was just eighteen and, like Jay and I, she could see him through the veil. They fell in love and he devoted his research and life to figuring out how he could bring her from Earth to Panacea. It took him forty-six years but he did it. Once she was here and they were married, he told everyone they had met overseas, in Escartes. It's all written in Thomas' journal."

I could see Sky's brain working overtime trying to digest the story. "Well, no wonder you look like... like that," she wafted a dismissive hand from my head to my toes as though my appearance was mildly offensive but not horrid enough to be 'tsked' or 'tutted'. "But how do you know it's true? Are you just believing the words written in one man's journal when he's not even alive to verify it?"

"No… there's more." I looked up at the flat, blue sky, now empty of frozen rainbows.

She sat up straight and took a long sip of her tea to steel herself. "Go on."

"As you know, the whole purpose of my visit with Elder Tunes was to show him Great-grandad's manuscript."

She nodded.

"It turns out there's writing hidden in invisible green ink inside that manuscript. Elder Tunes believes Great-grandad recorded how he managed to bring Aurora here from Earth. I think he wanted to test me. He wanted to find out if I could see the invisible script."

"And could you?" Sky squeaked.

"Yes."

She gasped. The blossom tumbled from her hair and fell beside her in the grass.

"Once he knew I could see the instructions, he told me the truth about everything. The ancient family secret that only he knew, and now," I shrugged, "I guess you know it too."

"Lilly, what in The Source's name have you gotten yourself into?" She was nervously winding her fingers in the cord holding her crystal. "So what did it say, this invisible green ink?"

"It needs to be deciphered properly. I've managed to decode a letter from Great-grandad, but the rest just looks like a collection of symbols that I've never seen before. Elder Tunes said I have to learn to read them with my heart; feel, rather than see their meaning. That's what I've been working on."

"What about Jay? Did you tell Elder Tunes about him, that you've been seen by a human too?"

"No," I shook my head. "I didn't really have to. I think he assumed. There were things he said that made me think he already knew somehow and that my great-grandfather's secret was meant to be known to me."

Sky let out a tense, strangled sound. Her face was a wide-eyed mask staring past me. "Okay then... excellent... I think my brain may have just melted." Normally I would have laughed at her, but I knew this was no laughing matter.

The late afternoon sun was sinking behind the neighbouring roofs, casting silhouettes of weather vanes across the lawn. The inky shadow of a whale was stretching toward my toes and I shivered as a fresh breeze brushed over my bare legs. Before she had a chance to say any more, Sky's uniter hummed in her pocket and she plucked it out, peering into the flat crystal tablet.

"Sorry, Lilly, I have to go. I told Gabe I'd pick him up from practice. But this conversation isn't over. Tomorrow, okay?"

I'd told her everything except for the teensy

part about falling in love with Jay. I think she may have suspected an infatuation; she didn't know the depth of my feeling or the intensity of the connection we shared. Although surely she would come to see, as I had, that mere infatuation was too puny a sentiment to charm open the veil between worlds. I was certain The Source was not in the habit of rearranging universal laws on so slight an inclination. Perhaps that would provide Sky with some comfort and reassurance and regain her support.

She gave me a quick hug and headed for her car keys, and I headed for the manuscript still lying on my bed. I flopped down beside it, sinking into my soft mattress and tossing aside a pile of embroidered cushions. I reached for its dark leather binding. It was worn and thin as the parchment inside, it's ragged corners bleached with age. My hands tingled as though coming awake. It was a strange, new feeling that had been happening whenever I was near the manuscript. A sense of aliveness that I didn't understand. I peeled back the cover and leafed to the page where I'd left off. I opened my heart and narrowed my eyes, focussing on the space between the lines of black calligraphy. Slowly, the invisible green symbols came into view and morphed into legible words, spreading on the yellowed page like creeping vines.

I had begun copying the words into a journal of my own so I wouldn't have to refocus every time I wanted to read them. It took a lot out of me to concentrate and connect with the hidden script, but more than that, I was afraid that my new found ability might vanish as quickly as those words and then my way of getting Jay here would be lost forever. As soon as that panicked thought entered my head, the script, so clear and vibrant a moment ago, faded and bled back into the parchment.

I had already copied down the first page which was a letter of sorts. I flipped open my journal and read through it again.

I have recorded these blessed events for posterity with the awareness that whomever comes by this knowledge will hold a great power, indeed. The one who is privy to these words, my life's work, has been chosen by The One Source and deemed worthy of receiving them and holding them secret. Until such a one enters this world, the legacy I leave will remain hidden within these pages, known only to myself, my extraordinary wife, and my most trusted friend and confidante.

So I say to the one who is reading this now, may all that you are and all that you do, be love and light. The time is right. You are to inherit a heavy mantle, as knowledge of this magnitude justly demands, yet you also stand at a golden door. Read on, my friend and I will reveal to you the key. All you require is coded herein. Would that I could offer guidance or some small inkling of what lies before you. Alas, I could no sooner predict the creation of the stars.

My discoveries have been guided by a divine hand for a greater future purpose. Of that, I am certain. My part in this unfolding story has ended and it now falls to you to play yours, whatever may come.

I write this in my eighty-seventh year as the final entry of my life's labour. Now, I close this book for the last time with unshakable gratitude in my heart for all the wonders I have seen and the successful discoveries I have made. But above all, I thank The Source for my many failures; for every time a fruitless effort brought me to my knees, without which, I would not have learned to pick myself back up again.

Your servant,
Grayson Flights

I touched my fingertips to the aged parchment and traced the elaborate, swirling hand of my great-grandfather. Goosebumps raised on my arms as I sat in the presence of a secret that had lay hidden for more than a hundred years. A shiver ran through me, bone deep, as I gently turned to the next page where I'd detected the invisible script. I closed my eyes and found my centre. Breathing deeply, I watched the constriction of my panic softening and releasing as I opened my heart and put my trust in myself and The One Source.

I could do this.

I *would* do this.

I could feel my whole body loosen, relax and open as white light flooded through me, just as it did when I was healing someone. It came pouring down from above and entered through my crown, it rushed up through the soles of my feet, and pulsed out from my heart, expanding in luminous brilliance. When I opened my eyes again, the script was crystal clear. It burst from the page, as vibrantly green and alive as a breathing rainforest.

It wavered slightly as I fought to maintain focus, blurring at the edges. This page contained only a few lines of the flowing symbols. I breathed deeply, every breath tethering my mind to every twist and turn of the script and anchoring my connection to the light.

A solitary note like an angel plucking a celestial harp rippled through me, awakening senses I didn't know I had. I'd heard the sound once before and had almost dismissed it as my imagination, yet here it was again. It had to be coming from the manuscript. It swelled from the ancient page as though pleased by my new awareness of it. Everything felt peaked and radiant and the love that flowed through me felt powerful enough to still the world.

My whole body thrummed, lifted, became acutely alive. I felt thin and light as mountain air. I was there but... not there at the same time. I glanced down at my body to make sure I hadn't suddenly become invisible like the script. Instead, it was the exact opposite. I could see myself, the book, the contents of my room with heightened clarity.

The ethereal note was vibrating like a tuning fork. I could feel my energy field rippling and morphing in response.

The note, so clear and bright, swelled, filling me up until I thought I would burst. Higher and higher it climbed. My head was spinning. I swayed as my entire being was overwhelmed. Just when I thought I couldn't bear it another second, it rose to a shrill, ringing climax and consumed the room like a blast wave. It shot through the energy particles of every object in it, including me, and left me reeling.

The profound silence that followed was deafening. A wondrous smile crept over my face. Time slowed. Everything was enveloped in softness and rendered vividly alive. I'd experienced the same sort of feeling during my deepest meditations but this was magnified to a whole new level. I couldn't wipe the grin off my face. Everything was sublimely beautiful, from the feeling of my eye lashes dipping as I blinked, to the sight of dust motes dancing in the golden lamplight. I could only think that this must be the wholly connected, peaceful state that go-lites worked tirelessly throughout their lives to achieve.

I marvelled at the book, completely awestruck. The symbols on the page shifted before my eyes, their flourishes and whorls rearranging themselves into words that I could now understand. I watched in wonder as the deep green ink came to life, lines and swirls slithering across the page and looping themselves together like fast growing vines. I waited until the page stilled, leaving two cryptic sentences.

*A silver cord lies within the sage heart.
Only it, holds the power to connect to a
sage heart in kind.*

I repeated the words slowly, out loud, puzzling through their meaning. Thanks to Elder Tunes, I already knew that Jay needed to heal himself of all his past hurts before he could ascend to Panacea. A sage heart, or Heart Wisdom, was earned through feeling all your pain and forgiving those hurts. The first part though - a silver cord lies within the sage heart?

My palms prickled as I placed them lightly on the page. It was instinctive; without thought, as though I could sense meaning through touch. My skin tingled as a memory came back to me: a day at the market with Sky; a sage heart seedling cupped in my hands to replace the one that had died; Swahelia, the old, blind fortune teller with rheumy eyes like pools of milk. Tendrils of sage heart smoke had twisted from the bronze burner in her tent. Her thin, weathered lips had parted and she had spoken just one line to me, 'Be careful, Little One.'

I didn't know what Swahelia had seen or what she had meant to warn me from. All I knew was that sage heart seemed to be a recurring theme in this mystery. Could the potent, medicinal herb have a part to play? I sprang from my bed and dashed out into the darkness of our back garden.

The stars glittered overhead and the pale halo of

the moon shed just enough light for me to find the little plant nestled in the warm earth. The night air was cool as I knelt in the dewy grass and plucked a silvery stalk. The smell was so strong – sharp, tangy and deeply green. I turned the thick, fibrous stalk over in my hand, dug my nails into its centre and split it down the middle. Long, silvery strands peeled away from the stalk, curling at the ends - *a silver cord.* I laughed. This was it! This humble herb was going to help me get Jay here... somehow.

Did I have to make a potion out of it?

Was there a ceremony?

I ran back inside, tripping over my own feet, to see what the manuscript said next. I flipped to the next page, and the next, scanning for another line of the strange symbols. *There!*

I tried for well over an hour, but no matter how much I strained and focussed, I couldn't reconnect with the music or the gloriously uplifted feeling it had brought. I could no longer conjure meaning from the symbols; they remained stubbornly static on the page. I huffed in disappointment and reclined back on my bed. I felt rather ordinary now, like the girl in one of my favourite stories as a child who was granted the power to fly, but only for a day.

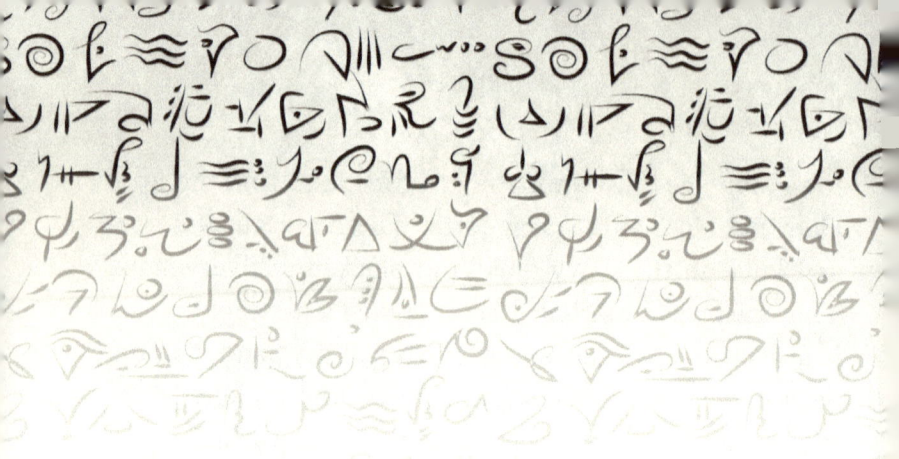

THREE

Lilly

Gnarled tree roots wrapped around Jay's legs. No, they *were* his legs. The wooden trunk ended at his waist and the rest of him was human. He was so far away from me, but I knew it was him. He was literally rooted to the spot, high on a ridge overlooking the ocean. I was battling the ocean's current, trying desperately to reach the shore, to reach him. The harder I swam, the bigger the waves grew, carrying me further out to sea. His human arms hung limply at his sides, his eyes glassy, fixed on the horizon. His tawny hair ruffled in the breeze while the rest of him stood stone still. My heart clenched, feeling how utterly empty he was. Like he'd been slowly scraped out over a lifetime and now there was nothing left inside except loneliness and a cold-hearted wish for it to all be over. I could feel the weight of his sorrow as though it were my own, so heavy, leeching the last of my strength. I was drowning.

I gasped and crashed awake from the dream, my arms and legs thrashing with fright. Jay's empty dream face was like ice in my mind while my outsides burned. *Why in The Source's name did I keep having this dream?* I'd not seen him since we'd sunk down into a field of wildflowers together; the day I'd told him that we'd known each other in a past life on Earth. Was it three days ago or four? Lack of sleep and the whirlwind of events had left me a bit bamboozled, but I knew with every fibre of my being that I'd loved him before, in another time, in another world, before I'd ascended to Panacea to become a go-lite. I felt so connected to him that it wouldn't have surprised me if we'd spent several lives together on Earth.

I forced my eyes open. The air in my bedroom was suffocating and I was desperately thirsty. The manuscript was still open next to me and the pungent smell of sage heart wafted from my hand where I'd clutched the stalk while I'd slept. I was uncomfortably hot. I looked down to see I'd fallen asleep in my blue sun dress from yesterday and its damp skirt was sticking to my legs. I peeled myself from the bedlinen and shuffled listlessly across the room to check that my windows were open. They were. The sun beating through the open panes was scorching the wooden floor. I poked my feverish head outside and felt the full weight of the heat haze that was blanketing the street. It must have been 35 degrees and it was only just past eight in the morning!

A tiny, magenta bird was begging for shade in

the bush outside my window. It's little beak was open as it sat forlornly, taking rapid, shallow breaths. Flowers bowed their heads away from the harsh light, the trees visibly sagged and blades of grass struggled to stand upright under the oppressive force of the sun. The street was eerily quiet. The insects had fled for shelter in whatever hidden pockets of cool they could find and there wasn't the slightest breath of a breeze. A blue trike lay abandoned outside the Tremmet's house across the street. I watched as waves of heat rippled off the cobblestones and I understood why young Lizzy Tremmet had given up on her morning ride. I was sure the trike would be a melted puddle of metal by day's end.

The heat was disorienting and unusual but 'unusual', 'bizarre' and 'impossible' were words that the people of Citrine were using a lot lately. We'd had runs of extreme weather and unexplainable appearances of Earth animals all over the city. No-one knew how they were materialising on Panacea but I was sure that if anyone in this world could get to the bottom of it, Christian would. My dad had told me that Chris' Gift as a Translator was the strongest the Elders of Citrine had seen in three generations. His ability to communicate with animals so clearly was 'astounding' one had said, 'spectacular' said another. He was probably out unravelling the mystery at this very moment. An image popped into my mind of our one and only kiss; how soft Chris' lips had been. I shook the memory away.

I stumbled to the bathroom and peeled off my damp clothes. Welcoming the thought of a revitalising, cold shower, I eagerly twisted the tap. The water rushed through in a warm stream. *Ugh,* it would have to do. I was so dehydrated I must have gulped down a litre of the stuff while I was standing there.

My shift at healaxis was starting in an hour and I had a feeling it was going to be a busy day. If it got much hotter, which it seemed bound to do, we'd be dealing with heat stroke and dehydration and possibly worse. I towelled my hair dry and chose a light cotton dress from my wardrobe. I couldn't remember if I'd replenished the store of fever pitch potions when I was mixing in the apothecary a few weeks ago. I prayed to The One Source that I had. It could mean the difference between life and death on a day like today.

When I went into the kitchen, Sky and Gabriel were competing for space in front of a rotary fan and each held a giant tumbler of juice brimming with ice. They were sprawled lethargically on their chairs, sitting motionless like a pair of melting ice-cream cones. The double glass doors to the garden sat wide open behind them. It provided a frame for the sad tableau of my melting friends against a backdrop of wilting green. Sky's usual chirpy 'good morning' sounded more like a monotone recording followed by a weak smile.

"How are you two?"

"They're saying that they can't explain this heat,"

Gabe reported, holding his uniter screen up for me to see. His other arm looped lazily around Sky's shoulder. The humidity had twisted his nutmeg waves into damp curls. "It came out of nowhere at around four this morning and there was nothing in our weather patterns to suggest it was coming. It has everyone stumped." Despite the draining heat, Sky and Gabe still couldn't help sitting wedged together. They were in the 'new love' stage of their relationship, trading frequent, blushing smiles and gravitating to each other like magnets.

"Are you headed to healaxis?" Sky asked.

"Yes, and I think it's going to be a hectic day. How about you two?"

"No work for me." Gabe's golden brown eyes were smiling. "The Council has declared a day of rest so most of the city will be closed, which means the Exchange will be closed," he grinned.

"And magistrument is closing for the day, too," Sky interjected, "so we're going to hang out here and try to stay cool. Maybe go for a swim at the beach this afternoon."

"Oh that sounds sooo good," I moaned. It was stifling in our small kitchen. The pale yellow walls made me feel like I was standing in a tub of melted butter. Even the flowers painted on our teacups seemed to be wilting. "What I wouldn't give to dive through the cool, ocean waves right now?"

"What time do you finish work? We can wait for

you," she suggested, "and you and I could continue our conversation from yesterday."

"That's sweet but I wouldn't want to intrude, and besides, I may have to work overtime."

"Well, let's just see what happens," Sky winked at me. "Have a great day!"

I shielded my eyes as I picked my way along the stepping stones to my car. It was like walking through a fire pit, the heat penetrating the soles of my shoes. The door handle of my car was red hot and as I opened the door, a wave of heat billowed out as though I'd just opened a kiln. There was no way I was sitting in there without airing it out first. I swung open all the doors and took a few steps down the driveway to stand in the shade of some overhanging branches from our neighbour's lemon tree. My car's solar batteries had never been blasted with sun this intense and I idly wondered if turning the ignition key would launch it like a rocket.

Houses shimmered through the blanket of heat and the weather vanes atop them sat lifeless and still. Stained glass windows blazed with colours so bright they seemed set to catch fire. The entire street stood empty apart from Lizzy Tremmet who had been sent outside to rescue her trike from the sidewalk. I was about to smile and wave but she was facing away from me, her eyes glued to something in the distance. She was stooped over the fallen trike, one hand on the handlebars, like she'd been welded to it. I watched her for a moment but she didn't move.

"Are you okay, Lizzy?" I called to her. She turned in the direction of my voice and her eyes were wide. I began walking towards her and then quickened my pace once I realised she was shaking. "I'm coming, Lizzy. It's okay."

She shook her head at me, her blonde curls bouncing, and pointed up the street. "Why is there a felephant?" She asked in bewilderment, her long lashes skimming her cheekbones as she blinked.

"A what?" I cast my eyes in the direction of her trembling finger and blinked a couple of times to register what I was seeing. Looming out of the heat haze was the grey bulk of a fully grown elephant thundering over the cobblestones. It's ears were flapping as it marched down the middle of the street, swinging it's leathery trunk like a metronome that timed out its racing pace. I scooped Lizzy up and scurried back across the road and into the safety of my house. I slammed the door and turned to see Sky and Gabe spring apart from where they'd been making out on the couch.

"What's going on?" Sky blinked at me, love dazed. Then with a confused look at Lizzy, "Why is there a small child clinging to you?"

"There's a felephant," Lizzy announced matter-of-factly.

"A what?" Sky stood up and straightened her clothes.

"Just look," I motioned both of them over to the round glass window where the four of us lined up with noses pressed against it as the colossal creature let out a mighty trumpeting blast and marched right by.

Lizzy clapped her hands and squealed with delight. "Do it again!"

Although all animals were free to roam in our world and shown the respect we held for all forms of life, elephants were not native to Citrine. The sight of one taking a morning power walk down a suburban street definitely qualified as bizarre.

"Where in the name of The Source did that come from?" Gabe's eyes jumped from Sky's to mine as he pulled out his uniter to report it to the Council.

"Can the weirdness get any weirder?" Sky asked of no one in particular and flopped back down on the couch with a lethargic huff.

After returning Lizzy to grateful parents I was extremely late to work, not that anyone noticed in the escalating chaos at healaxis. As predicted, exhausted bodies were arriving in a steady stream, mostly the old and frail and quite a few babies too. It was such a relief to enter the cavernous halls where cool air was being pumped from the underground springs below. Joren, one of my favourite orderlies, was easing a whip-thin old lady onto a slab of quartz crystal. Her skin was brittle like paper and she sighed in relief at the crystal's cool touch.

"Hi, Joren," I smiled, as he began wheeling her to

an examination room.

"She's looking for you, Acolyte Flights. Room 32," he jerked his thumb in the opposite direction to the way I was walking.

"Healer Cray, you mean?"

He nodded.

"Okay, thanks."

I headed for room 32, winding my way through the amber lit halls, past room after room of sick patients. Each door I passed gave me a three second window into someone's life. Worried voices, the sounds of pain, the chatter of family and friends. It was amazing how much you could glean in three seconds, but today I found myself savouring the pockets of peace and silence in between the open doors.

I reached the right room and tapped lightly on the open door. Healer Cray turned, her brow creased and her eyes sharp. She wore a light blouse of peach silk cotton and crisp beige pants, and in front of her, sat Garrick Leif, the gangly teenage boy I had examined once before and had the strange encounter with at the Crystal Pools.

"Healer Cray, Garrick," I smiled.

"I'm glad you're here, Lilly. Please come in."

The windowless room glowed with the light of solar stones alone. We were on the lower level which housed all the consultation rooms and were one floor above the labyrinth of caves running beneath healaxis. I closed the door behind me. "How can I help?"

"You remember Garrick, of course," Healer Cray chimed in her tinkling voice.

"I certainly do. I'm sorry to see you aren't feeling well again, Garrick." I gave him my most comforting smile.

Garrick immediately began to squirm on the icy blue slab of crystal and bowed his head.

"Garrick's mum thinks he may be suffering from heat exhaustion. Apparently he collapsed this morning and lost consciousness for about ten minutes. His hydration and tissue salt levels came back fine," she pointed at his chart. "I've done a preliminary muscle exam and his strength is depleted and I was about to conduct an energetic scan, but since you're here, would you like to take over?" Healer Cray was a kind and patient teacher who gave me plenty of opportunity to practice my skills.

"Sure." I remembered the last time she'd asked me to look inside this boy and the strange tears I'd seen in his energy field. It had also looked like there were things moving inside the tears. I approached the crystal healing bed where Garrick lay and was about to ask for his hand when he flung it at me with a resigned huff. I glanced at Healer Cray but her eyes remained focussed on the boy.

I took a few moments to centre myself and connect to The Source energy from above and below. The bright white streams joined at my heart and seeped into every cell in my body, bathing me in light. The energy built strongest through my hands and I zeroed in on anything that looked pale and lacking in vitality or dark and congested in Garrick's body. I carefully checked his limbs and head then moved on to his torso, holding his hand with my right and hovering my left hand above his body. I felt a pull toward his belly and followed the sensation. In my mind's eye I could see a dark gash that was about the length of my palm. It wasn't a physical wound, it was a gash in his energy field, and as I had before, I could see something foreign and moving inside it. Garrick shuddered and shifted on the crystal slab. I tried to magnify my vision to get a closer look this time but Garrick was starting to whimper and then moan until Healer Cray was bending over him and helping him sit up so he could be sick into a bowl.

When I'd first examined him the tears had been smaller. Although I'd only managed to see one tear this time, it was twice as big, at least. It stood to reason that the others had probably gotten bigger too. This was serious. I stood quietly while Healer Cray settled Garrick back onto a pillow and told him to stay still while we got his mum. She motioned me into the hallway and closed the door behind us. "It's worse than last time," I said before she asked. "I only had a chance to look at one tear in the energy field above his abdomen but the damage is greater than before and there are still… things moving inside the tear," I said for want of a better word. "I couldn't see what they were."

The hall was buzzing with activity. Healers moved with urgent purpose through the amber light, darting from room to room. Had there been a sudden influx of people suffering heat exhaustion? Healer Cray's eyes followed them with the same urgency. "I think young Garrick needs to stay with us a while," she decided swiftly.

"Agreed. I'd like to try examining him further, with your permission. Maybe I can get a better look at what's moving inside those tears."

"You are welcome to try."

"Oh, and Healer Cray, I don't think he's being completely honest with us or his parents. I think he knows something about what's causing this."

Her thin eyebrows rose to high arches as she weighed my accusation. Of course she would question me. Go-lites were an open, honest and kind race of people. What possible reason could Garrick have to lie?

"What do you base that theory on, Lilly?" she asked carefully.

"The fact that he locked me out of his energy field the first time I caught a glimpse of those tears and how fidgety and nervous he is."

"Or perhaps he's a fifteen year old boy with a crush on you," she smiled. Her pocket hummed. She retrieved her uniter and peered into the smooth tablet of crystal. "We're needed in emergency. Nine critically injured." She paused and squinted at the screen, then looked up at me with a baffled expression. "It says they were *trampled by an elephant.*"

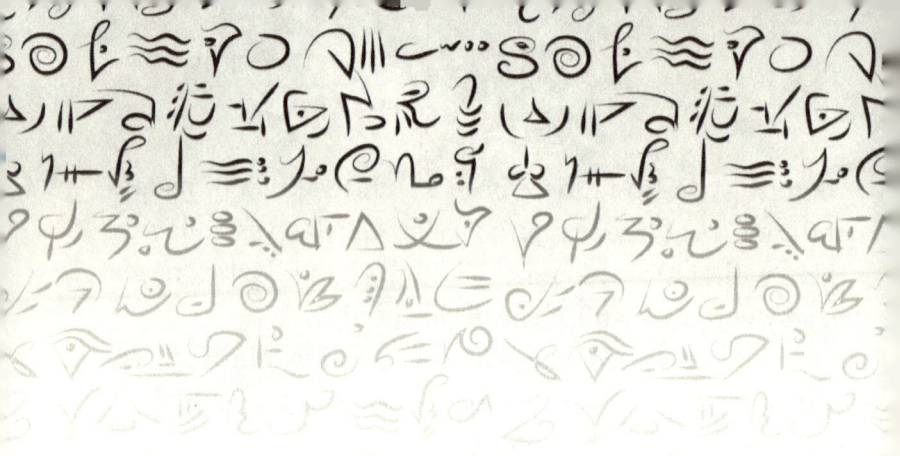

FOUR

Christian

The beast bellowed as if in pain. Two Elders took a startled step back through the trampled grass, a third hooded figure remained steadfast, extending an imploring hand - Grand Master Trill. The elephant's ears batted the air in panic and if it weren't for the magical enclosure holding it fast, I was sure the poor creature would still be running aimlessly for its life. I walked on, across the open field. The grass was speckled with tiny red flowers shining like droplets of blood. There was a strange smell in the air. If fear did indeed have a smell, I was certain I could detect it here: something bitter that came and went on the breeze as it sailed in circles around the open glade, penned in by a thick ring of rugged cedars.

The nearer I walked, the more I could feel her pain. Yes, the elephant was female, I could feel that too. There was fear and confusion, but there was also anger and grief. It tainted the air like a rippling smog, as bleak and grey as her wrung out hide. So this was the animal that had trampled nine people this morning. Three had died. I could feel her despair pressing down on me. Could feel the exhaustion wanting to overwhelm and the adrenalin that wouldn't allow it.

A group of Enchanters stood off to one side, looking weary but alert and debating something I couldn't hear. It was they who had subdued the elephant. I only knew that they had been called in to spin magical nets around the raging beast and haul it to this clearing on the outskirts of Citrine. Now, this small assembly was waiting for me. The Enchanters had woven an enclosure to mimic the tall, dry grasses you might see on a vast plain. It was a kind attempt to soothe the elephant but it seemed to add to the poor thing's confusion as she tried to charge forward only to be repelled backward by unseen magic.

The Enchanters nodded in greeting as I passed and made my way to Grand Master Trill. Her light robe of powder blue spilled to the muddy ground, its hem soaking up the earth. She turned to me as serenely as a planet moves on its axis, her amber eyes glowing, tight red tendrils escaping her hood and a smear of ashen soil on her ivory cheek. "Translator Palladen, thank you so much for coming."

"Grand Master," I nodded.

"I doubt there's need to explain why I requested your presence," the corner of her mouth quirked.

I merely raised my brows with a grin and turned to my task.

I took a slow step toward the fence of swaying grasses as the distressed cow let out a trumpeting wail and eyed me warily. "She's terrified... confused... angry," I told the Grand Master. "There's so much pain oozing out of her that it feels like a vice around my heart." I blinked away the feeling and took another step right up to the fence. I reached out with my mind, soothing, calming, seeking a connection. The elephant's mind was a jumbled wreck of broken thoughts all strung together in a panicked loop. I managed to focus and listen to the snippets she was repeating over and over. Her emotions were so strong I could picture everything she was feeling vividly in my mind. I saw a thunderous crack and the white terror of lightning snaking around her body as she was snatched away from her family. There was horror and fear as she'd stampeded through a strange coloured jungle made of something hard and impassable. *Where is my baby? Where is he? Where is he? Where am I?* There were people everywhere. Too many people. She kept running from the strange noises looking for a way out. I gasped. Her fear was so strong.

She stamped the muddy earth and charged at the fence. I stood my ground and held my heart open, waiting for her to see that I was no threat. "Please," I said quietly, so quietly that she would have to stop raging if she wished to hear me, "I'm here to help you." I spoke both out loud and into her mind so everyone could hear what passed between us. "If you'll speak with me I might be able to help you find your family."

She listened. She was so close I could see my reflection in her chocolate eyes. They shone with pain and desperation and her body sagged with relief.

"My name is Christian."

I am Uma.

Her voice reverberated like freedom in my mind. She was strong and in her prime, fiercely loyal to her herd, and I had only now noticed that she was gruesomely marred. Blood was leaking from three bullet wounds in her side. "We mean you no harm, Uma. We want to help. May I come in there and speak with you?"

One of the Enchanters, who I did not know, moved to spout a caution but Grand Master Trill silenced him with a raised hand. Uma took it all in, exhausted but sharp, and stoically gave her consent. "Thank you," I smiled at her and motioned to the Enchanters to drop the magical barrier so I could enter. The tall grasses parted to make a small doorway. I slipped through and they swished shut swiftly behind me. "You're hurt," I pointed at her flank.

I'll live. She was angry as she said it. *I cannot say the same for my family. My mate has been slaughtered and my baby... I have to find my baby.*

I felt her pain, sharp as a knife. "I'm so sorry, Uma, but you're safe here. No one here would ever harm another living thing. We only want to help you."

Where am I? This is not my home. I want to go home.

"I know you do but we need to tend to your wounds first. Will you permit one of our Healers to help you?" I looked to Grand Master Trill to signal that she should contact the animal Healers. "How did you get here, Uma?"

The poachers were firing at us. We were surrounded and my mate charged at them and told us to run. The poachers shot him again and again. I saw him fall. I saw Henu fall. She was shuddering – with fright, grief, rage. I felt it all tugging at the edges of my heart as I sent a wave of love to wrap around her like a warm blanket. She stilled and gazed at me.

"I'm so sorry," I said again. "I can feel and see how much pain you're in."

They're gone. My family and friends are all gone.

"Perhaps your baby is here somewhere too." I was loathe to get her hopes up, but it was possible. "If you can tell me what happened next, so we can help?"

I was so frightened I ran down one of the poachers. I felt his bones break under my feet and smelled his blood. We made it to a stand of trees, Ikar, my son, and me. There was shouting, shots fired, and I felt the hot sting in my side. Then there was a white flash, like looking into the sun, and the earth beneath my feet vanished. Everything vanished and suddenly it was like I'd been thrown into the night sky, like swimming through stars. I closed my eyes and when I opened them again I was in a strange place and Ikar was... Ikar was gone.

I sent her another soothing wave of love. "This must be very frightening for you, but was Ikar still with you after the white flash?"

I thought he was but when I opened my eyes, he was gone.

I hoped that meant they'd merely become separated somehow before landing. Perhaps there was a frightened baby elephant huddled somewhere close by waiting for his mother. "We need to organize a search party," I turned to address Grand Master Trill but she was already gathering the Enchanters and dispensing those very orders.

Then she turned to me. "We need to get Uma to the Haven," she said. "Can you remain with her and keep her calm while the Enchanters transport her?"

"Of course," I nodded and returned my focus to Uma. "We are organizing a search party for your son. If he's here, we'll find him, but in the meantime, we need to tend to your wounds. We have Healers that can help you. We're going to take you to a safe place nearby."

The Haven had been erected a few days ago by order of The Council of Elders to care for the Earth animals that had been mysteriously appearing throughout Citrine. The first report had come in from Mr Summers who'd been caring for Houdini, a horse that I suspected had been a mistreated circus animal on Earth. Despite the best of care, Houdini was weakening and becoming sickly. Then Mr Broadwood had raised an alarm when he'd found that two of the koalas that now called his property home, had suddenly died. It had been decided that all the Earth animals should be screened and treated by our Healers in an attempt to prevent further loss of life and gain some answers as to how they materialized here. As the only Translator in Citrine, it had fallen to me to get as much information from the animals as possible.

There was no telling what the consequences might be if animals kept appearing from Earth. It was unprecedented. The veil between worlds existed for a reason, and somehow, it was being breached. With so much uncertainty and too few answers, The Council had decided to keep the Haven and its purpose confidential, for now. There seemed little purpose in creating a public stir until we understood exactly what we were dealing with and what we were going to do about it.

Uma let out a startled bellow as the truck rumbled to a stop and sent her off balance. "It's all right," I soothed her, "we're here."

The pale green building sat low and long, camouflaged against the northern edge of Laurone forest. Uma stumbled off the truck, still unsteady on her feet, as we led her to an enclosure that ranged a square kilometre through the forest. Even so, she looked defeated as I explained the barriers the Enchanters had conjured to contain her. "It won't be forever," I reassured her. "We're searching for your son and we're going to try to find a way to send you both home. Back to where you came from." She rallied at that, and once I was sure she was settled, I left her with one of the Healers to clean her wounds. As I walked away, I wondered if once she'd been here for a while, she wouldn't prefer to stay.

I picked my way along the roughly cleared path that led to the koala enclosure. Scrubby trees rained silver leaves and were shedding the last of their blossoms for the turning season. A flock of cherry pickers squabbled in the branches as a sleek python curled around a low bough, a plume of crimson tail feathers poking from its' distended jaws.

Up ahead, I heard familiar voices; one spoken aloud, the others blending together in my head. As I rounded the last bend I saw a head of strawberry blonde curls and gentle hands reaching to scratch the belly of a very contented bear. Petra Honeywell was perched in a eucalypt tree, chatting and laughing, in a one-sided conversation with three koalas. She was dressed in khakis, as was her preference, and a white tee.

"Christian!" she beamed down at me, her green eyes bright and the smattering of freckles on her nose and cheeks looking like gold dust in the sunlight.

"Making friends, I see," I called up to her.

Friends? came a voice from one of the bears. *This one talks too much and never, ever listens. We think she might be dim-witted.* Empathetic murmurs passed around the group.

Perhaps she fell from a tree and landed on her head, suggested another. All three bears turned their soft, grey faces to Petra. *Poor thing, at least she has beautiful fur, even if she is dim-witted.*

I stifled a laugh. *She's not dim-witted,* I answered telepathically. *She can't hear you speak like I can. I'm the only one that can understand you.*

Ahhh, they all sighed at once, seemingly satisfied.

"How are they doing today, Petra?"

"Well, these three seem to be doing just fine," she grinned and gave the nearest bear a playful pat. "Give me a second to climb down and we'll discuss it inside."

"Here, let me help you."

She climbed down to a lower branch, sat, and slipped to the ground while I caught most of her weight.

A collective *'Oooo'* rose up from the koalas as they admired Petra's landing.

The smallest bear looked down in wonder. *He's right, that one could not have fallen from a tree. Her paws hold true.*

The others heartily agreed. *Yes, her paws hold true,* they echoed.

I started laughing and Petra gazed up at me in shy question, "What's funny?" she peeped through her lashes and smoothed her strawberry blonde curls.

"No, not you," I reassured her, "it's them," I said pointing back up the tree and squinting into the light shifting through the branches. "Bears say the darndest things," I shrugged.

We wandered back through the deep green scrub to the Haven's back entrance. "I've examined them all again and I've found some energetic anomalies I need to talk to you about." Petra's voice was grave as we pressed through the dusty glass doors.

"What about Houdini?" I asked her.

She nodded sadly, "Yes, him too."

My heart sank. "But you said those three koalas were doing better."

"They're doing better than the rest but all of them are dying, Christian, some quicker than others."

We walked the length of the grey hall, passing room after room of lab equipment, crystal screens filled with collected data, and many more people than had been here a few days ago. I spied Elder Zaph and Elder Avris being briefed by a group of Healers, and in the next room, Jordan Gray bent over a lab bench collating data. Seated on a narrow stool, he looked like a giant balancing on a needle. I gave Petra a sideways smirk, "Has poor Jordan moved from that room since yesterday?"

"He *volunteered*," she protested. "He's helping me compile all the test results."

I gave him a taunting smile as we went by and he groaned. I'd been friends with Jordan since childhood. Or maybe friendly rivals was more apt? I never had managed to beat him in a race to this day. He had a body carved from power, like a statue of some mythical God, coal black eyes, and hair so blonde it was plated with silver.

Although he and Petra were both acolytes and in their first year of studies at magistrument, their insight and skills were proving indispensable and I felt more confident in my duties with them working beside me.

"Let's talk in here." She directed me to an unoccupied room. Lab benches lined the walls. Upon them was a series of beakers, burners and vials, strung together with twisting glass tubes. A haphazard pile of hand written notes was weighted down with crystal recording tablets and a long rectangular window framed the endless green of Laurone Forest. She gestured to a block of solid crystal in the centre of the room and I moved to stand beside her. She waved her arm across its flat surface and it lit with a white glow.

"So what anomalies did you see?" I asked her.

"When I scanned their energetic fields there was something very wrong, like rips or tears. I've never seen anything like it."

"Yet, I can see you already have a theory, Healer Honeywell," I smirked.

"Why yes, Translator Palladen, as a matter of fact, I do," she smirked back. "We know the veil between worlds exists for a reason but until now we've only been able to speculate why." She pressed her palm to the glowing crystal screen in front of us and the eleven primary planets appeared, plus a shining sphere representing Source energy, which made up the twelve known dimensions.

"The veil separates the twelve dimensions of the multi-verse. Why? Because each dimension operates and exists within its' own range of understanding or its' own *scale*. We know, in theory, that the multi-verse is like a piano keyboard and every dimension exists and operates within its own scale, its' own range of 'notes', shall we say." She tapped the screen and the planets arranged themselves in ascending order, planet Ogden at the bottom, planet O at the top, and Earth and Panacea ordered in eighth and ninth position. "Ogden, being the lowest dimension, operates on the lowest scale and emits a very low vibration. All life there knows no notes or scales higher than the bottom register. We are only supposed to ascend to a higher dimension once we've learnt everything there is to know about our current one. And even then, ascension is a natural process that occurs after death, not while we're still in the midst of living a life. We live, learn, die and are reborn. We've either learnt enough to move up a dimension, or we're reborn to the same planet again to keep learning."

I slipped my finger over the luminous crystal tracing the ring of planets. "This is Grayson Flights' theory, isn't it?"

"It is," she said slowly, "but of course it's never been proven because no one has ever breached the veil."

"So in order to move up a dimension," I ran my finger from Earth to Panacea, "the vibratory rate of your energy field has to rise to match where you're going?"

"Yes, that's how it's *supposed* to work. So what do you think happens when the natural laws are violated and a living creature is plucked from their planet and thrust onto one in a higher dimension which is operating on a completely different vibratory scale to them?"

I stared at the screen and tried to imagine what it would feel like to be dropped onto Utopia, the next planet up the scale from Panacea. "I think the higher energy must be completely overwhelming. Possibly euphoric and dazzling at first, but dizzying and disorienting at the same time."

"And what do you think would happen after prolonged exposure?" she pressed.

"I don't know. Nothing good. You can't push someone into being something they're not ready to be."

"No," she shook her head decisively, "you can't. I think these animals may be dying because the higher energy scale on Panacea is literally too much for their Earth bodies to cope with. I think their energy fields are simply too small and too low in vibration to handle prolonged exposure to our world's higher vibratory scale. Their limited energy fields can't accommodate our higher, faster energy rate."

If what Petra was saying was correct, this was terrible news for the animals. "So you think the tears in their energy fields are being caused by the energy of our world being too different to theirs?"

"I'm almost certain of it. And because their energy

fields are damaged, their physical bodies can't be sustained. I know it's left of field and I have no way to prove it, but I can't see any other reason." She drummed her fingers against the crystal screen and brought up a list of all the tests they had performed on the animal's physical bodies.

To my surprise they were all negative. I shot her a quizzical look.

"We've been monitoring the animals closely, running as many screens as we can think of and there's no physical illness, no disease to diagnose. Their physical bodies are relatively healthy and yet they're dying. These animals aren't sick in a traditional sense. The ones we've already lost became nauseous, progressively weaker and slept more and more until their bodies simply stopped working." She tapped the screen again, bringing back the diagram of planets. "I believe the higher scale of our dimension is slowly tearing their energy fields apart and it's only a matter of time until their physical bodies stop functioning altogether. If we can't find a way to send them back to Earth, they're all going to die." Her lips stretched into a hard, thin line.

I gaped at her, horrified. "Who in The Source's name could do something like this? We know the poor animals aren't responsible, but someone is."

"I don't know," she walked over to the window and stared earnestly in the direction of the animal enclosures. "I'm also asking myself *how* they are doing it and for what possible purpose?"

"First we have to find the 'who' and unfortunately, our best sources of information have probably stuffed themselves stupid on eucalyptus leaves and fallen into coma-like sleep... again."

"Did the koalas see who brought them here?" Hope brightened her face.

"They did, but all I've managed to get out of them is that it was a male with fur lighter than mine."

She laughed and furrowed her brow at me. "Do you mean, *fur?*" she pointed at her strawberry curls.

"Sorry, yes," I shook my head, understanding her confusion. "Clearly I'm becoming fluent in koala. If I start yawning a lot and scratching my belly, I think it may be time to worry."

"No need," she held up her hand, "experienced bear Healer, right here."

"Good to know," I winked.

She walked back to the crystal screen. "So what do you think about my theory? Does it sound plausible?" Her eyes were soft and serious.

"I think it's time to tell the Council that you may have discovered the consequences of trying to cheat the vibratory scale."

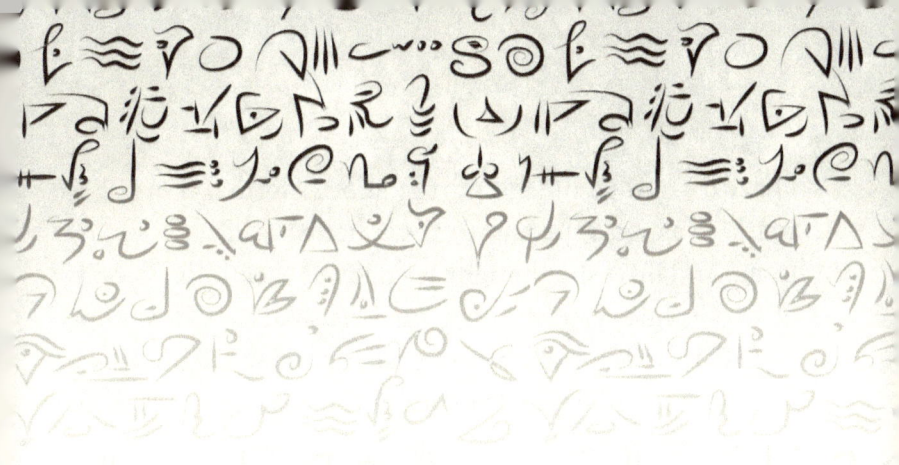

FIVE

Jay

There was a sharp and satisfying thwack as the cluster of coloured balls split apart and ricocheted against one another. I straightened, pool cue unsteady in my grip, and tried to conceal the sway of my body as I sauntered back to my barstool. The bourbon was doing a kick-ass job of numbing my mind but wasn't so great for my aim. I'd already lost $150 to this guy and couldn't have cared less. Our arrangement had been working out just fine since three this afternoon. He was happy to put up with a belligerent drunk so long as he could keep winning at pool and taking my money. Perfect.

It was Wednesday. Five days since I'd had any contact with Lilly. Five miserable days since I'd figured out what a useless idiot I was. I kept seeing her beautiful face and open, trusting eyes as she'd spilled out her past-life dream to me. She was so serene as she'd described her drowning; a life cut far too short. Her hazel eyes had sparkled as she'd speculated about her past-life connection to me and how she thought we'd loved each other deeply; how a tragic accident had torn us apart. I'd been too gutless to tell her about my past-life dream. About how I'd cheated on her one too many times and it had finally broken her in two. The dream was always so vivid that I knew it wasn't a dream at all, but a memory of that life. I'd felt the guilt of her suicide and my abhorrent actions as though I was reliving them, as though it was all happening in my present life.

I detested the thought that I could ever have been that person. It made me sick. I thought back on how much hatred I'd had for my ex, Jessica, when she'd cheated on me and the agonising pain it had caused. And I had done the same thing to Lilly in a past life, and worse! The girl had actually killed herself because of what I'd done! A wave of nausea rolled over me. It was hard to say how much of it was the bourbon and how much, guilt.

"It's your shot."

I raised my bleary eyes to the table. The dude leaned on his cue. He'd been taking my money for hours and I don't think he'd even told me his name. There were only two of his balls left on the table and I hadn't taken my first shot yet. He'd probably shoved all of his into the pockets while I wasn't looking. When I tried to stand, a fresh wave of nausea ripped through my gut. I gagged and quickly mumbled my excuses as I stumbled toward the bathroom to throw up, leaving my $20 on the table.

It was possible that I'd dosed off on the cubicle floor because the next thing I heard was, "For fuck's sake, Anderson! What the hell are you doing?"

John?

Next thing, two meaty arms were hauling me to my feet and a hand that smelled of stale cigarettes was patting my cheek. I peeled open my eyes. The fluorescent lights in the bathroom were blinding.

"Felt a bit sick," I grunted out.

He had on his angry face, which wasn't much different to his normal face except his eyebrows were scrunched slightly closer together. "Are you here alone?" He rattled me like a toy that's stopped working.

"Nah, I've been playing pool with some dude."

"And drinking yourself into oblivion, I see. Can I ask why? Shouldn't you be resting your damaged liver instead of abusing it?"

"Oh, shit. I sort of forgot about that," I laughed. It was the first time I'd laughed for days.

"You forgot that you only recently came out of hospital after being mugged, stabbed and nearly dying?"

"Yep. I guess so," I shrugged. Had it only been a matter of weeks since Lilly had found me unconscious and bleeding after some asshole had stabbed me for sport? She had saved my life. Ironic, given that I had been responsible for her last death. Maybe the asshole stabbing me was karmic payback for what I'd done to her in our last life together. Maybe she'd thrown a spanner into the Universe's plan by saving me. I laughed harder and John, losing his patience, yanked me out of the cubicle.

"Right. That's it. I'm taking you home."

"Steady on, big boy, you should at least buy me a drink first, don't you think?" I grinned patting him on the cheek. "Besides, I'm not really sure you're my type."

He swore and mumbled something under his breath and half carried me out of the bathroom and out of the bar, which was a very good thing because my legs weren't being cooperative.

I blacked out in the car.

Then there was jostling and swearing as I was thrown over John's shoulder like a sack of flour and hauled up the steps.

The all-too-loud jangling of keys and more swearing.

John finally dropped me onto my bed. "You're a fucking idiot. You know that?"

I could always count on my good friend John to say what he thought in ten words or less. "Yep," I drawled as my eyes closed of their own accord and I slipped into mind-numbing black, my reality falling away to be replaced by the terrifying world of dark dreams.

I felt like I was plummeting into a bottomless pit. A stunned-faced boy was staring at me with a depth of pity reserved for the hopeless and hell-bound. "Oh man, I'm so sorry," he stammered. "I thought her parents would have told you."

"No," I whispered. *They didn't tell me because they blame me. Why else would she kill herself?* "When?" I demanded. "When did they find her?"

"Yesterday. Search and rescue found her body washed up on the rocks at Broerson's Point. They'd been searching for two days. Didn't anyone tell you she was missing?"

"Why would they?" I shook my head. "We'd been broken up for over a month. I treated her like shit and dumped her. Her family and friends would sooner kill me than have to look at me again, and I don't blame them."

"Well, I'm sorry you found out this way. I just assumed you already knew she was gone."

Gone... I felt numb. I couldn't process it. *Gone...because of me and my lying, cheating ways. I always knew she was too good for me.* I could feel the bile climbing into my throat, the laboured shudders of my broken heart. *She was dead and it was my fault. She killed herself because of me. How could I have killed something so beautiful?*

"Jay." Lilly's voice floated through my dream fog.

A whisper.

A hand on my shoulder.

"Lilly?" I could smell white blooms, rich and full. I could feel tears on my cheeks.

"Hey, are you all right? Jay?"

I pushed down my grief and pried open my eyes, grateful to be out of the nightmare that had been plaguing me more and more. The morning sun was streaming through a crack between the curtains and the brightness made my eyes throb. She was bent over me, her expression impassive. My throat felt like the Sahara, dry and burning from retching last night. Oh, God. What must she think of me?

"Rough night?"

"Yeah," I rubbed at my face. Her features were slowly coming into focus, those hazel eyes wide and still.

"What are you doing here?" I blurted.

A flicker of disappointment passed over her features. "I can come back later if you like," she offered hesitantly.

My head said, *yeah that would be good,* but my mouth said, "No. It's okay. Just wait a second while I freshen up." *What the hell?* My head was pounding and I reeked and she was suddenly here. It had been days since I'd seen her. Of all the rotten timing…

"That's probably a good idea." She started to leave the room then turned back with a wry smile. "You might need a scrubbing brush."

"Yeah, I know. I probably smell like a bourbon barrel." *And B.O. and death breath.*

"No," she shook her head and bit her lip to stifle a laugh. She was pointing at my forehead.

"What?" I sat up in bed and looked across into the dresser mirror. There, scrawled across my forehead in black marker, was the word 'idiot'.

Fuck! I was going to kill John.

I found her in the back garden swinging in my hammock and tracking the clouds across the sky. The very spot I'd been sitting when she'd hurtled into my world for the first time. Yellow pollen from the wattle tree was sprinkling down around us. Her dark hair was loose, swirling about her shoulders and lifting and sighing on the wind. A rough spun dress the colour of the sea left her shoulders bare and skimmed her hips, falling loose to brush her calves.

"So, why have you been labelled an idiot?" she smirked.

"Uh, probably because my wonderful friend, John, thinks he's hilarious."

"He kind of is," she laughed and my world spun with notes of silver.

I was standing two paces away. I could smell her perfume. My heart screamed to close the gap and wrap my arms around her but my guilt rooted me to the spot. I hadn't even muddled through what I was going to do when I saw her again. I'd been too busy wallowing and berating myself and building an extremely strong case of why I wasn't worthy of her; this angelic girl from another world, who only saw the good in everyone.

For a moment I had thought that I could be good like her. She'd made me believe I could do anything. Now, reality was crashing in. Apart from the fact that my past-life dream had shown me how unworthy I was, I mean, who were we kidding? Lilly was practically an angel. She'd grown up in a world where attaining peace and love were the only agendas. My world was pretty much about two things: getting money to buy more shit to hoard in your house and making sure other people approve of you. *Just make sure you fit in. Don't say what you really think because you don't want to end up like Martin Luther King... or Gandhi... or Rosa Parks... Nelson Mandela... or Jesus!*

Lilly

"Jay? Are you okay?"

He snapped out of his daze. "Yeah, sorry. Just a bit hungover."

Whatever was bothering him, I knew it was more than a hangover. I had not looked inside Jay's mind since the last time he needed my guidance as a Soul Guardian, and as tempting as it was to know his thoughts now, I'd not been invited in and I would never disrespect his privacy. I watched as emotions passed over his face like the fast-moving clouds above. My shoulders sagged. This wasn't the relaxed and easy reunion that it should have been. It was actually something it had never been between us before: awkward. Was he tired, embarrassed, ashamed, or just not feeling well?

Five days ago Jay had materialised on Panacea after he'd had a vivid past-life dream. Thank The Source nobody had seen us as he'd tumbled out of thin air and collided with me in the magistrument hallway. He had been desperately calling out to me through his dream haze and had unwittingly appeared by my side in a very public place. It could have been disastrous. How would I have explained who he was or where he'd come from if someone had seen us?

I still knew so little about the bond that allowed us both to defy natural law, to pierce the veil between Earth and Panacea, to see and touch one another, to materialise on each others' worlds. But I knew a lot more today than I had five days ago. I knew there was a way for Jay to ascend to Panacea because it had been done before. My great-grandfather hadn't given up on his love for Aurora and I wasn't going to give up on Jay. I'd come here today to tell him about my great-grandparents and the manuscript and that I'd found a way to make this work. It didn't matter that he was a human and I was a go-lite, we could make the impossible, possible.

The joy I had felt at that realisation was intoxicating. I'd worked hard over the last five days to decipher the hidden instructions in that manuscript. I'd barely slept or eaten and had imagined telling Jay in a hundred different ways, as his face lit up and his green eyes danced with wonder.

Now, he was just standing there, not at all himself, not the Jay I knew. Where was the glorious, shining Soul who had sat opposite me in a field of wildflowers and kissed me and told me he loved me?

I stilled the hammock mid-swing and squinted at him, straining to find the real Jay under the layer of heavy energy that was smothering his light. It surrounded him like a murky fog. Trying to see through it was like trying to peer through lead. I had no idea what could have happened to make him this way. A squeezing pain hissed through my heart. This person was like a stranger to me.

He was silent, his face a blank mask and there had been no hug or kiss to greet me. A flock of birds wheeled overhead letting out short, sharp chirrups. I could hear the dull drone of bees. "Why were you drinking so much last night?" I asked it more to fill the awkward silence than for want of an answer. It became apparent very quickly that it was the wrong thing to ask.

Without warning, his eyes flared with unchecked anger. "It wasn't a big deal," he shrugged defiantly. "That's what we imperfect humans do sometimes."

"Even when you have a damaged liver that's still healing?" I countered. *Why, oh why did I just say that?* He was clearly baiting me and I'd bitten. It was as though my wisdom fled me in that moment and everything that made me a go-lite had short-circuited. It was a distinctly human reaction to be rankled by someone else's snarkiness. I reeled at how easily I had succumbed to his anger, at how unskilful it was to allow it to affect me and cause an angry response in return.

Jay eyed me defensively. He probably thought my slack jaw and furrowed brow were a pointed display of my disapproval. He was right, they were, but my disapproval wasn't aimed at him. It was directed squarely at me, at how *I* was behaving. I scrambled about in my own brain trying to find the serene, steady me. Trying to quiet the erratic feelings of indignation and defensiveness that had begun attacking me out of nowhere.

"I suppose go-lites are much more sensible," Jay ranted on, completely ignoring my question. "No getting drunk, throwing up and falling over for them, I'm sure." His frame was ridged, his chest was rising and falling so rapidly that his shirt buttons were straining against his chest.

I blinked at him, struggling to find a calm balance point inside. "Well, no," I answered, feeling bewildered, and even though it was the truth, again, it was clearly the wrong thing to say.

Jay made a noise that was somewhere between a scoff and a snarl. "No, of course not," he kicked at the tree trunk, which caught me by surprise because I'd never seen him be anything but completely respectful towards nature, and I'd not seen this hostility from him before. It completely rattled me.

"We don't get drunk because we don't drink alcohol," I retorted. "We don't feel the need for any type of drug."

At first his eyes widened with shock at that new piece of information about my world, then a small, incredulous burst of laughter sliced the air, followed by a smug, satisfied smile, as though he'd won some argument that I wasn't aware we'd been having.

I clutched the sides of the hammock until the course string bit into my palms. "Why are you being this way?" My voice had a prickly, nervous edge. He was being snide and hurtful and just plain mean.

We stared at each other, tension thick between us. "I'm sorry," he blew out. Now he was the one looking annoyed with himself. "I really am sorry, Lilly." There was genuine remorse now.

I didn't know what to say. I didn't feel like answering him. I didn't feel like being kind and asking him how I could help. I felt... I felt... hurt.

The realisation hit me like a slap and that overwhelming sense of tiredness, that was becoming such a familiar part of my life, washed over me again. Where was my patience? And what were the small, nagging whispers going through my mind? They were weaving little stories that made me question and doubt myself. I huffed in mild annoyance, trying to swat them away like flies. I was vaguely aware that I'd started Jay's hammock rocking in a nervous swing. I was starting to feel a little sick. I took a deep breath, searching for The Source's support and it flowed into me a few heartbeats later. Even then, I still didn't feel right. I felt hurt and all I wanted to do was go home and try to understand why I was acting like... like... *a human.* Finding out why Jay was acting like a complete stranger to me would have to wait.

So, I looked at him once more to see if he had anything else to say to me apart from a feeble, 'sorry'. He was still just standing there, barefoot in the grass, arms limp at his sides. *Couldn't he see that he'd hurt me? Why wasn't he making an effort to explain or tell me what was wrong with him?* I waited until I couldn't stand waiting anymore, and repaying the courtesy he'd bestowed upon me, said absolutely nothing to him, before vanishing through the veil with a deafening crack.

The vines of blue and white lightening snaked over my body, pricking and burning, as I hurled myself through the invisible membrane that separated our two worlds. The journey home was even more unpleasant than the journey there had been. My skin felt like a welter of stings, my head was spinning and I felt really nauseous now. Sky's words jumped into my mind: *We don't allow ourselves to be controlled by fleeting emotions. Right?*

My heart lurched as I landed back in my room, shivering, and tried to make sense of how that had turned into such a disaster. How could things get so out of hand between two people that were supposed to love one another? As a go-lite, I already knew the answer, but the part of me that was behaving like a hurt human didn't want to hear it. Maybe Sky was right. Maybe I was in over my head. But then again, this had happened before. These outbursts of anger and tension between us were another complication that I hadn't discussed with Jay. I suspected that feelings from our past-life selves were rising to the surface. The Soul never forgets. Jay and I finding each other was proof enough of that. The last time it had happened, it had been a powerful feeling that ensnared us both.

That night I dreamt of Jay again. He was still standing overlooking the ocean, this time with fear and pain in his eyes. There were fresh tears rolling down his cheeks. His tree trunk lower half was growing, slowly creeping up his body, replacing his skin with rough, crackled bark, and I wasn't drowning this time, I was right there with him. I could see him up close. I could hear his roots creaking as they grew, tunnelling deeper into the earth. And when I looked down, I saw myself tangled in them, being pulled under the ground and silently buried alive.

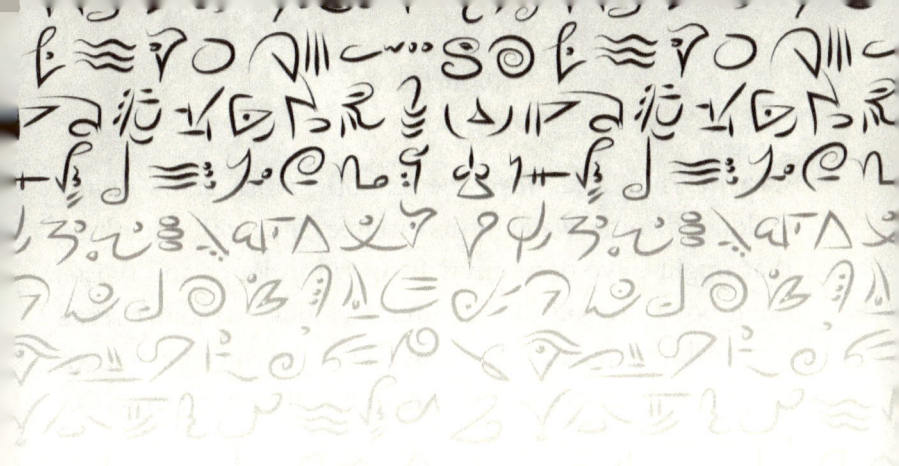

SIX

Lilly

I'd tolerated a mind-numbing day of mixing potions and pounding herbs at healaxis. My fingers were stained various shades of green and yellow from handling pulverised *twinet* leaves and *petchin root*. Sitting alone at the apothecary's wooden work bench, surrounded by bundles of freshly harvested herbs, had done nothing to distract me from thoughts of my failed reunion with Jay. I still hadn't recovered from it, I still didn't feel like myself. I had needed normalcy, something steady and solid to hold onto, so instead of going home after my shift, I wound my way through the purple hills to the place and the people that knew nothing about the situation I was in, who would make me feel safe, and return the world to normal for a while. I had wanted to see my parents, I had wanted to go home.

A sapient bird circled overhead; feathers flashing crimson, azure and gold, like a handful of spangles thrown into the sun. I climbed the smooth, worn stairs of my childhood home, watching its carefree flight with something that might have been envy. It soared in loops and twists, tying bows around the unmoving clouds. I couldn't recall ever feeling envious before but I'd felt the emotion enough times in humans to recognise it. I wanted to be carefree, like that bird.

I turned and walked through the door. Within the walls of this house was a softness, not in colour or light, but in *feel*. Walking over the threshold was like being wrapped in a warm hug while breathing in memories of the love and laughter that had been shared here. It was like a living thing that filled up every room: the spirit of love itself.

Mum had been delighted by my surprise visit and was fussing over teacakes she'd filled with fragrant spiced apples and arranging pastel teacups on saucers. The sweet smell of fresh baking perfumed the air. She was doing a fantastic job of looking busy but I knew she was just waiting for me to tell her what was bothering me. I twisted the corner of the pale pink table cloth between my fingers while she made sure everything was laid out just so. Through the window I could see the grey mountain peaks laced above the tree line, and above that, the untroubled sapient bird dipping and gliding around cotton white tufts of cloud.

"I thought things were supposed to get easier once you became an adult." I knew I must have sounded brooding.

The corner of her mouth twitched as she continued fiddling with the alignment of the silver cake forks.

"But lately, it seems like the more sure I am of my path and what I'm supposed to be doing, the more things don't turn out the way I thought they would."

My mother smiled kindly, swung her ebony braid over her shoulder and took a seat. The lime green *vida* crystal she often wore seemed to pulse at her chest. It hung from a simple silver chain and glowed against her white blouse. "Sweetheart, listen to me, we are so very proud of you. Your drive, your determination, it's one of the many things your father and I love and admire, but honey, all your life you've been running a race."

I fingered the rim of my patterned side plate. "You mean I'm always racing to catch up to my perfect friends and my super perfect parents?" I peeped up at her through the fringe of my lashes.

"No, Lilly," she shook her head. "No, that's not what I mean. The race you're running is a much lonelier one." She had a far away look in her caramel eyes, it was almost sad. She clasped her hands and placed them neatly on the table's edge and squared her shoulders. "You're always racing against yourself, Lilly, and that's why you find that you can never win."

The carved wooden clock that had always hung over our mantle ticked softly from the next room. She was right. I was always pushing to be better, to be more. I'd always felt like I was lagging behind the people around me but it wasn't them I was measuring myself against, not really. It was who I thought I was supposed to be. I felt incomplete like a half written book or an unfinished painting, as though there was an all-important piece missing from my life. I had no clue what it was. I just knew that I had to find it. I wanted to feel whole.

My mother picked up the teapot and poured. "At some point, we all have to learn to love who we are... just as we are," she smiled serenely. "Being a go-lite isn't about being perfect; it's about owning and loving every facet of you and every facet of everyone else, without judgement. Sometimes, my darling girl," she placed the pot down, "you are far too hard on yourself. Never lose your drive or your passionate determination to be your best, but love yourself enough to know when to slow down and let life unfold as it will. You don't have to hold on so tight." She lifted her arms into the air, her fingers dancing through empty space. "Just let go and everything will turn out the way it's meant to, you'll see."

I nodded quietly to show I'd listened and understood and Mum interpreted my silence as rumination. I picked at the teacake on my plate. There was a time when I would have trusted my mother's wisdom implicitly but I couldn't 'just let go' and believe the manuscript would decipher itself or that Jay would magically figure out a way to ascend to Panacea. It was all up to me. The Source had handed me a task and it was mine to complete, no matter what it took.

Everything that had happened between Jay and me was miraculous. We lived in different worlds separated by the veil and yet, we had been drawn to one another.

It defied everything I knew as a go-lite. He should never have been able to see me and we definitely shouldn't be able to physically feel one another or breach the veil into each others' worlds. The boundaries between worlds were safe, accepted, known. It would strike fear into the heart of every go-lite to find out what my great-grandfather had achieved or to witness what was happening between Jay and I now, unless they were given a good reason for why it should be happening. I still didn't know the answer to that myself. I had to keep holding on to my faith that The Source's plan would reveal itself in good time.

I watched Mum savour her cake and sip her tea with a small smile parked on her lips. I once again wondered what she would say if I told her the truth. With all of her faith and wisdom, would she see it as the impossible made real through a miracle unfolding in our midst, or would she see it as something broken and dangerous? I honestly didn't know the answer.

After clearing the table and doing the dishes, I wandered into the quiet of our backyard. I could breathe easier here. This was home. I closed my eyes and let the cool afternoon breeze caress my face. I stood perfectly still and felt every fluctuation as it skipped across my skin. It moved through the tall grasses and the leaves on the trees telling me to 'shhh' and I obeyed. I let all my thoughts fall silent for a moment and felt the beauty all around me.

The days were growing shorter. Leaf Fall was almost upon us. The shadow of Clear Mountain shivered across the lawn, creeping closer to where I stood at the edge of the creek bed that wound behind my family home. Here and there, leaves were already turning golden overhead like spits of fire trembling on the swaying boughs.

There were so many memories tied to this place. Good memories. Christian and I must have imagined a thousand different worlds where people lived in the clouds in cotton wool houses and had wings of leather and lace, or worlds where everything was made entirely of chocolate. I remembered that one had been my idea. He'd chased me relentlessly, claiming he was hungry and that I looked like a tasty treat. I'd squealed and told him to remember that he was made of chocolate too. He'd simply shrugged, declared that he was a cannibal, and kept on chasing me. A warm smile spread across my face and went through the rest of me as well, thawing some of the exhausted numbness. I could still see his long, gangly legs climbing trees like a spider and hauling me up after him. I remembered the way he would go very still when I was speaking, his grey eyes, soft and thoughtful. How he seemed, even then, to just know things, things that even grown-ups didn't seem to pick up on, or notice, or know.

I jumped the short distance to a rocky island that parted the waters of the creek. I crouched down and ran my hands through the flowing water. I was so blessed to have had a carefree and magical childhood. I thought of Jay and how he hadn't been so lucky, how he'd grown up fearing for his safety in a home absent of love. The beatings he'd endured from his father and how he'd fled at an early age, hoping the outside world would be kinder than the senseless violence he was trying to escape. I marvelled at the strength it had taken to haul himself out of that pit and build a life for himself. I'd seen many humans broken by far less.

Jay was a survivor, I told myself, and more than that, he'd risen above blame and bitterness and was learning to forgive. Not the traditional form of human forgiveness where apologies are exchanged on the surface while the wounds continue to fester beneath. Jay's heart was opening and he was learning to let go. He was discovering that everyone on his planet was just doing the best they could with the level of understanding that they had. He was learning the true meaning of forgiveness and I loved him for it.

I didn't know what challenges he was facing right now and he hadn't called on me for help, so I'd decided to give him a few days to sort through it for himself and then I'd go see him again.

The breeze rustled through the leaves and there was an inaudible hum in the air, an energetic charge that sent tingles across my skin, a familiar feeling. I turned back toward the house a few seconds before my father shimmered into view on the back porch. Mum had trained him well, claiming she didn't need dirt from all over the world traipsed through the house after his travels. So, for as long as I could remember, Dad would transport himself home to the same spot on the porch and dutifully remove his shoes before going inside.

His body, that was transparent and wavering moments ago, settled into a solid. His smile when he saw me reached into the recesses of my tired heart and shone like a million suns, filling me with a relieved kind of joy. The numbness I'd been feeling all day, thawed completely.

I ran to him, hard, and collided with his body as I threw my arms around his neck and clung to him, my fingers fisting in his rough spun shirt. My dad didn't say anything, he just held me, his arms wrapping me in a strong, steady cage while I buried my face in his chest and closed my eyes.

My father had always radiated a contagious peace. As well as being a Traveller, he'd been blessed with a second gift. He was also a Syphon, which meant he could draw unbalanced energies out of someone and send them back to The Source to be recycled. I rested against him now, knowing he would take away all my confusion and angst if I asked. I tugged on the back of his shirt; it was our signal that I wanted him to work his magic on me.

His syphoning didn't feel like anything in particular. It was just the warm, comforting feeling of being held by someone that loves you. He smelled like clean cotton and all the places he'd been. I could smell the unmistakable scent of newborn babies where he'd probably held them in an orphanage, and something else: finger-paint. As I pulled away from our hug, I could see splotches of red and daisy yellow splattered on his pale shirt. I looked into his impossibly kind face.

"Hi," he smiled, unleashing his sunbeam smile on me again.

"Hey Dad," I smiled softly, "how was your day?"

"Better than yours, I'm guessing."

I stooped to pick up his raggedy briefcase that he'd dropped when I'd crashed into him. "I'm okay. Just tired." It was the same one he'd had forever. His lucky case. When I was young, he'd told me that so long as it was with him, he'd always be able to find the orphans good homes. I had taken this to mean that the case had some kind of magical power, so, I had given myself the honourable task of bearing the magical case inside each afternoon when Dad returned home from work.

I grinned at him now and swung it happily in my hand as I skipped inside like I used to, making him laugh.

I woke up the next morning with a smile on my face. I hadn't slept that peacefully in weeks. My head felt light and clear, I felt back to my old self. I was even having an early morning chocolate craving and went to do some reconnaissance in Sky's usual hiding spots.

"Well, well."

I turned to see her in the kitchen doorway wearing a sweetly feminine nightie and a hand planted on her slender hip. She had literally caught me with my hand in the cookie jar which she hadn't even made much of an effort to hide. I lifted a cookie into the air like a trophy and grinned at her.

"Welcome back," she smiled, padding across the chequered floor.

"Want one?" I shoved the jar in her direction.

"I should have thought it obvious that I don't need much sweetening," she arched an amused brow.

"The girly nightie isn't fooling anyone, Sky. You definitely have your moments."

She scoffed and pulled a box of plain cereal from the pantry cupboard. "Where were you last night? You came home late," she said amidst the clatter of retrieving cereal bowls and spoons. She pointedly slid a bowl across the table to where I sat and grinned sweetly at the cereal box.

I surrendered, dropping the rest of my cookie on the table and poured myself a healthy breakfast. "I had dinner at my parents."

"Good, it's high time you ate a proper meal. You're skin and bone."

I stole a glance at my pyjama bottoms that were only staying up by clinging to the sharp jut of my hips.

"And that explains why you've got your sparkle back."

"What do you mean?"

"I don't know," she gave a flippant wave of her hand. "Your mum must lace her cooking with happiness pills or something. Every time you visit your parents it's like you've been fed a happy drug."

"Really?" I laughed. "Don't let my mum hear you say that. She prides herself on pouring pure love into everything she makes."

"Like I said: happy drugs," she winked, pulling out one of the wicker chairs and curling herself atop it like a resting panther. "Oh, and Christian stopped by last night looking for you, too."

"Oh?"

"He said to say sorry he's been out of the loop lately. Apparently Grand Master Trill had him chasing all over town with the Enchanters looking for a baby elephant. The good news is, they found it and mother and baby were reunited yesterday afternoon."

"I had to treat one of the people who were trampled." I munched thoughtfully on my cereal. "I hope Chris and The Council can get to the bottom of these weird animal appearances soon."

"Speaking of weird, what's going on with you two? Not that the concept of you and Chris is weird, I just mean, I walked in on you kissing a week ago and now, poof! Nothing! Are you avoiding him or something?"

The memory of Christian's lips on mine flooded my mind, his careful hands caressing my shoulders, the sound of his velvet voice breaking as he reached for me. Our one and only kiss had been pure and perfect in a way that confused me. It had taken us both by surprise. I couldn't honestly say I was sorry it had happened, it was just that now that it had, I wasn't sure what it meant. I was worried that Christian might think it was the beginning of something more than friendship between us, when really, it had just been an accidental kiss, if there were such a thing. I dismissed my worry as ridiculous. Chris had no shortage of admirers pining after him in any given week. It was silly of me to read too much into one little kiss.

Sky was staring at me in her catlike way, waiting for an answer. I wasn't avoiding Chris, was I? I'd been more than a little pre-occupied with others things. "Of course I'm not avoiding him and we *weren't kissing.*"

She raised her eyebrows at me incredulously. "*You weren't kissing?* Maybe your parents are feeding you more than happy drugs."

"I mean, we were," I fumbled, "but it was... it was an accidental kiss." I knew how ridiculous it sounded.

Sky's china doll eyes were dancing with amusement. She was laughing at me. "So, what? You accidentally fell onto his lips?"

"Actually, yes! That's exactly what happened. I tripped over his leg and landed in his lap and then... the kissing just sort of happened."

She looked at me dubiously. "That's the story you're going with? You're actually serious?"

"Completely," I blinked.

A mischievous smirk spread over her lips. She fluttered her lashes and suddenly became rather interested in the intricate pattern of butterfly wings on her silk nightie. "So do you think you'd enjoy tripping and *accidentally* falling onto his lips again... or...?"

I just stared at her. That one little kiss was made

even more confusing to me because it didn't feel like I'd betrayed Jay in any way. Christian was my dearest friend. The way I felt about he and Jay couldn't have been more different. Jay was sparks and fire, while Chris was so much a part of me that he was almost a second skin. The love I had for Christian lasted a lifetime but the love I had for Jay was much older than that. "Chris has a million girls swooning over him and this was one silly kiss. It was an accident," I maintained. But it hadn't been silly at all. It had been like... drinking cool water in the desert.

"Christian may have a million girls swooning over him but there's only one girl that *he* swoons over."

I gaped at her in shock. "What? You can't be serious. We've been over this before, Sky, when he invited me to the Midsummer ball. If Christian was interested in me in that way, he would have done something about it then. We're lifelong friends. The only time we've ever kissed was last week and it was an *accident*. If he'd wanted something more, he would have tried to kiss me at the ball, and he didn't."

"Maybe, that's because you're too distracted with other things."

"For The Source's sake, that's ridiculous! Christian doesn't know I'm distracted. He doesn't know anything about Jay or the manuscript."

Sky was looking at me like I was missing something that was blatantly obvious to her. She dropped her spoon with a clatter. "Lilly, that boy could read Braille through a brick wall. He's as sensitive as they come." Her tone was plaintive. "If I've noticed how off-kilter you've been lately, you can bet he has too. Do you honestly think he's going to try anything with you when you're like this? I think this is so important to him, *you* are so important to him, that he doesn't want to mess it up. He wants everything to be right when he makes his move and you've clearly been pre-occupied lately."

I knew I'd been so focussed on Jay and the journal that I didn't have room left in my brain for much else. *Oh...* I had a sick, sinking feeling. What if she was right? Had I been so wrapped up in Jay that I'd managed to miss what seemed so obvious to her. Maybe I needed to speak to Chris, clear the air and make sure there was no confusion.

Sky could see that what she had been trying to tell me had registered. "Anyway," she said softly, hoping she hadn't overstepped, "we never did finish our conversation about the manuscript and what you're going to do."

I pushed back from the table, the legs of my chair grating against the floor. "Another time," I told her. "I should go and get dressed. I don't want to be late for class, but I'm okay. I'll speak to Christian and figure this out. It's all under control. I promise."

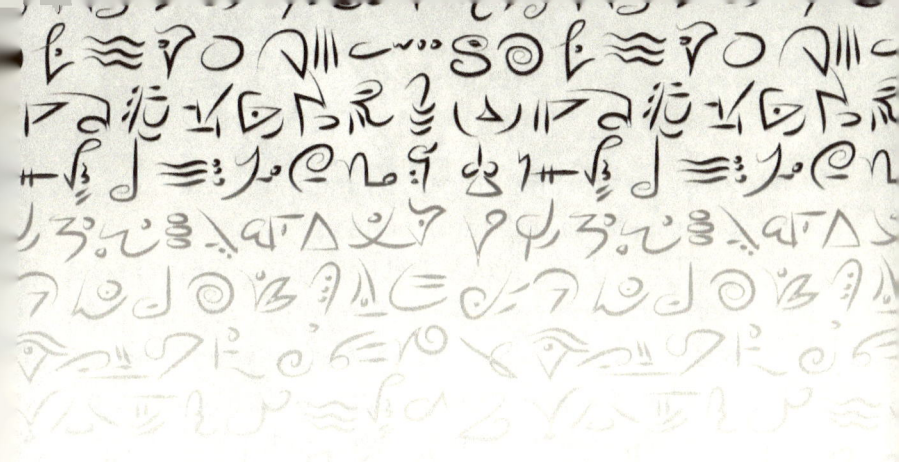

SEVEN

Lilly

The evergreen lawn at magistrument was swarming with students. Instead of the usual steady, harmonious flow of people, it seemed more like an agitated hive. There were people bent in groups talking in clipped voices while others flitted between clusters not knowing where to settle. I jostled my way, zigging and zagging through the crowd. It wasn't easy finding openings through the erratic throng. *What was going on?* I fleetingly considered fighting my way to the obsidian mirror pool and using it as a watery runway to the main entrance when I collided with a solid figure.

"I'm so sorry." I wrestled the strap of my heavy satchel back onto my shoulder.

"I missed you too, Lilly, but throwing yourself at me like that might be considered *slightly* overzealous."

I pushed the hair from my eyes and looked up to

see Christian smirking at me. His smile was at odds with the concerned faces milling around us.

"Hey, Chris." I could feel heat rising to my cheeks. We were practically sandwiched together and his right arm was caged around me, without actually touching me, to form a barrier against the jostling crowd. My own arms were hanging uselessly at my sides. Another body banged into Chris from behind and I instinctively raised my palms to stop Chris from toppling onto me. My fingers splayed across the hard muscle of his chest, the thin cotton of his faded t-shirt bunching up under my hands. I was expecting him to make another one of his flirtatious comments but he didn't say anything. He smelled like he always did, but now I found myself trying to describe it. Freshness... mountain air... cedar trees?

"I think we should try to move," he said.

I nodded as he took one of my hands and led me past the ancient tree that had stood vigil over the campus for thousands of years. I trailed behind him as he politely ducked and weaved, until we reached the sandstone stoop and towering double doors of the main hall. They stood twenty feet wide and two storeys tall, made from the ancient black wood of raven trees and adorned with mandalas of crystal and stained glass. The magistrument motto, *WISDOM FOLLOWS KNOWLEDGE*, was carved at their centres in bold, gold letters.

Inside, vaulted ceilings soared overhead depicting a map of the known universe. Stars and planets shone dully in antique gold against a fading wash of indigo. I stared up at them as we walked, going back over my conversation with Sky and wondering how to best broach the topic with him.

"It's sad news, isn't it?" Chris said as our shoes clicked along the white polished marble. His voice sounded even more rich and full than usual as it echoed back from the stars.

"What is?"

"The thing that has everyone talking out there. The terrorist attack on Earth."

"What happened?" I frowned.

Chris stopped walking and looked at me in utter confusion. "800 people are dead and 2,000 more are injured. They blew up five buildings. How do you not know this?"

"Is that what all the chaos is about outside?"

"Well, yes. Did you really not know?"

"Where?" I said in a panic, suddenly fearing for Jay's safety.

"London."

I audibly sighed in relief. So he was safe... but all those other poor people. I felt like the wind had been knocked out of me. I hadn't been called to help anyone. Since I'd met Jay, I hadn't been called to any other human at all. My Soul Guardian duties had effectively dried up of their own accord. In a crisis of this magnitude though, I would have thought I'd be needed. "I wasn't called," I said perplexed.

I caught the flicker of concern on Chris' face. "What about Sky?"

"I don't know. She didn't mention it this morning. Were you called?"

"Yes, to several different Souls. Last night I was with a poor woman who lost both her sons. They were all the family she had. Now she's 86 and alone. But it's not only the victims and their families that are suffering, there are millions of humans questioning what's to become of their world."

"How many Souls did you speak to?"

"Seven."

"Seven!" Usually we only counselled one or two Souls a night. Seven was an alarming number, far too many even for a seasoned Soul Guardian, and I hadn't been called once. Why, when clearly every available Soul Guardian was needed? "Chris, you must be exhausted."

"I'm okay." He gave a wan smile and breathed in the quiet of the great hall.

Lecture room doors of heavy, black ravenwood were set into alabaster alcoves. White columns stood sentry, either side, bowing to join in pointed peaks. They had been sculpted by masterful hands long ago and each archway depicted something different. We passed cascades of flowering vines and hidden in their brambles were nesting birds, beetles and silken spider webs. On the opposite side of the hall dolphins leapt above foaming ocean waves that teemed with life below.

"Do you ever struggle to remain hopeful? That they can change?"

He cast his eyes to the painted heavens as we passed beneath the dully gleaming stars – Avon, Zepper, Collastron, Dalybel – all the constellations that hung in our galaxy. "I remember feeling helpless sometimes when I was in training. It's normal, Lil. It's hard being on the front lines witnessing the pain humans cause each other. Exhibit A: the kerfuffle outside," he jerked his thumb in the direction of the campus lawn.

I didn't know if it was the bombing that had me asking the question or if it was Jay's backward step from the progress he'd been making. Wisdom was gained over many lives. Perhaps my wishes and dreams for Jay to evolve and ascend to Panacea in this lifetime were unrealistic. But if that were true, why had I been handed the means to bring him here?

"I wonder what it will take for them to learn?"

"They'll learn when they're ready," Chris looked down at me with an easy smile.

"But do you think they ever will?" My hope felt fragile, like the thin shell of a sparrow's egg with only a flimsy nest to keep it from falling and smashing to pieces. I looked into Christian's eyes and they were absent of the doubt and hesitation that I knew were clouding my own. He wasn't preciously guarding a fickle hope. His spirit wasn't being pulled this way or that; hitched like a cart to an unknowable future. It was buoyed along by something absolute and unshakable: the boundless surety of faith.

"Go-lites are proof that humans can evolve and shine. We did, didn't we? We were once human, after all." His conviction was easy, contagious.

I felt it reach into my chest and cup careful hands around my fragile hope. "Humans know so little of what they carry inside," I murmured.

"Wise words."

"Not mine," I corrected him. "It was something Dad said to me when I was made a Soul Guardian."

"It's true, and its why they'll eventually figure it out, just like you and I had to. You know I'm always here for you if you need to talk."

"I know, Chris. Thank you." I stopped at an archway adorned with tall river rushes. Birds with stilt-like legs fed in the shallows, their scythe shaped beaks slicing through the water. "I'd better go. I need to catch up on a few chapters of reading before my potions lecture."

Chris paused as though he wanted to say something else, then shook his head infinitesimally and gave me a swift peck on the cheek instead. "Go," he shooed.

"I'll see you later."

"Sure… later." As he walked back the way we had come to the south wing, I saw Petra Honeywell slip into step by his side. I noticed how her shoulder brushed his arm as they walked and how he watched her attentively as she spoke. Now they were laughing. She had always liked him. My heart hiccuped at the sight. I turned away and pushed open the lecture room door.

My day moved slowly but it was a comforting slowness. I fell into the easy rhythm of mixing potions and parroting the energy meridians of the body. All the chaos that I'd given more attention than it deserved, melted back into the periphery where it belonged. Thank The Source for my dad and his Syphon gift. I was thinking and acting like a go-lite again. Now that he'd cleared away the irrational thoughts and feelings that had frighteningly resembled a human, I could view everything from a balanced perspective once more; flow with life, instead of struggling against it.

I was grateful my father's Syphon gift didn't allow him to see the content or specifics of my troubles. I'd asked him about it once and he'd said it was a matter of reading the colours of a person's aura. Any colours that were muddy and lacking vibrancy indicated emotional imbalance. He'd target those, sucking away the oppressive and unhelpful energies, and freeing the person to be the truest version of themselves. 'Like a cosmic cleaner,' he'd joked.

I was going to take better care of myself from now on. If Sky was right, and Chris was in love with me, that was something I should have picked up on immediately. I was having a hard time believing it could be true because I just hadn't seen any sign of it, but maybe that was because my life was consumed with dancing green ink and a boy with greener eyes. I couldn't hope to decipher Great-grandad's manuscript if I wasn't balanced and energised. I needed to stop working myself into the ground, take a breath, and look around me.

I drove through the winding avenues that led home. The setting sun bathed everything in a dappled peach glow. Elaborate scrollwork, rainbow glass and recycled timber houses rose in an eclectic gallery of colour and ingenuity, a field of weathervanes sprouting from their pressed tin rooftops.

The cottage that Sky and I called home was shaped like an overturned teacup. It squatted quietly in greenery as though it had fallen at a garden party and been forgotten long ago. Oddly shaped windows of turquoise and sapphire glass were pressed into the fat little dome like jewels. The trailing blooms of a weeping willow draped a lilac curtain over half the scene and almost obscured the weathervane wobbling atop our roof. A host of crooked tin stars and worn copper planets spun lazily on rickety arms. There was no sign that Sky was home as I pushed open the peacock blue front door and headed straight for my bedroom. I decided I was in a good frame of mind to clear up the mess I'd made with Jay. I tossed my satchel full of books onto the purple velvet armchair in the corner and changed into some fresh clothes. I reached for the vial of white flower essence on my dresser, dabbing a little on my wrists. My uniter was humming from my bag.

I rummaged through and swiped my finger over the lucent crystal tablet. Mum's face was smiling up at me.

"Hey, honey. How was your day?"

"Hey, Mum. Great! How about you?" I asked, settling onto my bed.

"Busy," she blew a loose strand of ebony hair from her face. "I had a full day teaching cooking classes on the coast and your father has just been informed that The Council election has been set for tomorrow at midday."

"Oh, wow, that's short notice."

"Yes, well, it's been looming for a while and apparently Elder Sparks is too frail to continue on Council, so they've just decided that tomorrow will be his last day. Dad and I thought we could pick you up on the way to the ceremony at 11:30?"

Dad's beaming face popped onto the screen behind Mum's shoulder. "Hello my little flower." They were in the kitchen and Dad waved at me with a wooden spoon that he'd been liberating from a coating of melted chocolate. The evidence was smeared on his chin. His sandy hair was all messed up and there was a five-year-old twinkle in his hazel eyes.

"Hey, Dad. The big day is finally here, huh?"

"Yes, are you free to come along?"

"Of course. Where else would I be?"

The city of Citrine would come to a standstill tomorrow as citizens flocked to see the Elders and their spirit animals parade into Ophanim Dome. Ordinarily, the spirit animals were invisible to all but their Elder companions. Ethereal, glittering creatures, if my father's stories could be believed, unbound by form and born of purest light, only revealing themselves briefly when a new Elder was chosen. They stayed by their Elders' sides to lend support and guidance and as a symbol of the strengths each Elder had mastered. For as long as the Elder lived, the spirit animal would remain. When it was time for the Elder to leave this world, their spirit animal would depart with them.

It had been twenty years since the last Council election – Elder Tunes had been chosen in the year I was born – so tomorrow our city would be witnessing a rare, and wondrous sight. The stuff of bedtime tales and dreams. Dad had woven so many stories around their celestial beauty that they were alive and lucent in my mind.

I blew kisses at my parents. "Get a good nights sleep, Dad. And start preparing your victory speech! I'll see you both tomorrow."

"All right, sweetheart. Night." Their faces wavered in the crystal and disappeared, leaving an empty translucent screen. It was going to be a big day tomorrow, but there were also big things I had to deal with today.

I didn't need to think about what I would say to Jay. I knew the words would just come to me when I needed them. *I was a go-lite, it was our way.* The manuscript sat closed on my bed and I briefly considered taking it with me to show him, then thought better of it. What if inanimate objects couldn't pass through the veil between worlds and the book was destroyed? No, best it stay here where it was safe.

A low hum rippled the air raising goosebumps on my skin. It was coming from the manuscript. Its *voice* grew louder until it swelled into a bright, golden note. I stared at the dusty tome in wonder. It was almost as though it had *heard* me thinking about it. I eyed it warily. Was it trying to tell me something? *Did it want to come to Earth with me?* As soon as I had the thought, the note abruptly cut off like a wizard flicking his crooked wand and shattering a spell. I blinked in confusion and dismissed the book, drawing my attention back to the task at hand - finding Jay.

I sat in the centre of my patchwork quilt and closed my eyes, connecting with The Source and inviting that rush of pure white energy. I relaxed with it and expanded, my consciousness swimming out into the ether, searching through endless black for the familiar feeling of Jay's consciousness. I drew a vivid picture of him in my mind – the unfathomable green of his eyes, the gold lights glinting off the waves in his hair, and the permanent crease carved between his brows. My heart felt like a potion pot filled with a swirling red brew of love and pride... and then he was there, ghostly at first, until I pushed toward him with all the love I had and his form came sharply into view.

He was crouched in a bare garden bed planting seedlings. This must be the community garden he'd designed and overseen. He was shirtless and his back was to me. His olive skin was slick with sweat under the burning sun. His hair hung in damp twists, clinging to the curve of his neck. Dirt caked his hands and knees and there was ochre smeared on his waist where he'd probably been contemplating something with muddy hands on his hips. He was so beautiful. I smiled and reached forward to pass through the veil.

I wondered if this time it would feel like being thrust forward on a wave or if the stinging vines of lightning would carry me through. I still didn't know why I'd experienced the same journey in two completely different ways. Why the wave-like feeling left me elated and joyful and the lightning vines and thunder crack made me dizzy and weak. And then there'd been the time when I'd seen a strange white light in my chest. It had pulsed in the centre of my heart and pierced through the wall in a brilliant white needle. I hoped Great-grandad had recorded the answers to all of my questions in his manuscript, but as I pushed forward now, none of those things were happening...

...because I could not get through the veil.

I pressed forward again. Nothing happened.

I was still hovering in black ether viewing Jay from that space in between one dimension and another.

I tried again and my hands felt like they were pushing against a balloon, so I shoved harder, thinking the veil might burst like one and let me pass. My hands sprang back at me with equal force.

Jay had finished planting the seedlings and was shovelling mulch into a wheelbarrow. "Jay," I called to him. I tried to push through again. "Jay, can you hear me?" There was no response.

I felt the beginnings of panic rising up and breathed more white light through my being to calm myself down. I was going to be calm. I was a go-lite. I would flow through this with grace and ease. "Jay, can you hear me? I need to talk to you."

He stopped shovelling and looked up. Grabbing the t-shirt that he'd tucked into his back pocket, he mopped the sweat from his face and looked around.

"Jay, it's Lilly. Can you see me?"

He leaned on his shovel and cocked his head, listening. His eyes were looking straight through me.

"Can you hear me? I'm right here," I persisted.

But it was clear that he couldn't and as much as I shoved and pushed, I couldn't pass through the veil. I hovered there gaping at him as he turned and went back to work.

"No." It had never occurred to me that this might happen, not once! I had just assumed that once the door had been opened, it would remain open. I felt so stupid for not considering or planning for this. "Jay!" I pressed my shaking hands against the elastic membrane of the veil, a desperate longing rising up inside. I shoved against it again and again. "Please, Jay... please!"

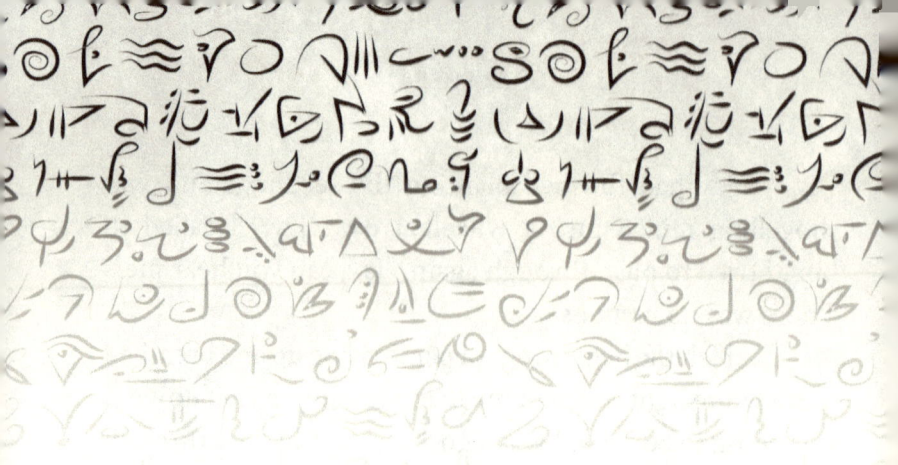

EIGHT

Jay

I'd been doing my best to keep Lilly out of my head. The binge drinking had been a crappy idea. It had only made me feel more depressed and my healing liver hadn't handled it too well either. So I'd moved on to plan B - getting back to work. The community garden had been put on hold while I was in hospital and now seemed a fine time to get stuck back in. My surgeon said I could try working half days with light duties. Thank Christ! I'd been going stir crazy. Surfing was out of the question at the moment and so was football... and I'd now proven that drinking was off limits too. Since I hadn't been inclined to resort to taking up knitting, I'd been left with far too much time on my hands to mope and worry.

The dreams, or rather nightmares, had been the worst part. Repetitive and torturous. It was always the same. I'd watch helplessly as the girl with pale blonde hair and sky blue eyes was sucked out to sea, powerless to save her. I'd had the same dream before I'd unintentionally crashed into Lilly's world. I remembered seeing her sink beneath the waves then there'd been a blinding flash and an almighty crack and I'd materialised out of thin air, slamming into Lilly in the middle of her university. She'd paled, her hazel eyes like saucers and she'd whisked me out of there like a thief in the night. I'd spent the afternoon lazing with her in a field of wild flowers and I hadn't been able to find the courage to tell her about the dream because I'd been so shocked and overwhelmed and disgusted with myself. Every night I got to feel the crushing pain, the guilt and the grief all over again for the abusive way I'd treated Lilly in our last life together. My secret had hung like a rotting corpse between us ever since and I still didn't know how to cut it down and bury it.

At first, I'd been ashamed to tell her, detested the thought of causing her pain and looking like such a lowlife in her eyes. The dream had made me realise how broken I actually was. How I'd been kidding myself to think I could catch up to where Lilly was at and walk beside her as an equal. She deserved at least that and so much more.

I loved her.

I was in awe of her.

She dazzled me just by breathing but I was starting to understand that my frail human feelings were probably a mere shadow of the way she loved.

In the last few days I'd realised that her way of

loving was unconditional. So if I did tell her the horrors of our past life together, everything I had done to her, I knew she would forgive me, without hesitation, and I could not let her do that. I was coming to the bitter conclusion that Lilly deserved better than me and our time together would have to come to an end. It was far more plausible to believe that she'd been sent to help me heal all my human problems than that she was my one true love, returned to me through time and space for a happily ever after. No. Humans were capable of such ugly things. I'd already ruined her last life, I wasn't going to risk ruining this one too. She was a go-lite now. A human would never be able to love her the way she deserved to be loved.

I stood alone in the quiet of the gardens. I closed my eyes against the sun and saw her in my mind. Flowing hair, piercing hazel eyes, the sweet, slow curling of her lips into a devastating smile. My heart ached for want of her.

"Jay."

I gasped. *Was she real? Was she there?*

My body shuddered as I was sucked through the veil. I felt drawn up to an impossible height and thrown forward toward her. I hurtled through black as lightning flashed in my periphery and landed with a thud on something soft and yielding, the smell of white blooms taking over all other senses.

Lilly's face came into focus only inches from mine and I felt her hot breath on my cheek as she exhaled in relief. "You're here," she beamed. "I thought I'd lost you." She threw her arms around me and nuzzled her face into my neck.

I sat stunned and mute. *Where were we?*

The room was lit by an extravagant lead-light lamp that threw shapes of colour onto the walls and ceiling. Rustic furniture painted in faded washes of blue and antique white stood on polished timber floors. An enormous triangular window was punched into a dusky blue feature wall, its glass pushed open, filtering the moonlight from outside. And I was sitting with Lilly in the middle of a wood framed bed, the headboard was a carved mural of water nymphs and nature sprites. *Her bedroom.*

"I tried to come and see you," she murmured into my shoulder – my bare shoulder – I remembered I wasn't wearing a shirt. "I could see you working away but you couldn't see me. I kept trying to push through the veil but I couldn't. I was so worried."

I tried to focus on what she was saying as her hand trailed down my spine and she pressed me closer, her soft breasts crushing to my chest. "I'm sorry," I breathed.

She pulled away from me and studied my face. "Why are you sorry?" She was holding her lower lip between her teeth and worry lines feathered her brow. Her skin was smooth and cool under my palms. I looked into her eyes.

For making you worry.

For not being good enough.
For what I have to do now.

The image I'd held of her in my mind was like a Polaroid bleached of colour. Here, in the flesh, she was vibrant beauty. Florid lips and luminous skin. Her irises flickered between blue and green in the amber lamplight and diamonds floated on the pools of her eyes. She was like a dream conjured in vivid colour, shifting in and out of the world; too bright, too brilliant to be real. She seemed to pulsate, life bursting through her edges, as she was all at once the most real thing I had ever known and something utterly fantastical. How was I ever going to let her go? "I'm sorry for not seeing you there," I answered finally. "I was involved in my work I guess."

"Well, I'm sorry for the way I behaved the other day." Heat was climbing high on her cheekbones. "I wasn't feeling... myself."

I stared at her, stunned. *Was she actually apologising to me?* I couldn't believe it. I'd been hung over, in a shitty mood and had pushed her away without explanation. I'd been irrational and cruel, like only a human can be, and she was the one apologising to me!

She wore a rueful smile and looked up at me through her long, dark lashes. "You were clearly upset about something and I should have stayed and helped you through it." She spoke with a soft and steady assurance. "You said things to me that I know you didn't mean, not really, and I let it get to me. I don't know why I let it get to me." She shook her head, clearly annoyed with herself.

"Lilly, no. Please don't apologise. You did nothing wrong. It was all me, okay?"

She waved her hands dismissively. "No, it wasn't. I had something really important that I wanted to tell you. Something that I thought you'd be excited to hear. When things didn't go as I'd planned, I was hurt and disappointed. I let it come between us and I'm sorry I wasn't there for you. It was behaviour unbecoming of a go-lite," she grinned sheepishly.

Before I could respond, she leant forward, her hazel eyes sparkling, and kissed me.

God help me, she was glorious.

Her lips were warm summer rain. Her hands moved like a sunset, sinking with impossible slowness from my chest down to my stomach and then glided around my waist. Her fingertips were cool, raising goosebumps where they trailed across my bare skin, tracing circles around my shoulder blades.

I'd blocked her out of my mind. I'd made myself forget the sheer force of her, how with one look she could melt the shackles I made for myself and lift me up into a soaring, dizzying sense of freedom.

Her lips, so careful at first, slid over mine with bolder intent. I tangled my fingers in her hair and crushed her to me. I drank her in. Tongues soft and hot, lips wet and gliding. Velvet skin beneath my hands. Her neck... her shoulders... her back arching. I was trembling. Her energy was wrapping around me and burning through me in pulsing waves.

And then we were falling, wrapped around each other, impossibly close. We could have been plummeting from a great height or floating gently down like feathers, I didn't know which and I didn't care. My head was spinning. Surrendering all I was, I couldn't feel where Lilly ended and where I began.

Lilly

We sank into a pile of pillows, a rampant heat building between us. I lay on top of him, our bodies joined in a slick, sleek line. Jay's calloused hands were moving frantically under my shirt, clutching at my back and pressing me hard to his chest. Our hipbones were grinding together, his sweat-damp hair sticking to my face as I trailed kisses across his forehead. His lips found my neck, wild and insatiable, as he breathed my name against my burning skin. His teeth grazed my collarbone and then he was dragging my t-shirt over my head and tossing it to the floor.

My breath was coming fast.

Everything was happening fast.

Too fast.

It felt strange, lacking, hollow somehow.

Our lips crashed back together, tongues tangling, needing to be closer, ever closer. I could feel the press of him at my thigh as his hands, hot and hungry, slid over my body, raking across my skin. I could feel his hands everywhere, but I couldn't *feel him.*

I wanted to look into his eyes, study his beautiful face, catch my breath, but he flipped me roughly onto my back and knelt between my legs, spreading them wide. His lips and tongue were on my stomach, hot and wet, working higher, while his hands squeezed my denim clad thighs.

My mind raced to the memory of us kissing in the meadow, the soft, open sweetness of it. This was something entirely different. This was dark and desperate. My body throbbed with want while my heart ached with need: the need to slow down, the need for a real connection, the need to see and be *seen.* Where was the boy I had connected with in a field of wildflowers? This felt empty, wanting, like a firestorm that mindlessly sweeps you up and devours. Something wasn't right.

There was a sharp knock on my bedroom door. "Lilly, are you in there?"

I froze and so did Jay. Sky was home. "Don't come in!" I barked. My voice sounded sharp to my own ears, almost angry.

There was surprised silence from Sky. I could feel it pushing against the closed door like a heavy weight.

"It's just that... I'm not decent," I explained.

Another concerned pause. "Gabe and I are going to The Cavern. Do you want to come?"

"Ah, no thanks. I'm... I'm kind of tired and The Council election is tomorrow. You two have fun."

"Okay. Well, you know where we are if you change your mind."

"Okay."

I waited until I heard the front door close before loosing my breath in a rush.

"Your flatmate?" Jay was still kneeling between my knees, his hard torso gleaming with a sheen of perspiration.

"Yeah, that was Sky."

"Well, her timing's just awesome," he gave a sardonic smirk and started crawling up the bed toward me.

"Actually..." I put my hands on his chest before he could swoop in and kiss me again. It was hot and slick under my palms. I managed to hold him still long enough to look at him, to really look. His hair stuck out at feverish angles and there was a glazed blankness about him that had me repeating the question: Where was the boy who'd kissed me in the meadow?

My heart was still hammering in my chest and I could feel his pounding under my hands. "Jay, can we just press pause for a second? I still haven't told you my important news." His green eyes were sharp, like harsh light on a choppy sea. "I need to get this out because it involves you and you need to know."

He gave a confused and reluctant nod as I slid

away from him and off the bed. I retrieved my shirt and slipped it over my head. I remembered I still had the t-shirt he'd lent me the day I'd tumbled through the veil and into his back yard. I fetched it from my dresser and threw it to him. Trying to talk to Jay shirtless would be far too distracting.

"You kept it," he grinned and I felt a little bit of his familiar warmth ease back around me as I settled on the bed beside him.

I rescued the journal which was teetering on the far edge of my mattress and pulled it between us.

Jay frowned. "What's this?"

"It belonged to my great-grandfather, Grayson Flights. He was a Master Scholar and this is his crowning achievement."

Jay tentatively touched his fingers to the battered leather cover.

"But it also holds a secret. I've just found out that he was married to a human and she lived here, with him, on Panacea."

The crease in his brow deepened to a slash and although his eyes were narrowed to the point of giving up and closing, they looked a little wild, like a cornered animal. "*What?*" It was barely a rasp.

Sweat was beading on his top lip and I watched as the colour drained from him like mercury plummeting in a thermometer. He was turning the colour of chalk.

I recounted it all: how Grayson was Aurora's Soul

Guardian and they fell in love, my great-grandfather's lifelong search for a way for them to be together, how he'd recorded the instructions in invisible ink, and that not a Soul on this planet knew except for Elder Tunes, Sky and me. By the time I'd finished, Jay sat bewildered, his mouth hanging slightly open and speechless.

"Don't you see what this means?" I picked up his listless hand and squeezed. "You were right from the start. There can be a future for us. It *is* possible."

A riot of emotions played across his face which was better than the blank shock he'd worn for the last ten minutes while I'd told him everything I'd discovered so far. I thought back to my own shock as I'd sat stunned, listening to Elder Tunes' story. "I could scarcely believe it either when I found out," I said, trying to mollify his discomfort.

"I don't understand." He was shaking his head, addressing his confusion not to me, but into the stillness of the room. He sounded breathless, disoriented. "None of this makes any sense." He had begun to sway like a spinning top that was running out of inertia and his face was ghostly.

"Jay, maybe you should lie down for a minute. I'll go get you some water." I gripped his shoulders and urged him to lie back on my bed. He was burning up.

"No," he fought me to remain upright, "I'm sorry, I think I need to go."

My hands dropped away and he looked into my

face with bleary eyes. Instead of startling sea green, his eyes were flat and pale, like the tide had been sucked away leaving only shallow pools. He looked ill and it wrenched at me to see him looking so lost.

A few months ago Jay didn't even know that other worlds and races existed, let alone that he'd fall in love with someone from another planet! And now I'd effectively just asked him to leave his world behind and join me in this one. If our positions were reversed, I'd be overwhelmed too. I pushed away my disappointment. "If you think you need to go, if that's what you want to do, I understand. It's a lot to take in."

Another slight shake of his head. He seemed too weak to give a coherent response. "I'm sorry," was all he could manage as he gave me a vacant look. My heart lurched as recognition struck. He was looking at me with the same hollowed out look that he wore in my past life dreams. He shimmered like a desert mirage and evaporated from my sight.

Understanding warred with disappointment. A heavy lump was lodged in my throat as though I'd swallowed a stone. Or perhaps the rest of what I'd wanted to say was stuck there, wanting to be heard and now there was no-one to hear it. My enormous secret that I was finally going to be able to voice had only been half told. The door to the vault that I'd stoically guarded left half closed when I'd wanted to throw it wide open. I hadn't had a chance to say that I was in the very early stages of deciphering the invisible ink or explain to Jay that his ascension hinged on the healing of his past hurts. That half of the secret would need to be shoved back in the vault for another time.

I sighed. A dramatic, sorrowful sort of a sigh and collapsed back into the pillows. In hindsight I supposed it was stupid to expect a starry-eyed, romantic scene when you're asking someone to give up their life, their friends, everything they know and move to an alien planet. And yet, I could feel myself being pulled into that awful place of self-pity that I'd been sucked into just days ago. I felt hurt again and it was the last thing I wanted to be feeling. I wanted to be joyful and full of hope for the future. I wanted to be filled with love and anticipation for the life that was now possible for us and I wanted him to be feeling these things with me.

Before my disappointment could take over and win, I forced myself up and reached for the manuscript. The only way we were ever going to be together was if I could decipher Great-grandad's instructions. I needed to centre and concentrate, let go of hurt and disappointment, and focus on the only thing worth focussing on in life - The Source. I closed my eyes and breathed. It may have been a simple choice, but it was a powerful one.

White light flooded through my being, lighting every cell until I could see myself, not as flesh and bone, but crystalline. I was lucent, shimmering. My heart thrummed as that pure and glorious note reverberated through my room and sent my spirit soaring. The louder it became, the more I could feel myself expanding, until I was once again, suspended in that elevated space of clarity.

Heat was building in my chest. My heartbeat grew louder in my ears. Every beat felt like it was powerful enough to shake the walls. I looked to my heart, pulsing ruby red in a body of diamond mist. A white hot spark had ignited within, illuminating it like a lantern, and then, there it was. I could see it clearly: a spiral of light coiled inside like a spring, just waiting to push its way through.

The ruby cracked and blinding white bled forth in a streak of brilliance. It snaked forward slowly, searchingly, and came to a stop. I sat mesmerized, feeling the fervent pounding of my heart and the strange power emanating from it. I watched and waited for something else to happen but the light only peeped a little way through the crack. I had no idea what it was for or what it could do and right now, it was doing nothing. There was a crack in my heart where silvery light seeped through and I had no idea why.

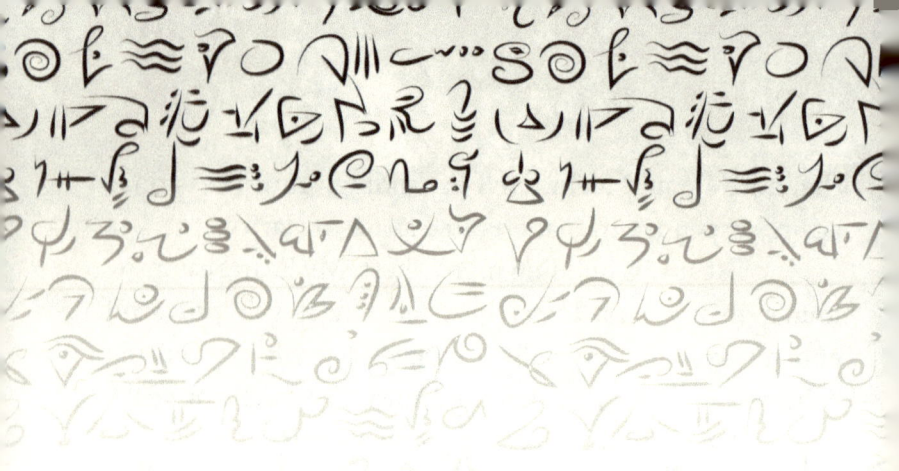

NINE

Lilly

I could hear dull echoes of laughter and music rising out of the ground as I crossed the street. The city was quiet tonight. My heels clicked against the vibrant mandalas of mosaic glass and tile set into the sidewalk. I fiddled with the plunging neckline of my dress, wondering if it was a little much and why I'd chosen to wear it. My head was still buzzing with questions about Jay, The Source energy I'd tapped into just an hour ago, and the strange beam of light that had emanated from my heart once again. I didn't understand what it meant and afterwards I hadn't been able to decipher any more entries in Great-grandad's manuscript.

I'd needed to clear my head so I'd decided to take Sky up on her invitation for a night out. The Cavern was a popular hangout with magistrument acolytes. Only a few blocks from healaxis, the underground club was, quite literally, under the ground. It was housed in one of the many crystal caves that lay beneath Citrine. A sprawling maze of damp tunnels twisted and merged with hundreds of tomblike chambers, home only to glow worms, cimmeran birds and lustrous gardens whose blooms lasted for millennia.

Enormous solar stones were mounted in wrought iron sconces on either side of the doorway, glowing like hot coals. The entrance itself was little more than an arch of soft orange light cut between buildings, no sign or symbol to mark what was hidden below.

Smaller solar stones lit the sloping tunnel as I padded down the smooth, well worn path, following my misshapen shadow. The further I wound to the belly of our city, the steeper the incline became. I could hear the music clearly now. It was one of Christian's favourite bands, Be Selene. The lead singer's voice wafted over the jangle of acoustic guitar and the slide of brushed snare, her voice a sultry concoction of smoke and brown sugar.

The tunnel levelled out to a circle of electric blue and I slipped through it, the massive cavern opening before me. The soaring roof was a neon sea, covered in glow worms that lit the cave in phosphorous blue. The floor was a thick sheet of solid crystal, clear enough to see water flowing beneath from the underground springs. Songless cimmerian birds flitted overhead, tiny as hummingbirds and black as night, their wings flashing sapphire and silver in the neon glow.

Acolytes milled, sipping wildly coloured power drinks from tall, twisted glasses. I scanned the room for Sky and Gabe, weaving around makeshift rock tables and up-cycled armchairs where people chatted and lounged on oversized cushions stitched with glass beads and richly coloured thread. There were familiar faces everywhere but no Gabe or Sky. There was a thick crowd on the dance floor. Maybe they were out there dancing.

I made my way to the bar where the jewel of The Cavern dominated the rocky wall behind it. It was a living work of art that rose from floor to lofty ceiling. A perennial garden of crystal clusters blooming from the wall like a field of gigantic flowers. Mineral rich water trickled down the rocks 'watering' the ancient blossoms and making them shimmer and glisten. The cimmerian birds flitted and hovered between the blooms like hummingbirds drawn to nectar. Instead they hovered to drink in the clean, clear water before it slid into a rocky pool behind the amberwood bar.

I cleared my throat loudly and the broom-thin bartender reluctantly tore his eyes from a leather-bound volume of 'Elemental Law: An Introduction to Properties and Power'. He was an Elemental then, like Sky.

"Sorry," he dithered, closing the book and pushing a tumble of curly, black hair from his eyes. "Big test tomorrow."

Poor guy. I felt sorry for him. He looked practically comatose from information overload. "That's okay," I smiled, "but you won't be having your test tomorrow. The Council election has been called."

He let out a relieved sigh. "Really? Thank The Source!" He clapped his hands together. Just once, but I got the feeling he wanted to raucously applaud that bit of news and then clap again in encore. "That buys me an extra day at least."

"I'm sure you'll do just fine," I kindly reassured him, then, "I hear Master Fallow is quite the task master, though."

"Yeah, he sure is." He blew out an exasperated breath and was nodding and shaking his head all at the same time. "Is he that infamous on campus?"

"No," I smirked, "my friend, Sky, told me. She's Elemental too."

"Oh, Sky... she's amazing!" he bounced, pushing his crazy curls from his face again, and looking slightly flushed. "And your name is?"

"Lilly."

"Nice to meet you, Lilly. My name is River, and yet," he gave a shamed, grimacing smile, "I'm letting you die of thirst. Sorry. Can I get you a drink?"

"Please."

He replenished a serving jug from the mineral pool behind him and waved his hand over a long line of fruit essences, juices and herbal infusions lined up on the bar. "What'll it be?"

The tall decanters of syrups and liquids glowed

like a bottled rainbow. "I think I'll have *sun spirit* and *calderberry*."

River poured the mineral rich water into an icy, fluted glass and added dashes of gold and magenta liquid that swirled like a lava lamp.

"Thanks," I winked. "Have you seen Sky tonight? I'm supposed to be meeting her here."

"She's right over there," he pointed to a table off to the side of the stage without taking his eyes off me. He sensed where his fellow Elemental was, without having to look.

The crowd in front of the stage had thinned out. The band were taking a break. I could see Sky and Gabe and several people gathered around their table, delightedly fixated on something. Walking closer, I saw a small flock of the tiny, iridescent cimmerian birds circling just above their heads, close enough to touch.

"They're just adorable!" one girl gushed.

A series of *oohs, aahhs* and giggles went up from the predominantly female assembly and seated at the centre of it all, was Christian. He smiled peacefully as the little birds alighted on his shoulders and hands, pausing only long enough to whisper something to him, then flit away again. His eyes had the half-here, half-not look he got when he used his Translator Gift.

"What are they saying now?" a girl next to him asked.

"This cheeky little mite wants to know if you

would part with a few strands of your hair for her nest," Chris grinned.

The girl plucked them without pause and delivered them to Christian's waiting hand.

"Lilly!" Sky exclaimed, spotting me behind Christian's fan club. "There's a seat here," she called me over, patting the shabby chic sofa cushion next to her. "You made it!"

The crowd parted allowing me through. All eyes had snapped to me, including Christian's. "Hey," I waved lamely, feeling extremely over-dressed under the appraising looks from all those girls.

"You look beautiful," Sky smiled as I sank gratefully into the seat.

"Stunning," Chris added.

My entrance had halted the chatter and merriment. I was fidgeting with my neckline again. Chris smiled at me serenely, an endearing sparkle in his eyes. His gaze captivated me for a moment, so light and cool, like mountain mist.

"I'm glad you came," Sky broke the moment and hugged me. "You needed a night out."

"Agreed," I said, downing the rest of my drink and banishing thoughts of Jay and cracked hearts from my mind.

I could feel Chris watching me. Could hear what he wanted to ask, but never would in front of all these people. Instead, he graciously and cleverly drew the attention away from me. "Who wants another drink?" he smiled brilliantly at everyone around him. "My shout." He threw his hands in the air, all cheer and bravado. His gaggle of groupies clapped as he led them away to the bar and the cimmerian birds circled back up to the cave's softly glowing ceiling.

I slumped gratefully next to Sky. I would have to remember to thank Chris later.

"Like I said," Sky arched her brows at me, and shot a pointed glance at Christian leading the masses to the bar, "he knows there's something up with you. He's as sensitive as they come and I think sometimes, he knows you better than you know yourself."

"I *know* he does," I agreed easily. She would raise no argument from me on that count. "He's been there all my life." A fond smile tugged at my lips.

"So how are you going to keep your family secret from him, Lilly?"

"I don't know," I shrugged. It was yet another complication I hadn't even begun to contemplate. How *was* I going to placate Christian and reassure him that I was fine? He had always been able to read me like a book. Sky was right. He knew something was bothering me and I could see that he'd wanted to ask if I was okay. How would I answer when we weren't surrounded by people? I didn't want to lie to him. There had never been anything but honesty and trust between us, at least, not until the day I'd met Jay.

Since then I'd been sneaking around in secret, unable to tell anyone that I'd fallen in love with a human. I could blame Great-grandad's manuscript and the duty I'd inherited to keep the secrets it held, but that wasn't entirely true. I'd kept Jay a secret long before I'd discovered my great-grandad had also breached the veil between worlds, fallen in love with a human and devoted his life to bringing her to Panacea permanently. I had eventually chosen to share my secret with Sky, not Chris. And then Chris had kissed me and confused things even further. My heart skipped and I squeezed my eyes shut, remembering him so close, so still. If it weren't for that kiss, I wondered if I would have eventually chosen to confide in him instead of Sky.

"Lilly?" Sky's hand was warm and gentle closing over mine. "Are you all right? Would you like to get out of here and talk?"

I slowly shook my head. "No, I just want to try and enjoy some normalcy for a while, take a breath."

She nodded and changed the subject. "I wonder where Gabriel got to?"

"Right here," he grinned, appearing out of thin air behind Sky and scaring both of us half to death. "Hey, Lilly."

"Gabe!" Sky squealed, her eyes flying wide. "You can't do that! Master Clay would have an absolute conniption if he knew. Source preserve us! You can't just stop time *whenever* and *wherever* you feel like it!"

"It was only for thirty seconds. Just enough time to sneak up on you." He kissed her on the cheek and plopped down beside her.

Sky was glowering at him while I was in hysterics. "Do you often use your Hand gifts to terrorise your girlfriend, Gabe?"

Gabe could barely contain his laughter either. "I may, or may not, *practice* occasionally without Master Clay's consent."

"So Christian was right!" I squeaked incredulously.

"What was I right about?" Chris had returned carrying a tray of brightly coloured drinks and minus his fan club.

"Gabe! He's been freezing us for practise, just like you said!" I could barely get the words out for laughing. It was funny but it wasn't *that* funny. It just felt so good to let go and laugh.

Chris' eyes went wide. "You!" he said, plonking down the tray and pointing an accusing finger at Gabe. "If I've swallowed bugs because of you..." He appeared completely affronted, annunciating each word with cutting precision, but then again it could have just been Christian in masterful ass mode.

"What?" Sky screwed up her face in confusion. "What are you talking about, Christian? What bugs?"

I was laughing so hard now that tears were streaming from my eyes. "I love you all so much!" I wheezed, trying to catch my breath. "You're the most amazing friends I could ever wish for." And my laughter, in that beautiful, contagious way that laughter has, had us all in hysterics as I explained Chris' irrational fear that bugs might fly into his mouth if he were to be frozen mid-sentence.

"It *is* possible!" he argued indignantly. "Gabe can only stop time within a certain distance from himself, so they could easily zoom into the area after he's frozen it, and then what's to stop them from flying into an open mouth?"

"You're actually serious, aren't you?" Gabe was almost doubled over with laughter. "You've seriously thought about this!"

"Oh, Christian, stop being such a big baby. It's not like you'd be swallowing a pill of poison," Sky scowled at him playfully.

"No," he shot Sky a look of cold steel, "it's far worse than that." His velvet rich voice glided over, and settled between the spaces in our laughter, commanding us to pause and listen. "Tell me, Sky," his steely blue eyes bore into her, "have you ever made a casual *snack* of someone you know?"

"Of course not," she scoffed.

"Well, maybe... I have."

Our laughter petered out as we connected the dots. Given Christian's Translator abilities, it *was* possible. Regardless of how absurd or unlikely, he *could* potentially swallow a buggy acquaintance or even a buggy friend whilst frozen! We couldn't help it. It was too ridiculous a thought. We all burst into laughter again, even Chris, albeit in between mock retching.

"I think the windshield of your car is a more likely weapon than your frozen, open mouth," I gave him a sympathetic smile and reached across the table to squeeze his hand.

"Agreed!" chuckled Gabe. "Can we please change the subject now? I think my stomach may burst if I laugh anymore."

"Dance with me?" Chris squeezed my hand back.

"I don't know if I feel like dancing."

"That's beside the point. We have to dance. We owe it to all these people." He gestured around the club.

"What are you talking about?"

"Since discovering at the ball that we're perfect dance partners, we cannot, in good conscience, deprive the world of our talent. It just wouldn't be right," he unleashed his killer smile.

The crowd roared with appreciative applause as Be Selene came back onstage.

"You see, they're hungry for us."

"Fine," I laughed, "I'll dance with you."

We moved through the swaying bodies to the centre of the floor where Chris scooped me off my feet and spun in circles. "Masterful moves, Palladen. You are a true talent."

He chuckled at my giddy laughter and planted me

back down on the lustrous crystal. He stood still, hands hot on my waist and looked down at me. His eyes were careful and tinted a brilliant blue in the light of the glow worms. "How are you?" he asked softly.

It was the question I knew was coming and the one I didn't know how to answer. If I were to answer truthfully, I would tell him I was tired; tired of all the complications I was yet to overcome, tired of keeping a mask in place in front of my friends and family, and tired from my efforts to decipher Great-grandad's manuscript. I couldn't tell him any of it but I knew a fraction of it had slipped through to show on my face. "I'm okay," I gave him a weak smile.

He didn't renew his offer to be a sounding board if I needed it, he just stood steady and gazed at me as people danced and sang and cheered all around us like water breaking against a rock. And I had that feeling again of a cocoon being woven around us, blocking out the rest of the world, until it was just Christian and me, held strong in this quiet, golden space while the world continued to heave and pulse outside. It felt just as it had when we'd kissed.

His eyes were soft and still, his face open and calm. He reached a lazy finger to sweep my hair back and placed a whisper of a kiss on my temple. His lips were warm and I breathed him in, trying to mentally describe what I smelled. It was crisp, mountain air with... cedar? Or was it musk? He drew back, leaving me guessing and recaptured me with a placid look before opening his arms in invitation for a hug. The corner of his mouth quirked as I stepped towards him, laid my head on his chest and wrapped my arms around him. His heartbeat was slow and steady in my ear, his body warm against mine. He was so tall he rested his chin on the top of my head and started to sway to the music. It pulled the world back into focus but I was content to rest against him for a while, lulled by the rhythm in his chest. And it occurred to me then that I would never have to tell him an outright lie to protect this secret because Christian would never press or pry. He only wanted assurance that I was safe and well, and that at least, I could give to him.

We danced like we were skating on a frozen pond. I stayed nuzzled into his chest and watched the steady flow of the underground spring moving below the crystal floor. A comforting swell of people ebbed and flowed around us, their carefree laughter and singing soothed me like a balm. I felt something shift in the way Chris held me. Like a part of him unfolded and collapsed against me too. I could feel what had begun as a friendly, supportive embrace, changing into something else. I was suddenly aware of Christian's palms on my back, his body pressed close, the way my left hand had fisted in his shirt. I could feel the silent smile on his lips without seeing his face.

Oh, Source above! It was true. Chris did want something more.

I fought the urge to recoil away from him, knowing

it would hurt his feelings. How could I have been so oblivious? And why was Sky always so infuriatingly right? I should have made the time to discuss our accidental kiss and clear the confusion straight after it happened, but I had been too busy with other things; too pre-occupied to notice that things had changed between Christian and me. Or maybe I hadn't wanted to accept that he had feelings for me because I didn't want to be placed in a position where I'd be forced to hurt my best friend.

The song finished, giving me an excuse to step out of his embrace and turn to applaud the band. I was too nervous to even look at him and feeling so rattled that I wandered off the dance floor without a word. I made my way like a zombie to the ladies room and locked myself in a cubicle. *This couldn't be happening.*

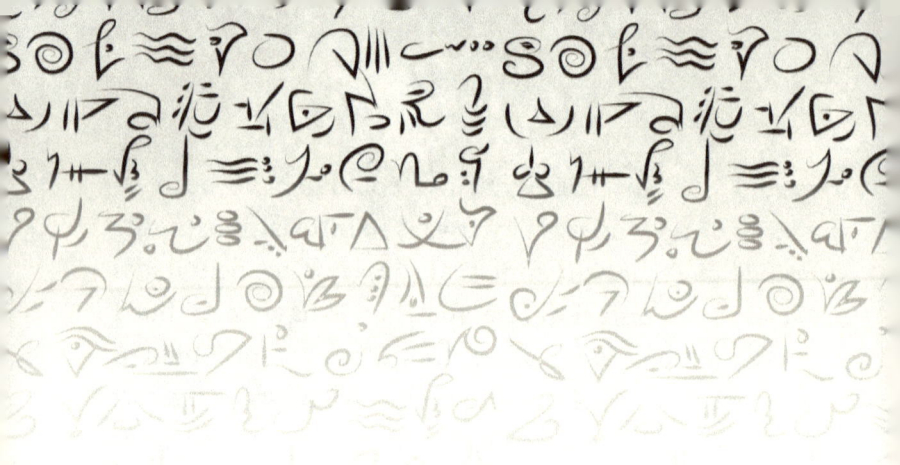

TEN

Christian

Sky and Gabe were plaited together on the sofa trading kisses and giggles when I cleared my throat and slipped into the seat opposite them.

"Where's Lilly?" Sky asked, searching behind me.

I let out a puzzled laugh, "I don't really know. Bathroom I think. We were dancing and then she kind of just took off."

Sky's eyes narrowed, taking in my confusion. She offered me a consoling smile. "She's had a lot on her plate the last few months. She's dealing with something very..." she paused, searching for the right word, "...challenging. But she's working through it."

So Sky knew what it was and I didn't. A pang of sadness tugged at me. I was relieved to know that Lilly had confided in Sky because I knew she'd keep an eye on her, but I was left to wonder why my oldest and dearest friend felt she couldn't share whatever was bothering her with me. Lilly knew all of my secrets and I knew all of hers. It had been that way since we were small, until now.

"Be patient, Chris. She'll get there."

I wasn't exactly sure *where* Sky meant by 'there'.

"I'll be back," she grinned and sauntered in the direction of the bathroom to check up on Lilly. I watched her go, feeling relief and disappointment in equal measure.

Gabe stretched his legs under the table and grinned broadly. "Don't worry. If anyone can whip Lilly into shape it's the Commando."

I chuckled and nodded, "So you know about Sky's nickname then? Did Lilly tell you?"

"No!" he barked an incredulous laugh. "I had absolutely no idea you called her that too."

"If it looks like a duck," I grinned and shrugged. "Can I ask you something, Gabe?"

"Sure, shoot."

"Have you ever had a long friendship with a girl and then wanted something more?"

"No," he rubbed his jaw, "I can't say that I have. I've never really been confident around girls, unlike some people." He jerked his chin at me with a smirk. "I was always the brainy guy with his nose buried in a book. Girls asked me to be their tutor, not their date."

"Until you met Sky."

"Until I met Sky," he agreed. "I'll never forget the first time I saw her, or rather, the first time she saw me. I was in the library on campus, dredging my way through tomes on time travel when I felt a wave of warmth rush through me. Usually when I'm engrossed in reading, nothing short of someone shouting *fire* can get my attention, but I felt the strongest urge to look up. When I did, I saw her, staring thoughtfully at me from three desks down. I didn't even notice how gorgeous she was because I was too captivated by the way she was looking at me. She saw past the piles of books scattered around me like a fortress, she saw past the shy guy that keeps to himself and she took the time to look deeper. She saw the real me, past all the layers to what's inside. It was like something unlocked inside of me and I knew, she was the one."

"Then what happened? Did our bold as brass Commando march up and introduce herself?"

"No. The exact opposite. I didn't even think or hesitate, I went straight over to her, floating on a warm wave of calm and purpose, and I asked her out. She said yes before we'd even introduced ourselves. We didn't even know each others' names!"

"I guess when it's right, it's just right."

Gabe nodded meditatively. "But back to you. I would have thought charismatic Christian Palladen would be very well versed in the intricacies of love. I'm not sure what help I could possibly offer with my limited experience."

"On the contrary," I took a long sip of my drink, "you've actually helped me a great deal. The connection you share with Sky is something Lilly and I share too. We always have, and I wonder..." I rubbed my jaw trying to piece my thoughts together. "I wonder if it hadn't been there all along if we wouldn't more readily recognise what a rare gift that connection is."

"You're wondering what would have happened if you'd met as adults instead of children?"

I nodded. "I wouldn't trade the friendship Lilly and I have shared for the world, but yes, I can't help but wonder how we would see one another now if we were just meeting for the first time. Last week I was ready to lay my cards on the table and tell her how I felt."

A deafening cheer went up from the crowd as Be Selene took their final bow and left the stage.

"So why haven't you?"

"Because now I'm second guessing myself and things have been strained between us since we kissed. She's distant... pre-occupied."

"But you can't assume that's because of you or the kiss. You heard Sky. She's struggling through something difficult at the moment."

"Yes, something she hasn't confided in me despite the fact that we've always told each other everything. It makes me think that *I'm* the difficult something she's struggling through at the moment."

"So talk to her."

"I can't. I don't want to pressure her or sway her in any way. If she *is* wrestling with how she feels about me, this is the one time I can't be there to support her. I have to give her the time to sort through her feelings on her own."

"If the Commando has anything to do with it you won't be waiting long." We both laughed. "But seriously," Gabe rested his elbows on the table and leaned in, "what about you? Have you sorted through *your* feelings?"

"I thought I had but maybe I'm making a huge mistake. The last thing I want is to jeopardize what Lilly and I share. When she ran off the dance floor, it made me think I already have."

"It sounds like you both need some space to think."

Gabe was right. I'd been going with the flow before tonight and I just had to trust that things would turn out the way they were supposed to. "What's for you won't go by you," I raised my glass and drank.

"What?"

"It's something I heard a Scottish priest say once: What's for you won't go by you," I repeated. "It struck me as such a beautiful saying that I've never forgotten it."

"Exactly. If you are meant to be more than friends, you will be. Take some time and think about what you really want."

"I will. Thanks Gabe."

He raised his glass in acknowledgment. "I don't claim to have Commando super powers but if you need a friend, I'm here." He jerked his chin in the direction of the bathroom door. The girls were coming back.

Lilly's expression was smooth as she and Sky rejoined us. There was no hint of her earlier turmoil. She was still looking like a dream in that dress. We had one more round and decided to call it a night. As we all tramped up the amber tunnel that led to street level, Lilly still looked calm and settled walking next to Sky. Whatever Sky had said or done, I was grateful to her because Lilly had looked suddenly and inexplicably torn when she'd dashed off the dance floor earlier.

A frigid breeze whistled down the tunnel raising goosebumps on our skin. Lilly shivered, pulling a jacket onto her bare arms and shoulders and hugging it tight to her chest. Gabe threw his arms around Sky to keep her warm. Had things not been strained between us, I would have done the same for Lilly, but I would not repeat my mistake of earlier this evening. Instead, I sped up and walked ahead of them.

The pale grey circle that led out into the night was getting larger, and with it, the air colder. My breath began forming clouds of steam and I looked back down the tunnel to see Sky, Gabe and Lilly huddled together, trudging upward as one. Curiosity got the better of me. I ran the rest of the way, bursting through the entrance and into a world of shocking white. I could never have imagined our city bleached of all its vibrant colour, yet here it was, every structure and statue, every treetop and roof, wrapped in a pale cloak. Stunned citizens were milling about looking skyward then back at the icy blanket that had swallowed our world. To my knowledge it had never snowed in Citrine, until now. Even stranger, we were only at the beginning of Leaf Fall and this was the second anomalous weather event to strike in the past week.

My mind clicked into connection. It was only days ago that we'd suffered an extreme heat wave, the same day Uma the elephant had materialised into our world from Earth. Was it merely coincidence? Now, nature's balance had been disrupted again.

"Oh my God! Is that actually snow?" Lilly bent down and grabbed a handful of glittering ice, sifting it through her fingers the way she always did with sand at the beach. She smiled in awe. "I've never seen real snow!"

Sky looked miserable beside her. "Ugh, this must be me having a nightmare about Endua. I moved to Citrine to get away from..." she made an irksome gesture all around her, "...this," she grimaced. "Pinch me, please."

Gabe immediately obliged and Sky squealed, swatting at him to stop.

"What in the name of The Source is going on with this city? Floods, heatwaves, snow!" Gabe was directing his question to me but I didn't have an answer... yet. I scanned the street, wondering if more animals were going to materialise out of thin air at any moment or if they already had.

"This is amazing!" Lilly was twirling in circles, her hands reaching for the heavens as stray snowflakes danced between her fingers.

More acolytes were emerging from the Cavern into a glittering, foreign world. They laughed and marvelled, trying to skate on patches of ice on the road, or flopping onto their backs to make angels in the snow. Before too long, there was a decent crowd frolicking and playing all around us.

"Look!" Sky cried, "Sebastian is making a giant snowflake!"

"Isn't that a little redundant?" I smirked, gesturing at the actual snowflakes falling from the sky.

Gabe chuckled while Sky ignored me. "Look, it's beautiful." She grabbed Gabe's hand and hauled him toward Sebastian and his snow sculpture.

Lilly skipped gleefully to take a look and I followed, while keeping an eye out for anything else strange. Sebastian's snowflake was nearly five feet wide. He had lovingly carved and moulded an intricate lace pattern on the snow covered ground. It looked like a mandala made of ice. At least it did until the first snowball glanced off Gabriel's shoulder and exploded in the snowflake's middle, showering us with the fallout of the obliterated masterpiece.

Sky squealed and whirled. "Who threw that?" she demanded.

Stifled giggles came from behind a statue of a voluptuous bronze lady. Her long hair draped around her body like a gown and tickled at her toes. Sky's eyes trained on the spot while she silently signalled for all of us to take cover behind a nearby bench.

"What are we doing?" Gabe looked puzzled as he squeezed in next to us and crouched down.

"We're bunkering down," Sky hissed, scooting in next to Lilly.

"*Bunkering down?*" I echoed, laughing.

"Are we going to have a snow fight?" Lilly was wide-eyed and sparkling. She had the same mischief-filled look I'd seen on her face a thousand times.

"Lilly, shhhhh! Don't you know what happens when somebody says *snow fight?*" Sky already had a modest arsenal before her, her hands moving deftly and with lightning speed. She'd been rolling snowballs on auto-pilot like a true snow fight veteran. I followed suit, as did the others. "Not like that," she directed Lilly, "you have to pack the snow hard so your ball doesn't fly apart when you throw it."

Sky's last words were lost as someone behind the statue yelled 'snow fight' and war was declared. I was fairly sure that Gabe was to blame. I looked up in time to see him holding a snowball high above the barrier of our park bench and pointing at it.

Cannon balls of white shattered against the front of our bench and sprayed us with snow through the slats. The girls shrieked, crouching lower between Gabe and I.

"Return fire!" Sky yelled.

We hurled our snowballs but they exploded

harmlessly against the bronze lady, except for a wicked curve ball from Gabe that raised a screech from one of our invisible assailants.

"Nice shot," Sky beamed at Gabe and kissed him on the cheek, "but this is no good. We can't win from this position. You three stay here. I need to break ranks. Cover me."

"Who – are – you?" Gabe laughed incredulously.

She ignored him. "On my signal, give them everything you've got." She had a wicked gleam in her eye. "Ready, now!"

Sky took off like a shot while we hurled a steady stream of snowballs at the statue. Gabe even got in a few more hits, raising shrieks of delight from Lilly.

Our distraction paid off. Sky had made it unnoticed to the other side of the street and was casually walking through the crowd, using other people as cover, to circle around behind our attackers.

"Where did she go?" Lilly was peeping through the slats searching for Sky.

"There," I nodded as she darted out of the crowd with an armful of snowballs and ran back across the street.

"Look at Commando go!" Gabe roared with laughter as Sky, lithe and graceful as a gazelle, launched a sprinting assault from behind enemy lines. She hurtled snowballs at their backs with unnatural accuracy as she sailed over the snow as lightly as a water spider. Screams of surprise pierced the air as our enemies abandoned their cover and ran out into the open.

"Attack, attack!" Sky yelled, herding them toward us. Lilly, Gabe and I were all laughing so hard at Commando we weren't capable of attacking anything. Sky's usually sleek, black hair was sticking out in all directions and despite our hysterics, she never lost her focussed fervour as she loosed her last snowball.

We pulled ourselves together and launched over the bench, firing and surrounding the enemy as we went but more people had decided to join in the fun. A cold, wet thud struck between my shoulder blades. Then another at the back of my head. Suddenly it was all out war and we were standing helplessly at its centre as we were mercilessly pelted. Within minutes, no-one could make snowballs fast enough to defend themselves. We were in the centre of a blizzard as people threw fistfuls of snow at one another instead. We were bombarded from every direction, squealing and laughing as Sky's organised assault descended into utter chaos and she and Lilly were holding hands and dancing in giddy circles. The only victor tonight would be childlike joy.

Moments later, drenched and freezing, we piled into Gabe's car across the street to head home. Lilly, shivering in the back seat next to me, had turned a pale shade of lavender but was still bouncing with excitement. Her hands and feet were always freezing at the best of times and I could only imagine that she'd be positively hypothermic by now. Had there not been this awkwardness between us, she'd already be sitting snug and close. I glanced at her, debating what to do.

"Scoot over and get warm if you like," I finally offered.

"I'm okay, thanks," she smiled at me.

"I'll turn up the heat," Sky suggested.

Gabe glanced at me in the rearview mirror and I read his look: *You both need space to think.*

So, for the rest of the drive I stared out the window watching Citrine fly by, its vibrant colours doused in white, while vaguely keeping watch for lost Earth animals.

We were almost at my place when I heard my name and felt an icy hand touch mine.

"Chris, would it be okay if I came in for a while?"

It caught me off guard. Lilly's face was smooth but I could see a flicker of apprehension in her hazel eyes. I had spent the ride home solidifying my intention to give myself space and the time to think carefully about what I truly wanted. I could see in her eyes that she was nervous, that she had something important to say. Had she already made her decision? I found myself agreeing to talk with her while a knot was forming in my chest.

We said our goodbyes to Sky and Gabe and I trundled ahead through the rainforest trees to open my front door. The house my parents had left me was enormous. It was all rustic redwood and glass panels, like a grown-up's version of a treehouse. But instead of being perched in a tree, the house had been built *around* them. A magnificent falisgus tree formed the heart of my home, rising from a courtyard at its centre and soaring a full two stories above the roofline. The house was far too big for one person, but it had seemed silly to part with it after my parents had retired and moved away. After all, I hoped to settle down and have a family one day and there were so many happy childhood memories for me here. Every mark on the walls and scratch on the floors told a story and so many of those stories included Lilly. I breathed a silent sigh and pushed open the door. Whatever she had to say, I would accept it because I loved her.

A bowl of solar stones on the coffee table lent an amber glow to the living room. I had left the windows open and a fine dusting of snow had settled on the sills. Lilly was following silently behind me and I could feel a pressure building between us. I turned to see her standing at the threshold of the room, not quite knowing what to do. She looked as though she'd just realised she was soaked through and freezing.

"Source above, Lilly, you're blue! You need a hot shower to warm up."

"Actually, that would be great. I didn't exactly think this through, did I?" She looked embarrassed. "Do you mind if I have a quick shower?"

"Since when do I mind? Your clothes are still hanging on the right-hand side of my wardrobe."

"Thanks," she smiled and hurried upstairs.

It had been months since we'd last been sailing on my parents' yacht, well, I supposed it was my yacht now, but Lilly had always kept dry clothes here for when we returned. Between my love of sailing and Lilly's love of the sea, there'd been countless lazy days of sun with salt on our skin and the endless blue of the ocean. I wandered over to the glass wall that overlooked the river and dock. Cleo's mast waved against the inky sky, like a giant magician's wand, lazily conjuring up the stars. I'd have to take her out again soon. Maybe invite Gabe and Sky.

I began closing windows to warm up the room and decided to light a fire. Although there was only a small amount of snowfall in my neighbourhood, the air was still frigid. I was stretching out on the fur rug in front of the fire when Lil padded down the stairs wearing a pair of ripped and faded jeans and a loose, linen shirt. I grabbed some more pillows from the sofa and laid them out so she could join me on the floor.

"You've already changed your clothes," she pointed.

"I'm sneaky and efficient," I winked. "Do you want some hot chocolate?"

"Not just yet. I need to talk to you."

She shifted her gaze from me to the fire as though she hoped to find the right words flickering in the flames. I had no idea what was coming. I couldn't get a read on Lilly lately. One moment she was with me and in the next breath, she'd disappear entirely. It was probably as much my own unbalanced head as it was her up and down behaviour of late that had bought us to this. We were sitting in awkward silence – something we never did. I didn't like these moments of unease that had been interrupting our easy flow. They were like a dam; unnatural and destructive. And it was because of this dam between us that I'd only just realised how desperately I missed how we used to be. How I'd always felt peaceful in a way that I only could with her. If what she was about to say returned us to our easy flow, I'd be grateful for it, no matter what; even if it meant setting aside my heart.

Lilly was a blue diamond. She shone a different kind of light. All go-lites were compassionate and sensitive by nature, but Lilly's instinct was to understand others completely, to *feel* everything they felt. She could dive inside another person and know what it was like to *be* them. It was as though she had an innate need to feel through their skin, see with their eyes and breathe through their lungs. Her complex sensitivity made her more vividly alive somehow but it also left her vulnerable.

I'd often had the feeling when we were growing up that her parents worried about her extraordinary sensitivity. Now that she was a Soul Guardian, I worried about it too. She'd seemed so off of late. I wondered if she'd been diving too deeply into the troubles of humans and neglecting her own well-being. But it was more likely that me kissing her had thrown her into a tailspin.

She was still staring into the flames. Her long

hair hung in wet waves of jet down her back. A rivulet of water was sliding down her temple, or maybe it was perspiration. "What are we?" she finally breathed.

And just like that, I found myself smack-bam in the middle of the exact situation I'd been hoping to avoid: helping Lilly sort through her feelings for me.

The chirp of crickets outside and the crackle of the fire stabbed at the silence between us.

"What are we to one another, I mean?" she clarified.

I already knew what she was asking, I just wasn't sure how to answer. Yet somehow, now that we were here, together, I wondered how I could have sorted through my own feelings without trusting and confiding in her as I always had. I knew what we had always meant to each other but I didn't know where we stood now. I kept my voice low and steady and answered her in the only way I could in that moment. "I don't know."

I waited.

I watched her slow, searching breaths.

"You've always been with me." Her face was blank, stunned, as though she was only just realising the interminable truth of it.

"Yes."

She turned her hazel eyes on me and they were glazed with feeling. "I don't remember a time without you in it." The firelight cut dark shadows along the line of her nose and under her cheekbones, her lips were licked red by flame. Her eyes swept over my face, tracing all the lines and angles that she knew by heart, as though she was searching for something. After a few intense moments she looked away, gazing once again into the flames. When she spoke, her voice was wistful. "Do you remember the things we used to imagine when we were kids?" A tiny smile played on her lips.

I stretched, reclining on a pile of pillows and propped my head on my hand. "I remember riding on the backs of tigers and making houses in the clouds."

"I was at Mum and Dad's place the other day, remembering the games we used to play. What about the hollowed out tree we made into a doorway to other worlds?"

"That's right," I chuckled. "I also remember pretending to glide over the water in a seashell boat with golden sails woven from mermaids' hair, and you deciding to jump overboard."

A coy little smile lit up her face and she gave a slight shrug. "I wanted to see if you'd be brave enough to dive into the sea serpent-infested waters and save me, and, of course, you did."

"Hmm, I seem to remember being more concerned about the sea monsters' safety than yours," I mused.

She scowled at me through her smile. "Hilarious as always, Christian."

"It's true," I placed my hand over my heart, "you were a bold and stubborn child, you know. Heaven help the sea monster that's foolish enough to capture you."

"Well, I might have been bold and stubborn, but *you* were annoyingly right all the time."

I sat up at that. "What do you mean *were?*" I teased. "I'm still right all the time," I grinned widely, "and you, are still bold and stubborn."

She burst into laughter. "I'd dearly love to argue but you're absolutely right... as always."

Smugly accepting my win, I gave a seated mock bow. "Are you sure you're not conceding just to appear less stubborn? Because it won't work you know."

We were both laughing. Lilly's eyes danced.

"No, I know. I can't ever fool you, can I?"

Our laughter softened and faded until there was only the whirring chirp of crickets. We stared at each other, sitting so close, the laugh lines giving way to searching looks and eventual awkward silence.

I looked into her eyes for endless seconds. Two round, deep, shining ponds. I could see sadness there, regret. My heart sank. "Are you trying to fool me, Lilly?"

Her brow furrowed and she flinched as though she'd been stung. It was the same torn look I'd seen as she'd wrenched herself away from me at The Cavern. One moment we'd been peaceful and contented in each others' arms, in the next, she'd jerked away and fled.

She exhaled loudly. She'd been holding her breath. "No, Christian, never." She looked away and back into the flames. "That's the last thing I'd ever want. You're one of the most precious people in my life and," she loosed a regretful sigh, "I think I've taken you for granted." She turned to me then, the full force of her sad eyes meeting mine. "I don't think I've ever thanked you for being in my life, for all the things you do, for the person you are."

I could feel and hear love brimming from every syllable and my heart swelled. I silently thanked The Source for her.

"I can't imagine what my life would be without you," she went on. "You've always been there and I don't want that to change."

"I don't either. You're a part of me, Lilly." It was the truth.

"And you are a part of me... an irreplaceable part."

There was no point in skirting the issue any longer. "But now you feel I've messed things up by kissing you?"

"No," she shook her head, "please don't say that." Her eyes were downcast, her cheeks flushed, whether from the heat of the fire or embarrassment, I couldn't guess which. I still didn't know where this was going or what she was going to say.

"I didn't plan for it to happen," I explained. "It took me as much by surprise as it did you. It just felt... right at the time."

Her eyes shot to mine and she seemed to search my face again.

"And then I realised that my feelings for you

had changed," I confessed, "that I must have been curious about us for a while and what we might be. I guess the kiss was me acting on that impulsive curiosity. I'm sorry for the awkwardness it's caused between us, but I won't say I'm sorry it happened."

"I'm not sorry either." A spark burned in her eyes, brighter than any ember, and then it was gone. "But..." she left the word hanging in the air as she braced herself to continue, "I came here tonight to tell you that I'm not free to wonder what could be between us, Christian."

My heart tightened in my chest as disappointment crashed through me.

"I'm involved in something... with someone and the last thing I want to do is mislead you."

Lilly was still speaking but I didn't hear her, I was too focussed on the sensation of my stomach dropping. I watched as recent memories of us played through my mind: Lilly balancing a butterfly on her finger at the Midsummer ball; her bursting through the water's surface at the Crystal Pools; the feel of her breath and her lips on mine.

So, she'd been seeing someone. That's why things had been strained, not because of the kiss but because she was already involved and didn't know how to break it to me.

Who was she seeing?
Why had she kept it a secret from me?
I felt numb and wounded all at once, as though

who I was had been cut in half, like the dam had been slammed between us, permanently this time. It felt wrong.

There was nothing stopping my own feelings though. I let them flow through me like water, the thoughts, the hurt. I watched it all tumble and churn and once the waters had stilled and I felt balanced enough to speak again, I did. "So Sky knows you've been seeing someone?"

"Sky knows most of what's going on," she admitted, "she's the only person I've told."

"Why the secrecy?"

"I wish I could tell you, Chris, I really do, but I can't. I'm not sure I should have even told Sky." She looked resigned, adamant. There was that stubborn streak again, for better or worse.

I couldn't make sense of what she was saying. I felt so disconnected from her. "You're scaring me, Lilly. Why in heaven would you have to keep it a secret? Is this why you've been so tired and out of sorts lately?"

"Honestly, yes." Her shoulders slumped. "Keeping secrets from the people you love is hard work, but in this case, it's necessary, for now at least. Please just trust that I'm okay and I'm doing what I feel is the right thing. The Source has presented me with a challenge, and it isn't easy, but I need to see it through."

I watched her for a long moment, trying to figure out what challenge she could possibly be facing in a brand new relationship. I could feel how exhausted she was, both physically and emotionally, but there was something more; a heaviness that I didn't recognise and her struggle to bear its weight. There was a list of questions forming in my mind which I didn't voice. I would not press her or pry. Eventually, I gave her a single nod. "I trust you," I said, "if you feel guided to do whatever it is that you're doing, I'll support you... always. And I know the Commando will keep an eye on you and make sure you're okay as well."

"She will, don't worry." She sat silent and adrift for a moment as though she was doubting her earlier conviction. I saw the instant she shrugged it off and claimed back her certainty. "And thank you," she whispered, "for trusting me. Your friendship means everything."

I looked at her squarely. "Did you really think you could ever lose it?"

· Her jaw tightened and she swallowed. "I was afraid... of losing *you*."

There it was again – that wistful, tortured look. I shook my head and reached over to hold her hand where it was fisted in her lap. She relaxed a little and gave me a ghost of a smile. I stared down at our clasped fingers and brushed my thumb over her knuckles. Her hand, for once, was warm. I wanted to reassure her, to let her know that I'd always be there for her. When I looked up again to speak, she was staring at me through glazed, expectant eyes and her lashes were dark with tears. I gave her a crooked smile. "You and I, we've played crystal xylophones in underground caves, and climbed ladders all the way up to the stars, we've even tamed wild dragons!" I smiled. "How many worlds do you think we've imagined?"

"I don't know," she said with a wan smile, "hundreds... maybe thousands."

"And in all of the worlds we've dreamt up, in all the adventures we've had, have we ever been apart?"

"No, it's always been you and me, together." Her voice was shaking. "And I don't ever want to imagine a world without you in it."

"Lilly, I don't think it's *possible* for me to imagine a world without you." I shook my head. "You know, some people might say that all the things we've dreamt up are nothing but childish fantasies, but I believe our dreams point to our greatest truths. If you believe in us, if you believe in the truth behind the dreams we've made together, you must know that we'll never be apart, because without you, Lilly, there wouldn't be a world worth dreaming."

Tears trembled in her eyes and she reached for me, burying her face in the crook of my neck, salty warmth spilling on my skin. I wrapped my arms around her and pressed my lips to her damp hair. Her tears came silently like rain drops from a sun shower. And when they had, she cupped my jaw with tender fingers and kissed my cheek, lingering to press her forehead against my temple. The thick scent of my cedar soap clung to her skin. She drew back and collapsed against me, going limp like a discarded marionette.

A log on the fire popped and crackled sending a swirl of sparks up the chimney like scattering fireflies. Lilly's eyelashes fluttered against my neck and stilled. I nestled back into the pile of pillows and she slid down to rest her head on my chest and curled her willowy legs against my thigh.

My mind was at a standstill, anchored in place by the flickering flames and the steady cadence of her breathing. It had only taken one sentence from her to dissolve the dream I'd barely begun to imagine. *I'm not free to imagine what more there could be between us.* But right now, we were here, together. I had meant what I'd said about always being together, no matter what form 'always' took. I believed in us.

I glanced down to see that she was drifting off to sleep. I was about to rouse her and take her home, when I realised that this could be the last chance I'd have to hold her this way. Tomorrow brought with it a new world where Lilly had given her heart to someone else.

Tomorrow could wait a while longer.

I wasn't ready to let her go, not just yet.

I gazed down at her angelic face, soft and flushed by fire, her feathered lashes dark with tears. She looked so little, curled up against my chest. I kissed her hair and held her tighter. She shifted and sighed, resting her cheek against my heart, her rose petal lips parted in an 'O'. Wrapped around each other, peaceful and warm, we couldn't have been any closer, yet we'd never felt so far apart.

If this moment was all we had, I was going to be here with her completely. So I pushed away my sadness and made a silent promise to be happy for her. I would keep my word, I would support her in whatever she chose to do and I would always be her friend.

I committed the feel of her to my memory and thought of all the love I'd been keeping inside just for her. I smashed down the dam between us and opened my heart. I finally let the feelings I'd been keeping bottled up inside, flow to where they belonged, to the only girl who had ever stirred them in me. I closed my eyes. "I love you, Lilly. Always."

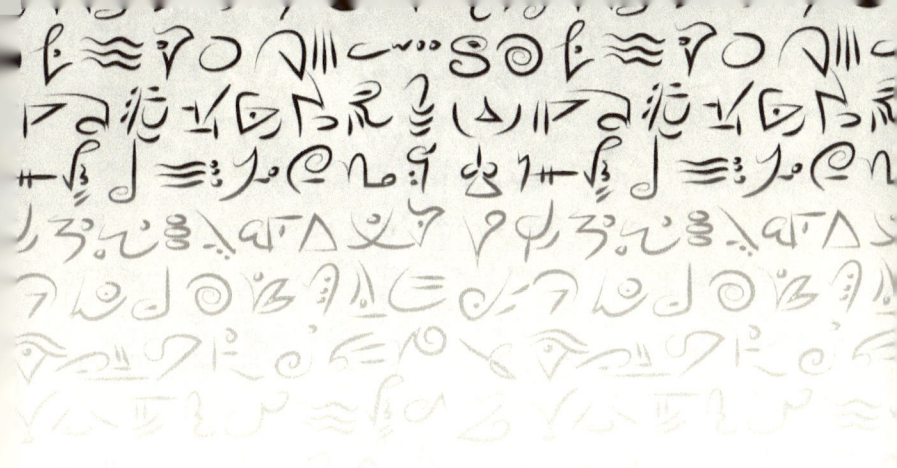

ELEVEN

Lilly

Ophanim Dome glittered like an icy egg, its opaque crystal walls slick with sunlight. Brass flagpoles had been erected to encircle the Dome, streaming pale ribbons of fluttering silk.

"Traveller Flights, second bay to the left, please, Sir." The parking attendant smiled at us through the window and waved us down the sparkling marble drive.

"My goodness! Did you see all the people?" My mother exclaimed, pointing through the trees to the expansive gardens surrounding the Dome.

I hadn't. My head was dazed with the events of the last 24 hours. At least I had patched things up with Chris. He knew the truth now, and as much as his disappointment was eating at me, it had been the right thing to do. I had already unintentionally given him false hope and I felt terrible for it. Had I not been so consumed with Jay and the manuscript, I would have seen it immediately. It wasn't like me to miss something so monumental. *You must pay more attention to your own life, Lilly.* But that was the point, wasn't it? I was trying to figure out how to build a life with Jay. But today was about my father. Jay's moody and detached behaviour and the bizarre burst of light that had radiated from my heart would have to wait.

We'd driven through the back entrance with the rest of the Council nominees. My dad cut the engine and hesitated in his seat. My mother and I both looked at him, waiting.

"Are you all right, sweetheart?" My mum touched his shoulder. He was wearing a gorgeous suit of the softest dove grey.

He breathed out a sigh and after a brief pause, nodded his head. "Yes, I'm all right." He caught my eye in the rear view mirror and flashed his sunbeam smile.

"Is that *confidence* I smell?" I winked at him.

"Actually, yes," he grinned, holding out his wrist so I could smell the fragrance Mum had bought for him.

"Well then," I urged, "shall we?"

He nodded again and we piled from the car, my mum fussing with Dad's silk tie, and me, smoothing down the skirts of my plum voile dress.

An attendant showed us through a set of iron gates and pointed down a pebbled path to a large platformed gazebo. It was reserved for Council nominees and their loved ones to view the ceremonial procession of Elders. It rose from the lawn like a sculpted wedding cake, frothing with white iron lace and cascades of flowering vines. My mother glided up the stairs. Her hair was arranged loosely in an artful twist over one shoulder, her pale, graceful neck swayed and curved as she greeted the families already seated on plump damask chairs. Around it, her green *vida* crystal hung from its silver chain. Her dress was the colour of ripe pears, strewn with dainty, white flowers. She was a picture of grace, moving like a song.

We took our seats and cast our eyes over the crowd. We had a birds' eye view, right next to the aisle where the Council would parade by. The air was electric. Thousands of people had gathered to witness the rare spectacle and their collective anticipation beat like a pulse. Some were dressed in finery to mark the occasion, others in work clothes; having abandoned their posts for the day. Everywhere there were banners waving with love and well wishes for Elder Sparks' retirement.

My dad perched between Mum and me, holding our hands tightly in his.

"So, when you're elected..."

"Lilly," he scolded gently under his breath, his eyes darting to make sure no one had heard.

I ignored him and tried again, "*When* you're elected," I persisted, but more quietly this time, "what spirit animal do you think you'll be partnered with?"

"I honestly haven't thought about it." He looked amused.

"Really? What do you think, Mum?"

"I couldn't even begin to guess," she blinked. "That's for The Source to decide. I'll never forget seeing Elder Tunes' spirit animal arrive at the last election, though. You were only a week old at the time and while I was utterly exhausted, I didn't want to miss seeing it. You were bundled up in my arms sleeping as that glorious eagle spiralled from the sky like a lazy comet."

"I remember," said my dad. "She looked like a falling star – white and bright and burning – until two magnificent wings unfurled and we could see that it was an eagle. And you," he nudged me, "slept through the whole thing! It was the first time your mother and I had seen you sleep soundly... ever!"

"Amid all the excitement and racket, there you were, as peaceful as can be," Mum agreed.

All I could say was, "Huh."

A bright chime rang out, sending a hush over the crowd and turning heads toward the garden's entrance. The parade was about to begin. Excited children were hoisted onto their parents' shoulders for a better view. The crowd shuffled and swayed toward the aisle as music arrested the air in sustained, chiming notes. All eyes were fixed on the still, empty space where the High Council would begin their procession.

There were awed gasps and cheers as Grand Master Genevieve Trill stepped into view and bowed. Her emerald green robes spilled around her like water as she took a gliding step down the aisle. Her auburn hair danced like fire and she wore a smile to rival the sun. Flower petals rained down in white, pink and blue, tossed from adoring hands. Trailing behind her skirts, I glimpsed a slinking shape. It appeared and disappeared as it wove through the folds of her green robes like a ghost moving through a forest. It looked like it was made of liquid glass; sleek, shining and transparent, there one moment and gone the next.

Everyone peered, trying to get a good look at the spirit animal that only ever accompanied an Oracle like Grandmaster Trill. Oracles were rare, so it was rarer still to have an opportunity to see the spirit lynx that always accompanies them.

The mysterious cat was living up to its reputation; moving in and out of shadows, silently drinking in the crowd and giving nothing away. It was said to be a keeper of secrets and to hold the wisdom of eternity. As they drew closer, I was captivated by each fluid step, by the way the lynx's diaphanous form shifted in and out of this world, a slick trick of the light.

Grand Master Aldos Mont came next, a rippling lion following in the wake of his scarlet robes. It moved with prowling precision and an immense power that was at odds with a body as insubstantial as air.

Elder Lucius Spry, who was a powerful Seer, bore a restless spirit raven on his left shoulder. Its glassy wings silently beat the air, its colourless body refracting the light like clear crystal. His robes were black as pitch and behind him, came Elder Roland Sparks dressed in goldenrod. He moved with effort as the crowd cheered and waved their banners, thanking him for years of faithful service. His animal companion was in spirit form no more. A fantastically coloured snake, solid and real, wound around his arm and draped across his shoulders. Its skin glistened magenta and orange flame, patterned with stars of obsidian and diamonds of kingly blue. As a Healer, it was fitting that his spirit animal had been a snake. Now his companion had taken corporeal form so that when it was time for Elder Sparks to leave this world, it would make the journey with him. They would shed their bodies together and their spirits would journey on to the next life in Utopia.

The path was now a carpet of soft petals, swished and stirred by the Elders' vibrant robes. The menagerie of spirit animals moved placidly with their Elders, without leaving a single mark of paw or hoof. A regal stag pranced by with Elder Lola Zenith, its antlers glinting like diamonds. A great, lumbering bear walked beside Elder August Melladon. The crowd gasped as it rose onto its hind legs, towering over the rest of the procession, its crystalline body reflecting the sun and shooting dazzling spears of light over the crowd.

Thirty-five Elders in all made the march down the long garden aisle to the sweeping scalloped stairs of Ophanim Dome. I grinned broadly at Elder Tunes as he seemingly bounced down the path with his magnificent eagle, Aquila, gliding high above him. He was even more excited than the children; waving to the crowd, shaking their hands and pausing to spread his infectious glee. To Atticus Tunes, every moment of life was cause for celebration. He existed in a state of perpetual joy and abandon, and to say it was contagious was to underestimate something very powerful indeed.

Grand Master Nevaya Willow was the last to make the walk. She carried with her an air of mystery, wearing deep purple robes that lit her violet eyes. Her ebony hair cascaded over one shoulder and swung in a shining sheet to her waist. By her side, stalked a sleek, hyaline wolf; its footfalls soundless, its thick fur translucent and glittering.

It was breath-taking to see the High Council, resplendent in richly coloured robes with their spirit animals at their sides. They stood in loose formation on the sweeping steps of the Dome, the spirit animals looking like a collection of life sized, crystal figurines as the crowd erupted in enthusiastic applause.

Grand Master Mont raised his ebony arms and stepped forward. His sable hair fell to his waist in dozens of tight braids, woven through with crystal beads that clinked together when he moved. His silvery lion planted his supple paws next to him and shook out his fluid mane. A hush travelled over the crowd. "Would the nominees please come forward."

This was it. My dad and the two other nominees

rose amongst a flurry of hugs, kisses and well wishes and made their walk to the foot of the Dome's wide, scalloped steps. The towering doors yawned open, the columns of ancient symbols on either side glowing gold, and the High Council flowed into the Dome like a rainbow wave. My father and the other nominees followed and the doors were firmly closed behind them.

I looked at my mother slack-jawed. The power of speech had fled me.

She laughed. "I think my face looked just as stunned as yours when I first saw it. And the best is still to come." She stroked my cheek.

"That was incredible," I choked out. "How long do you think it will take them to make a decision?"

"The Source only knows, but at least long enough to get a bite to eat I should think."

"That sounds great. I'm famished."

Stray petals swirled around the crowd like confetti as we walked, arm in arm, through the stalls. Spiced chickens sizzled over coal pits, groups of children ran with their hands linked like daisy chains, music wove through the scene, and everyone smiled and laughed, still in awe of the rare spectacle we'd been lucky enough to witness. Artisan's tents were clustered together like the bright squares of a patchwork quilt. Potters and glass blowers were busily crafting spirit animal figurines while Artists captured their likeness in pastels and paints. I bought a pocket portrait of the elusive lynx that had fascinated and intrigued me. The Artist had captured it beautifully. I held the picture up to Mum and the mysterious cat slunk towards her, its eyes wide and appraising.

"Beautiful work," she praised the Artist who smiled back with his paint-smeared face.

We were munching on some honeyed meat and flatbread when Sky and Gabe found us lounging on one of the many picnic blankets that had been laid out on the lawns.

"That was incredible!" Sky gushed. "I hope I get to see that again one day." Sky's fingers were interlaced with Gabe's and I felt a pang of longing seeing how easy it was for them, how simple. "Did you see Elder Gideon Loch's spirit dolphin swimming beside him... on thin air?"

"I know!"

"What about Rose Wynters' spirit spider?" Gabe crowed pulling Sky down to sit at the blanket's edge."

Elder Wynter's was the tallest woman I had ever seen. She comported herself like a swaying tree and her nest of brambled hair had been connected to her shoulder by a glass web with her spirit spider crouched at the centre.

"I loved Peaches Amaroo and her adorable little rabbit," my mother cooed, "tucked all nice and snug under her arm."

"Did anyone see Elder Petulla Zaph's spirit animal? I couldn't make it out," Sky asked.

"It was a dragonfly," grinned Gabe. "It was flitting around at a million miles an hour."

Hearty cheering was coming from the crowds closest the Dome's doors. It whipped over the gardens and rides, the stalls and hills scattered with picnic blankets, until everyone around us was cheering too. We stood to see the Elders filing through the doors and arranging themselves on the stairs with their spirit animals.

"This is it," my mother caught my hand and squeezed. "Let's get back to our seats."

We gave Sky and Gabe a hurried wave and set off into the thickening crowd.

We just made it back to the gazebo as the three nominees emerged through the colossal, glowing doors. My dad's expression was smooth, unreadable, as he lined up to Grand Master Mont's left. There was a reverent hush over the crowd. All the gaiety and cheering was suppressed in anticipation of the big announcement. Grand Master Mont stood proudly with his lion, bearing robes of sunshine yellow on his arm for the new Elder elect.

"Citizens of Citrine," he announced without preamble, "please join me in welcoming Traveller Jonathan Flights to the Council of Elders."

I hardly realised I'd been holding my breath as Mum cheered and threw her arms around me, crushing the air from my lungs. The people roared their approval and more flower petals were tossed into the breeze, fluttering like fragrant confetti. Grand Master Mont turned to my father and beckoned him forward. He clasped my father's hand and stepped close, bowing his head so their foreheads were touching in a gesture of oneness and welcome. My dad smiled humbly and accepted his new robes, pulling them on and tying the belt at his waist. Each council member welcomed my father in kind, heads bowing together in love and solidarity, a meeting of like minds. At last, he turned to the crowd and tipped his head in thanks for their support. They roared louder. "Love and light," they cheered, "love and light!"

Pride swelled within me for the man who had worked tirelessly throughout his life for others. He loved my mother and me with more joy and zeal than I'd ever seen anyone love and he shared that love with every frightened orphaned child he placed with a new family and every single person he met. He truly was like the sun; an inexhaustible source of light and warmth that reaches far and wide but never dims.

Grand Master Mont raised his arms, calling to the crowd for quiet.

"This is it," Mum whispered into my ear. "I wonder what your dad's spirit animal will be?"

A shiver of excitement ran down my spine as The Council's eyes trained skyward and the eyes of the crowd followed.

Grand Master Mont's voice boomed into the silence, his eyes shone golden; the colour of burnt toffee. "We call forth a brother or sister from the spirit realm to join with Elder Jonathan Flights, to be an extension of his consciousness, to guide his learning, and to inspire, so he may fulfil his Soul purpose and forever be a clear conduit of The Source's light."

A fierce rumble split the sky, scattering the clouds, leaving empty blue above. A Source driven wind whipped through the crowd. Grand Master Mont's braids clattered together and the Elders robes were caught like sails. The people gasped, then a reverent hush fell over the Dome as everyone gaped at the brilliant pinprick of light that had appeared from nowhere. It grew larger by the second as it hurtled toward us, arcing across the sky and leaving a trail of silver vapour like the finest glitter. Finding its mark, it rocketed toward us, picking up speed and looming larger by the second. It was exactly as my parents had described; a blazing comet of blinding white light.

As it shot closer I had to squint against the all encompassing brightness. People were shielding their eyes with their hands but were too mesmerised to look away completely. As the blazing ball neared, it slowed, coalescing into more than blinding light and vapour. Something was shifting within the sphere as though the light particles were rearranging themselves. It hovered high above us, a bubble suspended in the air as a fluid form began to take shape and the blinding brightness dimmed.

A slender leg was the first thing to emerge, followed quickly by a long face with a flowing mane. It was a majestic stallion; sleek and glittering and moving like quicksilver. Its mercurial body reared, hooves punching the air, then he set off at a gallop toward my father, leaving a dusting of stars trailing across the cornflower sky.

He zigged and zagged on thin air as though galloping down a steep, winding path. His hooves made not a sound as he alighted on the grassy, green aisle before the Council of Elders and reared, tossing his lucent mane. The crystalline creature bowed and shook out his transparent flanks then trotted up to the Council assembly on shining, liquid limbs. Only the bright sunlight lent form to the taut lines and ridges of muscle that rippled at his haunches. His mane and tail spilled like a clear waterfall.

My dad was already descending the stairs, his eyes locked with his spirit animal. His face was shining with awe and gratitude as he reached out and stroked the horse's forelock. The beautiful creature stood perfectly still and the crowd was as silent as a needle through silk. No-one dared interrupt the profound exchange occurring before their eyes.

After a few moments more, Elder Flights, dressed in his sunshine robes, and his new companion, climbed the stairs together and took their place among The Council. The crowd erupted with applause and cheers. My dad cast a glance our way and grinned. Mum's caramel eyes were glistening with tears.

With the official ceremony at an end, the High Council members walked among the joyful crowds, introducing their spirit animals to awed children and adults alike. I caught sight of a toddler trying to throw her chubby arms around the neck of Grand Master Willow's wolf, only to find purchase one moment, then stumble forward the next, as her hands passed through the wolf's ghostly form. As I reached out to stroke the mane of my father's stallion, I understood why. The lightest of touch was needed to feel the spirit animals lest your fingers pass straight through them.

"He's beautiful," my mother was saying. "What's his name?"

"Bo," my father replied.

"Did he tell you that?" I marvelled as his gleaming mane poured between my fingers like a mountain stream.

"In a fashion," Dad chuckled. "He didn't tell me so much as I just *knew*. The same way I know that Elder Zenith's stag is named Piccolo and Grand Master Willow's wolf is Vargas." He nodded to where the tenacious toddler was still trying to steal a hug. Vargas didn't seem to mind.

Then just behind them and off to the left a familiar gangly figure and a shock of russet hair drew my attention. Young Garrick Leif, my patient, was wandering through the throng looking lost and confused. Shouldn't he still be in a recovery bed at Healaxis? I gave a hurried explanation to my parents and wove through the crowd after him.

There were so many people clustered around the Elders it was difficult to keep sight of him. I was poised on tippy toes craning my neck when I spied him behind a crowd that had gathered around Elder Spry. Realising

I would have to double back and around to reach him, I turned sharply and collided with - of all people - Christian.

"This is becoming quite a habit for you. If you're going to continue to throw yourself at me all the time, perhaps I should invest in some sort of protective gear." His cheeky smirk was as familiar to me as my own heartbeat, but it didn't reach his eyes the way it always had. Then again, things were different now. Held safe and tight against him last night, it was easy to believe that we would go on as we always had, but in the sobering light of day, I knew I would have to watch how I acted toward him. I didn't want to give him any more false hope.

"Sorry," I mumbled, searching the crowd for Garrick.

He must have seen the concerned, distracted look on my face and slipped effortlessly from playful tease to alert protector. "What's wrong?"

"I need to find someone, Garrick Leif, he's a patient of mine. I saw him wandering through the crowd when he should be in a bed at Healaxis. He's gravely ill."

"What does he look like?" Chris was clipped and efficient.

"A tall, gangly teenager with red hair."

"Like that one over there?" he pointed.

We moved as one, Chris pulling me along behind him through the thickening crowd, his fingers curled securely around my wrist. For someone so tall, he was certainly agile; ducking and weaving around the masses of people, almost as though he could anticipate which way they were going to move before they knew themselves. If it had been me on my own, the journey would have been fraught with multiple bumps and repeated apologies.

Chris manoeuvred me to his side and pointed ahead. "Is that him?"

"Yes," I sighed and charged toward Garrick, landing my hand on his shoulder. He jumped in fright and spun to face me.

"Acolyte Flights," he stuttered. He was as pale as a full moon and sweat was beading on his face and throat. He was wearing the same worn jeans and t-shirt he'd been dressed in when I'd examined him a few days ago.

"What are you doing here, Garrick? Shouldn't you be at healaxis resting?"

His eyes were bright with fever and darted to avoid my gaze. But when he saw Christian's muscled figure standing stoically on my right, he must have decided I was the less threatening of the two and slowly met my eyes. "Healer Cray said I was well enough to go home." The lie rattled off his tongue without effort.

Chris shifted uneasily beside me and I knew I needed to tread carefully. This boy was like a frightened deer. So frightened that he'd just lied to us outright. What could be so terrifying that would cause a go-lite to lie?

"I see," I nodded slowly, trying to calculate my next move. He looked terrible. Dark shadows sagged beneath his eyes and his freckled cheeks were sad and hollow. I'd not had a chance to re-examine him or find out if Healer Cray had managed a diagnosis. I attempted to keep my voice light, cajoling. "I'm sure Healer Cray is quite right, it's just that you seem to be running a fever and you're very pale, Garrick. Perhaps it would be best to pop across the street to healaxis and make doubly sure that you're okay."

A frightened deer, indeed! Even Chris was caught off guard with the way that boy slipped away from us at lightning speed and vanished into the crowd.

"Where in The Source's name did he get to?" Chris hadn't even had a chance to react. "And why did he lie to you about being released from healaxis?"

"He's absolutely terrified of something. I've examined him twice and both times he wouldn't let me see the cause of his illness. He kept blocking me out."

"So do you have any idea what's wrong with him?"

"I know *exactly* what's wrong with him. I just don't know why or how it could have happened."

"What is it?"

I lowered my voice. "His energy field is compromised. I saw massive rips and tears in it. I've never seen anything like it before. I'm not sure what we can do."

Chris' slate blue eyes grew as wide as saucers and the muscle ticked in his jaw.

"I know, it's awful," I went on. "Healer Cray is taking care of him but I haven't had a chance to ask her if she has a formal diagnosis yet or any ideas of how we're going to treat him.

Chris nodded slowly, deep in thought.

"Anyway, I should go," I told him. "I need to let Healer Cray know that he's left healaxis."

"You should," Chris urged, "and I need to speak with Grand Master Trill while I'm here." A deep furrow had formed across his brow and his eyes were sharp with concern. "I should go too. I'll see you soon." He gave me a tight smile and turned abruptly to march back toward the Dome.

I felt a pang as he disappeared into the bustling crowd. He was gone before I had a chance to ask him what was wrong. "Bye," I whispered belatedly.

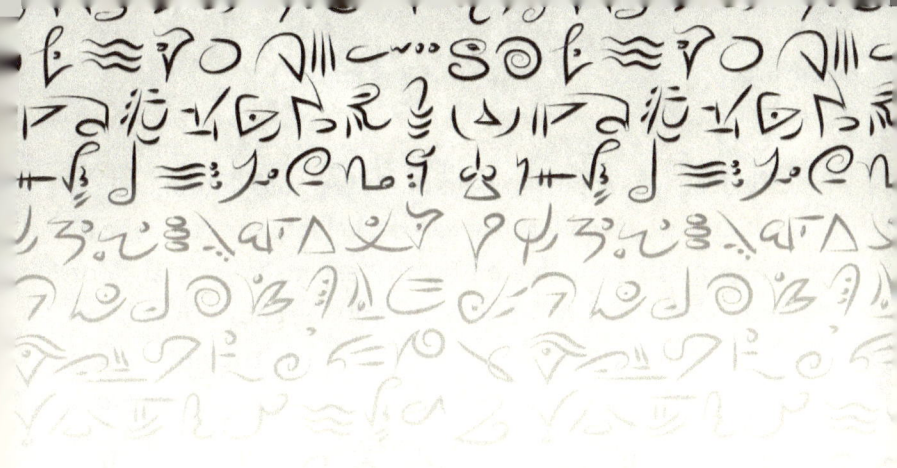

TWELVE

Christian

Grand Master Trill's amber eyes smouldered as I relayed the plight of young Garrick. Her lynx, Evangeline, stalked restlessly around her legs, her gaze alert and penetrating like her Oracle companion's. After finding her surrounded by adoring citizens and catching her eye, we had moved our conversation indoors where we wouldn't be overheard or interrupted.

"This is unsettling news," she drummed her long, pale fingers against a gleaming oak desk then resumed her pacing to the far side of the room. We were standing in her personal sanctuary within Ophanim Dome. All the Grand Masters were appointed a private room like this one, a place of retreat and reflection. I was honoured to be invited into hers.

The walls were painted from floor to ceiling with elaborate mandalas. It was as though we'd slipped inside a kaleidoscope. A plush divan of muted gold dominated the corner. Its curved legs appeared to clutch the rug beneath it like a raft as it floated on the expansive crystal floor. "But," she sighed, turning away from the enormous oblong window that overlooked the gardens, "as troubling as it is, it's the first real break we've had since Uma the elephant arrived. We need to find Garrick Leif and determine why he's suffering tears in his energy field like the Earth animals. There can be no mistaking this for a coincidence. The boy is clearly involved somehow and we need to find out what he knows, and quickly."

I nodded as my eyes drifted past her to the thousands of people milling in the gardens outside, completely oblivious to any danger or threat.

"Did you tell Lilly that the animals have torn energy fields too?"

"No, Grand Master."

"And you've not divulged Healer Honeywell's theory to anyone outside of The Council?"

"Not a Soul."

"Good, there's no need to alarm anyone as yet. It is fascinating though to think that being in the presence of an incompatible vibration can cause bodily harm. We've never had the need to contemplate the consequences of a life-form being brought from one dimension to another, given that it should be impossible to breach the veil. In any case, you've done well, Christian, very well." She spoke my name tentatively. Until now I had been addressed as

Translator Palladen. It seemed, given our predicament, that the time for formalities had passed. "I'll try to contact Garrick's parents and let them know you're on your way to their house. We might even get lucky and find him hiding under his bed," she winked mischievously. Even faced with a breach in the veil between worlds, Genevieve Trill still had a sense of humour. Such was the strength of the Elders.

"And when we find him, then what?" I asked.

Her amber eyes sparkled. "Then we enlist the help of the most talented Healer in Citrine and save the boy. But first..." she nodded toward her spirit lynx. Evangeline took a gliding step toward me, leaving the shelter of her mistress' skirts and revealing her full glittering form. Her graceful paws planted soundlessly on the crystal floor and her feline body swayed as she took another liquid step, and another, until she stood right before me. The afternoon light through the window set her sleek form ashimmer. Her translucent body served as a magnifying glass for the mandalas on the walls. I was completely mesmerised.

I sank to my knees to be closer to the creature I would probably never see again in my lifetime. The spirit animals had only allowed themselves to be seen to welcome a new council member and his spirit companion. When the day's festivities were over, they would only be visible to the Elders.

I grinned at Grand Master Trill. "I think she likes me." The myriad of colours on the walls were undulating through her body as she arched her back in a lazy stretch.

"Evangeline *has* always been a faultless judge of character," she arched a perfect brow and grinned back. "She wishes to speak to you. She has a message to deliver."

I was absolutely stunned and humbled. "For me?" I questioned incredulously. "How do I hear her?"

"It's a little different to your Translator abilities. You simply have to open your mind to her. Don't go searching for her words or try to hear her. Just open your mind and allow her to come to you."

Evangeline was staring into my eyes, her slitted pupils still and hypnotic. All the bright colours of the room faded as she drew me in deeper. It was like staring into a bottomless well. All sights and sounds disappeared until I was floating in endless velvet black, a living, breathing void where all yesterdays and tomorrows are possible. Out of the darkness, images rose like reflections on water. I saw broken buildings and rubble; the aftermath of some great force of nature. A sick feeling of pain and loss darkened my heart. Then the scene changed. I glimpsed a man with haunted eyes, the colour of the sea. He was lost and empty. I saw Lilly's face contorted with pain, her eyes swollen from too many tears. A memorial candle wreathed in white flowers - a tribute to the dead. The flowers were white lilies. The sick feeling grew. Where was Lilly? I scrambled through the darkness searching for another glimpse of her but the images had faded.

Fear snaked through my gut. *What does this mean?*

I pleaded with Evangeline. *Is Lilly going to be all right?* My heart beat was too loud, too fast. My head began to swim with fear and panic. They had been the briefest of flashes but the images were so weighted with emotion that I felt like I couldn't breathe. The echo of Evangeline's voice sprang from the darkness. It reverberated in my mind. *A life is made up of a million journeys and each one, seemingly good or bad, is a necessary step toward the great becoming - the journey of becoming ourselves.*

Why are you showing me this? I begged. *Please, I can't lose her.*

Lilly's true journey is just beginning. If you love her, you will not interfere with her choices. You will not seek to save her from the heartache and tragedy that paves the path to her true purpose. You will let her become what she was made to be.

The power of Evangeline's words vibrated through every cell in my body – both warning and wisdom. My mind battled the darkness of what I'd seen and wrestled with her words. What was Lilly destined to become? Was she going to die? Was she going to leave this world and move on to somewhere that I couldn't follow?

Since we were small, my first instinct had always been to protect Lilly. Not because she was younger or my responsibility, it was because of the deep-seated connection we shared. But, I was a go-lite and I understood acutely how imperative it was that others be allowed to find their own way in life. I didn't usually have any trouble adhering to that philosophy, until it came to Lilly. I'd spent my whole life learning to watch her fall down while fighting the urge to rush in and catch her, but what Evangeline had shown me wasn't a scraped knee or a poor choice in boyfriend. It was frightening. It looked like Lilly's whole world was going to be torn apart and what terrified me the most was not knowing who's memorial I had seen. I couldn't bare to think about it. *Please tell me it's not her.* I did not expect a response and Evangeline wasn't inclined to offer one. I had promised Lilly I would trust and support her always and now Evangeline was demanding that I do the same. Lilly had told me that The Source had set her a challenge. Evangeline had predicted that Lilly's true journey was just beginning. I loosed a shuddering breath, trying to expel my fear. *Did you show me that to prepare me for what is to come?* I asked her.

Would you have been strong enough to keep your promise to Lilly if I did not prepare you? she asked.

I sighed and answered truthfully. *When I made that promise, I didn't know Lilly would be facing such tragedy. I'm not sure that I'll have the strength to watch her go through that much pain, even though you've told me I must. I just want to keep her safe, and the thought of losing her...*

Evangeline pounced on my words and I could almost hear laughter in her voice. *Keep her safe? From what? The path her Soul directs her to take? You wish to keep her safe from the life The Source has planned for her? Lilly has an important part to play in what is to come. Would you hold her back and rob her of her right to fulfil her true potential?*

No. I want her to be all she can be. I love her.

Then you must love her enough to let her fall on her own, for each time she rises again, she'll have the knowledge and wisdom to scale an even greater mountain. Every choice you make writes the future, Christian. Choose wisely.

Her words were dizzying, the power behind them so intense that it was becoming difficult to hear much more. I had so many more questions but I could feel myself slipping out of Evangeline's grasp as I naturally yearned to return to the present, where the energy wasn't so overwhelming, where I wasn't swimming in a sea of every possible past and future.

A warm wave of love swept over me, so immense and complete that my body hummed and softened in surrender. Doubt and fear fled and my heart filled to bursting point with pure, golden love. The Source was giving me the strength I needed to keep my promise. I sat still for several moments and allowed everything I'd seen and heard to soak in. Eventually, the room and Grand Master Trill came back into focus and Evangeline was once again weaving in and out of the Grand Master's forest green robes, half hidden from my view.

"She's rather direct, I'm afraid." An apologetic simper crept over the Grand Master's lips.

"Yes, she certainly is," I breathed, feeling quite overcome and dazed. I blinked away the brightness of the room and slowly rose to my feet. That golden energy was still washing through me making me feel as light as a feather.

Grand Master Trill grasped my forearm and gently steered me to the divan. I drifted down onto the velvet seat. She remained standing. "Whatever Evangeline has shown you," she spoke in her quiet, commanding way, "take heed. Her instruction comes directly from The Source." Her eyelashes fluttered upward in a gesture of reverence. "I have never known a spirit animal to advise anyone except their Elders. You have been blessed with a rare gift today, Christian. I hope you use it wisely."

I hoped I would too. I hoped I would have the strength to let Lilly find her own way, no matter where the path led.

I felt exhausted by all I'd seen and heard but the influx of pure Source energy overrode it, leaving me with a peaceful sense of surrender and trust. I couldn't have mustered a panicked thought, even if I'd wanted to. The bonds of fear wound tightly around my heart had been snipped away and my mind felt clean and clear. I knew it wouldn't last. It would fade eventually and then it would be up to me to dig deep and honour my promise.

My floating euphoria buoyed me all the way to the Leif's front gate, a gate that was lying broken on the ground, along with half the front fence. There was no doubt that something large had caused this damage and a certain hefty, high-spirited lady sprang to mind - Uma. I turned a splintered paling over in my hand, examining where it had been trampled in half. A little yellow house sat proudly behind the wreckage, rising from a lush, green lawn like a giant buttercup. It wasn't so much that it was shaped like a flower, but the unlikely number of bees swarming around it that brought the metaphor to mind. Were they drawn to the colour? There wasn't a single flower growing in the Leif's garden. There were thick, low lying shrubs with dark waxy leaves, and under clusters of tall trees, pale ferns ran into the lawn. Yet, there wasn't a single bloom to attract the dozens of bees I counted buzzing at the window panes or sticking to the walls of Garrick's home.

I approached the house, picking my way through the strewn rubble, to the white front door. All the windows were shut tight, presumably to keep them out. I could sense the bees' agitation as I neared and reached out with my mind to forge a connection. They descended in an erratic frenzy, unsure if I was friend or foe. *Hello again,* I greeted them all. This was definitely the same swarm I had rounded up in the city centre and led out to Laurone forest; the swarm that had attacked and killed innocent people. I could feel their energy and they were still angry.

Where is the rest of your hive? I tried lightly. *You're a long way from your new home in the forest.*

A chorus of angry voices spoke at once, *Gone, dead, lost.*

I'm so sorry, I raised my hands in supplication. *Can you tell me what happened?*

Weak, falling, dead, came dozens of voices.

I could feel their grief and their anger as sharply as a sting. *How can I help?* I asked, knowing full well that there was little I could do to save them.

We must go back. We do not belong here.

And you came here for help? I guessed. *But why here?*

Their reply came slowly this time and when it did I had trouble interpreting the message. It was confused, uncertain, and the only word I could glean from the cloud of agitation hovering around me was, 'instinct.'

You felt drawn here, is that it, to this place? I gestured around me.

A decisive and collective, 'yes' came back.

I was having trouble reconciling my recollection of the gangly, timid teenager I'd met earlier with the dawning realisation that he could be an inter-dimensional mastermind. Could this boy truly be at the centre of it all? Was it he who had somehow brought the swarm of bees from Earth to Panacea? Houdini the horse, the koalas, Uma too? Was this all him? I fumbled for my uniter and focussed on the opaque crystal screen, reaching out energetically to Grand Master Trill. Her face wavered onto the screen in moments, an intrigued look in her eyes. "You were right," I told her. "We need to escalate the search for Garrick."

Convincing a riled swarm of bees to get into my car was probably the most ridiculous thing I've done in this lifetime. After knocking on Garrick's front door and finding no-one home, I decided that I couldn't very well leave them there, especially if they were angry enough to attack again. I needed to transport them to The Haven. Maybe Petra and the team had stumbled upon a miracle and could save their lives after all.

It was like trying to drive in a black and yellow blizzard, a blizzard that buzzed. They were so terrified that all my pleading for them to stop flying was largely unsuccessful. As soon as I opened the car door, they spilled into the fresh, still forest air and clustered in a quivering cloud above Petra and Grand Master Trill. I practically fell out of the car, a lather of sweat where I'd had to keep the windows and vents closed.

Petra bit her lip, stifling a giggle. "I'll get these fellows stowed away in an enclosure, if you'd be kind enough to tell them to follow me."

I did as she asked and filled the Grand Master in on what I'd found at the Leif's home: the broken fence, the bees, and unfortunately, no Garrick huddled under the bed.

By the time Petra returned, Grand Master Trill was standing in the shade of a nearby tree and had managed to orchestrate a search party with a few messages projected from her uniter. The party was made up of Elementals, Projectors and a Hand, and she'd also arranged for one of the Haven's Healers to go with them. We didn't know what shape Garrick would be in by the time we found him. After what Lilly had told me about the tears in his energy field, and the ever growing surety that this boy was responsible for breaching the veil between worlds, hopefully he would still be breathing.

Petra emerged from the scrubby trail that led to the animal enclosures. "You two should go home and get some rest," Grand Master Trill instructed. "There's precious else to be done until we find the boy and get some answ..." Her eyes rolled back in her head and she sucked a small gasp through her lips. Her face fell flat and still as a blank canvas. Coloured mist began to marble and roil across the orbs of her eyes like dye dropped in water. They looked like two crystal balls stirring to life. Her body went rigid and she threw her head back in a blind salute to the skies, her lips working fast in intelligible whispers.

Petra cast me a sidelong glance, her strawberry curls bobbing in the warm breeze. We both fixated on the swirling spheres and silently waited for the Grand Master's vision to run its course. She shuddered, her rigid body jerking awake as though from a violent dream. Her pale fingers flew to her face, fingertips pressing to her mouth, her eyelids. With a sigh, she blinked, coming back to herself, her eyes clearing to burning amber. She staggered and I rushed forward, scooping my arm around her waist, fearing she might fall. She slumped gratefully against me.

"Are you all right, Grand Master?"

"I would be glad of a chair and some cool water," she breathed.

Petra dashed to the Grand Master's other side and

we shuffled up the leafy walk to the Haven's back door, supporting her weight between us.

"The visions have been taking their toll of late," she confessed as we seated her on one of the crystal healing beds in the lab.

"Is that a usual thing?" I tried to keep the concern out of my voice.

"No," she replied flatly. Petra handed her a glass of cold water and she drank deeply, emptying it whole. "My visions have been troubling." She opened her mouth as though she wanted to say more then closed it again. She drew in a laboured breath and stared into her empty glass.

Petra and I exchanged a glance. The Grand Masters were the wisest of us all, leading with grace and certainty. It was easy to see them and the rest of The Council as infallible. Yet they hadn't sprung from the gilded loins of gods or been spun from silken dreams. They had been born and imbued with the same power as every go-lite and had devoted their lives to becoming leaders and examples to us all.

When she finally spoke, her strength and calm had returned. She stood, smoothing her robes and lifting her chin. "You can inform the search party that they're no longer required," she commanded. "I have found Garrick Leif. I know precisely where he is going to be and when. Translator Palladen, my vision has shown me that you are the one who'll bring him in."

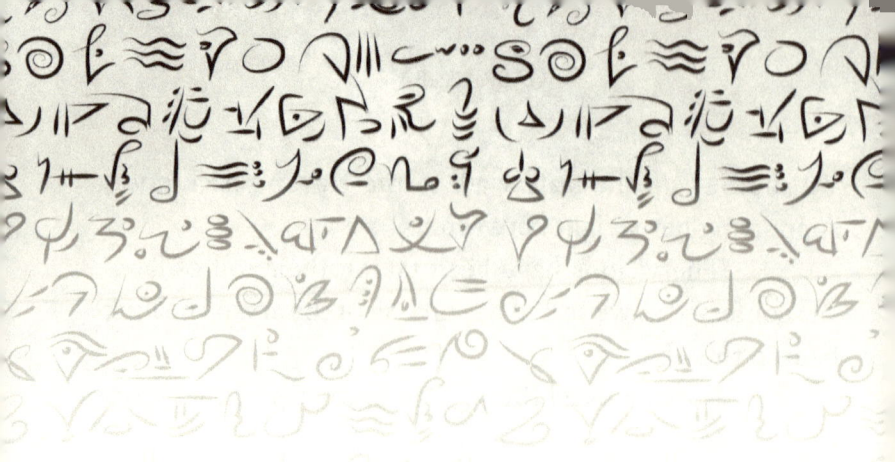

THIRTEEN

Lilly

I ran across the city square that lay between the grounds of Ophanim Dome and healaxis. The thin soles of my sandals slapped against the pale sandstone, stinging with each stride. The square was empty save the statues that rose from bursting flowerbeds. The only sound was the cascading waterfall splashing at its centre. A mosaicked wall of gold and ultramarine depicting naked water maidens blurred beneath the flow of water.

I prayed Healer Cray wasn't in the middle of performing a healing. Garrick had looked ghastly and I feared that if he wasn't returned to healaxis, the consequences could be dire. I dashed over the arched footbridge that traversed the cobbled road below and barrelled through the wrought iron gates of healaxis. Honeysuckle and daybright filled my nostrils as I ran through the gardens, past the healing springs, and toward the sparkling spires that towered over the treetops.

My lungs were burning as I scrambled up the sandstone stairs and into the cool, amber-lit entryway of healaxis. I bent over grasping at my knees, breathing hard.

"Source above, Acolyte Flights! Are you trying to outrun the wind?" Vianne hurried over from behind the marbled front desk and placed a soothing hand on my back, her eyes alight with concern. "Are you well, dear?"

"Yes, I'm fine," I straightened up. "I need to see Healer Cray. Where is she?"

"In the library, dear. She's been down there for hours. She said she wasn't to be disturbed."

"I'm afraid this can't wait," I said, walking toward the service elevator behind the reception area. "Can you please contact Garrick Leif's parents and tell them Healer Cray needs to speak to them?"

Vianne nodded once as I threw open the vine patterned grille and stepped inside the lift.

The library at healaxis was no ordinary library. Buried deep below the sandstone structure was a living, breathing wealth of knowledge dating back to the birth of Panacea. There weren't any mile high shelves laden with dusty, crumbling books. The records here were of a more enduring kind. The elevator door creaked open and I slid back the heavy grille. It screeched and whined, echoing into the cloying air of the cave. A labyrinth of tunnels lay before me, each leading to caverns brimming with knowledge collected over thousands of years.

I stepped from the elevator and felt smooth rock beneath my feet. Solar stones glowed in elaborate wrought iron sconces from the damp walls.

"Healer Cray?" My voice echoed through the still space.

"Is that you, Lilly? I'm down here."

I turned right and followed Healer Cray's echo down a slightly sloping tunnel. It was lit so dimly I could barely see. I moved carefully, sliding my feet over the bumps and ridges of the tunnel floor and feeling my way along the rough walls. As I stepped into the open expanse of the cavern I almost had to shield my eyes. Enormous pillars of crystal sprouted from the floor, from the walls, the ceiling. They jutted at every angle capturing and refracting the light from the solar stones in a towering, glittering forest.

Healer Cray was crouched by the far wall, her palm pressed to a rod of aquamarine as luminous as a sunlit sea. Her fine, straw coloured hair was escaping her bun and curling in tendrils around her heart shaped face. Her eyes were closed, her head bent, listening to ancient whispers. She looked uncharacteristically dishevelled. Her usually crisp shirt was limp with heat, sleeves rolled to her elbows, and she was caked from head to toe in dust.

I wove around the glittering spikes and spires to join her. She tipped up her chin and dazzled me with her glorious smile. Her teeth seemed to glow like the crystal forest around her.

"Garrick Leif has left healaxis," I blurted.

"Oh my." She rose slowly to her feet, her bright eyes widening, her smile draining.

"I saw him at Ophanim Dome just now. I tried to get him to come back with me but he fled and vanished in the crowd. He looks really sick, Healer Cray."

"Oh my," she said again. "I was just down here trying to find any information about energy tears."

"I've told Vianne to contact his parents. Did you manage to find anything?"

"No, not yet," she sighed. "I'm not convinced that there's anything to find. These crystals hold the histories of disease and healing," she brushed off her dusty hands on her linen trousers, "thousands of years of the past recorded and preserved in rock." I followed as she ducked under an amethyst rod jutting out from the wall. "But I doubt that anyone has ever been afflicted with a ruptured energy field before. Honestly, I'm at a loss."

I placed my hands on a six foot shaft of crystal that had grown up through the cave floor. It was cool and smooth and glistened green, like sweet grass beaded with morning dew. It hummed as I closed my eyes and asked the question, *how do you cure tears in the energetic field?* Snippets of images flashed through my mind like flipping through the pages of a book. The crystal was searching, looking through all the records it held, trying to find an instance of a compromised energetic field. I waited, watched and listened for several moments as the images continued to flip by but never settle. I opened my eyes and shook my head at Healer Cray.

There were dark rings under her eyes and the light, tinkling chime had gone from her voice. In all the time I had known her I had never seen her look exhausted. She was usually a boundless source of love and light that she showered on her patients and all she met. Now, she just looked worn out.

"When was the last time you went home or had a good night's sleep?" I asked her as we wove around a brilliant cluster of iolite.

"I'm not sure." She wiped a dusty hand across her forehead, leaving a streak of dirt behind. "I've been keeping a close eye on Garrick, channelling healing energy into him three times a day. I don't know what else can be done."

So that's why she looked so exhausted. She was giving over as much of her own life force as she could in the hopes it would heal Garrick. "Healer Cray, you need to rest. You can't do all the healing yourself. The damage to his energy field is too great." My voice bounced and amplified off the cave walls, making my declaration sound more forceful than I'd intended.

"I know," she slumped against the entryway to the cavern, "and that is why you are my star acolyte. You're never afraid to speak your mind and I thank you for it, Lilly. Even experienced Healers sometimes need reminding that we are flesh and blood like our patients.

There are limits to what we can do."

I wanted to save Garrick as much as Healer Cray did. He was only a boy. He hadn't even had enough time in this life to grow into himself. But sometimes, regardless of what we want, The Source has other plans in store. I had no idea what those plans might be but that wasn't going to deter me from giving it my all. There had to be a way to help him. I took in Healer Cray's weary expression, a plan forming in my mind. "What if we gathered a team of Healers to help us treat him? If the power of one Healer isn't enough, perhaps we need more, working in shifts?"

"You see? Star acolyte," she smiled. "It's a smart plan – simple and smart," she nodded her approval. "Now, all we have to do is find our run-away patient before it's too late."

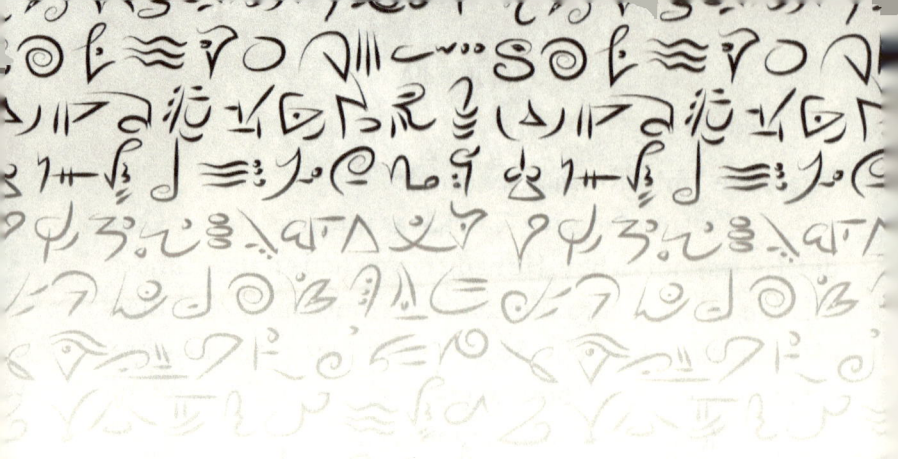

FOURTEEN

Jay

My trip back from Panacea was a rough ride. As soon as my feet hit the floor in my living room, I'd fallen over and thrown up. Hurtling through the black ether between worlds had felt like a million needles pricking my skin. The snaking vines of lightning twisting around my body had been blinding.

While Lilly had been speaking to me I'd barely been able to keep track of what she was saying. Dizziness and nausea had left me faint. I must have caught a stomach bug from somewhere. I'd been lolling about all day feeling dead tired and terrible for skipping out on her. I was also reeling with shock from what she'd told me. I'd spent days convincing myself that she and I weren't meant to be, that I could never be worthy of her. Then she'd turned all my theories and justifications on their head. Could it actually be true? Had this magical book fallen into her hands at precisely the right moment so I could join her in her world? It seemed too big a coincidence to ignore but at the same time, too fantastical to swallow.

My stomach gurgled loudly, through nerves or sickness, I couldn't tell. I groaned, burying my face further into the pillow. My sheets were damp from fevered dreams and my bedroom smelt stale. My phone buzzed. I fished around in the tangled bedding and found it. "Hey, man. I'll be there a bit later. I haven't been well all day."

"You all right? What's up?" Ryan shouted over the blaring music.

"Stomach bug I think. The worst of its done. I'll be okay for tonight but I don't think I'll be making it over to help you set up. Sorry."

"All good. The oaf has already carried in the kegs…" I heard a string of curses from Ryan that weren't directed at me. "Jesus Christ, John! What the hell are you doing?" I heard a muffled retort in the background and more cursing. Ryan brought the phone back to his ear. "And he's started drinking already," he sighed.

"Of course he has," I laughed. "Would you expect anything less?"

"I'm sampling for quality control!" John yelled. "Sometimes kegs can go flat."

"Is that true?" Ryan asked me.

"Not even remotely."

Ryan groaned. "So you'll be here later?"

"I wouldn't miss your birthday, Ryan. I'll be there."

The full moon was dangling a pale silver ribbon on the surface of the river. The lights of the city winked from the far bank. I breathed in the warm, muddy air of low tide and sat down on the bench seat that ringed the gazebo. The party was in full swing. Ryan's house was lit up like Gatsby's mansion, music and laughter spilling down the lawn to the river's edge where I sat, seeking a moment's peace. I could hear mud crabs clicking in the mangroves, out for their evening meal. I could hear the shiver of a moth's wings somewhere in the dark. Then I heard my name.

I turned to see her shimmering into view at the gazebo's centre. She was a vision in a pale grey dress that shone silver in the moonlight. A shy smile crept over her face as she came fully into view. "Hello Jay."

"You look gorgeous," I whispered.

She shrugged. "When I saw where you were, I thought it best that I dress to blend in. Are you enjoying the party out here on your own?"

"I just needed some air," I grinned.

"How are you feeling? I was worried about you."

"Yeah, I'm so sorry I bailed on you like that. I think I must have caught a stomach bug or something. I still don't feel a hundred percent."

"There's nothing to be sorry for. I just wanted to see if you were okay and I was hoping we could pick up where we left off. I still have more to tell you."

"More?" I was still trying to come to terms with what I'd already heard. "How could there possibly be more?"

She clasped her hands together and stared down at the weathered boards of the gazebo floor, thinking. "Not exactly *more*. I probably should have said I have *details* to add… important details."

I stared at her blankly, not knowing whether I wanted to hear anymore and as per usual, Lilly saw my fear. Those hazel eyes missed nothing. She moved toward me like a fish gliding through water and sat down. I could feel the swell of her closeness, the power of her presence, and it lifted some of the heaviness that had been weighing me down.

"You're still pale," she said softly, her fingers fluttering to my forehead. "Your temperature is back to normal though." She studied me for a moment, waiting for me to respond, questions burning in her eyes.

"It's just a stomach bug," I said, "I'll be fine." I found myself reaching for her hand and pulling it away from my brow.

A flurry of confusion passed over her face. "What's wrong, Jay? I can feel that you're keeping something from me."

I didn't know what to say. I'd been bottling up my fears and doubts, knowing full well that I'd have to tell her eventually: about my past life dream, how I didn't feel good enough for her, and now, how confused I was by the discoveries in her Great-grandad's journal, and how bewildered I was by the prospect of relocating to another dimension!

"If you don't speak with me, I can't help you."

"I thought you could look inside my mind anytime you wanted," I stalled.

Her serene expression didn't waver. "You know I won't do that. I'm not your Soul Guardian anymore." She stood and walked to the railing, leaning out over the city view. Below us, the river was lapping at its banks and above us, the party was raging on. Between Lilly and I, there was only silence.

I knew it was time to come clean. She deserved the truth. I just had no idea where to start or how to begin. Then three little words fell out of my mouth, not the three little words that she wanted to hear, but they needed to be said. "I'm a coward."

She didn't move a muscle and she didn't speak. I couldn't see her face as she leaned out over the water. Her bare arms and shoulders were pale in the moonlight. Her dark hair was swept forward over one shoulder and I counted the ridges of her spine down to the deep V in the back of her dress.

"I don't deserve you, Lilly."

I watched her ribcage heave in a silent sigh.

"I've kept things from you because I'm ashamed of myself and I was afraid to show you who I am. I was afraid to admit out loud that I'm not good enough for you."

She slowly straightened up and turned to face me. "What has happened to you, Jay? I left you for a few days to decipher my great-grandfather's manuscript and something changed. You were this beautiful, shining light in the meadow. You kissed me and told me you loved me. You were radiant. But ever since then, something has been eating away at you. What's wrong?"

Fresh shame pulsed through my heart. I stood and took a hesitant step toward her. "I'm so sorry, Lilly. I do love you, I do." My voice faltered and I swallowed hard. I needed to say this quickly before the very sight of her made me lose my conviction. "I wanted to believe that we could make this work but the truth is, you deserve so much better. Better than the love I can give you." I felt numb, gutted. The words were out and there was no taking them back. We stared at each other, the short distance between us like a gaping chasm.

"Why?" she winced. "Please, tell me why you feel this way."

Even now, I couldn't find the words to tell her what I'd done in our past life together. I *was* a coward, through and through. The silence stretched out between us. I felt like I was shrinking under the scrutiny of her gaze.

"Do you honestly think I don't know you?" She looked quietly stunned. A breeze whispered around us, picking up strands of her hair and blowing them across my cheek. "I've been inside your heart," she went on, "I've felt what you feel. I've seen the pain you've suffered in your life and I've seen you stand strong and face it. Now you're telling me you're a *coward?* That just isn't true, Jay. I know who you are."

I could see how strongly she believed it, but she was wrong, she didn't know. She only knew parts of me, the parts I had allowed her to see. I had not been completely open with her. Hearing her defend me like some courageous hero was more that I could stand. I couldn't bear the guilt another second. "You don't know!" I shouted. "You don't know how I cheated on you and tormented you in our last life together. You don't know how I drove you into depression and caused you to kill yourself!" I was breathing hard, my heart pounding with rage. I could feel my features twisting with the sickening memory of it and I fought hard to smooth my expression, to erase all the anger that I didn't want to feel.

She was stone still. Cool and composed, taking in my struggle and waiting for me to rein in my temper. When she spoke, her voice was careful, measured. "Is that what you'd dreamt about the day you came crashing into my world in a wild panic? Was that what your past-life dream showed you?"

"Yes," I admitted with a heavy heart.

"And is that the reason you think that you're not good enough for me?"

"I think it's a pretty damn good reason."

The corner of her mouth twitched. *Was she*

actually trying to stifle a smile? Why the hell was she smiling?

"Did it occur to you that your past-life self may have gotten it wrong?" She arched an eyebrow.

"What?"

"Well, I would have thought that the best person to ask if 'past-life me' killed themselves would be *me*."

"I saw it, Lilly."

She shook her head. "You saw and felt the guilty beliefs of a grief stricken Soul that thought his girlfriend's death might be all his fault. That doesn't make it true. I can tell you unequivocally that 'past-life me' *did not* kill herself. Her drowning was an accident. I can also tell you that she died doing what she loved in her favourite place in the world." A look of contentment softened her face. "I could feel it so clearly; her love of the ocean. In the end there was acceptance and peace because she knew she was going home." Then she did smile; that stunning, mesmerising, dazzling gesture that was like heaven's gates opening.

I collapsed back onto the bench seat and buried my face in my hands. Relief and gratitude flooded through me. *It wasn't my fault, it wasn't my fault.* "But I still repeatedly cheated on her, made her life – your life – a living hell."

"And I wonder what horrible things I've done in my past lives? Maybe I did horrible things to you. Humans hurt each other every day in countless ways and most of the time, they don't even realise they're doing it. So you were a crappy boyfriend in our last life together, so what? In all the lives you've had, you've probably done far worse than that. And I'm sure I have too. For all I know, I could have been Genghis Khan in a past life."

I barked an incredulous laugh. Her suggestion was completely absurd.

"No?" she smirked. "Maybe Hitler then?" She donned a finger moustache. "Can you picture it now?"

"You're being ridiculous."

"Am I?"

"Yes. Obviously someone like *you* could never have been *Hitler*."

She dropped her grin and pinned me with those piercing hazel eyes. "How do you know?" she paused, letting me take her question seriously. "Some Souls learn harder and faster than others because they make bigger mistakes."

I looked at the hazy skyline in the distance. Silhouettes of buildings glowed with clouds of artificial light. "And some people never learn at all," I countered.

"True," she shrugged. "Change is always a choice, not a given."

"See, you're too smart for me," I teased.

"My point is, who you want to be in life isn't dictated by who you've been. You always have a choice. The only question is; what will you choose?"

I stared out over the river trying to assemble my thoughts. How did she always know the right things to say? It seemed incredible to me that something that had felt so overwhelmingly important, now felt insignificant in the grand scheme of things. "I meant it when I said that you're too smart for me. Or maybe I should use the word 'wise'. How can a human ever see the world the way a go-lite does?"

She came to sit beside me on the wooden bench and angled her body to face me. "Because all go-lites were once human and all humans have the choice to evolve into go-lites one day, just like I did."

"But I'm still human." I felt stupid stating the obvious but I had no idea where she was going with this. "I think, act and feel like a human," I added for emphasis.

She gathered up my hands and looked at me intently. "That kind of brings me to the *detail* I didn't get to share with you last night. In order for you to live on Panacea with me, you have to evolve enough to think, act and feel like a go-lite."

I gaped at her. I could feel my eyes go buggy. "You're kidding," I scoffed. "You think *I* am capable of doing that?"

"Not right now maybe, but one day, yes I do." Her face was so serene, so full of belief and conviction… belief in me. "It would mean completely healing yourself of all your past hurts, which you're well on your way to clearing."

I stared at her, open-mouthed. She said it like it was the simplest, most natural thing in the world and her absence of doubt seemed to erase all of mine. She was absolutely incredible. I could feel her faith in me entering my lungs like air. "One day? So you're going to wait for me?"

"Aurora waited for forty-five years while my great-grandfather pioneered a way for them to be together. When love is real, that's the strength it holds."

I blinked at her, speechless.

"But all of that is irrelevant until you figure out what you want. We've done a lot of talking and you probably need to do an equal amount of processing. I know this entire situation is extremely overwhelming but I just want to say one more thing. The reason I believe in you, the reason I know this is right, isn't because you somehow saw me through the veil between worlds. It isn't because of a magical manuscript with invisible writing, it's because of the connection my heart feels to yours." She squeezed my hands and stood, drawing me up after her. "Sometimes, when I'm near you, my heart fills with brilliant white light. I've seen it fill to bursting point and crack through the walls like a beam from a lighthouse." Her fingertips brushed over my chest and then she placed her palm flush over my heart. "All my life I've felt a bit out of step, as though some part of me was incomplete. I think you are what I've been searching for. I think you are my missing part, Jay."

As she spoke I could feel my own heart ignite and any fear or doubt that was still lingering burned away. Because I knew what she was talking about. I'd felt it too. Not as a beam of light, but more like a golden fire.

Her eyes were filling with tears because she could see the recognition on my face, she could feel it in the quickening beat in my chest. I slowly stretched my hand toward her and touched just below her collarbone with two fingers. Her breath rose and fell more rapidly as I pressed my palm to the bare skin over her heart. Her eyes were like lanterns in the moonlight, so full of love and hope and all of our tomorrows. I breathed in an unsteady breath and stepped closer until the backs of ours hands were pressed together and we were breathing as one.

"I feel you like fire," I told her. "Like a pure, golden flame. The first time I kissed you it was as though my heart came back to life." Her face melted into a smile and I bent to kiss the perfect lips that had saved me more than once, just by uttering the truth. They parted, soft and full against mine and we stood there, motionless, in a long, lingering kiss. I broke away and wrapped my arms around her, holding her close, sliding my hands down her back, feeling the velvet of her bare skin. I wondered how I could have ever thought of letting her go. "I'm so sorry, Lilly," I whispered against her hair, nuzzling my cheek to the top of her head. "I'm sorry for keeping my past-life dream from you and for all the heartache I've put you through. But I'm here now. I won't go anywhere again, I promise."

She tilted her chin and pressed soft lips to my jaw. I dipped my head and found her mouth again, letting my eyes fall closed. Touching her, kissing her, feeling her, was to be overwhelmed by an impossible sweetness. We moved languorously like the slow flow of molasses, our arms and lips finding the shape of each other and then melting into one.

Lilly's strength, her power, was love. It ran through her like a current. I could feel it whenever she was close. I could feel it in every touch, in her words, in the way she cradled me with her gaze.

She *was* love. Pure and simple.

Standing here, holding her in my arms, I suddenly realized that I had been starved of it.

Starved of the way she made me feel.

I pulled her in closer, winding my fingers in her midnight hair. Her eyes were shot through with starlight and her mouth was silk. Whole galaxies could appear and disappear in the slow blink of her eyes. Our lips met again and she glowed. She was bright and precious in my hands. A golden mountain too smooth and flawless to climb. A moan rose from my throat as I kissed her like my life depended on it, like she was oxygen. I could kiss her like this forever but it would never be enough.

A loud whistle cut the air, closer than the ruckus of the party. I broke away from Lilly and looked around in a daze. She slumped against me, breathless. Two burly figures were stumbling across the lawn in our direction.

"Hey, shit head! What are you doing out here?" John yelled down the hill. "Who's that with you? Is that? L-i-l-l-y!" he slurred and galloped toward the gazebo with all the grace of a palsied stallion, dragging Ryan behind him by his Armani shirt tail. The drunken pair tripped in a divot and almost went down in a heap, roaring with laughter at their own stupidity. Lilly's eyes were wide as she watched my two best friends make thorough imbeciles of themselves.

"Inebriated much?" I enquired as they tripped up the gazebo's stairs, a six pack dangling from Ryan's hand.

"I-n-e-b-r-i-a-t-e-d," Ryan crooned. "I-n-e-b-r-i-a-t-e-d, it's such a brilliant word." Fits of laughter followed as the pair sang the word over and over, sweeping their arms about like drunken yogis.

"Anyhow," I interrupted loudly, "you guys remember Lilly?"

"L-I-L-L-Y!" John yelled again as though he'd forgotten she was there and threw his arms around her in a crushing hug. Lilly stumbled as the bulk of the great oaf, swaying from too much drink, nearly sent her sprawling across the gazebo. Ryan, the eternal gentleman, shot forward, ready to catch her, but Lilly had already twirled out of harm's way and the two drunkards ended up colliding with one another in a spectacular display of sheer idiocy. Lilly laughed, high and bright, like all the delight of the world was sung from her lips.

Ryan collected himself and plucked up her hand, planting it with a theatrical kiss. "It's so good to see you again, Lilly. Sorry John and I are so..." his eyebrows shot up in gleeful anticipation, "...i-n-e-b-r-i-a-t-e-d!" he sang. He and John began chanting the word, stumbling over each other, choking on their own laughter and waving their arms about like maniacs. "I-n-e-b-r-i-a-t-e-d!"

"Oh, god. Okay fellas. That's enough now... seriously," I begged.

"Happy Birthday, Ryan," Lilly beamed.

"Thank you, lovely one, but you're missing all the festivities. Here, have a drink."

"Lilly doesn't drink," I shook my head at the proffered bottle.

"No?" Ryan's unfocussed gaze turned quizzical.

"Never acquired the taste," she answered smoothly.

"Well, music and dancing then? Come on!"

Without pause for protest, we were marched up the gently sloping lawn, away from the twinkling city lights and the slow crawl of the river current, and ushered into the glass panelled, lower floor of Ryan's riverside mansion.

The room was a turmoil of sequined beauties with collagen stung lips spouting pretty, empty words. They hung on the arms of expensive suits like portable works of art, alongside Rolex watches and Cartier cuff links. I guessed these were Ryan's stockbroker mates from work. He'd been entrenched in that world for the last five years, had made a name for himself early, but he'd never turned into an arrogant dick, despite his success. Ryan was one of the most real, down-to-earth people I knew. He might dress and live like a king, but his heart was firmly grounded in what truly mattered. He'd never let the glitz and glamour fool him or steal his heart away.

Behind the glamour crew, the boys from our touch football team were domineering the bar playing drinking games. Raucous chants and cheers rose above the loud music and rowdy chatter as Billy slopped a quarter of a pint down his front and was booed into forfeiting. Ryan steered us through the press of bodies, the smell of booze and too many perfumes mingling together. I was clutching Lilly's hand, wondering what she thought of it all, but when I glanced back at her trailing behind me, her expression was unreadable.

Ryan led us through the crowded room and out onto the raised pool deck that extended from the side of the house. John was bringing up the rear, herding us along with drunken enthusiasm. The pool was a thrashing, splashing, screeching turmoil of bodies in various states of undress. Those that hadn't thought to bring bathing suits were swimming in their underwear while others had clearly been too drunk to bother taking off their clothes. There was a scream as one shimmering beauty was pushed into the pool. She burst to the surface, long hair plastered to her head like wet paint, her sequined cocktail dress clinging to her like mermaid's scales and rivers of black mascara running down her cheekbones. A DJ was pressed into a booth against the far railing, and what available space surrounded the pool, had become a dance floor.

I felt Lilly stumble behind me.

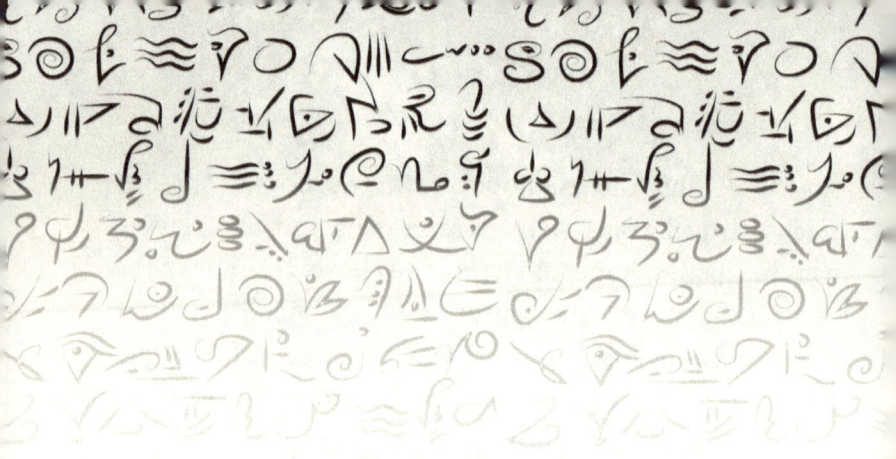

FIFTEEN

Lilly

There was so much noise, bright and jagged, blurred conversations and pounding music. I tipped my face to the night, gulping in air while the stars wheeled above me. Too loud, too much confusion, too many people and their energies sweeping through me. I was here, on Earth, among hundreds of humans and it was completely overwhelming. There were so many thoughts and feelings, secrets and insecurities, all swirling in a soup that felt ready to boil over at any moment.

I felt weak, a shadow of myself. I had never been in the physical presence of so many humans at once. I had watched it from behind the veil, of course; their pain, their jealousies and fears. But to be thrown *physically* into the middle of this many Souls with their unresolved emotions was a feeling I could never have anticipated. One person's pain, viewed from a distance, was manageable. This was something else entirely! I felt nauseous and dizzy, desperate for some stillness and peace to revive me, and for the first time, I felt plagued with a sense that I should not be here. I did not belong on Earth.

I could see Jay's green eyes, wide with concern. I could see his lips moving but I couldn't focus on what he was saying to me. In the periphery, a blur of bodies danced and shouted and were crammed together until one was indistinguishable from another. Jay's rough hands were gripping my bare shoulders as he stooped to peer into my face. It was as though I was drowning in a million fears. I could feel anxiety, loneliness, envy and struggle coming at me from all directions. It was in that moment that I truly understood what clever masks humans wore. The things they did to sweep away the pain and soldier on. They danced and laughed and drank and joked, but underneath all that, I could feel what was buried inside them. There wasn't a single person here who was truly happy and satisfied with their life.

Jay's arms came around me as I wavered on my feet. He cradled me to his chest as I fell against him. "I need to get out of here," I gasped.

"Is she all right?" I could hear Ryan fussing. "Here, Jay. Bring her over here."

I was bustled through the wet, dancing bodies and propped against the railing of the deck. The river breeze felt good on my face but did little to abate my nausea.

Jay's hand cupped my cheek. "God, Lilly, you're all

clammy and pale. Can someone get her a chair?"

I could feel my gut twisting and a rush of heat surging through my body. I turned away from Jay just in time and threw up over the railing. A cheer rose up from the people behind me, followed by a cascade of raucous laughter. Having emptied my stomach, I turned back around to see people pointing at me and laughing. I was so confused. Were they actually making fun of someone who was sick and in need of help?

Jay's hand smoothed down my back. "Ignore them," he said. "They're a bunch of idiots."

I slid to the floor, resting my head against a wooden post. *I really did not belong here.*

Jay crouched down beside me. "I think maybe you caught the bug too," he smiled apologetically. "Sorry."

"Sorry if I embarrassed you in front of your friends," I returned limply.

"They aren't my friends. Do you think you're okay to move? I think we should get you out of here."

I nodded and he lifted me to my feet as Ryan came back with a chair and John with a half empty glass of water. Presumably he'd spilt the other half.

Jay threaded his arm around my waist. "Mind if I take Lilly upstairs to lie down for a while?"

"No, not at all. You can use the last bedroom on the right." Ryan walked ahead of us cutting a path through the crowd and left us at the staircase.

Everything in his house was shiny and new,

unlike Jay's broken down little cottage or the mishmash of salvaged treasures that made up a go-lite's home. I trudged up the floating stairs, sliding my palm along the cool, chrome railing, and arrived at a long hallway. It was hung with mirrors of all shapes and sizes. Some were in elaborate gilt frames, others had no frames at all.

Jay gave me a secretive smile, "Ryan is obsessed with the story of Alice through the looking glass. But don't tell him I told you. He'd kill me," he laughed. "You're getting some colour back," he brushed his thumb over my cheek.

I was feeling a little better. Even the short distance of one storey seemed to offer some relief from the chaos downstairs. He took my hand and led me down the silver hall. "Isn't that a children's book about a girl that slips into other worlds?"

"Yep. Can you imagine what he'd do if he found out about you? He'd worship you as his real life Alice," he chuckled and pushed open a door to a spacious bedroom. A king-size bed was positioned in the centre like a podium and glass doors gave a stunning view of the city lights beyond the river. Jay slid them open letting in a rush of fresh air. "The bathroom is in there if you want to freshen up," he pointed to a mirrored door.

Every surface in the bathroom gleamed. I found toothpaste and spare toothbrushes under the vanity and splashed my face, watching the cold water spiral around the glass basin. The nausea was gone but the fatigue was crippling. I felt barely strong enough to muster a smile, let alone make the journey back to Panacea. I'd been gone just over an hour - not long enough to be missed. I really needed to lie down for a while and rest.

When I came back into the bedroom, Jay was standing on the balcony with his feet apart and his hands in his pockets admiring the view, but he wasn't looking at the city lights, his head was tipped up to the stars. He was more dressed up than I'd ever seen him in a deep green collared shirt, that brought out the beautiful colour of his eyes, and slim pants that hugged his long legs. His sleeves were rolled to his elbows showing the hard cords of his forearms. He cut an imposing figure, all lean muscle and long lines, staring serenely at dusty clouds of stars. If it weren't for the mop of tawny waves, it could have been Christian standing there, hands relaxed in his pockets, quietly thinking.

"I need to lie down for a while," I called to him, sliding onto the plush bed.

"Sure thing," he answered, his attention pinned to the stars. I watched him for a while, standing peaceful and still, until I couldn't keep my eyes open anymore.

I woke with a start. An angry man was yelling something about 'that bitch's big booty' and asking said 'bitch' if she, 'wants to slide down his pole?' It took me a few dazed seconds to realise that it was music coming from the party downstairs and that someone had turned up the volume to a deafening level. Jay groaned beside me and rolled over, throwing a sleepy arm across my waist. How long had I been out? I picked up his wrist to read the time on his dive watch. *Oh no!* I'd been asleep for hours. I sat up, feeling woozy and shook Jay's shoulder. "Jay, I have to go."

He groaned again and forced his eyes open. A lazy smile spread across his face as he pulled me to him and kissed me. "I have to go," I said, pushing him away.

"Are you feeling better?"

"It doesn't matter. I've been here too long."

He looked as unconvinced as I felt. I didn't want to leave him but I couldn't stay any longer. I might be missed. I went into the bathroom and splashed more water on my face. My reflection in the mirror was deathly pale, powder blue bruises sat under my eyes and my collarbones looked oversharp. I knew I had lost some weight but the face staring back at me looked gaunt. I didn't bother drying my face, I marched back into the bedroom and bent to give Jay a quick peck on the lips.

"Hey," he protested, grabbing my hand as I pulled away, "when will I see you again?"

"Soon," I told him.

"Don't I get a proper goodbye kiss?" His eyes were liquid green, like a love potion – bright and startling and persuading. If I stared into them too long, I'd be lost. He drew me down with his gaze alone. I sank onto the edge of the bed and smoothed my fingers along his knife-blade jaw. His lashes swayed like golden grasses in a breeze, before laying still against his copper skin. Staying a few more minutes wouldn't make any difference now. I bent over and touched my lips to his eyelids; soft and fine as suede. His warm, supple breath spilled through parted lips and whispered at my throat. My skin prickled and hummed. And then he was whispering my name, his mouth trailing hot kisses down my neck.

His arms coiled around me and his mouth found mine. His kisses came like surging waves, crashing through every part of me until I knew nothing but him. I sank against his chest, dizzy and wanting, the feel of him blocking all other sight and sound. The world had turned to a wash of soft foam. "I have to go," I said again.

"Stay," he breathed into my ear. "Just a little while longer." His hands were roaming down my spine and playing at my hips. "I want you, Lilly." His wet lips stamped heat across my cheeks, my jaw, the tender hollow at the base of my neck. His hand slipped to the inside of my thigh. "Stay with me."

He rolled, bringing me down to lay beside him. His fingers traced a slow line up my leg, teasing at the hem of my dress. He kissed me again with so much longing that I thought I would come apart. I wanted him too. Badly. But I couldn't stay. I'd been gone for hours and someone was bound to notice I was missing. "I love you," I whispered, "but I really do have to go."

He let out a tortured yowl and flopped back against the pillow clutching at his heart.

"I'm sorry," I laughed. "I'll see you again soon. I promise."

He opened his eyes and shot me a mischievous grin. "If you're really going, I suggest you do it quickly because you have roughly five seconds before I pounce on you again."

I laughed and jumped off the bed. "I really am sorry." I kissed his forehead and pressed my palm to his heart before shimmering out of his view.

As soon as I penetrated the veil, the nausea struck in full force. The lightning vines wrapped around me, needling my entire body, and I felt like I was going to be electrocuted. The flashes were blinding and dizzying. My body felt weaker than it ever had. I struggled to remain conscious as I hurtled through the ether, praying I'd make it home. I had a delirious epiphany that I'd outstayed my welcome on Earth. Evidently, the longer I stayed, the harder it was to get back. My whole body was burning up and I knew I was about to be sick when my feet hit solid ground and a scream pierced the air - Sky. I had landed right in front of her in our living room. She was on her feet, wide-eyed and shaking as my stomach erupted all over the floor. I vaguely remember smiling weakly because I'd actually made it back. Then, I swayed… once… twice… and passed out.

I was in bed again. My bed. I was still wearing my grey strappy dress. Where were my shoes? I must have left them at Ryan's house. That reminded me of another fairytale from Earth - Cinder something - a love story sealed with a shoe, of all things. Humans had such silly stories about love. How could you possibly know you loved someone because they fit into a shoe? There would have been plenty of other girls that fitted that shoe! How did the prince know that he'd found the right girl? Did he look into her eyes? Did he talk to her? Did he say, 'Hey, were you the girl I danced with at my fancy ball?' No! He just grabbed her foot, shoved on a size 6 glass slipper and said, "Awesome, I love you, let's go!"

I could feel my body shaking with laughter at my own joke.

"You're awake."

I stopped laughing and cracked open my eyes. Sky was coming into my room with a tray and a chilly expression. She was wearing a swirling paisley top that made me feel dizzy and I had to squint away.

"What's so funny?" she asked. "Because I know it can't be the fact that you materialised out of nowhere last night and threw up on our rug. Not to mention that you nearly gave me a heart attack." She stood sleek and poised as a statue, the tray balanced on one palm.

I fell silent, remembering the whole unfortunate scene last night with Sky as my witness. I still felt giddy and hollowed out somehow and I was talking nonsense to myself about glass shoes! Maybe I had a concussion from my fall. I touched my fingers to my head and winced. They came away greasy and sticky.

"Don't touch that," Sky scolded. "You've got a nasty bump from where you passed out. I've put some healing balm on it so don't go wiping it all off. Maybe next time you decide to faint, aim for the rug instead of the hard, wooden floor, but only if you haven't thrown up on the rug first." She put the tray of tea and toast on the bed next to me and stepped back with her arms folded, eyeing me. "I hope you're feeling better because you've got some serious explaining to do, Lilly."

A go-lite's version of angry is nothing like a human's but I could see I had pushed Sky to her limit. I could feel worry radiating off her in waves. Her tone was cutting, her posture oozed annoyance, but I knew once she got whatever she was feeling off her chest, that would be the end of it. Negative emotions, when they did arise, were dealt with simply and swiftly. After all, what would be the purpose of holding on to them?

I had really messed up last night. I'd been so weak I couldn't even navigate my way back to my bedroom. I knew it was a small miracle that I'd even made it back to Panacea at all, but to land in front of Sky like that... she must have been terrified. And then to pass out cold? I looked at her with all the compassion my foggy head would allow me to muster. "I'm so sorry, Sky."

"I don't want an apology. I want to know what's going on," she said coolly, grinding her knuckles into her hipbones. "Look at you. You can barely lift your head off that pillow, you're so weak. While you've been unconscious for the last seven hours I've been forming a rather disturbing theory on where you materialised from and what's been going on. I'm hoping to hear it contradicted because I know what I'm thinking is impossible. But then again, it wouldn't be the first time you've done the impossible. In fact, you seem to be making a habit of it and it's starting to scare me, Lilly." Her eyes were drilling holes through me. "You're not well. Your whole life is careening out of control and the worst part is, I think you've barely noticed."

I gaped at her in disbelief. I'd never seen her so upset. I cringed back against my pillow, a hot rush of guilt colouring my cheeks. Logically I knew that I had asked her to look out for me and keep me on track, but now I was annoyed. Sky was supposed to support me, not make me feel like a child. "I know what I'm doing," I spat.

Her lips parted in surprise and I felt a fleeting sense of satisfaction that I had wiped that superior look off her face. Then it was my turn to look shocked while I wondered why I was thinking such a horrible thing. Sky was my friend, she loved me and only wanted the best for me. I was feeling dizzy again but I managed to calm myself and offer an apologetic smile. "I'm sorry for snapping at you," I said gently. "I'm still feeling quite sick... dizzy and queasy." She was unmoved. Her lips were pursed in the most perfect pout I'd ever seen. "I know you're worried about me but this is the first time anything like this has happened. I'll be okay, really."

Her eyes narrowed. "Meaning this is the first time you've ever done the stupid thing that caused you to throw up and pass out?" she paused. "Or do you mean this is the first time you've passed out from doing the stupid thing that you've secretly been doing for a while?"

I winced at her, not wanting to admit the truth. "The second one," I said reluctantly and braced for her reaction.

Her blue eyes flashed like they'd been struck by flint and hectic crimson splotches were rising on her china white skin. "I'm terrified to ask, but you need to tell me right now. *How* did you materialise in our living room? Because I know you haven't suddenly acquired your father's Traveller Gift."

I stared at Sky, dumbfounded, my lips rounding in a shocked O. Her words were like a revelation.

My father's Traveller Gift?

It was such a simple explanation for why I could travel to Earth. A barrage of thoughts ran through my mind as I entertained the idea that I had been blessed with a second Gift that I never knew about. Could I be Healer and Traveller at once? It was rare, but not unprecedented. My father had two Gifts. He was both Traveller and Syphon. Maybe his Traveller abilities had been passed down to me, just not in the same way as his Gift presented itself. What if instead of being able to travel between different cities, I had the ability to travel between worlds?

"Great Source above, Lilly! Will you please tell me

what's going on?"

I blinked at her, stunned. "I think I do have the Traveller Gift," I told her, "only I never realised it. I think I might have inherited my dad's abilities and that's why I can teleport to Earth."

She yelped. Her eyes were wide and terrified. She buried her face in her hands and shook her head back and forth. "I was really hoping you weren't going to say that. What have you done? Doesn't it violate some natural law to teleport to Earth? This is insane!"

I ignored her panic and chased my thoughts to their conclusion. "But Sky, I think you're right. It makes sense, doesn't it? It's the same Gift as my dad's, just in a different form. My great-grandad must have been a Traveller too."

"Are you telling me Grayson Flights sashayed back and forth to Earth making personal house calls? *'Carry on, don't mind me, oh and sorry I threw up on your rug.'* Seriously?"

I sat up too quickly and my head reeled. "I don't know, but that's a really good question. Maybe he says something about it in here." The manuscript started to hum as I reached for it on my bedside table. My fingertips tingled as I drew close and the feeling was so strong I wouldn't have been surprised to see tiny lightning bolts shooting from my fingers.

Sky clicked into Commando mode. "Oh, no," she shook her head vehemently, "you're not burying your nose in that book right now. This conversation is far from over."

My arms dropped back onto the bed. The

manuscript fell silent and so did I, slumping back against the pillows. Poor Sky. She did deserve answers.

She sat there blinking at me. "Well, you've successfully melted my brain for the second time this week, so just give me minute to catch up, okay?" She frowned, trying to put all the pieces together. "So before you crashed landed in our living room, you were on planet Earth - like actually, physically there?"

I nodded.

"You somehow used a Traveller Gift you didn't know you possessed to get there and presumably, the reason you went there was to see Jay?"

I nodded again.

"Are you completely insane?" she exploded. "Lilly, Earth is dangerous! Have you learnt nothing from being a Soul Guardian? You've seen what humans do to each other. You could have been shot... or kidnapped... or killed!" she huffed.

I waited for her to catch her breath. "I didn't join a gang, Sky."

She threw her hands up in exasperation. "No, you just turned up here half dead from the effort of your travels. Do you realise I had to drag you in here by myself? When you didn't wake up I was going to call healaxis for help but then I realised that would risk revealing your secret. I didn't know what I could or couldn't tell them so I sat by you all night to make sure you kept breathing."

"Oh no, Sky. I'm so sorry." I felt terrible. I reached

out for her hand and she offered it to me reluctantly. "I'm sorry to have kept you up all night and for all the worry and upset. Thank you so much for looking after me." Her eyes were beginning to soften, the fear draining out of her. "Thank you for everything you've done for me, Sky. You're a beautiful friend and I love the way you love me."

She nodded and squeezed my hand. "My brain is still melted though." The beginning of a smile tugged at her lips.

I laughed and sat up to hug her. "That's probably not such a bad thing. You always were too much of a smarty pants anyway."

She laughed, resting her chin on my shoulder for a few moments, then my stomach growled like an angry bear had taken up residence. "Eat," she said, pulling away from me. "You must be hungry." I was suddenly ravenous. Sky had piled toasted blackbread with cottler cheese and fresh berries. I couldn't remember anything ever tasting so good. And she'd drizzled honey over it too. "How many times have you been to Earth?"

I stopped chewing to do a mental count. "Five, no, six times," I corrected.

She flinched at my answer and hurriedly collected herself again. "How did it happen? I mean, were you trying to do that?"

"Of course not, given that it's supposed to be impossible. It was a complete surprise. Jay and I were having a conversation one day through the veil and next thing, I landed in his back yard, in the flesh."

"You're kidding!"

"No, it was absolutely surreal. He had the same look on his face when I appeared before him as you did last night."

"So you're saying you did nothing to make it happen, it just happened, out of the blue?"

"Not exactly. I wasn't aware at the time what caused it. Now I know that it's the connection we feel to one another. I just have to focus on the energy of Jay's Soul and I can find him, wherever he is. After that, it's just a matter of pushing through the veil to join him." I took a sip of mint tea while I watched poor Sky's brain melt a little bit more.

"This is unbelievable." She was looking at me with a mixture of shock and awe. "*You're* unbelievable. Do you realise that you might be in possession of one of the most powerful Gifts this world has ever known?"

I narrowed my eyes in question, my brow knitting with confusion. I'd never thought of it that way. All I knew was that Jay's heart was connected to mine and not even time, space or death could alter that. We had known each other in a previous life and The Source had brought us back together. Sky might be right; I could have a latent Traveller ability but that didn't explain how Jay had materialised on Panacea. Was he a Traveller too? Did humans possess abilities like go-lites? They were just more questions I didn't have answers to.

Sky was looking at me the same way Christian did sometimes; with a mixture of admiration and bafflement that I'd never truly understood. "I'm not powerful, Sky. I'm just in love. But I suppose," I mused, "there's no greater power than that." I sighed with giddy relief. I'd finally voiced my feelings for Jay. Saying the words out loud for the first time sent a rush of pleasure through me.

Her expression was neutral as she registered the fact I'd just professed my love for a human. My heart hummed at the thought of it, of the life we could have together, of all we could be. Sky was watching me in her catlike way, her head tilted to one side. I could see the cogs turning in her mind, fitting all the pieces together. She glanced at the manuscript lying closed on my bedside table. "And you intend to bring him here, just like your great-grandad did Aurora?"

"I know in my heart, that's what The Source is guiding me to do."

She was silent, thinking, scrutinising. Her eyes drifted around the room as though she could gather more information from the still air around us. I could see her unspoken questions through my drooping lashes. My body still yearned for sleep. So instead of pressing me further, she brushed her thumb over my hand and released it. "Rest," she said. "We'll talk more when you're feeling better." Her weight lifted from my bed and I watched her leave through blurry eyes, shutting my bedroom door behind her.

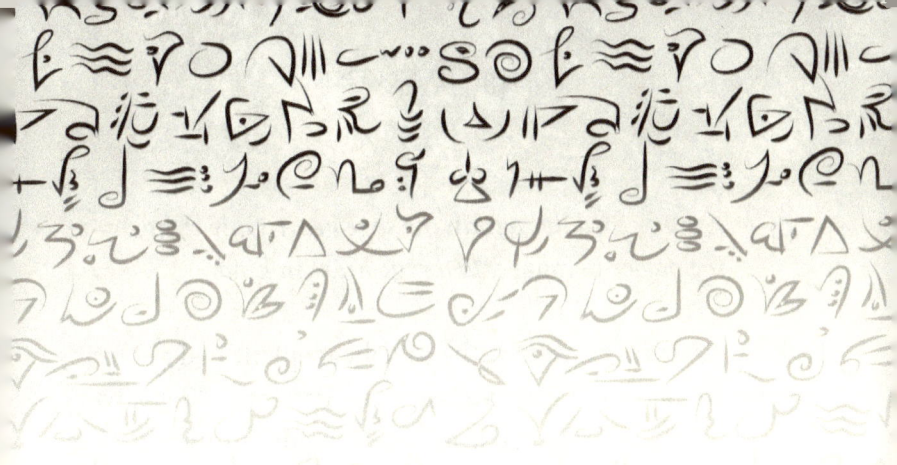

SIXTEEN

Lilly

I woke again at around midday. The house was quiet and the day warm. My mind still felt like it was moving through a blanket of fog but my body felt lighter, better. I instinctively reached for the manuscript and my journal on the bedside table. My barely awake mind was already filling up with the questions and possibilities that my conversation with Sky had stirred.

Could I really be a Traveller?

And was Great-grandad a Traveller too?

And what of Jay and Aurora? Did they also have the Gift? Could humans really possess Gifts like that?

I opened my journal and flipped to the page where I'd neatly set down the translation of Grayson Flights' hidden messages. For all my strain and effort, I'd only managed to decipher a few lines from the invisible green ink so far.

A silver cord lies within the sage heart. Only it, holds the power to connect to a sage heart in kind.

I was confident the sage heart plant had a starring role to play in Jay's ascension to Panacea. The silvery, cord-like stalk was most probably made into a potion of some sort. I was expecting to find the recipe on one of the pages I had yet to decipher.

I hauled the leather-bound manuscript onto my lap and leafed through its yellowed pages. It still had that medicinal smell like the apothecary at healaxis. I turned to where I had left off and prepared myself to centre and focus. Much to my surprise, it didn't take as much effort as usual and before long, emerald green ink became visible on the page between the lines of my great-grandad's scholarly writings. As I watched lines of ink twist and curl across the brittle page, I realised why. This wasn't another set of cryptic clues. It was a journal entry where Grayson was describing what it had been like when he first saw Aurora.

Curious, I flipped to the next page where I could sense the hidden text looming. Again, the writing slipped easily into view, and again, it seemed to be a diary entry. I leafed through all the remaining pages, refocussing on each one. The magic on this book was strong because there was a definite pattern. The strange symbols remained stubbornly illegible on some pages while Grayson's personal recollections revealed themselves with only moderate effort. The pages that seemed to hold specific instructions for ascension in my great-grandad's rhyming riddles, were much harder to decipher.

I turned excitedly back to his first journal entry. I devoured line after line while Grayson described how he had been drawn to Aurora with 'urgent force' during his Soul Guardian duties. She had been grieving over the death of her brother when Grayson was sent to her and he had fallen under her spell from the first.

Buttermilk skin and starlit eyes. Willowy and light as a dancing swan. Her pain flows through her like music and she is all the more beautiful for it. I watch the solo dance of her grief. She spins and leaps, rises and falls and with each lithe turn, I am mesmerised. If only she knew that she wasn't alone and that there is someone, so close, who would like to take her hand.

He was besotted with her and wanted nothing more than to ease her pain. It was an achingly familiar tale. I shut the book and closed my eyes.

I suddenly felt the need to get out of the house. I was craving a swim. I imagined cool ocean waves clearing my head and bringing me back to myself. I knew where I wanted to be... what I needed.

I glided around the winding coast road, hugging the bends, my gaze drifting over the grey cliffs to the turquoise waters below. I had used the drive to clear my mind, to focus on myself and replenish the energy I had lost on Earth. The pain and discontent of too many humans at once had thrown me. It had been more than I could handle and I'd paid the price. From now on, I would visit Jay in private. Lesson learned.

I wondered if someone stronger and more balanced than me could have coped? I imagined Elder Tunes with his infectious joy and felt sure he could have handled the emotional bombardment. Any of the Elders probably could. I even thought that Chris or Sky would have managed it a lot better than I had, but that was true of most things.

I'd always known that I was different. Even as a little a girl. No matter how much my parents and Chris loved me, I still felt apart somehow, like I wasn't quite the same as them. I felt like the wrong Cinderella, like I was trying to shove my foot into a shoe that didn't quite fit. It was true what I had said to Jay, how I'd always felt a part of me was missing. Maybe now, things would be different. Maybe now that I had found Jay and I knew what I had to do, I would finally feel whole. I had never felt so driven, so pulled in a specific direction, and yet somehow, I recognised the feeling, as though it had been simmering beneath the surface, waiting for the right moment to emerge.

An eagle drew a lazy spiral around the sun and I could smell the tang of salt on the breeze. It was like a tonic. I relished the hypnotic sound of the sea air buffeting through my open windows. My hair flew in wild twists, dancing to its rhythm while the sun slanted through the windshield, heating my skin. I was almost there.

The road dipped slowly at first, then dove into a scrubby forest, stealing the water from my view. I turned down the track to my favourite beach, jostling over rocks and divots, and ambled to a stop at the end. I turned off the car, sat still and listened. Nature was singing. The tremolo note of cicada song pealing through the white-barked trees, the bright chirp of birds, the wind sighing and rustling through pale leaves, and beyond, I could hear the low bass of the ocean.

I gathered up my bag and towel and padded along the sandy track. Up ahead, glints of blinding blue winked through the scrub. I scrambled up the rise in the dunes aching to breathe in that first wave of cool, salt air from the top and look out over the edge of the world. But as I made the last step, I froze, the elated smile drained from my face. The pristine shoreline was littered with sleek black shapes as big as boulders and ribbons of red were leaking into the sea. I gasped. And then I ran.

Intense grief ripped from my heart and tore up my throat. I screamed in horror at what was all around me. The ancients of the deep lay slashed up and twitching in the shallows, labouring under their last breaths. Scarlet rivers ran from their mangled flesh, their life force draining into the sea.

I charged frantically into the bloodied waves and reached for a whale that was barely alive. His great eye was upon me as I threw my body in a protective embrace across his back and channelled healing energy into him with all my might. He sang one low note that vibrated to my core and I squeezed tighter, compounding my strength and willing him to live. "Don't leave," I pleaded. "Who has done this to you? Who could do such a thing?" If he managed an answer, I wasn't the right person to hear it. Christian was. I wished he were here. I needed him. These whales needed him.

The gentle giant heaved once more and I felt the spirit drain from his body as my trembling arms dropped helplessly to my sides. I spun wildly in a vertiginous stupor, not knowing where to turn next. So many already lay heavy and vacant. Desperation flung me from carcass to carcass, straining through tears for any signs of life. *They're dead, they're all dead!*

I stumbled and fell, slamming into one of the wasting giants. My hands struggled to find purchase on its slippery skin as my face landed inches from a deep gash in its side, revealing pale flesh devoid of its life blood. I regained my balance and moved trembling fingers to examine the gaping wound. There, lodged in the lower edge was the sickening sight of ugly, grey metal. I cried out in horror and toppled backwards. I felt sick. My body buckled and I lurched forward emptying the contents of my stomach and fighting the urge to pass out.

My mind struggled to accept what was too painful for my eyes to see. "That can't be...no...it can't be!" I knew it was the head of a harpoon and that these weapons were used for senseless slaughter of the ancients on Earth. I stood staring inanely at my white cotton skirt being gruesomely consumed by red. I watched in a daze as the bloody saltwater soaked higher toward my waist. *I'm wearing death.* I buried my face in my hands and unable to feel my legs anymore, slid defeated into the scarlet sea.

"Christian," I sobbed, "I need you." The grief was crippling, a crushing weight on my heart as though a part of me was dying too, as though *I* was the one bleeding into the sea.

I sat there in a daze feeling completely helpless until I realised I was probably in shock. I had to call for help. I had to call Chris. I rose on legs that felt barely there. I managed to place one foot in front of the other until I was out of the water and floating in a daze, up the beach to my bag. I sank to my knees in the sand and found my uniter. I focussed on the dull crystal tablet and thought of Chris. Within seconds his face appeared on the screen.

"Lilly, what's wrong?"

He would have felt my fear and shock vibrating through my call before he ever looked at his uniter screen. "You have to come. I need you. They're all dead." My voice sounded hollow and very far away.

"Where are you? Is that blood? Are you hurt?" he demanded.

My heartbeat was loud in my ears. "What?" I looked down at my shirt and it was stained red. "Yes, it's blood but I'm okay." The world was beginning to go wonky.

"I'm coming. Just tell me where you are."

It was an effort to force out the words. "At... at the beach." Everything tilted sideways. I felt the uniter slip from my fingers and something rough grazing my cheek.

Christian

"Lilly!" Her eyes rolled back in her head and I watched helplessly as she swayed and collapsed. Her uniter landed in the sand next to her still body and all I could see was blood all over her. Not the bright crimson that pours from a wound, but pale pink from bloody water. "Lilly! Can you hear me?" My chest tightened like I'd taken a blow and fear bloomed across my skin like hot needles. She wasn't answering me. She wasn't moving. I couldn't even tell if she was breathing.

Fingers brushed my shoulder and I jumped. "We're almost there." Petra was looking at me, her face pale and eyes full of concern. "The turn-off is just up ahead."

The truck rattled down the hill. Petra twisted in her seat to tell Healer Dwano that there would be two casualties when we reached the beach instead of one, Garrick Leif and Lilly Flights. Thanks to Grand Master Trill's vision, we knew exactly where Garrick would be and when. But what in The Source's name was Lilly doing there? And what had happened to her?

I couldn't tear my eyes from the screen. She still wasn't moving. My heart was pounding and fear was rising in my throat like the tightening of a vice. I could feel Petra's eyes on me, searching for the right thing to say. I gaped at the still body on my screen. "She isn't moving," I told her.

"Almost there," was all she said.

Then Evangeline's prophecy leapt into my mind. I could see the memorial flame as if I was standing in front of it. I could smell the wreath of white lilies and wild jasmine. My world tipped. *No... no, no, no, no, no!*

I was about to lean forward and tell the driver to go faster when the truck ground to a halt. I threw open the door and sprinted down the beach track, my heart feeling like it was ready to explode. I fought up the soft sand of the dunes, gritting my teeth and pushing myself as fast as I could go. The sand was collapsing under my feet. The muscles in my legs screamed, taking twice as many strides and advancing half the distance. I'd never felt hatred for anything in my life but now I absolutely *hated* sand.

I could hear the echo of Evangeline's voice, could

see her hypnotic eyes. '*A life is made up of a million journeys and each one, seemingly good or bad, is a necessary step toward the great becoming - the journey of becoming ourselves.*'

I clenched my jaw in defiance, not wanting to hear where my mind was taking me. Death was a journey, a new becoming. In the end, it was the ultimate journey. Is that what Evangeline had meant? Was Lilly going to die? It was the question that had plagued me since Evangeline had delivered her warning and a question she hadn't been inclined to answer. That had only been 24 hours ago. I hadn't even had a chance to play my part and not interfere in Lilly's choices. I had been trying to steel myself for any possibility, replaying Evangeline's words over and over in my mind. I was trying to be strong and love her enough to let her fall and find her own way. And fall, she had, right in front of me while I sat powerless. And now, she might already be gone. And for what? Was this guy and whatever secret quest she was on worth dying for? And where was he now, when she was in trouble?

I stumbled and fell, scrambling to see over the rise. My eyes flew left, scanning the beach from the rocky spires and caves of the Record Keepers and sweeping the shoreline. A figure lay prone in the distance - Garrick - and then my eyes shot to a patch of red sea lapping against a collection of sleek, black boulders that hadn't been there before. No, not boulders - whales - dead whales bleeding into the sea. That's what Lilly had meant.

It was gruesome, gut wrenching, incongruent in

a way that tipped my mind askew. Then I saw her, curled motionless on her side. "Lilly!" My heart dropped into my stomach. I screamed her name again, pushing to my feet and pelting down the other side of the dune. I watched anger and panic rise up in my mind like a sinister fog. It took all of my presence to not let it overwhelm my better judgement. Lilly needed me and she needed me focussed and in control. I was no good to her made impotent by negative emotion. I blew the laboured breath from my straining lungs, choosing instead to focus on my love for her, that warm, bright feeling that enveloped me whenever she was near.

I ran like I'd never run before and skidded to a halt beside her, kicking up sand and dropping to my knees. Now that I had reached her, I found myself hesitating. My shaking hands reached for her, praying she was alive and not wanting to know if she wasn't. I cupped her shoulder and smoothed her tangled hair. "Lilly, please, can you hear me?" I rasped.

Her white cotton skirt was stained pink to her waist and it was crumpled around her sand covered legs. Her shirt was marked with brighter smears of blood and I felt sick at the sight, praying none of it belonged to her. I gently rolled her onto her back. Sand was sticking in her dark hair and in a bloody graze on her left cheek. She was deathly pale, soaked from head to toe, and she was cold. So still and so cold.

I was breathing hard and tears stung my eyes. I

clasped her shoulders and lowered my head to her chest, pressing my ear to her heart. A desperate sob escaped me and I shuddered against her, blindly reaching to cup her face in my hands, to smooth her hair, to wind my arms around her and hold her tight. I could hear her heart drumming faintly, giving mine permission to start beating again too. She was alive.

"Lil, I'm here." I sat up and squeezed her hands. "Can you hear me?" I stared intently into her face, searching for any small movement. I slipped my arm under her neck and lifted her up, cradling her to me. I heard shouting as the others stampeded onto the beach. Petra and Jordan ran up to us. The others had already spied Garrick further down.

"Is she all right?" Petra asked breathlessly but she didn't stop moving.

"She's alive," I said as she kept running toward the whales.

The shadow of Jordan's huge frame hovered, "Is there anything I can do, Chris?"

"No, go," I told him. "Help Petra."

I watched them stagger into the red waves, weaving between the slick, black mounds lying lifeless in the shallows. We were too late. There was nothing to be done. I knew it because there was silence in my mind. No pleas for help from the gentle giants littering the shore.

Grand Master Trill's vision had been a little off. She had given us the precise place and what she thought was the precise time but we had arrived too late. Petra and I had witnessed the toll her troubling visions were taking. I prayed that we were still in time to save Garrick Leif. I could see the rest of the team gathered around him now, Healer Dwano signalling to lift him onto the stretcher. Like Lilly, he wasn't moving either.

I looked down at her, so slight and still in my arms. I'd often wondered how such a little person could hold so much love, so much stubbornness and determination. I held her to my chest. "I need you to wake up," I pleaded. My voice was beginning to break as fresh tears pricked my eyes. "I need you to pull out that famous Flights obstinance. The kind of wilfulness that makes sea monsters cower and think twice about eating you," I laughed as a tear rolled down my cheek and splashed onto her forehead.

Lilly's brow furrowed and she moaned softly. "Lil? Lilly, can you hear me?" Her eyelids battled her fatigue, straining to open. Her bloodshot eyes rolled around in her head like loose marbles. I smoothed my palm over her cheek and wiped my tear from her face but soon enough, she began crying tears of her own.

Lilly

"It's okay, it's okay. Ssshhh, you're all right. I'm here, Lil."

Chris was here.

His solid arms were wrapped tightly around me

and my frozen shock melted with the heat of his embrace. He touched his lips to my hair and rested his cheek to my head.

"I came as soon as I could. Source help me, if anything had happened to you..." He gave me another desperate squeeze before grasping my weak shoulders and pushing me back to search my face. His expression was wild. His steel blue eyes locked on mine. "Are you all right? Do you need a Healer?"

"No, I'm okay. I think I collapsed from exhaustion," I croaked. "I was trying to save the whales."

"This is horrific. Did you see what happened to them?"

"No, I... I don't know. They were dying when I got here. All slashed up and bleeding. I saw a harpoon lodged in one ancient's side." Chris sucked in a pained gasp. "I tried to heal him but I wasn't strong enough. I couldn't save him." My voice was a weak whisper. I was struggling to reconcile what I had witnessed. I didn't dare look back to the water. "They're all dead aren't they?"

Chris nodded.

I felt numb. A pained, strangled sound burst from my lips. I pulled him closer burying my face in his chest, the trauma of it all erupting to the surface. I could feel my throat closing over and it was hard to breathe. I sucked in the heavy air. The bodies lying in the shallows were vacant but the energy of violence that had been unleashed here remained, putrefying the air.

Chris held me quietly while I cried. Every now and then he ran his hand down my back like he wanted to wipe away the sadness. "This can't be happening," I sniffled, looking up into his grim face.

"It can, because those whales were from Earth," he said gravely, shutting his eyes. "Just like the elephants, the bees, the dead butterflies, the koalas."

"And Houdini; the horse that magically appeared on Farmer Summer's property."

"Him too," Chris nodded.

I shivered and he pulled me close into him again.

"Do we need a stretcher here?" came a voice across the sand. A group of people were walking toward us.

"No, I've got her," Chris answered. "Come on, Lil, let's get you home. You're wet and shivering. You need to get warm and rest."

I nodded robotically and he plucked me up in his arms in one easy movement.

"I can walk." My voice was as dead and lifeless as the old ones' bodies. He said nothing and strode ahead of the group. Their voices were all a blur. Their faces a shocked mirror image of my own. I closed my eyes and pressed my face into Chris' warm chest willing it to all disappear. I couldn't process any of it. I just wanted to be away from here. He trudged up the steep dunes and down the other side. All the while I kept my eyes squeezed shut, clinging to his warmth.

I remembered Chris putting me in my car and rummaging around in my bag for the keys but I remembered nothing of the drive home.

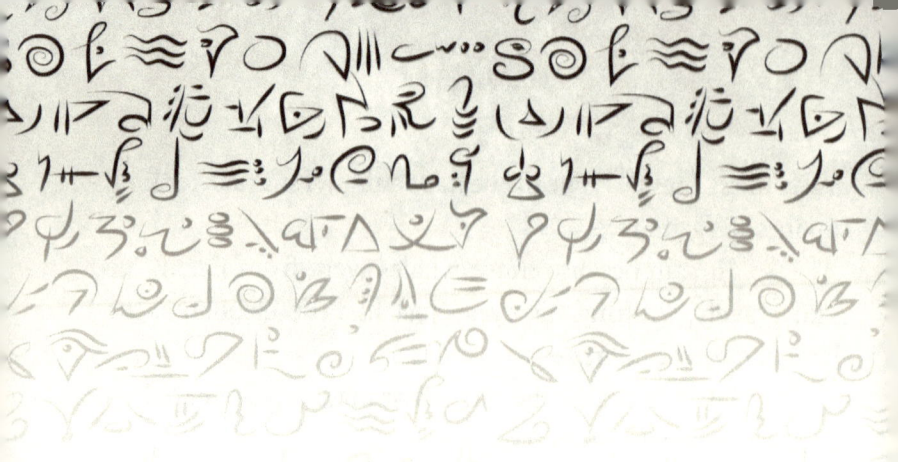

SEVENTEEN

Lilly

Christian was hovering in the living room while Sky paced outside my bathroom door. "Call me if you feel dizzy," she cautioned. I couldn't be bothered answering. The steaming hot shower thawed my bones and reddened my skin but did nothing to wash away the horror and confusion. I still felt so cold. I fumbled to shut off the water and dried myself in a daze.

Sky had laid out my favourite pyjamas on my bed. I could hear she and Chris talking in low voices in the other room.

"What do you mean?" Chris asked her in a guarded tone.

"You should talk to her about it. It's not my place to say."

Of course Christian was going to ask questions. He was worried. He'd just found me unconscious and covered in blood. He would be probing her for an explanation that she wasn't at liberty to give. My stomach clenched and started to churn as though a stampede of horses was thundering inside it. I had trusted her implicitly with my secret because there was no questioning Sky's loyalty. But the fact was, last night, I had roused in her a very real fear. Admitting that I'd been Travelling to Earth and that I was in love with a human had elicited the very reaction I'd anticipated. My confession had warped the accepted reality etched in the hearts and Souls of every go-lite. She had been afraid – afraid of what it meant to the way of our world and afraid for me and my safety. I wondered: when loyalty and fear are pitted, one against the other, which is victorious?

I couldn't hear them talking anymore and then I heard Sky in the kitchen, rattling canisters and boiling the kettle. I dressed quickly and appeared in the living room doorway to see Christian slumped on the midnight blue sofa with his face buried in his hands. The Blue Lady of Flowers on the wall behind encircled him in a wreath of blue blooms. I hesitated, watching him as he pressed the heels of his hands to his eyes, his long fingers threading through the dark wave of his hair. He looked so vulnerable and I wanted to curl up on the couch beside him, hold his hand, make him smile. "Hey," I said quietly.

He tore his hands away from his face and came to attention, looking me over with troubled eyes. "Are you feeling any better?"

"A little," I nodded. "I'm a bit hazy on everything that happened after you found me. Those other people on the beach, they were carrying a stretcher. Did I see Healer Dwano there? Was someone hurt?"

Chris levelled his gaze. "Yes, someone was. We found your missing patient, Lilly. We found Garrick Leif."

My jaw dropped. "Where?"

"A few hundred metres down the beach from where I found you."

"Is he alive? Source help me, I didn't even see him there!"

Chris crossed the room in a few long strides and gripped my hands. "It's okay. He's alive. At least, he was when we found him." He steered me to the sofa and sat me down. "I'll call healaxis and see how Garrick is doing. You need to rest, Lilly. Sky's making tea. "

Now I was the one slumped on the sofa with my head in my hands while Chris went through the kitchen and into the garden to make his call. I could hear the low, soothing bass of his voice drifting through the open glass doors; a supple, sagacious murmur. Sky bustled in, setting a tray on the coffee table. Steam rose in twining fingers from the spout of a purple pot. She'd made a plate of sandwiches cut into triangles and arranged chocolate brownies dusted with sugar in a tower.

"Thank you," I sighed. I was starving.

"Well," said Chris, coming back into the room and sitting next to me, "Garrick is alive, but barely." I'd never seen Chris look as troubled as he did today. It was as though someone had tipped him upside down and rattled out all his confidence. "They said his energy field is practically shredded and they don't know if they can save him. He's in a twilight sleep and they aren't holding much hope of him waking up."

I felt dizzy. *What in The Source's name was going on?* "No," I protested. "What was he doing at the beach? He's only fifteen years old. He can't even drive! How did he get there?"

"I wish I knew, but until he wakes up – *if* he wakes up at all – we aren't going to get answers to those questions." Chris gave me a long look. "Why were you there, Lilly?"

I shrugged. "I wasn't feeling well. I took the day off and thought I'd go to the beach to recharge. Instead, it ended up being a complete horror show." My attempt to look after *me* for a change had backfired completely.

Sky was perched on the edge of the tapestry armchair, quietly sipping her tea. I looked at Chris and he was studying me, reading me as though there might be more to it than that. "What?"

"Nothing," he said. "I was just thinking."

Irritation flared unbidden and spread like a brushfire. "Well, do you have to stare at me while you think?" I snapped.

Chris went very still, blinking in bewilderment. I turned away from him, my body brimming with annoyance. Sky was peering at me through narrowed eyes, clutching her mug with both hands. Now they were both staring at me. Chris shifted on the couch beside me and it creaked loudly through the silence.

"What?" I looked from one to the other. "I'm fine," I flung my hands up in exasperation. "Can you both just relax and stop worrying about me, please?" I could hear the strain in my voice; high and tight.

Sky frowned. "Lilly," she began.

I brusquely cut her off, "Look, I may not be as wise and perfectly in control of my life as you both are, but I'm not made of glass either." I was hearing the words spilling from my lips but I couldn't seem to make them stop. What's more, it had only taken a scrutinising expression, a lingering look, to set me off. Insecurity was bubbling up from somewhere deep inside of me. I felt as though I was being weighed and measured and found wanting. That small voice that had always made me question myself and had driven me harder to be better was turning into a roar. "This is my life and I know what I'm doing!" I yelled. "Why can't you ever just trust me and believe in me as I believe in both of you?"

Christian's mouth was hanging open. He was completely dumbfounded, confusion etched on his frozen face. Sky was inching toward me with sympathetic eyes and her arms outstretched as though she were about to diffuse a bomb. She was too late. I'd already exploded.

I sat there, shivering in the wake of my outburst,

then I hung my head in shame and cried. I cried because I was embarrassed. I cried because I was frightened and confused and I didn't understand what was happening to me or why I'd said those things. I cried because I'd lashed out and hurt my friends in some petulant, childish display. And most of all, I cried because the part of me that didn't feel good enough wasn't remorseful at all. That part of me had felt a rush of satisfaction at being heard. With every rash word from my mouth, it had grown larger; from a small, dark shadow to a towering monster looming large enough to open its jaws and swallow the room. *It* was glad I'd said all those things and for a moment it had felt bigger than me. *Source help me,* it had chased away all peace and reason.

Sky's hand was resting on top of mine as she crouched in front of me. Christian's hand was on my shaking shoulder. When had I started shaking? I couldn't bring myself to look at either of them. I squeezed my eyes closed, forcefully wringing out the remaining tears. I swiped them from my cheeks and stared studiously at my hand glistening with salty water. Tears. I'd cried more of them in these last weeks than I had in my entire life.

"I'm so sorry," I whispered. "I didn't mean..." What could I possibly say to them? I didn't understand what had happened so how could I explain it to them? Another wave of exhaustion chewed through me. The monster had gulped down what little energy I'd had left. "I think I need to sleep. I'm sorry." I still couldn't meet their eyes as I lifted myself up, burning with shame, and went to my bedroom and hurriedly closed the door behind me.

I tossed and turned all night. I dreamt of a boy with forlorn green eyes, his wooden limbs rooted in place while I was carried out to sea...

I dreamt of a girl with hair like wheat whose heart broke clean in two. *"When you discover the one you love isn't who you thought, it's the unmaking of the world."*

I came awake, her words bleeding from the dream world and into my conscious mind, playing over and over in haunted echoes.

I stared at the ceiling, suspended in mute melancholy. It was almost daylight. The sky turned from indigo to violet to bronze, tinting my bedroom walls a hundred different shades in between. I listened to see if I could hear the sunrise. When I was a child I was convinced that I could. I would lie perfectly still, straining into the silence just before dawn. And then it would come; a distant, fiery rumble as the sun climbed over the horizon, like the sound from the belly of a great furnace and God had just opened the door.

My body felt heavy, my head light, like I'd been lying in this bed for an age. My muscles were so stiff from lack of use that I wondered if I would turn to stone. I needed tea. Truth be told, I needed a lot more than just tea. I had said I was going to take better care of myself but I had done nothing to make that happen, save a failed trip to the beach. Before I had met Jay or discovered my family secret, I had lived my my life as all go-lites do. I'd meditated everyday, visited the crystal pools often, fed myself well in body, mind and spirit. How else could we be of service to others if we were depleted ourselves? These days I was always too busy – busy thinking about Jay, busily bent over the manuscript, busy Travelling to Earth – to give myself what I needed to function.

I crept into the hallway and started for the kitchen. Right now I would settle for tea. When I reached the living room I stopped. Chris was curled up on the couch. His long legs were contorted like a sleeping jack-in-the-box just waiting for someone to crank that handle and free him. I smiled, wondering how anyone could sleep like that, but I knew full well that Christian could sleep standing on his head if he wanted to.

I owed he and Sky a proper apology. After a restless night of dreams and disconnected thoughts, I couldn't offer an explanation for how I behaved but I *could* tell them how sorry I was.

Shards of morning light were angling through the window and creeping up on Chris. I was tip-toeing past to draw the curtain so he could sleep a little longer, when he woke. His eyes fluttered open and focussed on me hovering over him. A lazy smile lit up his face. "Hey. How are you feeling?"

I shrugged, unsure how to answer. "You slept in your jeans," I grimaced. I had never understood how anyone could sleep in jeans.

"Sky graciously offered me a frilly nightie but I declined," he smirked. "Although, I have to admit, it was rather tempting." He sat up and ran a hand through his mussed hair. "A saucy little black number with Enduan lace."

"How in The Source's name do you know about Enduan lace?" I choked a laugh.

"You might be surprised by the things I know," he winked. "Man of taste and all that."

I left him there grinning and went to seek out breakfast. A few moments later I heard him shuffle in behind me. "Do you want tea?" I asked placing the kettle on the stove.

"Do you have any juice?"

"I can make some," I said, turning to find him hanging from the door frame in a lazy stretch, his shirt riding up to reveal a slice of toned bronze where his jeans hung below his hipbones. I quickly turned away and began rummaging through the icebox. I emerged with lila melon, mangoes, blinderberries and armfuls of The Source only knows what and started to chop.

"I can do that," he said, rounding the kitchen table and taking the knife from me.

"You stayed... last night."

He shrugged, cutting the lila melon in half with one, clean slice. "I wasn't sure you'd want me to but I didn't feel good about leaving you either."

"Thank you. It was nice to find you here when

I woke up. I'm so sorry about what I said and the way I acted. I don't know what happened."

He was looking at me thoughtfully and was about to say something when Sky appeared in the doorway in a dusky blue robe. "You'd had a trying ordeal." It felt like she was saying it to soothe herself as much as me.

Images of the dying whales slammed into my mind. "Even so, I'm not sure what came over me. I'm sorry, Sky."

"Today is a new day," she grinned, banishing the heavy mood. "What's for breakfast?"

Chris seemed to dismiss whatever it was he was about to say and gave me a reassuring wink instead. "You just need a decent meal and some rest. Poached eggs anyone?"

We spread a blanket in the garden and sat down to freshly squeezed juice, poached eggs on rye and myrtle tea. The pixie roses that Sky had planted were just starting to bloom, now that the weather was turning. The miniature, blue buds polka-dotted the branches, no bigger than the nail on my littlest finger, and filled the air with a perfume of spun sugar.

Chris was lounging on his side, idly picking at his plate while Sky and I hoed in. She was chattering away, telling us how Gabe had just broken his own time freezing record, the type of news that would normally make Chris whoop and whistle, but he was uncharacteristically quiet. "What's going on in that clever brain of yours?" I finally asked him.

"More than I would like," he tipped his face into the sun and closed his eyes. "I'm worried about you, that's all."

Two little words – *that's all* – weren't enough to subjugate a lifetime of caring. I could feel his worry as a remote cave where he sat alone in the dark. I wanted to throw my arms around him and tell him everything was okay. I was so tired of secrets and the toll they were taking on me and the people I loved. I was tempted to just blurt out everything and be done with it. But knowing the truth carried its own burdens and it felt safer to follow my great-grandfather's example and keep the secret, at least until I had deciphered the entire manuscript. My dearest friend was reaching out to me but I couldn't let him in, not without defying The Source's wishes and placing a heavy burden on his shoulders. I had already seen the strain it had placed on Sky. "I'm aware that I'm not myself, Chris, but I don't have an explanation for you yet."

His eyes were wistful and they were more grey now than blue. Sky was sitting quietly smoothing a blade of grass between her fingers. It pained me that I couldn't say more. He had always been my protector, a constant rock in times of need, and now, I was asking him to abandon the way he'd always been and stand idly by while I was crumbling in front of him. It went against every fibre of his being, I knew, yet he accepted my response and said no more. I could see soft blue return to his eyes as he chased away the grey. I could feel him letting it go simply because I'd asked him to. He was honouring his promise to me. He was trusting my choices and supporting me just as he said he would. My heart swelled with love, and in that moment, I knew he deserved more from me in return. If I could at least shine a bit of light into his dark, lonely cave, I would.

"Chris, I can't tell you everything, but I can at least tell you *something* so you won't wear yourself out worrying about me."

A flock of birds twittered overhead and Sky glanced up from pouring more tea to shoot me a relieved smile. I could see Chris' energy shift, his head craning forward expectantly.

"I'm decoding a discovery that my great-grandfather made."

"Grayson Flights?" He looked as though that was the last thing he expected to hear.

"Yes, well, it turns out, that after Dad gave me his manuscript, I found coded writing and symbols hidden inside."

"What do you mean by *hidden?*"

"There are passages written in invisible green ink, hidden between the lines of the main text."

"What? Are you saying the book is enchanted? How in the world did you know?"

"It was Elder Tunes, actually." I could see him visibly relax at the mention of Elder Tunes. "I told him my dad had gifted me the manuscript and he could barely contain himself. I promised to pay him a visit so he could have a look. When I showed it to him, he must have seen immediately what I hadn't. He didn't say anything though, he just placed the open book in front of me and told me to read it energetically, with my heart, as though I were reading a patient. Next thing I knew, swirling lines of green ink were snaking across the pages in between the black text. He was testing me. He wanted to know if I could see the invisible symbols, and I could."

"Can you read it?"

"I'm attempting to read it. Grayson wrote a letter saying that whoever can decipher his writings will be entrusted with great knowledge."

"So what does it say? What did Grayson discover?"

"Ah, well, that's the bit I can't tell you. Sorry," I winced, knowing the curiosity must be killing him. "Grayson left instructions from The Source to hold the knowledge secret. I've only deciphered a fraction of it anyway. It doesn't make much sense at the moment. My great-grandfather went to extreme lengths to keep this knowledge hidden. The magic on the manuscript is strong and I don't know how it decides who to share its secrets with."

Chris' dark brows climbed higher. "Now I understand why you've been so determined to see this through." He looked relieved which was exactly what I'd hoped to achieve by giving him part of the story. "So

Grayson's discovery has been passed on to you now. Lil, that's amazing! Can you show me the manuscript?" Chris asked.

I couldn't see what harm it would do for him to look, so I retrieved it from my room and handed it over. Now I was curious if he or Sky would be able to detect the invisible script. Sky wriggled over next to him on the blanket so she could peek inside too. Chris peeled back the leather binding and opened to a random page. The two of them were quiet as Chris slowly flipped through the pages, pausing to admire intricately rendered diagrams or Grayson's calligraphic writing.

They'd already passed over three pages with the invisible ink and had given no sign that they'd seen it materialising on the page. Not that it meant much. I hadn't been able to see it without instruction either. "Go back one page," I told Chris. "That one has invisible writing on it. Now focus on the page. Elder Tunes told me to feel and see the content energetically, not intellectually. Don't try to read it with your head. Feel the meaning with your heart."

Light dimmed and flared through billowing clouds. Chris stilled the thin page as it fluttered in the breeze. They both went very still, heads bent over the aged parchment, focussing and waiting for something to happen. Nothing did.

"Nope, definitely not *chosen*," professed Sky.

"Me neither." Chris handed back the manuscript

and reclined on the blanket again. His uniter vibrated in his pocket and he drew it out, frowning at the crystal screen. "What's happening? Are you all right?"

A female voice answered, shouting to be heard over a cacophony of squawks and shrieks. "We need you here right away. It's mayhem! The city streets have been turned into a zoo."

"Was that a monkey I just saw behind you?" Chris' eyes were wide and Sky leaned in to see what he was gawking at.

"There's dozens of them! And flamingoes, moose, gazelles, and The Source only knows what else."

"I'm on my way. Where are you exactly?"

"I'm on the corner of Sunspirit and Palladia – just opposite Wax 'n' Wicks." The screeching cut off as Chris swiped his thumb over the screen and ended the connection.

"What in the name of The Source was that?" Sky gaped. "Petra was surrounded. I saw a rhino... and swans, I think. I saw a peacock land on the head of Scholar Wymis' statue. It pooped on him!" Sky failed to mask her glee and approval for the creature. It had staged a poopy protest against the Scholar whose theories bent her brain and inevitably lowered her grades.

I looked back to Chris. "Are you and Petra working together?" I asked him.

"She's an incredibly gifted animal Healer." He rose from the lawn, patting down his pockets, looking for his car keys. "Grand Master Trill wants to make sure our *unexplained guests* are well looked after."

I nodded. "I have the day off work today but I wanted to go to healaxis anyway and check on Garrick. Will I be able to make it in there? Have they blocked off the city streets?"

"I'm pretty sure they will have, but you can come with me if you like," Chris said. "I'll drop you at healaxis."

"Go," Sky shooed us. "I'll bring all of this back inside," she waved an arm over the remains of our breakfast. "And Lilly, take it easy today, okay?"

I nodded reluctantly.

"Look after her, Christian. I love you both. Be careful."

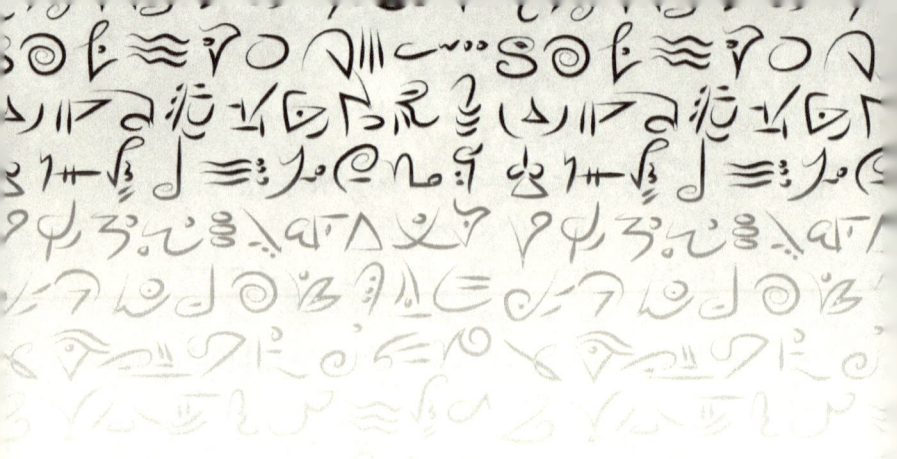

EIGHTEEN

Lilly

"Have you seen the menagerie outside, Healer Cray?" The wide halls of healaxis' upper floors were eerily quiet as we made our way to Garrick's room. There wouldn't be any visitors today, what with the Enchanters' boundaries containing the animals and blocking off the city centre.

"I've only seen glimpses through the windows on my rounds."

I'd always loved the view of Citrine through these high, cathedral windows. You could see clear to Mount Glorious on a bright day. Today, a grey sky shadowed the Dome's lustre and dulled the sparkle of Ponderence River as it slowly snaked its way around a city of pressed tin rooftops. Even Healer Cray's footsteps sounded dull against the parquet floor. She still looked tired, but better than when I'd last seen her.

"Translator Palladen had to move along a herd

of moose blocking the gates. Monkeys are dangling from trees all over the gardens and there are swans floating in the healing springs! The whole city is in chaos," I reported.

She cast me a weary look. "Chaos seems to be the new normal these days. Are the Council any closer to understanding what in The Source's name is going on?"

"I'm sure they are but I couldn't tell you how. Chris – Translator Palladen – isn't forthcoming about it."

"While I'm certain they have the matter in hand, people are starting to worry. They really ought to make a public announcement in light of this latest *development.* A swarm of bees and a heat wave are one thing, but a pod of dead whales with harpoons in their sides? And now this… " she waved her hand at the menagerie outside the windows.

My stomach turned at her mention of the whales. Those poor, gentle Souls had met with a barbaric death. At least the animals downstairs were alive and well, for now. "How did you know about the harpoons?"

"I overheard Healers Dwano and Honeywell telling Grand Master Trill when they brought Garrick in."

Healer Cray looked as sickened as I felt. I wanted to know if she'd figured out that the animals were from Earth. Chris had shared that much with me but the Council had kept it quiet until it could be definitively proven and explained. "And what do you make of that *development?*" I probed.

"If what they said is true, logic would dictate that

the whales were not of this world. There is only one place that harpoons whales - Earth." She turned to me, disbelief clouding her eyes. "But how can that possibly be? The very notion seems pure fantasy."

"I think that's what they're working so hard to find out."

"And they honestly think Garrick Leif has something to do with it?" she chaffed.

I stopped walking and frowned at her. "Why do you say that?"

"Grand Master Trill is keeping a very close eye on him. She seems extremely interested in the tears in his energy field and I've just had word that she'll be back today. She's bringing Elder Sparks along with her."

"Source above! You mean they're dragging poor old Healer Sparks out of retirement to treat Garrick? I thought he was so frail he'd be moving on soon?"

"Well, apparently he's agreed to it. They're going to try to wake Garrick from his twilight sleep so they can get some answers. Maybe they want to ask him what he saw. They'll probably want to speak with you too."

I ignored the prospect of having to endure endless questions from the Elders. "And *will* he wake?"

"I honestly don't know." She looked tired again. "He'll wake when his body is healed enough, *if* it can be healed enough. We're doing everything we can. I acted on your suggestion, by the way. Healer Dwano, Healer Everglade and I have been working on him in shifts."

"Well, I can step in today and help. I could give you a break."

"No," she shook her head, "absolutely not. Not after your ordeal with the whales yesterday. You must still be exhausted from trying to save them. You really should be at home resting, you know."

"I'm fine," I promised her. "I wanted to check on Garrick. I feel terrible that I didn't see him lying unconscious on the beach."

Her face softened and she reached over and squeezed my shoulder, immediately recognising the things I wasn't saying out loud - *that he might not have slipped into a twilight sleep if I'd gotten to him sooner.* She shook her head decisively and gave me a knowing smile. It was enough to bring me back to myself and chase away my self doubts.

"I'm happy for you to visit with Garrick and watch him while I attend to other patients, but you are here as a visitor only, Acolyte Flights. The Source only knows what tomorrow will bring and I need you well-rested."

"Yes, Healer Cray. Are his parents here?"

"They just left. Grand Master Trill arranged for Hand Tellis to escort them safely through the havoc outside. They've been here since yesterday and they're exhausted. A few hours at home will do them good." She lowered her voice as we entered Garrick's room and after she checked him over, she left me to it.

He was skin and bone, lying motionless on a healing bed of quartz crystal topped with a thin mattress.

His pale skin had turned a sickly grey and his russet hair, once as bright as flame, was doused and lifeless. Even his freckles seemed to have faded. If it weren't for the subtle rise and fall of his chest, I would have thought him already dead. How awful for his poor parents, to see their only son wasting away.

A synthesis line had been inserted into his arm and was connected to a glass sphere hanging by his bed. Deep violet liquid swirled within the sphere like a living thing - a life-preserving concoction of fluids, nutrients and healing essences. I took up the chair that his mother had probably sat in all night and moved it closer to his bedside.

I peered at his still face – strain pressed into putty. "Garrick, it's Acolyte Flights. You've given us all quite a fright, but you're safe now. Your mum and dad will be back soon and you're being well looked after." I watched for any slight movement, any indication that he could hear me, even a twitch, but there was nothing.

I was desperate to know if the tears in his energy field were worse since I'd examined him last. I didn't see the harm in having a quick peek, so I stood and held one hand above his head and hovered the other over his body. I took a deep breath and reached out for a connection to The Source. It was slow in coming and it made me realise exactly how tired I was and how bogged down I felt by everything that had been happening. I had to focus for several minutes and tune my mind before white light flooded my body and flowed through my hands. It was such a relief when it finally did.

I gazed at Garrick's still body and watched the many layers of his energetic field come into my view. I winced at what I was seeing. The damage was so much greater than when I'd last examined him. Ugly rips had appeared everywhere. The boy looked like he'd been attacked by sharp claws and I could see why he'd fallen into a twilight sleep. My eyes darted from one tear to the next, wondering how the Healers knew where to begin working. His whole energetic field was a heartbreaking mess. "What did this to you?" I whispered. How can a person's lifeforce, their spirit, be torn to pieces this way?

Then I saw something move and it wasn't Garrick. It was coming from inside one of the tears. A lightning-fast flash of movement, just as I'd noticed before when I'd tried to examine him. The difference now was that Garrick wasn't awake to stop me from looking closer. I zeroed in on the large tear above his stomach. I waited, my eyes fixed to the spot. The room was still and quiet, apart from the sound of my breathing and the slow drip of the synthesis line. There it was again - just a flash of shadowed shapes, too fast to discern.

Healer Cray had told me to rest but seeing Garrick lying there, so weak and helpless, I had to try. I couldn't stand by and do nothing. I called on The One Source for more energy, anchoring my feet to the floor at Garrick's bedside and willing pure, white, healing light to flow through me. A giddy wave swept over me as the burst of raw energy shot down through my crown, flooded my entire body, and spilled out through my hands. It was instantaneous and intense, flowing into the ragged tears in Garrick's energy field and filling them up with blinding white.

My vision blurred and I swayed on my feet. I felt myself tip forward and tried to grab the edge of the bed to keep my balance. My hand connected with Garrick's arm instead and his eyes flew open. I started and we both drew in a panicked gasp. I hadn't noticed until now how intensely blue Garrick's eyes were and they were blazing with fear... and something else... remorse. "Garrick, it's okay. You're in healaxis." He was gasping for breath and his heart rate was through the roof. "Please, just calm down. It's all right."

"I never meant..." he coughed, "I only wanted to do the right thing."

"Of course you did. Now just breathe slowly for me. Nice deep breaths, okay." I placed my hand over his heaving heart and breathed with him, willing it to slow. Once it had returned to normal, I poured him a glass of water from a crystal jug next to the bed and helped him to sit up and take a few sips.

"What happened to me?" he croaked.

"You were found unconscious and brought to healaxis. You've been here overnight. Healer Cray has been taking very good care of you. She's even bringing in Elder Sparks to treat you today and you're parents will be back soon."

"Elder Sparks? Is coming here?"

"Yes, and Grand Master Trill is coming to visit you too."

Garrick grabbed my wrist, hard. "No. They can't come here. I don't want to see them!" The crazed look had returned to his eyes. I tried to pull my hand away but it only made him grip tighter. "They can't know. They won't understand."

"Garrick, please, you're hurting me." I felt woozy again and leaned against the bed but he wouldn't let me go. I was starting to feel nauseous. Bright bursts of light exploded behind my eyes and I reeled, feeling weighted down. And hot, my whole body was prickling with heat. *What was happening to me?*

Panic, alarm and giddy sickness punched at my insides. It was exactly how I'd felt at Ryan's party, being around so many suffering humans. Only now, that feeling was coming from Garrick. It didn't make any sense. I tried to focus on him through my confusion and the roiling nausea. He was painfully wrenching at my arm, his grip insistent, while he ranted a string of unintelligible protests. He was terrified.

There came a muffled buzzing in my ears that slowly drowned out his pleading. My breath was coming in harsh gasps and the sound of it filled my head. The room was blurring around me like a lit pinwheel. I swayed on my feet, then all sight and sound was smothered completely and I fell into black.

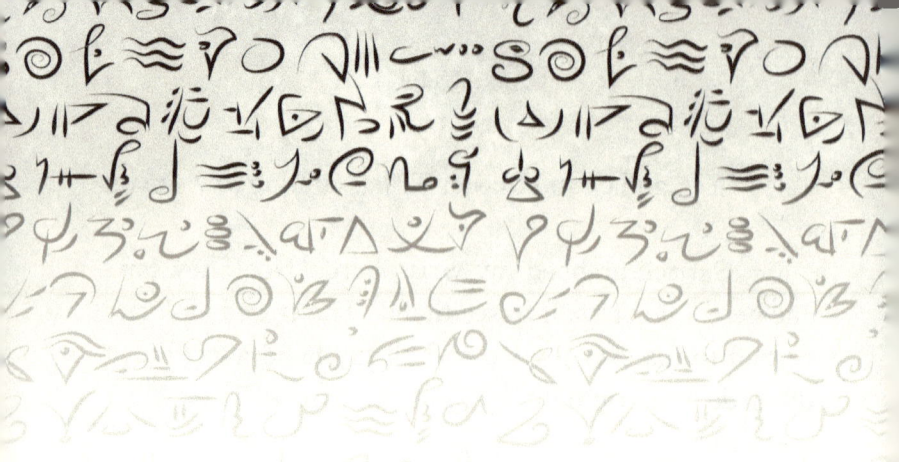

NINTEEN

Christian

A drizzling rain had begun to fall and the strong musk of wet fur and hide clung to the air mingling with the smell of fear. The Enchanters had cordoned off the city centre, penning hundreds of animals inside, turning the central shopping district, the grounds of Ophanim Dome and healaxis into a temporary zoo. The pale blue, scalloped facade of The Exchange where Gabe worked had been transformed into an angry rainbow. Exotic parrots with multi-coloured plumes were hanging from the scrolls and flourishes that adorned the magnificent archway, screeching and squabbling. The front doors below had been shut tight and the workers sent home. There would be no barter or trade in Citrine today. For the second time in as many weeks, merchants had barricaded their doors and the city was emptied, save for sick patients within the sandstone spires of healaxis.

I stood by Petra in the middle of Palladia Street feeling lost in the din going on around me. By contrast, she was efficient and focussed. Her strawberry blonde curls were pulled back tightly in a ponytail but several had escaped and were bouncing around her face like runaway slinkies. Her green eyes were sharp chips of adventurine as she triaged her way through makeshift enclosures of subdued Earth animals and birds. She was wearing her favourite khaki fatigues with holes in the knees and nubuck suede hiking boots. The tails of a button up shirt trailed behind her, hanging open over a slim fitting singlet. "You can load the chimpanzees and the moose onto the trucks but I'm still checking the gazelles and parrots."

The Enchanters got to work, loosening the webs of glowing energy they'd woven around the herd of moose to keep them contained, then gently pulling on the threads to coax them forward. They bellowed, their hooves slipping and clattering on the rain slick ramps that led onto the trucks.

They were frightened. These animals were wild and most of them had never seen people before, or trucks, or cities. My head swam with their panic and fear. There were so many frightened voices, and the noise coming from outside my head wasn't much better. The chimps were screeching and so were the parrots. The moose were making some sort of barking sound. It was pandemonium.

"Chris, can you help me?" Petra was beckoning me over to the enclosure. The energetic gold net glowed in the misting rain.

"Sure. What do you need?"

"These gazelles are such timid, skittish animals." She'd hypnotised one slender creature onto its side and Jordan had woven a glowing web around it to keep it still. It twitched slightly against the wet cobblestones. "Every time I calm one to examine it, the others disrupt what I'm doing and upset everything. Do you think you could try talking to the rest of the herd?"

"I'll try." There had never been a time when I was surrounded by so many terrified animals at once. There were roughly eighty frightened voices coming from four different species in my immediate vicinity alone, with hundreds more yet to be captured in the surrounding streets, and... there was only one of me. I was the only Translator in Citrine and the only one who could speak to these animals and try to calm them. This was going to be a challenge.

I dug deep, blocking out the noise and centring my focus on The Source. Ever since I was small, I'd felt The Source's presence as a calm, empty expanse. There was a softness to it where time slowed, and if you drifted in it for long enough, time eventually ceased all together. I sought that place now, slipping into the familiar, practised connection. The challenge, was allowing the hundreds of frightened animal voices to just be; much like floating through a chorus of human suffering while on Soul Guardian duty. I felt compassion, of course, because that suffering was remembered and understood from my time as a human, but it was never adopted as my own. It was a feat that was only possible by viewing the world from that calm, empty expanse. It was only possible by connecting to The Source.

It was the same with animals. You needed to *hear* without becoming overwhelmed by so much discord that you held onto it in your own heart. I allowed their fear to pass through me like a storm. I heard their pleas for help like battering rain, I felt their terror like the lash of screaming winds, and then, once I knew, once I understood how they felt … I let it all go. It was a skill every go-lite worked to perfect over a lifetime; cultivating enough strength and balance to feel the pain of others but not be altered by it. It was the mastery of true compassion and, perhaps, the hardest thing The Source asked of us. Lilly was my biggest obstacle to mastery because I struggled to see her in pain, but in that, she was also my greatest teacher.

The silence around me brought my focus back to the street where I stood with rain running in rivulets down my face. I had intended to only calm the gazelles so Petra could continue her work, but as I looked around at the trucks brimming with animals and the crew of Enchanters, all was quiet. The monkeys had stopped screeching, the moose were no longer bugling, and the parrots had ceased their squabble. Grand Master Trill gave me an appraising smile from across the street and went back to issuing orders. Lilly's dad was with her.

It was the first time I'd seen the newly appointed Elder Flights on Haven business.

"It's okay, beauty. You're all right. I'm nearly done," Petra cooed at the wriggling gazelle. "Can you hold her a little firmer, Jordan?"

Jordan flicked his wrist and the net of golden light glowed brighter and cinched in slightly. His fine, blonde hair was plastered to his head in thin, dripping whips. He held his solid arms wide, his face fixed in powerful concentration. He looked like a Viking God from human mythology. Petra was kneeling next to the gazelle's sleek head, holding a curved antler in one hand while she hovered the other above the creature's velvet hide. She was scanning her body for injury and her energy field for tears. She'd been at it for hours now, moving from patient to patient, never seeming to tire or lose focus. She was drenched from head to toe and smeared with mud. We all were, except for Grand Master Trill who had only just arrived with Jonathan Flights at her side.

"Are you under control here?" I asked Petra. She gave me a silent nod, remaining entrenched in her work. "I'm going to speak with the Elders. I'll be back."

As I strode down the sodden street past the velvet draped windows of Wax 'n' Wicks, Grand Master Mont walked up to Jon and Genevieve. His huge frame towered over them both as they stood talking in a circle. The rain was painting his pale yellow robes with splashes of deep saffron and making his ebony skin shine with silver. "Do you think it's possible?" I heard him ask Jonathan.

He looked up to meet Grand Master Mont's eyes. "It seems to be the most plausible explanation. The lad may have a type of Traveller ability that we've not seen before."

"So you're saying it's an elevated Gift? That he may possess the ability to Travel between dimensions?" Grand Master Trill's face was neutral but there was an eager edge to her voice. She and I had been seeking a concrete answer since the first animal appearances. I too, longed for an end to the mystery and for peace to return to Citrine. What Lilly's dad was saying did sound plausible and as a Traveller he could lend unique insight into how Garrick's Gift might function. It also gave me hope that we might be able to have Garrick return the animals to Earth, *if* the Healers could save him.

A terrified shriek pierced the air and the calm blanketing the street was torn away by the frantic pounding of trapped hooves inside trucks and the screams of frenzied apes. I spun around to see Petra standing alone in the middle of the puddled street. Jordan was gaping at her from inside the gazelles' enclosure and between he and her, was a patch of air that was shimmering. It looked like a mirage at first, like waves appearing then evaporating into the air. And then I saw something moving inside it – something large.

I was already running. I couldn't see what was materialising in front of her but I knew it wasn't good.

Petra was glued to the spot, arms outstretched, paralysed with fear. The glimmering waves in the air were slowing, making it easier to see what was coming through. My heart stuttered. *Source above! No!* I was almost to her. One stride...two...three. My arm caught her roughly around the waist as a fully grown lion wavered into this world and unleashed a guttural roar.

I heard the wind whoosh from Petra's lungs as I scooped her up, threw her over my shoulder and bolted for our lives. Jordan was safe in his enclosure with the gazelles. I couldn't ask him to let us in and risk them escaping with a lion on the loose so I ran to the nearest truck. I threw open the door and hoisted Petra up into the cabin. She flopped across the seat. I was about to push up behind her when I heard a low growl that was much too close.

I turned in a slow circle, my hand still on the door handle, and was met with a pair of stony yellow eyes. They were locked on me, still and hungry. The lion was poised to pounce. The chimpanzees in the back of the truck screamed and jumped in fear, rocking the whole truck. Petra whimpered and her arms came around my chest, urging me to climb inside with her and slam the door. But I knew it was too late for that. The lion was far too close, well within striking distance. If I turned to try, I knew it would lunge for me and then Petra would be next.

I'd never had occasion to converse with a lion before and now that I was about to, I could see why it hadn't made my wish list. *You don't have to be afraid. I know this is a strange place but you're safe here. No one will harm you.* I wondered if he could hear the tremor in my voice even though I was speaking telepathically.

He took a sinuous step forward, sniffing the air, but made no reply.

"Chris, please," Petra begged in a whisper, "get in the truck."

"If I do that, it will attack." A thousand things were running through my mind including the clamour of voices coming from terrified animals. I had to calm down. I had to connect and make this creature pause long enough to evade being eaten. *Source save me! Were those eyes designed to hypnotise prey?*

They were liquid amber with black beads in the centre, like stones suspended on the surface of a pond. A shiver ran through me as I felt their cold, calculating intent. *Please,* I said, *my name is Chris and I'm here to help you. You're not the only one who is lost and wants to go home. There are many others that we're helping.*

Three Enchanters had slowly crept up behind the lion but maintained a good distance so they had time to react if needs be. They caught my eye, signalling that they were about to cast a net over him, just as he released a low, protracted growl and spoke into my mind. I gave a short, sharp shake of my head and the Enchanters halted, dropping their arms.

What is this place? The lion's voice rumbled

inside me.

You are far from home, my friend. Just like these others.

The pale fur on his nose was the colour of desert sand and bore a pattern of scars. The rest of his short, dusty hide was battle-worn and a piece of his left ear was missing in the shape of a half moon. He warily eyed the rocking truck at my back and the herd of panicked gazelles to my left as they bleated and ran against Jordan's golden net. His tail flicked back and forth, his posture rigid.

We only want to make sure that you weren't hurt during your journey here and to show you to a place more comfortable so you can rest and recover.

He released me from his hypnotic gaze and tossed his brittle mane. *You are but a cub,* he snorted. *Bring me your king. I would speak with him.*

I let out an audible sigh, relieved that I wasn't about to become lunch. *Certainly,* I replied, suddenly feeling like a page boy. *I will send my friend Petra to fetch our, er, king. Who may I say seeks an audience?* I asked, playing along. Did all lions speak this way?

You may tell him Sadascus, King of the eastern plain.

"Petra, can you please tell Grand Master Mont that King Sadascus would like to speak with him?" I heard her open the door on the other side of the truck and slip out.

Sadascus growled as he watched her go. *Do you*

have your eye on that one for your pride one day, young cub?

Um, no, your Majesty.

A pity. He harrumphed and continued to hold me in his intimidating gaze. He said nothing more until Grand Master Mont approached and came to stand beside me.

Your Majesty, I will have to translate. I am the only one that can speak with your kind. This is Grand Master Mont and he bids you welcome.

King Sadascus was silent, his royal bearing seeming to wilt suddenly, like a rose left in the desert. His amber eyes were fixed, not on the Grand Master, but to his side. He looked *awestruck.* He extended a mighty paw forward and gave a sweeping, reverent bow. *Old one, I am honoured,* he rumbled.

It took me a moment to realise that Sadascus was addressing Torro, Grand Master Mont's spirit lion. While the spirit animals were usually only visible to their Elders, it was apparent that Sadascus could see him and was humbled in his presence. *Fascinating!*

"It seems Torro will be my spokesperson," Grand Master Mont inclined his head to his left, the crystals in his long braids clinking together.

I nearly jumped out of my skin when I heard Torro's ancient voice echoing through my head in reply and seconds later, his translucent body became visible to me too!

Welcome, Brother. He nodded to Sadascus. Torro's

crystalline form took on a violet hue under the blanket of rainclouds. His eyes, powerful and intense, almost looked blue. *I regret that you have been pulled from your world and cast into another, but the cub speaks truth.* Apparently I was the cub. *None will harm you here. My companions seek a way to return you to the plains and right the wrong that was done to you.*

As you say, Old One. I defer to your wisdom.

Torro rumbled his approval. *I ask that you go with this cub to a place of rest and comfort while we make way for your return home. It is not an easy task so we ask for your patience. The cub, Chris, will have questions for you. Can we count on your help, Brother?*

Sadascus bowed again by way of an answer and then stood tall, puffing his chest with pride.

I hope we have occasion to speak again, Torro said. *It has been eons since I roamed the great plains with the wind at my back. I still remember how the tall grasses whispered. I remember days bursting with life, sound and scent, and peaceful nights spent under a sea of stars. But time has dulled my precious recollections. Perhaps you would share a tale or two and give my faded memories new life.*

It would be my honour, Brother, Sadascus growled.

Grand Master Mont bowed in gratitude, his eyes like warm coffee. "Thank you for being so understanding, King Sadascus. We will try to make your stay as comfortable and as short as possible. If you would like to go with Chris and Petra, they will take good care of you." Grand Master Mont gave me the nod to take over and in a swirl of saffron robes and clinking braids, made his way back to Grand Master Trill and Elder Flights. Petra sidled up to take his place and grinned at Sadascus.

Young cub... Sadascus floundered, trying to remember my name.

"...Chris," I supplied, speaking out loud so Petra could hear at least half of the conversation.

Cub Chris, he began again, *about the manner of my arrival...*

"There's no need to apologise, Your Majesty. I..."

Sadascus interrupted with an agitated growl. *Apologise? Why by the Earth Mother would I apologise? Every living creature has a right to defend itself and a right to eat, do they not, young cub?*

"Well, yes, I suppose they do..."

Yes, indeed, he huffed. Whatever he had originally planned on saying was swallowed by his regal air which had returned as soon as Torro had departed. *Well, are you going to stand aside, cub?* He was staring at me quizzically, head cocked to one side.

"I...what?" I'd seen him soften like butter before Torro but he was anything but soft now. Those liquid amber eyes were hypnotising me again.

If you don't stand aside, he annunciated slowly, *I cannot enter the moving cave.*

I frowned, wondering what in The Source's name

he was talking about. I was still standing in front of the truck's open door, Petra waiting patiently beside me. Wait, surely he didn't mean... "The moving cave? You mean the truck?"

Insolent cub! Do not tell me what I do and do not mean, he growled. *You think me simple? I am well acquainted with moving caves and the roar they make. Now step aside.*

His powerful voice rattled through me like thunder and I hurriedly stepped aside, shuffling Petra out of the way. Sadascus barged past us and leapt through the open front door and into the cabin. The chimpanzees in the back started going crazy again. He settled in the centre of the bench seat and stared expectantly down at Petra and me.

"King Sadascus, I'm sure you would be more comfortable in the back. We have an empty truck... sorry, cave over here," I pointed.

More insolence! First, you presume to know what I know and now, you presume to know what I wish?

"Forgive me, Your Majesty. I only meant there would be more room for you in the back and the moving cave over there is empty and quiet."

He let out a roaring laugh and glanced through the window behind him at the screeching chimps. *Foolish cub. Their cries are music to my ears. They know who is king!* He tossed his mane. *Come, let us be gone.*

I looked at Petra and groaned. "And I thought

driving with a car full of bees was the most stupid thing I've ever done."

She laughed and squeezed my arm. "Thank you for saving me. I panicked. I froze."

"I don't think that's any reason to be ashamed. Anyone would have panicked when faced with a wild lion."

"You didn't," she smiled wistfully. "You never do." She rose up on her toes and kissed my cheek. Strawberry curls brushed my face. Her skin smelled like wild violets and deep purple lavendulum flowers. "Thank you," she breathed, pressing her palm to my chest. Then she turned and walked back toward Jordan and the rest of the gazelles that needed to be checked before they were loaded into trucks. I stood stock-still as she walked away, my eyes fixed on her loose shirt tails fluttering behind her.

A funny feeling came over me, like a call from somewhere inside. The shriek of monkeys faded into nothingness. I could feel my eyes glaze over. It felt as though the world around me was being sucked away, receding to a distant point on the horizon. All I could see was Lilly, pressing and urgent in my mind and I knew something was horribly wrong. Something had happened to her, I could feel it.

I wasn't a Seer but this wasn't the first time I'd had a feeling or vague premonition that Lilly was in trouble. It had happened only yesterday before she'd collapsed on the beach and the truth was, it had been happening all my life, although I'd never shared that with her or anyone else. I'd always chalked it up to the natural, intuitive connection you have to people you care about.

When Lilly was four, she'd run away. I had been playing on the swing in my backyard when an image of her, clear as day, came into my mind. She was determined pouting lips and a nest of tangled hair, clutching a wax crayon in one hand and a drawing she had made in the other. I had pestered my mother until she finally made the call to Lilly's parents and found that I was right, Lilly was gone. I would never forget the look on Dawn Flights' face that day when I led them straight to her. In my vision I had seen exactly where Lilly was hiding, huddled in a hollowed out tree by the creek on the Flights' property.

"Christian!"

I snapped out of my daze, the world coming sharply back into focus. Through persistent drizzle, I saw Jonathan hurrying across the road, clutching his uniter.

"It's Lilly. She's collapsed at healaxis." He ran a frantic hand through his wet hair. "She's not good, Chris. They said she has tears in her energy field, just like the tears that are killing Garrick Leif."

My blood turned to ice in my veins and my whole body felt weak, as though I might fall down where I stood. The images from Evangeline's prophecy crashed through my mind like dominoes, each angst-filled image careening into the next until they lay ominously still in a lifeless pile. "Lilly."

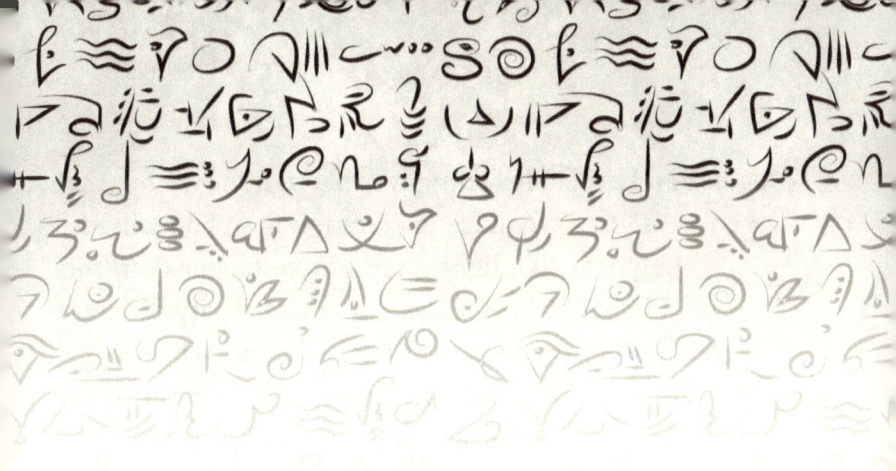

TWENTY

Jay

I was soaring again. I was floating on the incredible wave of love that was Lilly. She had swept in and righted my world, just like she always did. I could hardly believe that I'd talked myself into thinking that we shouldn't be together. My argument had felt so justified. Now, I couldn't see how I'd managed to create all that self-doubt. Not when I was feeling this elated.

I missed her. It had been four days since Ryan's party and I wanted to pull her close, to feel her lips and tangle my fingers in her hair. There was an ache in my heart where she now lived and I knew that the only way to make it stop was to hold her again.

I felt terrible for passing on my stomach bug and making her sick. I guess it proved one thing though - go-lites weren't invincible. Maybe Lilly was more vulnerable than I knew. It was a comforting thought - not that she was sick and probably feeling terrible right now - but that she and I might have more in common than I'd realised.

Lilly was like lightning; a force bigger than me. She was a light in the darkness, a jolt of clarity. When I pictured her in my mind, I often saw her as a silver angel with billowing black hair whose feet barely skimmed the ground. Of course, she *was* other-worldly, in the most literal sense, but perhaps I'd had her on a pedestal for too long, seeing her as something beyond my reach. Now she suddenly seemed more reachable than she ever had before; the distance between us not so great that I couldn't leap over it. And she had given me her heart. She was willing to wait for as long as it took for me to heal all my broken parts - to be whole and complete, with her.

What she felt for me and what she was offering was real. For the first time, the thought of spending my life with Lilly didn't seem like a fantasy that left me giddy and flying high, believing I could blaze a trail around the sun. The gloss and glitter of dreams had been stripped away to show a future I could touch and hold.

I had spent days wandering her world in my mind. I had only been there once but I'd stashed away the memories like treasured photographs, taking them out often to sigh and dream. Now, I had the chance to be a part of a world that heaved with life and colour and would continue to thrive for the simple reason that it was cherished.

I loved Earth and I had done my best to defend

her, but it was clear how her story would end. Not because it was inevitable, but because most of the people she housed, fed and allowed to breathe, didn't care.

I had begun daring to imagine what it would be like to live in a world where people did care, and through the miracle that was Lilly, it was within my reach.

"What are you looking all doe-eyed about?" Ryan hefted another bag of trash onto the truck. It was clean-up day on our local beach and the guys always came along with me and did their part.

"Someone's in loooove," John made a disturbing kissy face and came at me with terrifying blubbery lips. "Piss off, John!" I shoved him away from me. "I would sooner kiss a blowfish than you."

"Leave Jay alone, Oaf. You can hardly blame him for being besotted," Ryan laughed. "Lilly's the real deal. If only we were all lucky enough to find someone like her."

"You don't have to tell me that," John groaned and pointed down the beach at a group of bikini clad girls who'd been taking selfies for the last half hour. He turned to us with a mystified look. "Why?" he pleaded. "Do you get this? I really, *really* don't get it."

I burst into laughter. "Do you honestly think any of us do?"

Ryan was grinning and shaking his head. His look was somewhere between amused and pitying. He dumped his sack of trash on the truck and took a long swig from his canteen. "Where is the angelic Lilly, anyway?"

Lilly

A dull, steady thudding seeped into the black ocean of my consciousness. Feeling slowly returned and I became aware that I had a face that felt like swollen foam and limbs that refused to move. The thudding intensified to a shattering pound as my head swam about looking for its lips. I tried to cry out but a weak, frightened whimper was all I could muster and my eyelids were weighted shut.

"Lilly? Lilly, can you hear me?" The voice floated down and settled over me like a warm blanket. A hot hand clamped over my clammy cheek - Dad. "You're okay. Everything is going to be...fine." His voice cracked on the last word and I could hear the strain and worry.

My lips tingled with pins and needles and the pounding in my brain became louder. "What... happened?" I twisted my numb tongue to form the words.

"Honey, you fell." My mother's soothing voice came close in my ear. "You hit your head on the floor. Healer Cray found you unconscious in Garrick's room."

"Garrick..." I choked out.

"It's all right," asserted my father from near by. "Rest now, Lilly. Healer Cray says the gash on your head is deep and you've likely sustained a concussion."

"I... fell? Why did I...." my weak voice trailed off as the fractured memories assembled themselves in my mind. Garrick had woken up. He'd been terrified. He had grabbed me.

"That's what we're trying to work out, honey. Healer Cray is doing all she can to get you well." I could hear the reassuring smile in my mother's voice as she spoke.

"What's wrong with me?"

There was a long silence, punctuated by the insistent ping of fluids dripping into a synthesis line. Finally, my dad spoke. "Healer Cray says you have tears in your energy field, Lilly."

"What do you mean? How?" I forced my eyes open. Bright sunlight streamed through the windows and bounced off the stark walls, turning the room into a glaring, white haze. Blurred silhouettes of my parents were hovering over me. My mother was clutching my hand. I blinked my vision clear and spied Sky looking drawn in the far corner of the room. It looked like Gabe was physically propping her up. And then there was Christian, standing preternaturally still at the foot of my bed, his shirt rumpled and collar askew. His face looked ashen, drained of the golden sunlight that his skin drank in so readily. The thick lick of hair, that he always raked back, hung in an unkempt wave across his forehead. His lips were pursed and the line of his jaw, tense. He was trying to keep his expression neutral but I new him too well. I could read the truth in his eyes. On the surface they were like cold steel left out in the rain, but beneath there was a deep well of emotion and I knew I was in trouble.

"We don't know how you sustained the tears, sweetheart. Elder Sparks says the damage isn't as extensive as Garrick's but you've still got a lot of healing to do."

I could barely make sense of what I was hearing. "No, that can't be right. There must be a mistake." *How could I have a torn energy field?* I glanced back at Christian, he was no longer staring at me, he was pointedly looking at Sky, his expression see-sawing between frustration and resignation. My eyes didn't want to stay open as I willed my rubber neck to arch forward in a feeble attempt to sit up. "Sky," I croaked. "Sky, I need my manuscript." She gave me a look that was full of sorrow and nodded. My pounding brain rocketed into the front of my skull and ricocheted back again as I collapsed onto the bed. Concerned voices chorused at me to lie still and three sets of hands steadied my trembling body.

"You're in excellent hands, Lilly. You needn't be worried," said my dad. "Healer Cray is here now to check on you." I hadn't even noticed her enter the room. "Just rest. We're all here for you."

"Sky, can you bring it now?" I could hear the desperation in my voice but I didn't care. She looked as though she were about to cry.

Healer Cray moved to my bedside, her kind face hovering over me and blocking Sky from my view. "Just relax, Lilly," she smiled. She produced a glowing wand of timalight crystal and pointed it at my third eye. My vision split into facets of radiant orange and my eyes fell shut.

I felt the smooth, vibrating surface of the crystal sweep over my swollen forehead and heavy eyes. Its cool face calmed me and I drifted into a deep, dreamless sleep.

Christian

I almost fell out of the room. I didn't think I could hold myself together for another minute. The last four days of seeing Lilly helpless had finally caught up with me. I left her parents speaking in whispers with Healer Cray by her bedside. I needed to breathe for a moment, to process that she was fully conscious, although we all knew that it likely wouldn't last. Garrick had been in and out of twilight sleep for days, his wrecked body struggling to mend while the Healers pumped as much energy into him as they could, and still, no-one knew if it would be enough to save him.

Lilly had been shocked and confused when her parents told her the diagnosis, genuinely at a loss for how it could have happened. But of course she would look confused. Lilly never gave a thought for her own well-being when someone else was in need. Like her dad, she was one of the most selfless people I knew. She'd given everything she had in an attempt to save those dying whales and then she had wrung out her heart and given more to help Garrick. He had been her first thought when she opened her eyes.

I shuffled across the hall to an arched leadlight window and braced myself against the sill. I stared out at

Citrine, peaceful for now, but for how long? Here on the upper level, I could see over the dense trees and tangled vines of healaxis's healing gardens, past Ophanim Dome, glittering in the midday sun, to the field of copper weather vanes rising from hundreds of rooftops. They spun and whirred, caught up in the ever-changing wind. A tired laugh tumbled from my lips. I too, was at the mercy of that wind, never knowing which direction I'd be pushed in next. *'Heed the will of the wind,'* the old saying went, *'lest you veer off-course.'*

I'd been desperately trying to stay on course, paying close attention to all of the signs, playing Evangeline's prophetic warning over and over in my head, and still, I was floundering. I'd never felt on edge in my life or so unsure of what I was doing. For every challenge I'd faced in the past, it was faith that had seen me through; a steady rhythm that beat at the core of me, driving me in the right direction. Now I could feel my faith fraying at the edges, my trust in The Source, wavering. Never before had I felt so tested.

"Christian."

I whirled around. Sky had appeared in the hallway, her eyes pleading. Watching Lilly balance on the edge of life had been excruciating for her as she skulked in the corner of her room and said little. She knew exactly what Lilly had been up to these past months and judging by the torn look on her face, I could tell she had a theory on what had caused the tears in Lilly's energy field. I had not asked her if she thought Lilly's secret mission and her illness were somehow connected and she had carefully ignored my knowing looks. I had not once pressed her to reveal what she knew or suspected, but I could see her buckling under the burden of secrecy a little more each day.

"Have you decided what you're going to do?" I understood the difficult position Sky was in and I could see how hard she was battling to make a decision. She hung her head and swallowed hard. Her slender shoulders were trembling. I didn't want to make her situation any harder but Lilly's life was at stake and I had held my tongue for four whole days. I had given her more than enough space to decide if what she knew might be helpful. "She might die, Sky. Do you understand that?"

She flinched. "Healer Cray is hopeful, now that she's woken up."

"She's been in a twilight sleep for four days!"

"And now she's not. We have to hold on to that and be thankful."

I squeezed my eyes shut and ground the heels of my hands against them. "I am thankful," I blew out. "The Source only knows how thankful I am that she's still alive." I was angry. I felt completely helpless. My hands were clenched in fists, shaking at my sides. I turned away from her and stared out the window. I traced the smoky lines of the purple mountains that ringed Citrine. "I know this is difficult, Sky, and I'm sorry you're burdened with Lilly's secret. I don't envy the choice you have to make but you need to decide one way or the other. Now, Sky."

When I turned back, her lip was quivering. I doubted she had ever seen me angry before and I was definitely angry now. The world was spinning out of control and the most precious thing in it was slipping away from me. A huge tear spilled down Sky's cheek. I threw off the grip of my anger and went to her. I walked back down the hall and reached for her hands. She looked up into my face, her eyes blinking like a china doll.

"I'm so sorry. Forgive me."

"You don't have to say you're sorry," she whispered, "I know how much you love her."

I wrapped my arms around her and drew her into a hug. We slumped against each other, sharing our exhaustion and fear, but we held each other up, too, like a pair of leaning towers. "Can I just ask you one thing?"

She nodded slowly.

"Do you know why Lilly's energy field is torn?"

"I don't know. All I have are suspicions. I couldn't say anything for sure which is why I haven't spoken up. I could be completely wrong."

"But you don't think you are?"

"The only thing I know for certain is that Lilly believes in her heart that she's on a mission from The Source and she needs to see it through, no matter what. There are reasons she needs to keep it a secret and she trusts me to do the same."

I could see the rest of what Sky wanted to say, but

didn't: that she wasn't entirely convinced that Lilly knew what she was doing and that she was frightened by what she'd seen. "A part of me wishes that I didn't know and that she'd confided in you instead of me. You always know the right thing to do."

I gave a bland laugh, "I wouldn't be so sure of that. Where Lilly is concerned, my heart tends to skew my judgement. I think she made a wise choice confiding in you."

She laid her head on my chest and her breath hitched. "What if we lose her, Chris?"

I was silent for a moment, Evangeline's prophesy whirring through my head. As much as it pained me, I knew the answer and the promises I'd made. I dropped my cheek to Sky's glossy hair. "Then we'll have to let her go," I breathed, "to her next life with our love and blessings."

We stood there for a long while, holding on to each other. Sky, burdened with a secret that she didn't know whether or not to share, and me, held back by a promise made out of love and a prophetic warning to let Lilly choose her own fate. It was as though The Source itself had bound our hands, and even though Sky and I had been soldiering on, trying to keep the faith, we were both struggling against the ropes.

When we broke away from each other, Sky looked a little less lost. I could even spy a hint of her sass returning, a shrewd twinkle in her eye, a jaunty jut to her chin.

"Is Lilly still seeing someone?" I asked hesitantly.

"As far as I know, yes."

"So it's serious?"

She nodded.

"Just not serious enough for him to be here when she needs him most? She's been lying in healaxis for days and where is he? Has he even called?"

"It's complicated, Christian."

"I hardly see how. If you love someone, you're there for them." Sky looked pained. "And don't give me some elaborate excuse as to why he can't be here. When someone you love is hurting, you move the heavens to be by their side. There isn't anything that could stop you."

"There isn't anything that would stop *you*," she said pointedly.

I frowned at her, baffled. "Am I really so unique?"

"More than you know." Her comment was without mirth. "Look, I don't think he's even aware that Lilly collapsed."

I stared at her, aghast. "You're joking. Well, shouldn't someone let him know? He'll be heartsick to find out that she's been in here and nobody told him. I know I would be."

She breathed a tired sigh. "You wouldn't need to be told she was ill. You'd have felt it in your bones."

I didn't tell Sky that I *had* felt it when Lilly collapsed, standing in the middle of Palladia Street while the rain misted down. She had filled my head, holding back the world until all I could feel was her. I pushed aside Sky's comparison. Whoever this guy was, Lilly had chosen to be with him and he deserved the benefit of the doubt.

"If I knew how to get in touch with him, I would have," Sky said.

"So, you've never met him? I asked in surprise.

"No."

"But surely you've seen him."

"No, not once."

"Well, Source above, Sky! Does he even exist?"

"Yes, Christian, Jay exists!" she huffed, her voice echoing down the long hall.

"Okay, fine. I'm dropping it," I raised my hands in surrender. "You should get out of here for a while, go have a nice lunch with Gabe at a swanky restaurant or something."

"And will you be following your own good advice and joining us?"

"Not right now. There are some overdue questions that I need to ask Garrick Leif."

"Excellent," she rolled her eyes, "you can go interrogate someone else for a while." She patted me on the shoulder and walked back to Lilly's doorway where Gabe was waiting for her.

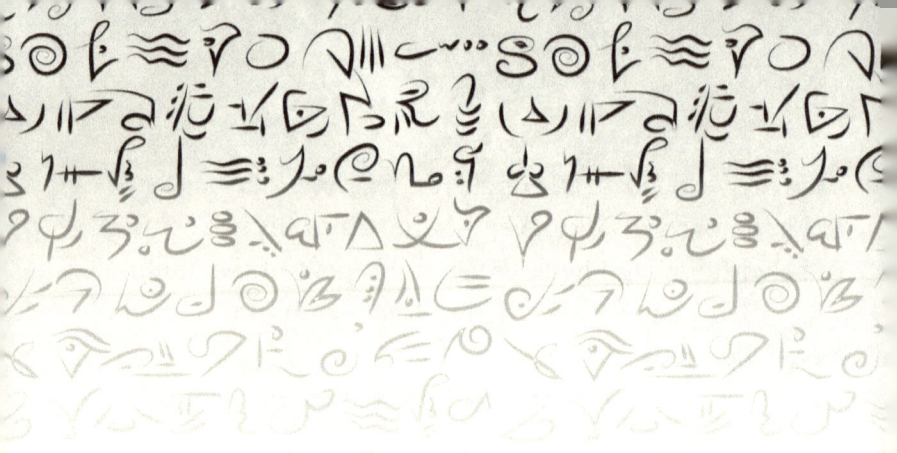

TWENTY-ONE

Christian

Garrick's room was only three doors down. I might not be allowed to ask Sky for answers, but there was nothing stopping me from questioning Garrick Leif. So far, the Elders hadn't gleaned much from him at all. He'd been slipping in and out of twilight sleep while his body was healing and he was often too terrified and agitated when he was conscious to make any sense.

I peered around the doorway. He was alone, staring out the window at the treetops that only days ago were filled with squabbling birds and countless monkeys. It had taken us the best part of twenty-four hours to round up the visitors and transport them to the Haven. Now, all was quiet. The only sound was the high-pitched ping of fluids dripping from the glass sphere suspended above Garrick and into the synthesis line in his arm. I tapped lightly on the door frame, "Mind if I come in?"

He craned his neck off the pillow and I could see a look of relief flood his face, although I had no idea why. "Sure, come in," he mumbled.

"Do you remember me? I'm Chris, Acolyte Flight's friend." I settled myself in a chair by his bed.

"I remember." He paused, chewing his lip. "Is Acolyte Flights okay? My mum told me she's still in healaxis and that she has the same things wrong with her that I do." He looked distinctly curious about that, just as I was.

"Actually, that's why I'm here. I'm hoping you can tell me anything at all about how this happened to you, and then maybe we'll know how to help you and Lilly." The boy seemed remarkably lucid today, and calm. Elder Sparks must have been working his magic. "At the moment, Garrick, the Healers are doing their best to make you both well but they're not certain that they can. They don't understand what caused the damage to your energy fields and there's nothing in Panacea's medical archives to suggest that it's ever happened before."

"Never?" he blanched. Finding out that he was a medical oddity seemed to disturb him far more than the the fact that he'd almost died. An intense sadness welled in his features. It made him look even paler than he had. He turned away and his voice was muffled against the pillow. "I always knew I didn't belong," he sniffed. "I'm different... strange."

I stared at a nest of russet hair flattened to the

back of his head from lying in bed for too long. What could I say to ease this teenage boy's mind? He was shy and awkward and oozed ordinariness. It was had to imagine him as anything but. "You don't seem strange or different to me, Garrick. What makes you think that you are?"

He turned back to me, his deep blue eyes blazing. "I can't tell you because you won't understand. No-one will. I don't even understand it myself. I just wanted to help them, that's all, I just wanted to save them." He went back to staring forlornly out the window.

"The animals, you mean?"

He nodded.

"And how were you trying to help them?"

There was a long, anxious pause and when he answered I had to strain to hear him. "By saving them from danger. By giving them a better home."

I had to stop myself from openly gawking at him in shock. He'd all but admitted what we'd suspected and needed to know. This shy, self-conscious teenager possessed a power beyond anything we knew. He was red-cheeked with embarrassment and fidgeting with the bed sheet, avoiding my eyes. I understood how hard it must have been to tell me his secret. I knew he was too sick to skitter away like a frightened deer again, but I wanted to ease his discomfort. I decided to change the subject. "Did Acolyte Flights tell you I'm a Translator? I love animals too."

He stole a shy look at me. "She didn't need to.

I already know who you are." His lips wobbled into a tentative smile. "I want to be a great Translator like you one day."

I stopped, stunned for a second time in the space of twenty seconds. Was he actually saying what I thought he was saying? "Garrick, are you telling me you can talk to animals? Do you have the Translator Gift?"

He grinned and nodded.

"That's amazing!" I whooped, because it was! I had always been the only Translator in Citrine. The last one had died when I was twelve and still coming into my Gift. "We'll have to put you to work as soon as you're well," I ribbed him.

The smile drained from his face. "*If* I get well."

"You seem much better today."

"Yeah," he shrugged, "but if I can't make it stop..."

The helpless look in his eyes told me the rest. He had no control over what was happening to him and no-one to turn to. He'd been struggling through this on his own because he thought he was strange and didn't fit in and I honestly couldn't fault him for that. He *was* different. There had never been anyone like him and no-one had ever breached the veil between worlds.

"Here's what I think. I think you have an extraordinary Gift that you've kept a secret because you were afraid. A power that no-one in all of Panacea has ever seen before. Am I right so far?"

Garrick studied my face for a few moments and

gave a resigned nod.

"You have the power to bring animals from Earth through the veil and into our world. But because you don't know how to use this power, it's made you sick. Am I still right?"

He let out an exhausted sigh, clearly relieved that someone finally knew the truth about him. *Thank The Source!* We finally had confirmation that he was responsible, that our improbable theory was actually fact.

"Garrick, listen to me, I understand why you've been scared. You are different. Nobody else can do what you can do but you're not strange, you're miraculous," I laughed.

He eyed me warily through russet lashes and then a ghost of a smile tugged at his mouth.

"So here's what we're going to do, you're going to tell me as much as you can about how your Gift works and the Elders and I are going to find a way to make it stop for a while and give you time to heal. Then we're going to work out how to use your Gift in a way that doesn't hurt you. Deal?"

"Okay, deal," he nodded.

The room felt lighter. Garrick's pall of helplessness, suddenly lifted. "So the first rescue you did were the bees? What were you saving them from?"

"A farmer was spraying pesticides."

"But how did you know that bees on another planet needed your help?"

"They came to me in my dreams, asking me to save them."

"And is that how you knew that all the other animals were in danger, because they came to you for help in your dreams?"

He nodded.

Unbelievable. So, Garrick was like a Soul Guardian... for animals. I'd never heard of such a thing. But he went on to tell me how the koalas, Houdini, all of them, had come to him in dreams, asking for help, and of course he could understand them because he was a Translator. It was perfect! Beautiful! I was so busy marvelling at this amazing kid that I almost forgot why I was there. I needed to find out *how* he was doing it.

"So the first time, with the bees, how did you actually shift them from Earth to here?"

"I didn't mean to do it. It was an accident. I felt so sorry for them, watching their brothers and sisters dropping from the sky, and I wished that I could make it stop. Then, when I woke up, there was a swarm of bees in my bedroom. I didn't understand how it had happened. I panicked and opened the window to get them out. I didn't know they would attack people." He looked guilt-ridden.

"And the next time with the horse?"

"I don't know. It was sort of the same, I guess. I saw him being whipped and beaten and I couldn't stand it anymore. I had to do something."

"You could feel his pain and you wanted to make

it stop?"

Garrick's fingers touched his chest. "I could feel it in my heart."

This was all starting to make sense. Garrick talked and talked, telling me all the dreadful things he had seen on Earth and how cruelly they treated animals. His heart had gone out to them with an overwhelming desire to stop the cruelty, stop the pain. Although he couldn't articulate how his power worked, I felt sure that the key to it lay in that heart connection. At least it would give us a starting point for understanding this new power.

Garrick was only fifteen. That was much too young to be thrown into Soul Guardian duty - five years too young. He'd gotten his first glimpse of Earth life only a few short months ago and was understandably perturbed. Worst of all, he'd shouldered this entire ordeal on his own, never uttering a word to his parents or friends. He'd been given an incredible Gift that he didn't know how to control and it had almost killed him. I didn't have the heart to tell him that all his efforts were in vain and that the animals he'd brought here were dying or already dead. Nothing good would come of sharing that right now and it begged an even bigger question. Why would he have been gifted with the extraordinary ability to teleport animals from one dimension to another, only for them to wind up dead because they don't belong here? That part made absolutely no sense at all.

"Chris, is your friend, Lilly, like me too?"

I hesitated. In all our talking, it was the one thing I couldn't reconcile. Where *did* Lilly fit in to all of this? I was fairly certain she hadn't been staging secret rescue missions of Earth animals. So why was she suffering the same energy tears as Garrick?

"Or..." he bit his lip, looking ashamed, "...did I somehow *hurt her* when I grabbed her arm?"

"You grabbed her arm?"

He nodded. "Right before she collapsed." He slumped back into his pillow, suddenly looking pale again.

"And you think that by touching her you made her sick?" He didn't answer. A sheen of sweat had broken out across his forehead and he was fighting to hold his eyes open. "Garrick, what's wrong?" He didn't answer. I sprang to my feet. "I'll go get Healer Cray." I don't know if he heard me. His head had lolled to one side and he was very still. His eyelids were pale lavender and the hollows beneath were the dark shade of a bruise. He'd fallen back into twilight sleep again.

A loud thunk made me spin around. I scanned the far side of the room searching for the source of the noise and saw nothing. I turned my attention back to Garrick. "I'll be right back with Healer Cray."

Thunk! There it was again. It sounded like it was coming from outside. A circle of sky quivered directly outside the window, warping and shimmering in wavy lines across the air. A flurry of white feathers emerged from the portal, just a few short feet from healaxis's towering sandstone wall. I watched in horror as a flock of white birds hurtled through at speed, heading straight for Garrick's window.

"Stop!" I yelled, my hands flying instinctively out in front of me. I was shouting, pleading, but they didn't have time to register what I was saying. The portal was too close to the window. I shielded my head as they hit and bounced off the glass.

Whack, thunk, bang!

The window rattled as more and more collided with it. They were snow geese. The ancient, leadlight glass finally began to crack as the sickening sounds of wings snapping and necks breaking against it fired through the room. I felt ill. I could do nothing as they torpedoed the glass and fell from the air right in front of me. It probably only lasted for a matter of seconds but it felt much longer, and then, mercifully, the horrible sounds stopped and it was over.

I walked over to the window and wondered how it had held without one of them breaking through. Blood was spattered and smeared down the glass with snow white feathers sticking here and there. I braced myself and looked down. The lawn below Garrick's window was dotted with tufts of white and red, wings spread like bloody fans, necks lying at odd angles.

I looked back at Garrick. He was still sleeping, his eyes darting rapidly beneath lavender lids. *Great Source above, this poor boy desperately needed The Council's help.*

I wondered if he had seen what just happened, or if the view in his mind's eye was different. Was he lying there, trapped in twilight sleep, horrified and guilt-ridden or did he think he'd successfully saved them?

I pulled out my uniter and briefed Grand Master Trill on what I'd just found out and showed her the grisly scene outside Garrick's window. Her amber eyes were intense and unreadable. "I'll assemble The Council. I will need you to present what you've discovered in fine detail. Between all of us, we should be able to gain some understanding of how this new Gift works and devise a way to help Garrick."

"He's still sleeping, so it might be wise to station the animal Healers and Enchanters outside healaxis. The Source only knows what else he might allow through while he's in twilight sleep."

I had an hour until the meeting at Ophanim Dome and I wanted to check on Lilly before I left. Her room was quiet. Everyone had left her to rest. She was sound asleep, curled on her side with her knees tucked almost to her chest. Her thin arms were wrapped around her knees like she was trying to gather up all the parts of herself and hold them together. Deep hollows were carved under her cheekbones and her lips were parched and cracked. She had become so painfully thin and she looked so vulnerable. A wave of sadness went through me.

I sat down by her bedside and wondered for the

hundredth time why she was lying there fighting for her life. There weren't any animals pouring through portals outside her window. Even though Lilly had been there when the whales had died, it seemed it had just been a coincidence. She had flung all of her energy into trying to save them and had collapsed with exhaustion. The following day she had pumped enough healing energy into Garrick to rouse him from twilight sleep; a feat that a team of experienced Healers had not managed. Perhaps the damage to her energy field was the result of extreme over-exertion? But then why hadn't other Go-lites ever suffered from such a thing? No, I was certain that she and Garrick were connected somehow. Lilly had been looking after Garrick since he was first admitted to healaxis and Garrick was concerned that he may have hurt Lilly through his touch. I would need to mention that to Healer Cray and The Council and hope they could offer some answers.

I was so relieved Garrick had told me the truth. At least now we had a real shot at saving him. Even though we were facing something completely new, a Gift that our world had never seen, I had to believe that the collective insight and wisdom of the Elders would be enough to save Garrick. I'd also hoped I would come away from that room with answers about Lilly, but I couldn't reconcile what was happening to her at all.

She winced and hugged her knees tighter to her chest. I noticed her synthesis line was tangled around her wrist and if she twisted it anymore, she'd pull it out. I carefully touched my fingertips to the back of her hand so as not to startle her. Her knuckles were white where she clung to herself, her skin, clammy and cold. Not that freezing cold hands were unusual for Lilly. I slid my palm to cover her knuckles and gently picked up her hand. She sighed and I could feel some of the tension drain from her body. I untangled the line and lowered her hand back down but before I could let go, her fingers curled around mine. Our hands lay against the stark sheet, hers pale as putty, mine like clay. I had promised her we would always be together, but what if she was going somewhere that I couldn't follow?

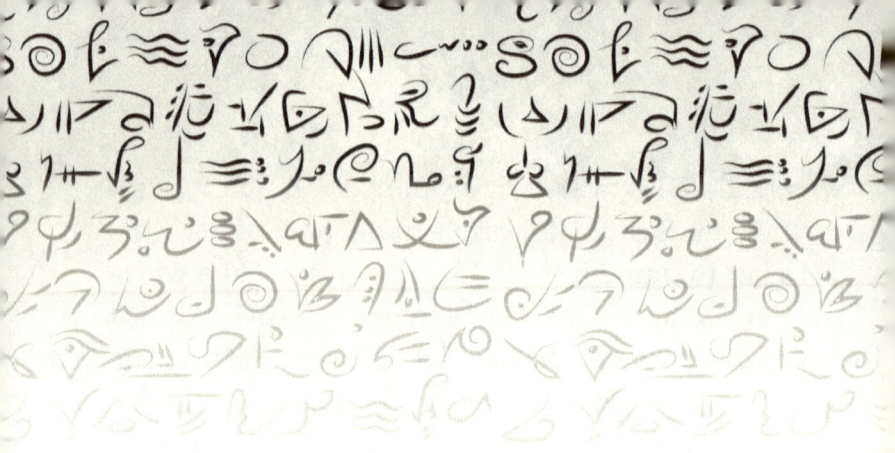

TWENTY-TWO

Christian

I pushed through the heavy chamber doors to find The Council already assembled. Light streamed through the Dome's glistening crown throwing faceted patterns of light onto the opaque crystal floor. The Elders that weren't away on Council business were gathered around the circular oak table. It gleamed like honey and was polished to such a high sheen that the Elders were mirrored on its surface. Their robes of saffron, wine, deep plum and indigo were drenched in milky light as it filtered through the thick crystal walls. The whole chamber seemed illumined by the moon.

Grand Master Willow was presiding today. Grand Masters Trill and Mont were seated beside her. She gave me an insouciant smile as I entered. "Translator Palladen, welcome. Please, sit," she gestured to an empty carved back chair between Elder Loch and Lilly's dad.

"We owe you much gratitude for your fine work today and we're all very eager to hear what you've learned from Garrick Leif." Her violet eyes glittered with interest. Her ebony hair was braided into a circlet around her crown, the rest falling in a black wave to her waist.

My eyes swept around the table. Twenty-six of the thirty-five Council members were present. As benevolent as The Council were, I didn't know how this news would be received. I was about to shatter an ancient and accepted truth: the veil could not be breached. So, I was aware of a stray butterfly flipping around in my stomach in anticipation of mixed reactions and certainly a good deal of shock. What Garrick could do was at once wondrous and in direct contradiction to everything we'd ever known. "Garrick has confirmed that he's responsible for the animal appearances throughout Citrine. After a long conversation with him, I've discovered the extraordinary extent of his Gifts. It appears Garrick is twice Gifted. I can confirm that, like me, he is a Translator and he also possesses a new and powerful Gift that allows him to breach the veil and transport animals from Earth to Panacea."

Intrigued murmurs passed around the table. Perhaps Grand Master Trill had graciously done the job of dismantling our world beliefs before I arrived.

"We have been told Garrick is but fifteen years old," said Elder Spry, raising his tangled, black brows.

"Yes, that's correct. He's told me that he doesn't

know how to control his power and if we cannot find a way to help him, it could cost him his life."

"And the lives of more of our citizens." Elder Spry wore the grave look of a troubled Seer. Beneath his black robes he was made of wire and sinew. He had a hooked beak of a nose and dark glass beads for eyes. His wiry fingers were knotted against the table, his thin lips pursed in thought. "Nyx is growing wilder by the day. I fear tragedy lies ahead." Nyx, Elder Spry's spirit raven, was not as powerful as Evangeline. Nor was Elder Spry's Seer Gift as mighty as Oracle Trill's, yet I could see his dread of the things he'd glimpsed as he inclined his head toward the seemingly empty space on his shoulder where Nix was perched. Grand Master Trill looked on with careful eyes but said nothing.

"Was he able to tell you how his Gift works?" A sing-song voice lilted through the chamber. I turned to a plump, motherly figure in peach robes; Elder Amaroo. A robust sculpture of yellow curls formed a fan-shaped bob about her head. She was petting something invisible in her lap. I guessed it was her spirit rabbit, Trixie.

"He explained as well as he was able. It seems young Garrick sees endangered animals in his sleep, just as a Soul Guardian sees struggling humans. He told me they call out to him for help."

"And he can understand them because he's a Translator," Grand Master Mont nodded, stroking the beginnings of a ropey beard.

"Precisely. So we're dealing with a boy who is too young to be a Soul Guardian, who desperately wants to save Earth animals from abuse and death, but what he can't explain clearly is *how* he's been rescuing them. The best explanation I can offer is that his heart connection to their pain is so strong that he's able to penetrate the veil and draw them to him. I think the desperation he feels to save them from suffering is an energy so potent that the veil literally gives way to it."

The chamber filled with consternate discussion and Lilly's dad leaned in, bumping my shoulder. He was bearing up admirably under the circumstances. Lilly wasn't out of danger yet but I could feel his faith in her recovery radiating from him like a beacon.

"Nice insight, Translator Palladen," he wore a small smile of approval. "Are you often in the habit of challenging 300,000 years of accepted universal law and doctrine?"

"Only when warranted," I grinned.

Jon cleared his throat and darted his eyes across the enormous round table to Elder Melladon. "Consider the first feather ruffled," he whispered.

"That's an interesting theory, Translator Palladen, but the veil exists for a reason." Elder Melladon rose from his chair and began to pace, his crimson robes shushing against the crystal floor. "The veil serves to protect the free will of all Earth's inhabitants. Their choices are their own and we, as go-lites and Guardians, respect that." He raised his arm and pointed an indignant finger toward the heavens. "Our job is to offer emotional support and guidance to those who ask for it, nothing more."

It was true what Elder Melladon had bluntly pointed out, or at least it had been since the inception of the go-lite race. Now, Garrick's Gift was calling all that we knew and believed into question. The chamber fell into reflective silence as everyone considered the implications of what Garrick had done.

Elder Amaroo cleared her throat. "Translator Palladen makes a valid point about Garrick being too young for Soul Guardian duties. Had he been older with the benefit of five years more training, perhaps he would have the grounding to function like any other Soul Guardian and remain compassionate but impartial. Perhaps we would be singing his praises as a new breed of Soul Guardian for animals," she smiled kindly.

Neveya Willow steepled her fingers, the ice blue sleeves of her robe cascading to her elbows. "Elder Amaroo, what you are suggesting would mean that every go-lite has the potential ability to pierce the veil, providing they have an emotional connection to an Earth Soul."

I glanced at Elder Melladon and the very thought of it was turning his face as crimson as his robes.

"Yet," Grand Master Willow went on, "throughout our histories, there has not been one mention or clue of another having this ability. No," she said resolutely, "I think this is much more than an accident of youth and lack of training."

"Neveya is right." Grand Master Trill paused, collecting her thoughts. Her amber eyes had a far away look as they roamed over the elaborate crystal mandala set into the dome above. "Garrick is unique and confounding in multiple ways. Firstly, he should not yet possess the ability to function as a Soul Guardian, given his young age. Secondly, there has never been a Soul Guardian for animals before, and thirdly, he can teleport living beings from another dimension into our world. I firmly believe that his ability is a new power emerging."

"I agree with Genevieve," said Grand Master Mont. "We've seen portals open up before our eyes and watched as animals have charged through. It is the most extraordinary thing I've experienced in this lifetime, and yes, it raises many questions, but our primary concern at this moment must be preserving life. Garrick is lying in a healing bed with his energy field in shreds. We believe his lack of understanding about his Gift and his inability to control it has caused him serious harm. Elder Flight's daughter, Lilly, is also seriously ill with a damaged energy field, although we have no knowledge or evidence of her possessing the same Gift and she is currently too ill to question. Plus we have hundreds of Earth animals being treated at the Haven, all to no avail. They continue to sicken and die because, they too, have tears in their energy fields."

"So," Grand Master Willow looked at each Elder

in turn, "our immediate task is not to speculate about why a new Gift is emerging or what it means for the go-lite mission. There will be plenty of time to debate Soul Guardian tenets after Garrick, Lilly and the animals are out of danger. We must put our heads together and try to determine how Garrick's Gift might function. The Source willing, we'll be able to devise a way to control it and prevent any further harm."

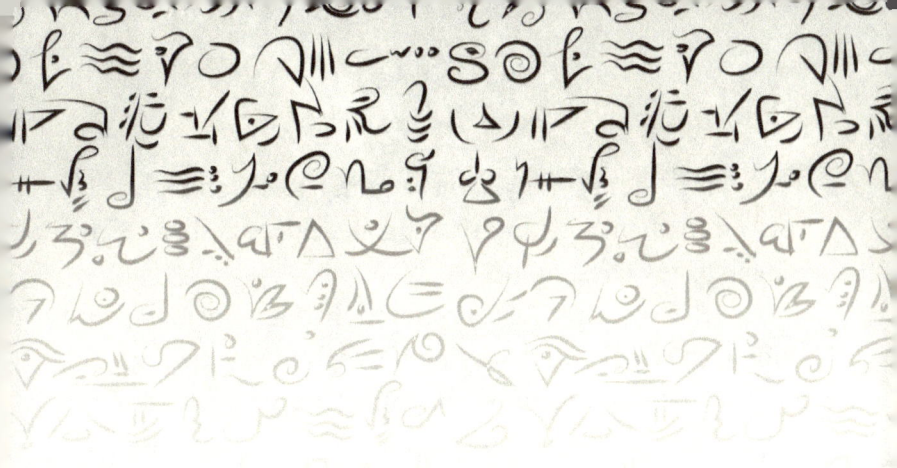

TWENTY-THREE

Lilly

When my eyes finally opened, the room was black as pitch except for the silvery river of moonlight that spilled onto the floor and pooled at the foot of my bed. My head was leaden and my neck felt like it was encased in concrete. A voice gnawed at the edges of my blurred consciousness.

"Lilly... Lilly.... are you okay?"

Jay's warm hand touched lightly to my forehead as I struggled to form words. "Jaaayyy," I breathed out.

"I'm here, Lilly. I'm here. What happened to you?" His soft lips brushed my temple like velvet rose petals and I could feel his hot breath on my swollen cheek. My whole body warmed and I relaxed under his touch.

"I...I fell," I managed, forcing my leaden eyelids to remain open and find his face. He was right here, with me. My heart swelled and I tried to reach for him with weak arms as unbidden tears escaped down my cheeks.

"Hey, it's okay. You're going to be all right." He placed his hands on my shaking shoulders and rested his cheek to my chest.

"No, it's not," I stammered through my tears, but I didn't know why I was saying it or why I was crying.

His lips came down on mine and silenced me with a kiss that was soft, deep and all consuming. My sobs ceased and I wound my arms around his neck, losing myself in the moment. The sharp emotional pain that was trying to pierce my heart, softened around the edges, becoming a dull ache and eventually dissolved into the ether. His presence lulled away the fear and soothed my weary body. He just held me and kissed me and we floated together in a blissful delirium, as I clung to him like a life raft. I don't know for how long and I didn't care. I wanted to drift away, carried by the ebb and flow of his breath and buoyed by the beat of his heart."I love you, Jay," I whispered. "I love you."

"Lilly, wake up. Lilly..."

There was a hand on my shoulder.

"Jay?" I slurred, trying to open my eyes.

When I did, bright daylight was bouncing off the stark, white walls and Sky was at my bedside, her expression tense.

It had been a dream.

My heart sank.

I had lost count of how many days I'd lay here,

falling in and out of twilight sleep and when I was conscious, enduring endless questions from Healer Cray and Healer Everglade. Jay must be frantic, wondering where I was, wondering why I hadn't been back to see him. Had he been trying to contact me? Maybe he had been here while I was asleep, even though I'd told him it wasn't safe for him to come to Panacea. Had he come to find me anyway?

"You were having a dream. Or is it considered more of a nightmare when you cry in your sleep?" Sky poured me a glass of water and handed it over.

My heart leapt into my throat. "You heard?"

"I heard enough."

My face felt sticky from where the tears had dried on my cheeks. More tears! And I had absolutely no idea what I'd been crying about.

"So, how are you feeling?"

"Much better than I was. Is Garrick okay? Is he still awake?"

"He's in and out, thanks to you it seems. You shouldn't have over-exerted yourself, Lilly. You should have listened to Healer Cray and rested."

It was the first time I'd seen Sky in private since my collapse. My room was always full of people - Healers, my parents, Chris and Gabe. Sky had hovered in the background, never saying much. "What made you pull a stunt like that when you were already so weak?"

"You know I don't believe in lost causes. I had to

try. Anyway, the most pressing question at the moment is, what in The Source's name has caused these tears in our energy fields? Sky, my manuscript. Did you bring it?"

"I primarily came to see how you are, but yes, I brought it," she said flatly. She reached into her suede backpack and handed it over with a sigh.

"What?"

"I sort of thought collapsing through exhaustion might have slowed you down a bit. Silly me."

"And I thought you'd be a bit more enthusiastic about helping me understand what made me collapse in the first place."

Waking up in a healing bed at healaxis and being told that my energy field was torn like Garrick Leif's had been a terrible shock. In the precious moments before I'd slipped back into twilight sleep I'd realised that it had to be because of my trips to see Jay. The pain I had felt before I'd collapsed had been overwhelming and all too familiar. The nausea, the dizziness, the bombardment of painful emotion, was exactly how I'd felt at Ryan's party. Falling in and out of twilight sleep, it had taken days for my hazy brain to piece together what should have been obvious. I really did not belong on Earth and if I'd taken the time to study my great-grandfather's manuscript more closely, I would have known why. Even more shocking, I'd been forced to confront the possibility that if I had tears in my energy field and so did Garrick, that maybe I'd been wrong in thinking that my ability to Travel to Earth was unique.

What if Garrick had the same ability as me? But this was all just wild theory until I pored through those pages and saw it confirmed.

"Look at the title." I held up the battered volume so Sky could read the words stamped into the worn leather.

"The Vibratory Scale of Ascendency." She shrugged.

"There's a diagram in here depicting the vibrational order of our universe." I opened the heavy book on my lap and leafed through until I found the right page. Stars of black ink swirled around the eleven known planets that were drawn in an unbroken circle. "Here," I pointed. "I should have paid closer attention to this."

Sky frowned at the page then scooted her chair closer. Her eyes roamed over every carefully rendered shape and line, analysing. Every go-lite was familiar with my great-grandfather's theory: that the planets were arranged like musical notes in an ascending scale and that every new Soul starts at the bottom note - planet Ogden. The greater mission of every Soul in the universe was to progress up the scale, learning through multiple lifetimes and being reborn to a higher planet, functioning at a higher vibration, until ultimately, when they have learnt all there is to learn, they return to The Source.

"It's just a theory, Lilly. What does it have to do with the tears in your energy field?"

"That's just it. I don't think it was just a theory to him. I think through his research and travels to Earth, he proved it as fact. I think he actually knew what happens when you try to bring a Soul from one planet to another. He knew because he spent his life trying to find a safe way to bring Aurora to Panacea and that probably took a whole lot of experimenting and failed attempts. If I'd bothered to look closer at his journal entries, I might not be lying here right now because I'm pretty sure he discovered that foreign planet = incompatible vibration = tears in your energy field. I'm so incredibly stupid!"

Sky shot me a worried look and it took me a moment to realise that it was because I'd just degraded myself without a second thought, and I'd done it out loud. The negative voices inside my head had been becoming more vocal, and it wasn't just since I'd wound up in healaxis. If I was being honest with myself, it had been getting worse for a while, only I'd been too stubborn to slow down and think about what it meant. I barely wanted to think about it at all. It was a nagging annoyance; an obstacle I'd kept pushing down, but I couldn't ignore it forever. Lying in a healing bed gives you a lot of time to think.

"I had considered that going to Earth was having a bad effect on you," Sky nodded thoughtfully. "It stands to reason that taking a living thing from one planet and dumping it on another will have consequences. But do you really think that a difference in vibration is capable of shredding your energy field? That seems extreme."

"How else do you explain it?"

"Well, while I've watched you run yourself ragged on your mission from The Source, I've considered a few theories of my own. But when you were diagnosed with a torn energy field and I learned that Garrick had the same thing, I thought that with your overly empathic nature, you might have somehow taken on his sickness. I wondered if you weren't so determined to heal him that you drew too much of the sickness from him and then couldn't shift it from yourself."

"That *can* happen if a Healer doesn't know their limits, but I'm thinking this is the key," I tapped the manuscript. "My trips to Earth, my time spent in a lower energy environment, has done this to me. Earth is incompatible with my vibration."

"And what about all the time you've spent with Jay? He's from Earth, he has a lower vibration. Isn't that a gross incompatibility?" Her left brow rose to a pointed peak.

I glared at her. "*Gross?*"

"Yes, as in, *huge.*" She rolled her eyes. "Look, you're the one postulating, I'm just seeing it through to it's logical conclusion. If what you're saying is true, then being in the physical presence of someone with a vibration lower than your own will cause tears in your energy field, i.e... it will eventually kill you."

Anger spiked through me, sharp and hot. I could feel my body go rigid and my face harden to a scowl. I wanted to lash out at her. My jaw was already clenched but I clenched it tighter to prevent the angry tirade I wanted to loose. "Well obviously it didn't kill Grayson," I annunciated through gritted teeth.

Sky was looking at me with her head cocked to one side, her face, calm and neutral. She was looking at me the way I used to look at Jay while I was waiting for him to calm down. She was looking at me like I was human.

And there it was; the thing I'd been trying so hard to ignore. Not only was my energy field in shreds, I was acting and thinking like a human. Admitting it to myself felt surreal but I couldn't ignore the truth of it any longer. What had I become?

"Are you going to see if you're right?" Sky urged. Go ahead, see what Grayson has to say," she nodded toward the manuscript.

The page opposite the diagram went into a detailed explanation of the vibrational scale. I squinted at the page to see if I could detect any hidden script and there, dancing between the lines of flourishing black ink were glimpses of swirling green. "There's something here."

"What does it say?"

"Give me a minute. I have to concentrate." I sat up straighter in the bed and drew on every scrap of strength I'd regained. If it was one of Grayson's diary entries it shouldn't be too hard to see.

Sky sat silently while I wrestled with myself, trying to form a connection that should have come with relative ease. After several laboured minutes the words started to appear. I read halfway down the page looking for something that would prove my suspicions, and more importantly, for a way to overcome this mess.

It was extremely slow going in my weakened state and what I found in the end was disappointment. Sky waited patiently while I struggled through six pages of diary entries. My great-grandfather had been much smarter and wiser than me. After three visits to Earth, he had recognised the toll it was taking on him and had stopped. His best friend Thomas had been a Healer and had been the one to detect the beginnings of tears in Grayson's energy field.

Tears were streaming down my face. Sky was clutching my hand. "He only got to hold her and kiss her once, then it took them decades to finally be together again." I could feel my features contorting with grief. The bright, airy room suddenly felt claustrophobic and small.

Sky's sympathetic smile was a blur. "I'm sorry, Lilly. Truly. But you have your answer. Now you know the truth of why you've been so ill."

I blinked and was too slow to stop two huge tears splashing onto the journal. I smudged them away with the corner of my bed sheet leaving two damp, puckered dimples on the aged parchment. "This is unbearable," I winced, my voice cracking.

Sky breathed audibly - in and out - and held me with a look that had no beginning and no end. "Nothing... is unbearable."

My sobbing came in spasms, stabbing the quiet air. I didn't want to hear Soul Guardian philosophy right now. My heart was breaking. The thought of not being able to hold Jay was terrifying, unthinkable, cruel. To be able to see and hear one another but never touch would be pure torture. How had Grayson and Aurora survived it, wasting year after tedious year separated by the veil? My head was a riot of emotions I had never felt before. Desperation clawed inside. I wanted to feel Jay's body hot against mine. I wanted to crawl inside his skin and feel every part of him. I wanted to give him everything I had, everything I was. "I need to see him... I have to explain."

"Lilly, calm down. Just breathe, okay. You're having a panic attack."

I was about to snap out an angry contradiction when I realised she was right. I was sweating bullets and gasping in great gulps of air that were never enough.

"You're okay. Lilly, look at me." Sky was leaning over me, her hands bracing my shaking shoulders. I blinked away more tears to see her face close to mine, her serene gaze holding me steady. "This isn't who you are." Her eyes were soft, still, an endless blue sky. Her voice was a lullaby. I felt a wave of love wrap around me, the air shimmering gold.

I sagged back against my pillow and Sky took the manuscript from my lap and placed it on the chest of drawers by my bed. "I understand that you want to be with him but you have to accept that for now, that isn't possible. If it's meant to be, you'll figure out Grayson's instructions and what he did to get Aurora to Panacea and if your love for one another is strong enough, no amount of time apart will break it."

Sky had settled my hysteria and now I just felt hollow, deflated. I scrubbed the tears from my cheeks and reached out to her with forlorn eyes. "I already know part of what has to happen. Jay needs to heal all of his past hurts. He has to rise up and become like a go-lite before he can ascend here," I said in a meek voice.

Sky was very quiet. Hearing myself say it out loud made it seem completely improbable. The determination and faith that had driven me forward through these trying days had paled to a distant star. "I know it will take years," I amended quickly in case she thought I was delusional. "I told him I would wait for as long as he needed. What I didn't know was that we'd be forced to stay apart, to live our lives separately until the day he ascends. I thought I'd be able to keep visiting him on Earth until he was ready."

"If your great-grandparents managed it. You can too."

She was right. I had to believe that our love was strong enough and that it wouldn't break. "But I have to go and see him one last time. I have to tell him in person."

Sky visibly flinched. Her lips parted in shock. "Lilly, you can't. It's too great a risk," she said breathlessly.

"I can't abandon him, Sky. I have to see him, reassure him. I don't know how he's going to react when I tell him and I have to be there for him."

"Lilly, no!" She was resolute.

Why couldn't I make her understand? "He has no idea where I am. He probably thinks I've abandoned him already. How many days have I been stuck in here? Seven?"

"Nine," she corrected.

I felt frantic. "I can't wait any longer. My chest aches like someone's kicked a hole in my heart. I have to see him. I love him!"

"*Love?*" Sky blinked at me with incredulous eyes. "You know what another trip to Earth will do to you. It sounds more like obsession than love. An obsession that's slowly killing you."

Her words pierced me like a knife. *How could she say that to me?* She was the one person I had entrusted with the truth, with my heart and everything in it, and now she was turning on me.

I recoiled away from her, my face twisting with pain. An invisible wall rose up, shielding me from further hurt.

She had betrayed me.

Pain and anger were weaving themselves into a nasty storm while she sat watching me with infuriating calm. She'd just trampled all over my heart and now she was sitting there as though it were nothing at all. She didn't deserve to be calm! "Why did I ever trust you?" I spat. "You know, for all your righteous ways, you sure took a long time to tell me how you really feel. I suppose I should thank you for finally mustering up the guts to be honest with me."

She was a picture of poise, her spine straight, her mouth soft. "Lilly, you're not yourself," she said quietly.

"What about you?" I retorted. "I don't even know who you are anymore!"

There was actual *pity* in her eyes and it enraged me even further. "I trusted you and you betrayed me!" I bellowed.

Her hands fluttered in front of her; a plea for calm. "Please, stop, before you say something you'll regret."

"More righteous advice from one who knows better than me how to live my life!"

"Like that," she shook her head. "Can't you see that this isn't you? You've changed. You're not well."

"I can't believe I ever trusted you. Just get out... leave... I don't want you here." Fresh, hot tears spilled over. My whole body was trembling.

Sky sat in an aura of sorrow. She closed her eyes and hung her head. The moment seemed to stretch on for an eternity.

There was a light rap on the open door as my mother breezed into the room. Her blue linen dress was creased at the waist where she'd cast off her cooking apron. She must have come from teaching a class. In her hand was a slender green stem, blooming with a snow white lily. "How is my little flower?" she beamed, then catching sight of Sky crumpled on the chair, her face fell flat. "Sky, darling girl, how are you?" She placed a warm hand on her shoulder and kissed the top of her head. "I hope I'm not interrupting."

"Not at all, Dawn. I was just going," Sky said rising to her feet and forcing a thin smile. I lay mute, staring at them both, feeling too wretched to hide the tears that had spilled moments before. Sky turned back to me, her eyes blank. "Feel better soon, Lilly." Then it was as though she vanished from the room. I didn't remember seeing her leave. She just wasn't there anymore and I was left staring at an empty chair.

"What's happened, Lilly?" My mother's hand was squeezing mine and she was sitting in the space that Sky had just occupied. Her perfume curled around me – freesia, bosun lilies and midnight amber – that comforting smell that sparked memories of a calm voice soothing away my nightmares, careful hands tending to cuts and grazes, loving words when you needed them most. I stretched my arms toward her as fresh tears stung my eyes. She stood and embraced me, nestling her cheek to mine. I clung to her and sobbed. All the while she just held me. My whole body shook with the anger and grief, as though if I could only shake hard enough, I could expel it from my being. I cried for a long time, until I was sweating and hot from the effort and my hair was wet with tears and plastered to my cheeks. I peeled myself away from my mother's arms and gulped in some fresh air. She sat back down and picked up my hand again but said nothing. "I'm sorry," I blurted.

She paused, puzzled. "Why are you sorry?" Her caramel eyes were soft like a deer's.

It was such a small question, much too small an opening to shove this colossal mess through it. I fashioned a small answer. "For being such a mess, for snapping at everyone, for being too stupid to see what's right in front of me."

"Oh... oh... honey, hush now. You've been seriously ill. It's not your fault." She was rubbing my arm and serving up her starlight smile.

But it *was* my fault. I'd bought all of this upon myself. The warning signs had been there and I'd ignored them and the embarrassing fact was that the warnings were clearly documented in my great-grandfather's diary entries and I hadn't bothered to read them! I'd been so consumed with seeking out and deciphering the pages that would get Jay here that I'd dismissed the rest as unimportant. I stared out the window feeling utterly useless. The day outside was eerily still. There wasn't even a whisper of a breeze which made the treetops look painted on a flat, blue sky.

"Healer Cray says this emotional turmoil is being caused by your damaged energy field." She said it with acceptance and calm.

I shot her a stunned look. "What?" Had I been this emotional the entire time? I couldn't remember. The days were all a blur, drifting in and out of twilight sleep.

"It's all right, you're behaving much more like

yourself than you were. We think the emotional outbursts will stop once you've completely healed. Did you snap at Sky just now when I came in?"

I'd done more than snap, but she'd deserved it. I just nodded at my mother.

"Sweetheart, no-one holds you responsible for the things you've said in your hysterical state so you have nothing to worry about."

Hysterical? What havoc had I been causing for the last week? What horrible things had I said and done to the people I love? I honestly couldn't remember. I felt wretched; like there were things writhing under my skin. I shrank back against my pillow. I was so embarrassed I wished the damn thing would swallow me whole.

"Sky understands and so does Christian," she soothed, taking in my stricken look.

"Christian?" I gasped. *Source help me, what had I said to Christian?* I cringed to think.

My mother patted my hand. "That boy loves you, Lilly, with every beat of his heart and every breath. He always has. But," she shrugged and shook her head, "if lightning has struck elsewhere, I'm happy for you. I can only say that whoever he is, he must be extraordinary to outshine our Christian." Her eyebrow arched, challenging the notion.

So everyone knew about Jay! I let out an involuntary moan. It was shame, dread and desperation expressed perfectly with one animal sound. My heart was racing. I'd blabbed about him during some overwrought hysteria, and while I had no idea what I'd said, judging by my mother's breezy air, it seemed I hadn't included the fact that he was human. *Thank The Source for that!*

She was waiting patiently for confirmation or denial of my delirious rantings about a new boyfriend. "It's not that straight forward mum."

"Oh, darling," she shook her head again as a sympathetic little laugh escaped her lips, "love never is. It's one big roller coaster ride and all rides have a beginning and an end."

I stared at the openess of her face, the mellow warmth in her eyes, at her heart unfurling a little bit more through her smile. I suddenly felt a desperate need to tell her the truth. If there was ever a time that I needed my mum it was now. I'd kept Grayson's discovery a secret, just as The Source had asked, but everyone has their limits and I had reached mine. I had done my best to be strong and brave but I could no longer see my way forward. I needed help. I was trying to find the words to explain when she changed the subject and the moment was wiped away like a wave smoothing rough sand.

"I have good news. Guess who's allowed to come home tomorrow?"

"Really?" I felt sure she was mistaken, but scepticism had been burrowing its roots into my broken brain, so I didn't argue.

"Healer Cray says you're strong enough and she

believes you'll heal more quickly at home. But, there is a caveat: you'll have to come back for a thirty minute healing session every day."

It was highly preferable to being stuck in this bed. "Sure," I shrugged.

"I'll be here tomorrow morning to collect you." She bent down and placed a kiss on my forehead. Her long, black braid tickled at my cheek. "Sleep, my little flower. I love all that you are."

I looked up into her melting caramel eyes. "Even the crying, irrational, messy bits?" I grimaced.

"Especially the messy bits," she smoothed my hair. "Struggles are the building blocks of wisdom."

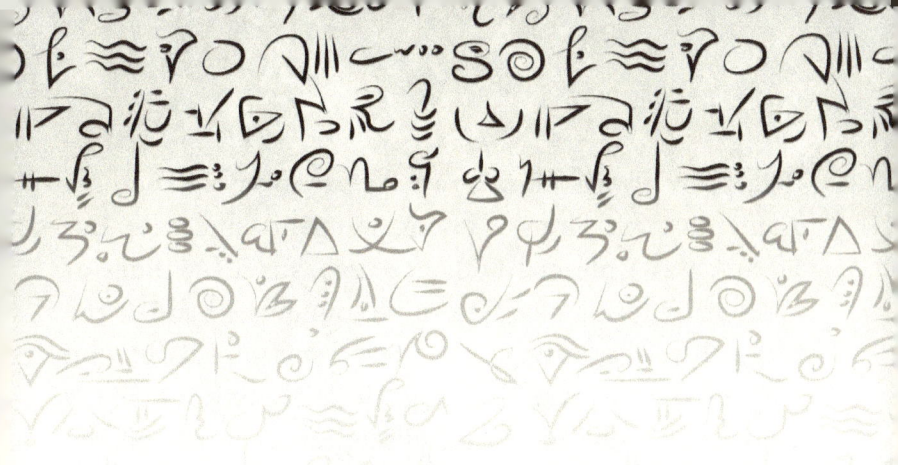

TWENTY-FOUR

Lilly

I'd made up a hundred different speeches in my head to tell my parents the truth but I couldn't find the courage to do it. I hated myself for it. Apparently I was now incapable of something as basic as honesty and worse still, I was capable of something as insidious as hate.

I barely recognised myself anymore. My argument with Sky had been a huge wake-up call – the way I'd yelled at her, the awful things I'd said – she was right, I was not at all myself. I was acting in a way that was so far removed from the person I used to be that I was disgusted I hadn't realised sooner. It had been a slow and steady decline – hurt feelings one moment, a snappy comment the next – a mounting collection of clear warning signs that I had industriously ignored.

When I searched my memories, looking for the girl I once was, it was like watching a character in a play.

That Lilly always knew exactly what to say to soothe a human in pain. She was loving and gentle and wise. But as much as I pleaded with her now, for a few lines of wisdom, she was nowhere to be found, she had left the stage. I was beginning to wonder if anything about who I used to be had ever been real. Healer Cray was sure my emotional outbursts would disappear once my energy field had completely healed. But what if Healer Cray was wrong?

My parents had given me a wide berth since bringing me home yesterday morning. I could hardly blame them. The angry scowl I saw reflected back in the bathroom mirror would be enough to scare anyone. Even my eyes looked different. I kept blinking at my reflection, wondering where I had gone and where the girl with eyes as hard as flint and an even harder jaw had come from.

Looking back on all that had happened, I knew I had screwed things up. There was no way this was The Source's intended result for my mission and now that I knew how my energy field had been damaged, it also solved the mystery of Garrick's illness. It meant I wasn't the only one who could Travel to Earth and that Garrick had been keeping a huge secret of his own. I could not fathom why The Source would give a young boy the power to breach the veil and Travel to Earth. He wasn't old enough to be a Soul Guardian so he couldn't see or talk to humans. There would have been no reason for him to Travel to Earth because there would be no-one for him to help and no-one he knew. I couldn't see the point of it. I pictured the intense blue of his eyes and the smattering of freckles over his nose and wondered if he was struggling as much as I was.

I was feeling better physically. I had not slipped back into twilight sleep, but it was little consolation when you were mourning the loss of your mind. I had spent the last 24 hours examining every facet of myself and had realised how far adrift I was. I was completely out of control and it had left me with one terrifying question: Was I even still a go-lite anymore or had the damage to my energy field transformed me into a human?

I was panicking, scared out of my wits and I had no idea what to do. I needed guidance. I needed to tell my parents the truth of how I got the tears in my energy field and hope the Elders could find a way to help me, and Garrick, too. Or maybe Garrick had already told them what he could do. I shuddered, unable to decide if that was a good thing or a bad thing.

The problem was, I was too cowardly to face them. I'd imagined every nightmarish reaction I could think of and kept playing my personal horror show over and over in my mind. It was insanity! Logically I knew my parents would not judge me, they were go-lites, not humans. They would do anything to support and help me, but the shame I felt at my naivety, the fear I felt for the consequences of my actions, had me tying myself in knots.

"Enough!" I slammed my hands down on either

side of the bathroom basin. "Stop being such a pathetic weakling!" I glared at my reflection, at my lip that had started to wobble, at my eyes wide with tears, and sank pitifully onto the wooden floor. I sat with my back pressed against the cabinet and tried to steady my breathing. All sense of rightness, of my mission, had gone. All I could see was an ungodly mess and the prospect of being stuck like a human, forever.

"Lilly, sweetheart, can I come in?"

I stiffened in fright and tried to train my expression into something that resembled calm. I didn't want to shame myself further in front of my mother. *What must she think of me already?*

"Just a second. I'm coming out." I scrambled to my feet and washed my face. I paused with my hand on the brass doorknob and took a breath.

My mother's face on the other side of the whitewashed door was serene but her eyes were watchful. "Everything okay?"

"Sure, I'm fine," I lied. I was a skilled liar now as well. I walked past her and into my bedroom before she could study me too closely. This was the room I'd grown up in and it was exactly as I'd left it. My single bed was nested under the window to catch the morning sun and Mum had made it up with my favourite coverlet, so I could sleep beneath the ocean in a coral garden, surrounded by mermaids. My collection of seashells, rocks and crystals were arranged on narrow shelves lining the far wall amongst faded pictures of the people I loved. My father carrying me on his shoulders. Christian and I covered in mud and holding hands. A six year old me looking earnestly at the dubious contents of a mortar which contained the first potion I'd ever attempted to make. I stared at the memories of my former life, reaching for the familiarity I desperately craved. Everything here was untouched, unchanged, except for me. In the midst of it all, I was a stranger.

"You know that if there's anything you need, I'm here."

"I know, Mother," I snapped, then immediately regretted it. I was so frustrated with myself I wanted to scream.

Ever patient, she kissed my cheek. "This won't last forever, Lilly. You just have to be brave for a while longer."

What if she was wrong? What if I was stuck this way, doomed to be tortured by the negativity of my own mind? I drooped onto my bed. "Sorry. I'll be okay, it's just..."

She waited expectantly.

"Nothing. It's nothing," I shook my head.

"Well, I came in to tell you that I'm heading out. I need to get some things for dinner and I'll be gone a while. I should be back by six and your father said he won't be home until seven."

"Six? Where in The Source's name are you

planning on buying groceries? Endua?"

"Not quite that far," she looked down and began shuffling the silver bracelets on her wrist.

I didn't ask questions. It was obvious she had a surprise in store for us. No doubt a spectacular homecoming dinner infused with all the love she could muster.

"Rest, my little flower." She kissed the top of my head and breezed from the room.

In spite of the risk, I'd been waiting for a chance just like this one to slip away and see Jay. It was the least I owed him after raising his hopes and telling him we could be together, with such faith and conviction that it had almost been bewitching. I couldn't find a scrap of that faith now. My head was spinning with a hundred and one thoughts about what he might say and what he might do once he learned the truth: I could never go back to Earth and we would be forced apart, perhaps for many years, bound to different worlds until he ascended to Panacea.

Sky's warning was looming large in my mind but what harm could a last trip to Earth do that hadn't already been done? Things were as bad as they possibly could be. I'd already diced with death and I was still here, and as for my mind, it was so broken I failed to see how it could get any worse. You couldn't lose something that was already lost.

It seemed impossible that anything could feel more urgent than telling Jay what I'd learned, but there was an empty, dragging ache in my heart that wouldn't subside and I knew the only way to ease it was to hold him again. I'd imagined it over and over, branding the feel of him into my skin. Those precious snatches of memory distilled with fancy were the only things sustaining me.

I eyed the manuscript with suspicion as it lay closed on my night stand. I'd not opened it once since coming home from healaxis – I had more than enough to cope with for now – so I almost jumped out of my skin when it began to hum into the still room. "What?" I demanded impatiently as the sound built bright and true. Was I expecting an answer? A mystical voice to come booming out of nowhere? The high note began to warp into a whine, sharp and insistent, until I wanted to cover my ears and cringe away. "Stop it!" I yelled, and much to my surprise, the whine was plucked from the air like a star being swallowed by a black hole and my bedroom was restored to peace. I gave the dilapidated journal a long warning look before I left it where it lay and strode from the room.

I wandered outside and followed the crooks and curves of the creek. Thin streams of water trickled over smooth stones, weaving their song on the air. I stirred through a patch of waist-high grasses and tiny moths rose up in a white cloud. They hovered lazily as though aroused from sleep, then sank back down into shadow.

Was there a simple and painless way to break this news to Jay? Or was trying to find one the only dream left for me to chase? It would be so much easier if I was still thinking and behaving like a go-lite. The real Lilly would know the right things to say. She would know what to do. But the real Lilly wasn't here and she had taken all of her faith and wisdom with her.

Just ahead, I spied the flat, black surface of my *listening rock*. While some people had thinking rocks to sit upon and ponder, this rock had been allotted a very different purpose. 'If there's ever a time when when you don't know what to do and you can't solve it by thinking, stop, close your eyes and *listen*,' my mum had said. The eight-year-old me had thought the rock magical, and maybe it was. As she'd seated me, cross-legged, on its warm, black surface, shot through with sparkling veins of mica, I'd felt better.

I followed her directions now and *listened*. I listened to the creek burble happily over smooth stones. I heard the high cheer of birdsong – bright and close, then far and fading – sung in surprising bursts and fickle keys. Dragonflies whizzed above tall grasses on the far bank and skipped over the surface of the water. I tried to follow the elusive path of their flight but they were winged magicians; capturing the light and spinning it into flashes of amethyst and emerald green – there and gone in an instant. *Why can't I be a dragonfly?*

I sat and forced myself to simply listen and I did feel better for it. I would have sat longer but time was short. I needed to get to Earth and back before my parents came home. I stood, brushed off my skirt and closed my eyes to search for him. I didn't know if I was healed enough or strong enough to make this journey or even locate him. The effortlessness with which I'd always entered the black space between worlds now took all of my focus and concentration.

At long last, I felt the velvet pull of the darkness and I was drifting through empty space. The silence was thick, absolute, and almost made me weep with relief to meet it. I lingered, drinking in its nothingness like an antidote, wishing I could stay here for hours... days... suspended in soft stillness.

A familiar tug came at my heart and I turned, searching the blackness. A window to Earth was opening and I could make out a sun-kissed figure, lying face down at the edge of a rock pool with one hand stirring the surface. I shot toward him, my heart beating faster. His eyes were like the palest green glass as he stared into the water, so deep and dark, that it mirrored the trees and the wafting clouds above. He'd been swimming. His bronze skin shimmered with water droplets that trickled down his bare back and arms.

The ache in my heart grew and I lurched forward, pressing my palms to the veil. The thin membrane stretched as I pushed, but did not give way. My hands sprang back with elastic force. I tried again, digging in with determined fingers until I broke through. Great shocks of lightning splintered up my arms and flashed down my torso, the heat of it biting and stinging my skin. I hurtled through black and finally, mercifully, my feet touched down on the other side of the water hole under a scrubby stand of trees. I felt dizzy, but apart from that, I was okay.

The air was steamy and thick with the smells of leaf litter and fresh, still water. The sun was high and the day was scorching. Already beads of sweat slicked my brow. There wasn't another Soul in sight. We were all alone in this hidden place that reminded me so much of the crystal pools at home. I lingered out of sight, not wanting to walk forward. While I stood here, I could exist in a space of craving his touch instead of mourning its loss. The longer I stalled, the more time I had left before our last precious moment together would be over.

Jay lifted his chin to follow the flight of a bird in the pool's wavering reflection. Flashes of colour glinted on the water's surface. *Is that?* I looked up to see a sapient bird, or at least Earth's version of a sapient bird, circling and swooping above Jay. It was the strangest thing. These birds seemed to show up at life altering moments. The same kind of bird had been there when I'd seen Jay for the first time. It had been perched on his window sill and was the only thing that had made him smile. Then, when Jay had been stabbed and was bleeding out on a deserted street, a sapient bird had appeared at my window. If it hadn't been for that bird's insistent pecking on the glass, I might have dismissed my vision as a nightmare and Jay would have died that day. And now, here it was again; a lofty witness to the hard truths I needed to tell. Truths that could tear us apart.

I blinked the sunlight from my eyes and looked back to Jay. He was staring straight at me, his lips parted in astonishment. His green eyes were awash with a tumble of emotions, his lips; speechless.

"I'm so sorry, Jay. I would have come sooner, only I've been in healaxis... hospital... I was too sick to reach you." I snapped through the sticks and decaying leaves until I was standing at the edge of the pool. The heat radiating from the dark rocks rose up and wrapped around me in waves.

He scrambled to his feet. "Are you okay? I was out of my mind with worry." Water dripped from his bare skin speckling the dark rocks at his feet.

"Not really," I answered honestly. "I probably shouldn't be here but I needed to explain. I owe you that much."

He studied me, weighing my words. "Why do I feel like you're here to say goodbye?" He looked emptied and exhausted.

I hung my head, unable to meet his anxious eyes. The crushing feeling in my chest was making it hard to breathe. "I don't want it to be. I'd never want that, but I'll understand if that's what you choose."

"What's happened, Lilly? What's going on?"

I could hear him fighting to keep the panic out

of his voice. I sighed and started picking my way over the rocks to his side of the pool. "I have so much to tell you and it's hard to know how to start."

"Whatever it is, just tell me. We'll figure it out."

He was moving closer, leaving a trail of wet, black footprints behind him. I could feel myself being pulled into his orbit. It was a force I still didn't understand; a magnetic attraction with an inevitable outcome. Jay and I would always gravitate to one another. It was like a universal law.

We met in the middle, Jay wild-eyed and panting, our bodies colliding with want and need. He crushed me so fiercely his arms were like vices, and still, I wanted him to hold me tighter.

"God, I missed you," he exhaled.

I squeezed his waist, laying my cheek against his wet shoulder and breathed him in - sandalwood, salt and rain clouds. "I missed you, too. So much." I tipped my face into the sun and kissed him, raw and deep, a kiss to make up for all the kisses I would miss. I ran my fingers through his wet, silky strands and cupped his stubbled jaw - soft and sharp, all at once. I wanted to burn him into my memory; his taste, his smell, the heat of his skin under my hands.

"I love you," he gasped, drawing back to search my face. His eyes were bright and fevered and I didn't know if the rapid rise and fall of his chest was born of desire or panic.

I touched my lips softly to his cheek and slipped out of his arms. "Sit with me," I coaxed, taking his hands and lowering us to sit at the pool's edge. I kicked off my sandals and gathered my skirt up to my thighs. The cold bit as I lowered my feet into the dark water. Jay's long legs dangled beside me, his body pressed up close to mine, our shoulders joined together.

"Lilly, please tell me what's wrong. What happened to you?"

"After I left you at Ryan's party, I collapsed."

"From the stomach bug? I'm sorry I made you sick."

"It wasn't a stomach bug, Jay." The trees rustled as a dry gust of wind rattled through their limbs. Leaves bleached of their colour rained down around us. "You and I were never sick in that way. I'm a go-lite and you're a human. Our bodies aren't built to live in each others' worlds."

Confusion clouded his features. "What do you mean?" he struggled. "Are you saying I got sick because I went to Panacea?"

I gave a weighted, single nod. "The energy field of Panacea is too high for your body," I explained gently, "and the energy field of Earth is too low for mine. Being somewhere we don't belong causes our energy fields to tear. It makes us sick, Jay, really sick."

"But you said your great-grandmother was human and she lived on Panacea," he argued.

"Yes, she did, but only after she'd raised the vibration of her energy field enough that she could survive there."

He plucked up a dried leaf and began picking it apart. "By learning to think and act like a go-lite?"

"Yes, and by completing whatever cosmic ritual is hidden in the pages of my great-grandfather's manuscript. I'm still trying to decipher his instructions." I waited for him to piece together the awful truth. There would be no more visits like this. This would be the last time I would stand on planet Earth and the last time I would hold Jay in my arms, until he grew into the strong, wise and beautiful Soul I knew was inside him.

I had no illusions. I knew it could take years of waiting. All I had now were my hopes and dreams and a thundering beat in my chest that told me to hold on.

"How sick were you?" Jay's hands were fisted on his thighs, his knuckles bloodless and pale. The vertical line carved between his brows deepened.

"They said I almost died."

Jay gasped and grabbed my hand, squeezing it tight. He needed to hear just how serious the consequences were for what we had done. I had to make him understand that visiting each others' worlds was no longer an option.

"I was unconscious and delirious after my third collapse. My energy field was torn to shreds and it took a team of Healers to save me."

"And now? Are you okay?" Panic was rising in his

voice.

"I feel like I'm halfway there. My body feels better each day but it's my mind that worries me. I've been emotional, erratic, not my usual self."

"Lilly! You should not be here! Jesus Christ, what were you thinking? You can't risk yourself like this for me."

"I was thinking," I winced, "that I had to kiss you one last time."

Tears welled in Jay's eyes, the bright sunlight knifing to the depths of two aquamarine lagoons. His sandy hair ruffled in the hot breeze as he reached for me. Supple lips brushed over my cheeks, my forehead, as light as feathers. His arms came around me and scooped me up, lifting me onto his lap. Our cool, wet legs twined together. Rough palms ran the length of my spine and circled my hips.

"I'll still be able to see you and talk to you through the veil," I whispered, laying my head on his shoulder. "If you want me to, I'll still wait... for as long as it takes."

I closed my eyes and let his scent fill up my senses. We sat still and quiet for a long time, our bodies moulding together, breathing as one.

Jay eventually stirred. He turned to nuzzle his lips to my ear. "I want you to know that you mean everything to me," he whispered, "and that's why I'm going to try as hard as I can to be someone who can walk beside you as an equal. You've shown me what it means to be truly loved and I want to be there for you, the way you've always been there for me."

I lifted my head to look into his eyes. They were fierce with determination. "But," he sighed, "this isn't going to be a short or easy road, so I need to know that you've really thought this through. Are you positive this is what you want?"

"Yes," I touched my lips to his, "I'm sure."

His hand came up to cup my cheek with such tenderness it sent a shiver through my whole body. I returned the gesture, stroking my fingers across his olive skin. I stared into his eyes, my head swimming with the love I felt for him and when he kissed me, the heat that coursed through my body like fire was almost unbearable. He pulled back and gave me a wicked grin before pushing off the rock and sliding us both into the chill, inky water.

I managed to squeal before my head plunged below the surface. I came up gasping, wide eyed from the cold shock, as Jay's laughter rattled off the rocks and carried into the trees above. "Come here," he laughed, scooping me into his arms.

"You're a beast!" I swatted at him.

"And you're a beauty."

He kissed me deeply, stealing my ragged breath and sending a rush of fire over my cooling skin. I tasted the sweet, fresh water on his lips, felt him steering us from the centre of the water hole to it's warmer, rocky edge. My back met the hot stone raising goosebumps of delight on my skin. Jay pressed his body against mine and kissed me again, working his way along my jaw and neck, tangling his fingers in my dripping hair. He eased me onto a ledge and my legs wrapped around him, drawing him hard against me. The trees groaned in the rising wind. It blew in hot gusts, sending showers of frenzied leaves skittering around our twined bodies. His hands explored my shape, moulding to every dip and curve, skimming the jut of my hipbones, gliding over my thighs. I tipped back my head, sighing into the sun, feeling his fingers slick on my skin, delving to my core.

"I want you," he breathed into my ear.

My hands spasmed, gripping the hard muscle of his back.

"I'm yours," I gasped.

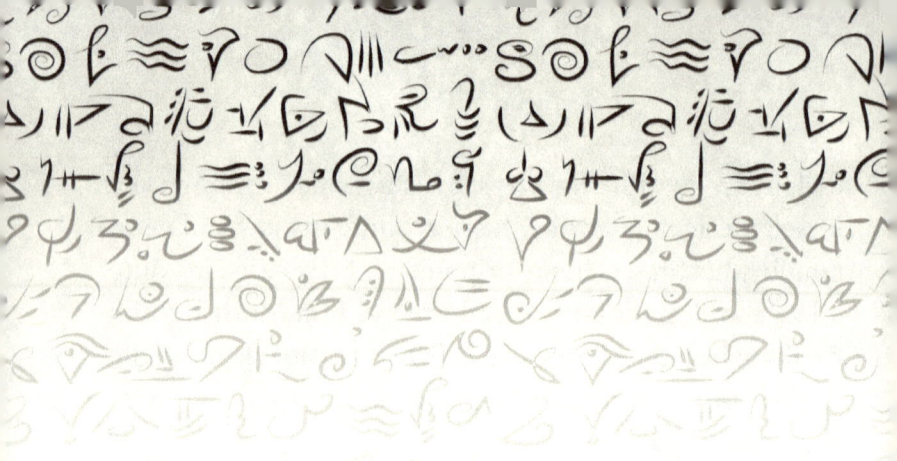

TWENTY-FIVE

Christian

I smoothed my hand down Houdini's ebony neck and stroked the faded scars on his flank. He lay on his side in a bed of fresh hay, a white cloud of foam bubbling from his mouth. I had asked Lilly's dad here to ease Houdini's passing, knowing that his spirit horse, Bo, would be a great comfort to him now. Jonathan stood just outside the stable, listening quietly, as Bo soothed and reassured my dying friend. I had visited him often and had tried my best to counsel him through the pain of what had been his life on Earth. He was one of the first animals Garrick had brought to Panacea and while Petra had worked tirelessly to keep him alive, after all he'd endured, he just didn't have the will to keep going.

Too many beatings had all but extinguished the light in his Soul and debilitating fear had settled in its place. Even if I'd had months or years to prove to him that he was safe, I doubted the terror would have left him. Some wounds were etched so deep that they took multiple lifetimes to heal. I prayed Houdini's next life would be kinder.

Petra knelt beside me, a wet cloth in her hand and squeezed small amounts of water into Houdini's mouth. He barely responded. It wouldn't be long now.

We'll miss you, my friend. I spoke into his mind and ran my fingers through his course mane.

I'm old... worn out. I'll be glad to end it, he rasped.

Then, may we meet again in another life, Houdini, where I'm sure we'll be the greatest of friends.

I hope for that too... and... thank you.

For what?

For having the care to give an old, broken-down horse a name.

I lay my head against his neck and stroked his mane until his last breath left him.

Petra scrubbed her hands over her face and sighed.

"You did your best," I told her. "He wanted to go."

"He did," Jonathan agreed from the stable door.

"Thank you so much for coming," I said to he and Bo. Even though I couldn't see the spirit horse, I had heard what he'd said to Houdini and I was so grateful that his words brought the old stallion some measure of peace.

"Of course," he smiled. "You're doing fine work, Petra. And not just with the animals. You were first to consider the vibratory scale as a key factor in all of this and you were right. You've given credence to my Grandfather's life's work, so thank you, and very well done."

She stood, brushing the straw from her knees and gave him a weary smile.

"Half the Council are inside with Garrick Leif. I think it's time we joined them. The poor boy will probably feel less intimidated with you there, Chris." He shrugged on the sunshine yellow robe that had been hanging over his arm and looped the cord at his waist. "You've both done all you could for Houdini, but now there's a young boy inside who needs your help too."

Petra and I both gave Houdini a lingering look, lying peacefully in a bed of hay, and followed Elder Flights up the leafy track to The Haven's back door. The halls were a bustle of activity. There were twice as many people here as there had been last week. Jordan strolled past us with a chimpanzee clinging to his hip and pulling at his long, pale hair.

"What in The Source's name are you doing?" Petra frowned at him.

"They're questioning Garrick and the animals about his Gift. They want to hear both perspectives."

Petra shot me a worried look and stopped to check on the chimp. We continued down the hall without her. I had purposely kept the animals' failing health from Garrick. I hadn't wanted to burden a sick boy with such terrible news.

"Is that a good idea?" I asked Jonathan.

"It was decided late last night that the best way to dissuade Garrick from teleporting any more animals was to tell him the truth. We've explained the vibrational scale to him and that all of the animals he rescued are slowly dying. Healer Dwano has also explained that if he continues this way, he'll die too."

My heart went out to Garrick. It must have come as a terrible blow but he *did* need to know the truth. "Has it worked?"

"We think so and we're hoping it continues to work because we have no idea how to stop him, otherwise. Did you know Lilly came home this morning?" he asked, changing the subject.

"No," I brightened. "How is she? She must be doing better if they sent her home." I grinned widely at the wonderful news. After so much worry, it was like being struck and finding you could still produce a high note.

"The Healers can't tell us why her energy field is torn. Has she said anything to you, Chris? Or did you see anything out of the ordinary that might explain it?"

"I can tell you that she's definitely not teleporting animals from Earth, so, no, I don't know why. Garrick told me he grabbed her arm just before she collapsed at his bedside. He was worried he might have caused it somehow, but that seems flimsy at best. I have nothing else to go on except she's been tired and distracted for a while now. And I'd noticed that she was acting strangely before she wound up in healaxis."

"Dawn and I are going to sit her down tonight and ask her if she knows why her energy field is torn. She hasn't been well enough or coherent enough until now, but she seems to be healing, and we need to get to the bottom of what happened to our daughter."

I had to forcibly hold back my relief. *Thank The Source.* I hoped her parents could find the explanation that I had failed to uncover and prevent this from happening to her again.

When we reached the conference room, Grand Master Mont was slowly pacing the floor, taking in all the data displayed on the crystal screens, his saffron robes billowing behind him. Grand Master Willow sat placidly with her violet eyes trained on a wrung-out looking Garrick. Grand Master Trill was not there. She had retired to her sanctuary for rest and recuperation. Apparently the quality of her visions had not improved. Half of the Council were assembled, dotted about the room in animated discussion while a forlorn peacock drooped in the centre of it all by Garrick's feet.

Petra appeared beside me at the doorway, her lips pursed in consternation while I fought to stifle a laugh. I couldn't help it. I could have blamed my impropriety on lack of sleep, too much work, or the need to balance out all the gloom of late, but the wilting peacock was solely to blame. You see, I couldn't help but wonder if it was the same peacock Sky had applauded for pooping on Scholar

Wymis's statue. If so, this sad looking creature was Sky's unlikely hero.

Jonathan slipped in ahead of us and took a seat next to Elder Jasper Avris at one of the laboratory benches.

"Translator Palladen," Elder Wynters threw up her spindly hands at the sight of me, "thank The Source you're here." Rose Wynters was slight and stretched. She was uncategorically tall. Her hair was a perpetual bouffant of snags and snarls which added convincingly to the argument that she was more tree than woman. "Can you please reiterate your thoughts on the boy's heart connection and how it allows him to pierce the veil?"

I hadn't even entered the room and my work had already begun. "I'm not sure I can be of much help beyond a rudimentary theory, Elder Wynters."

"Nevertheless," she waved a limb at me, "we are agreed that your insight may prove correct and would appreciate hearing how you arrived at the notion."

"Please, come in," Grand Master Mont motioned us forward, his beaded braids swinging.

I went to stand by Garrick and placed a steadying hand on his shoulder. His head jerked up and he cast me a relieved look that soon turned to pleading. I wondered how long he'd been sitting here. I said a silent hello to the peacock. It gave a despondent ruffle of its feathers and ignored me, but cosied up to Petra quickly enough when she knelt to check on it. I looked at the gathered Elders, clustered on lab stools in their colourful robes and colourless expressions, and cleared my throat.

"Garrick is a Translator," I addressed the waiting crowd. "I understand his compassion and empathy for those endangered Earth animals, and yet, my own compassion has never caused an Earth animal to magically appear in our world. So what makes Garrick different?" I bent down to speak to Garrick directly, "Can you try to explain to them how your heart feels when you see an animal in trouble?" The boy sighed and nodded. "Don't be shy, just tell them the truth."

"I can feel their pain," Garrick said simply.

"We are go-lites, Garrick. We can all feel the emotions of Earth Souls," Jonathan said in his gentle way, "but we also understand that they have been born into that world for a reason and we do not have the right to interfere with their destiny or take them away from their homes. By removing those animals from what you have judged to be horrible circumstances, you are robbing them of the very experiences their Souls went there to have. Every experience holds a lesson. It isn't up to us to judge the ways in which they learn them."

"I know that, Elder Flights, but I can't help it," Garrick winced. "I don't have any control over what my heart does when I see these things."

"But you seem to be controlling it now. You haven't let any animals into Panacea since we made you aware of the consequences."

"It isn't easy, but no, I haven't let any through. I

don't want them to suffer any more than they already are. I don't want to be responsible for any more deaths."

Many of the Elders had their heads bent in silent consultation with their spirit animals. For the first time, I noticed Elder Tunes tucked into the far corner at the back of the room. I smiled at him in greeting and his face lit up like a firework. He had not been present at any of the recent Council meetings and he listened now with studious intent.

"When you say you had no control over your heart, can you describe to us what it did, how it felt in those moments?" Grand Master Willow encouraged.

"It felt like it was going to beat out of my chest... like it suddenly became stronger and bigger and I could feel something inside it reaching out to those animals. And then... I don't know... it was almost like that energy poured out of my heart and lassoed them and pulled them to me."

It was a much better description than Garrick had originally managed from his bed in healaxis and one that had the Elders knitting their brows together and talking in low, puzzled voices... all but Elder Tunes. His already jolly face seemed lit from within. His clear, blue eyes twinkled as he gazed at Garrick, held in thrall by what he'd just heard. He seemed... excited.

"And how does our peacock friend describe the experience of being pulled through the veil? Can one of you translate, please?" Grand Master Mont looked from

Garrick to me.

"Go ahead," I urged Garrick, hoping it would settle him and boost his confidence.

I listened while he asked the peacock, Rodriego, what it had felt like for him. It was similar to what Uma the elephant had told me - hurtling through black, blinding flashes of lightning - but the peacock also described a hot, needling sensation.

My eyes kept drifting to Elder Tunes and I noticed he was mildly perplexed by that last piece of information. I wondered if Lilly had been in contact with him about her work on the manuscript. *Did Elder Tunes even know Lilly had been diagnosed with tears in her energy field and had nearly died?* If he was the person who had encouraged Lilly to decipher Grayson's manuscript, maybe he could tell me if it was dangerous work, if it might be connected to her illness. I decided I should definitely speak with him after this meeting was over.

Elder Lola Zenith rose and addressed the room. "Piccolo has a question for Garrick." She and her spirit stag had been engaged in conversation for most of the meeting. Like Lilly's dad, she was a Traveller. They were the only Travellers on the Council and probably stood the best chance of understanding Garrick's strange, new Gift that seemed to be an amplified extension of their own. "He wants to know if you have ever Travelled yourself. Have you ever teleported yourself from one place to another or is your Gift limited to transporting others?"

Garrick sighed so deeply and his shoulders sagged so low, I thought he would disappear into the floor. "I can't say for sure. I was delirious. But while I was in healaxis I think I might have Travelled to Earth for a few seconds."

A shocked silence blanketed the room. This gangly, freckled kid was a maverick. He had single-handedly turned the go-lite ethos on its head.

Elder Zenith came forward and squatted next to Garrick's chair. Her lips were stained the same magenta as her robes. She pushed back a tight ringlet of black hair that was skimming the rim of her glasses. "What do you remember?"

"Tall grasses, heat, dust. It looked like Africa and for a moment it felt like I was there, not just watching through the veil, but really there."

"Do you remember anything else? Did you have the same feeling in your heart? Did you see lightning flashes like the animals or feel the hot needles they've described?"

"No, I felt like I was being lifted up on a giant wave and thrown forward toward Earth. It felt so wonderful I thought it must be a dream, but then I felt dirt under my bare feet and could smell the air. It was only for a few moments but it felt so real."

"Thank you, Garrick," she patted his hand and stood.

I looked at her; shell-shocked. Urgent murmurs passed around the room bearing the weight of worlds.

As though it weren't incredible enough that Garrick could teleport Souls to Panacea, now he'd admitted to teleporting himself to Earth.

"When did this happen?" asked Grand Master Mont.

"Acolyte Flights came to visit me in healaxis. She healed me enough to wake me from twilight sleep. I was panicked and afraid and grabbed her arm and then she fainted. I remember seeing her fall to the ground and a few seconds later I blacked out again. Then I felt my heart beating out of my chest, felt a rush as I was pulled forward and then my feet hit the dirt."

A light voice drifted from the back of the room quieting the hubbub. "Excuse me, my dear boy," Elder Tunes' glacial eyes fixed on Garrick, "earlier you described how it feels to transport these animals from Earth. You said it was as though an energy reached out from your heart and lassoed them. So, it begs the question, whose heart reached out and lassoed you? Whose energy pulled you to Earth?"

Gasps of understanding escaped more than one of the Elders.

"A two-way connection," Grand Master Willow mused. "Do you know who your connection is on Earth, Garrick? Did you see anyone else?"

"Just a lion."

I looked at Elder Tunes. "Sadascus the lion," I breathed. "He appeared that day."

Elder Tunes' expression swelled with elation. "Wonderful!" he clapped. "Just wonderful."

"Hundreds of animals appeared that day," Petra shrugged.

"Yes, but King Sadascus arrived at the same time that Lilly collapsed and Garrick touched down on Earth. I doubt that's a coincidence."

"A lion?" Garrick blinked. "Are you saying there's a lion with the magical power to lasso me and pull me to Earth?"

The entire room hesitated while they contemplated how outlandish that sounded, everyone except Atticus Tunes. "My, but you are a marvel!" he hooted. "That is precisely what Translator Palladen is saying... in theory, of course."

There was only one way to find out if there was any truth to it. We would have to introduce Garrick to King Sadascus and see if a magical connection made itself apparent.

"I apologise for my absence these last few weeks," Elder Tunes continued. "Much has happened while I've spent long days in silence seeking guidance from The Source. I have been given leave to share information that's relevant to this inquiry. It concerns my father, Thomas Tunes, and his lifelong friendship with Grayson Flights. I am in possession of my father's personal journal which states that Grayson also breached the veil and Travelled to Earth. Garrick is not the first go-lite to do so."

Jonathan's head whipped around to the back of the room, as did all the Elders.

Aldos Mont was the first to recover himself and speak. "Atticus, why have you never shared this information before?"

"Grayson and my father were bound by The One Source to keep his work a secret unless a time came when it was needed. Until now, there hasn't been a need to make Grayson's discoveries known, but while I was meditating in The Blue Caves, The Source revealed that the time had come to tell you what I know. I have returned to share this message: Grayson Flights' greatest work was not postulating the vibratory scale of ascendency, but proving it. He was tasked with finding a means to cross the veil and transport Souls from Earth."

"And did he? Did he transport Souls from Earth to Panacea?" Jon was pale as parchment.

Elder Tunes smiled at him kindly. "Just one. His wife, Aurora."

I was biting back a list of questions, and I could see Petra was too, while the Elders, with the exception of Jon, slipped into tranquil rumination and quiet discussion of all that had been laid bare here today. Before too long, Grand Master Mont called an end to the meeting, saying there was more than enough information to digest for one day and that Garrick would need his rest for meeting Sadascus tomorrow.

"Well, I think I've heard more than enough mind

bending testimony for one day." Petra plucked up the sad peacock and cradled it to her chest. "I'm taking him back to his enclosure. See you tomorrow?"

"Sure." I nodded.

Garrick stood wearily and shuffled for the door. "You're doing great," I told him. "Get some rest. Tomorrow you'll have more work to do."

"Chris, what does this all mean? What's going to happen?" He was nervously chewing his lip.

I wished I knew what to tell him but I wasn't privy to The Source's greater plan. "I don't know, Garrick, but the Elders will work it out. Don't worry. The important thing for now is that you aren't bringing any more animals to Panacea and you're getting well."

He nodded uncertainly and disappeared through the door like a ghost.

Elder Tunes was at the back of the room and had been waylaid by Elder Melladon, a powerful Projector. He paved the path of my approach with a serene smile. He was dressed in the un-dyed robes of the Seeker. His white hair was like thin wisps of cloud encircling his moon shaped face.

"I've been studying the disruption of our weather patterns and believe they have been caused by the veil being breached," Elder Melladon was saying. "Whenever Garrick penetrates the veil and draws Souls through it, I think a rush of Earth's energy is pouring through and wreaking havoc on the delicate balance of our world.

Everything we've witnessed – the tears in the animal's energy fields, their failing health, and the changes in our own environment – all supports Healer Honeywell's assertion that the vibrational scale of ascendency can be proven as fact."

"Fascinating," Elder Tunes grinned, "but if you will excuse me, I think this young man would like a word. Translator Palladen, how may I serve?"

"Elder Tunes, I'm sorry to bother you when you've only just arrived back from retreat."

"Yes, *I have* only just returned," he said holding up a section of his dun coloured robe. "A thousand pardons if I'm less than fresh. My body yearns for a cake of hard oatmeal soap and a deep, hot tub, yet my spirit wishes to climb back up to the caves. The Blue Mountain is glorious this time of year."

"So I've heard."

"Oh, but you must go and see for yourself! There is nothing quite like *mantyla* crystal for opening the mind and purifying vision."

The mountain housed a labyrinth of blue crystal caves where go-lites had journeyed for thousands of years to seek higher wisdom.

"And now you've returned to a city in crisis. Have you been away long?"

"Well, let me see," he drummed his stubby fingers against his chin. "I believe I've been away precisely as long as I chose and not a moment more than was needed," he cocked his head with a grin.

"I only wondered if you were aware that Lilly has been gravely ill. She was diagnosed with tears in her energy field. The Healers cannot fathom why. I'm fairly certain she hasn't been transporting animals from Earth like Garrick."

The smile drained from his face. "No, I was not aware. Is she all right? I must go and see her."

"She's healing and I'm sure she'd be glad of the visit. I know that you've given her some pointers on how to decipher Grayson Flights' manuscript, which she has been dedicating herself to." He seemed entirely unsurprised that I had this knowledge. "But then she collapsed and almost died."

"So you're wondering if her work on translating the manuscript is to blame?"

"The question has been on my mind, yes."

Elder Tunes considered me with soft, still eyes of glacier blue. The longer I looked into them, the more I felt as though I was being gifted with the serenity of the Blue Mountain.

"So, do you think it's possible?" I asked again after a long silence. "Could Lilly's efforts on the manuscript have caused her energy field to tear?"

"Oh! You were expecting an answer?" he giggled ruefully. "I'm terribly sorry, my boy, but I fear I don't have one to give. At least not one rooted in fact or understanding."

"Your best guess, then?" I pressed, knowing full well that the sky would have to be falling down before he'd share in my feeling of urgency. The Elders were largely unflappable, preferring to hold fast to their faith through any storm. They rarely wasted energy on asking 'why?' Instead, they repeated a choice to go with the flow, cultivating faith in The Source's larger plan.

"At a guess, I would say, no. I wouldn't think the act of deciphering and reading script from a book to be detrimental to one's health, even a magical book like Grayson's manuscript." His voice drifted off with his thoughts and I could hear a silent 'but' on his tongue. After a few moments his smile returned, mapping his face in jolly crinkles. "I sense we are on the brink of great change; I have sensed it for a while now and I know the other Elders feel it too. It's the reason I retreated and sought guidance from The Source. I was instructed to share Grayson's discovery because the time was right."

"Do you know why, Elder Tunes? Did The Source show you what's going to happen?"

"Patience, my boy," he waved a stubby hand. "If you rush to reach the last page, you'll miss your own story. There's nothing to fear. We are always given precisely what we need at the time we need it. The Source makes it so," he winked.

I paused, hesitant. "Elder tunes, I have to ask, Lilly wouldn't tell me, but is she attempting to translate Grayson Flights instructions on how he breached the veil? Is that what is encoded inside his manuscript?"

"We cannot know for certain what the invisible writings hold, not until she deciphers them. But yes, I have long suspected that he hid the keys to his discoveries and his life's work inside The Vibratory Scale of Ascendency. Since inheriting my father's journal and the secret knowledge of Grayson's inter-dimensional feats, it seemed like a logical place to look. Then the discovery was made that Lilly has the ability to read his hidden writings. Clearly, she is meant to translate the invisible script but reading the symbols with one's heart is a challenging skill to perfect and I doubt she's made much progress as yet. These things take time. I'll pay her a visit in the next few days and see if she's made any headway."

I was suffering from information overload and instead of making things clearer, I still didn't have an answer to the question that haunted me most.

Elder Tunes gave me a gentle clap on the shoulder. "Don't fret, my boy. She's doing The Source's work."

I realised I had been staring over Elder Tunes' head at the blank, grey wall. That one question kept repeating louder than all the rest: why was Lilly's energy field torn?

"I must speak with Elder Flights," Elder Tunes was saying. "He'll no doubt have questions about my father's journal and the surprising news of his grandfather's Travels to Earth. But before I go, Translator, may I ask you a question?"

"Yes," I blinked myself from my daze, "of course."

"Had I said that Lilly's work *was* detrimental to her health, what would you do?"

I paused, reliving Evangeline's disturbing vision in my memory. None of it had come to pass yet. Lilly was still alive, no-one else had died, the city hadn't been reduced to a pile of rubble. "I would tell her what I'd learned; in facts as plain as I could manage and let her decide her own course."

"No colouring the facts with your own fears and judgements?"

I shook my head. "No, I made a promise."

"Good," he smiled. "Very good. With that, he floated serenely over to Lilly's dad who was waiting for him.

I sat on the stool that Elder Tunes had vacated. My head was swimming. The answer to my question was becoming clear. There was no other explanation for why Lilly's energy field was torn and her father, Elder Tunes and the rest of The Council must surely have arrived at the same conclusion. With all we had learned today, it seemed undeniable – Lilly had the ability to breach the veil. If the Elders had forgotten about her in the whirlwind of information that had been exchanged, it wouldn't be long before they made the connection.

I sat there, stunned. It was inconceivable that this could have happened to her and I didn't know. Had the distance between us become so great? Was the dam dividing us so impenetrable that I no longer knew my best friend? I'd been completely engrossed in my work at Haven and solving the mystery of Garrick and the animals, not to mention wrestling with my feelings for her and then finding out she had a boyfriend, that it hadn't occurred to me that Lilly might share Garrick's confounding ability.

Garrick's Gift had seemed to manifest spontaneously; perhaps the same thing had happened to Lilly. Had she been caught unawares and frightened by her power, as Garrick had been? My heart went out to her. I wished I could have been there for her but Elder Tunes had said that The Source had demanded it be kept secret. I remembered snippets of my conversations with Lilly, she had said The Source had presented her with a challenge that she couldn't share with me. But once she came clean about deciphering the manuscript, I'd thought that's all there was to her secret. I never for a second imagined that she was like Garrick. How had she kept her Gift hidden from everyone? Then I remembered, she hadn't. Sky knew. Sky had known what Lilly could do all along.

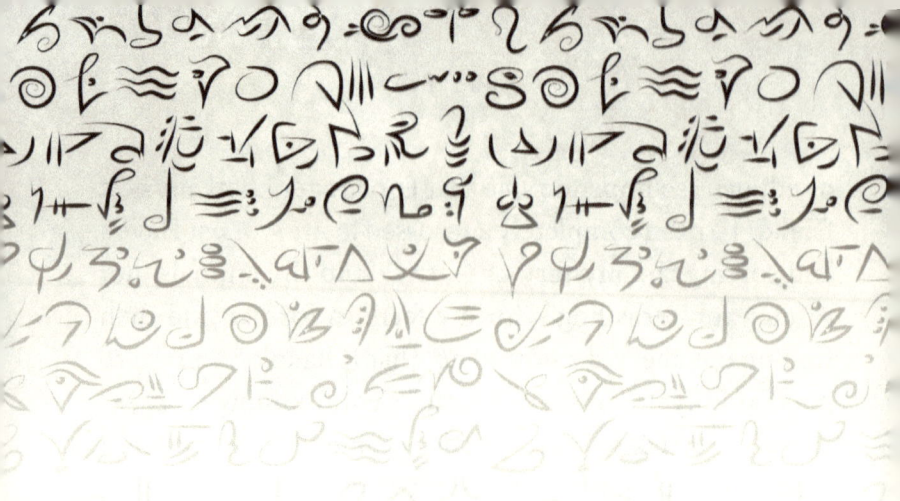

TWENTY-SIX

Christian

I went home and showered, standing for a long time under the steamy spray to sort through my thoughts. I'd barely slept for a week. Instead, I'd lay awake for hours staring at the canopy of trees through my bedroom window going over all the puzzle pieces. When I did manage to snatch an hour or two of sleep, I was inundated by Earth Souls needing guidance. It was nothing these days to help four or five Souls in one night, as opposed to the usual one or two. It was taking a toll on all of us... everyone except for Lilly.

She'd had no knowledge of the last two major crises on Earth until Sky or myself mentioned it. She had openly admitted that not a single Soul had called on her for help which she attributed to all the energy she was expending on the manuscript. Now I wondered if she wasn't spending that energy on taking trips through the veil.

Now that we had a better grasp of the power Garrick held and the consequences of using that power, the more likely it seemed that Lilly shared his Gift. I was worried about her. I was walking around with a permanent knot in my stomach because I could feel she was in trouble but I was shackled by my promise to not interfere.

I shut off the water and slung a towel around my hips. If what I was thinking about her was true, if Lilly truly could travel to Earth, she needed to have all the facts about her ability. I felt an urgency to speak with her, to tell her everything I'd learned today. I would arm her with all the information we had gathered and trust her to use it wisely. I'd almost lost her once and I never wanted to feel like that again.

Violet clouds strangled a pewter sky and rain lashed down in sheets of silver. A squalling wind was bending trees and tossing debris like confetti. This storm had sprung from nowhere.

I ran from my car and dashed up the Flights' front steps. The wind tore at my clothes and I was drenched in seconds. I pounded on the door. I'd messaged Lilly to say I was coming round. I'd made it three quarters of the way before this freakish storm hit.

Lilly opened the door and a blast of wind sent her

hair flying. "Thank The Source you're all right! Quick, come in." She grabbed my hand and pulled me inside, slamming the door. Her hair floated back down like feathers. "You're soaked through. Stay there and drip in one spot while I get you a towel."

I took off my soggy shoes and put them by the door. "How are you feeling?" I yelled after her down the hall.

"It's nice to be home. I don't miss lying in bed all day, being delirious, and not remembering what I've said to anyone."

A wry smile tugged at my lips as she reappeared. "Who told you?"

"My mother," she huffed, filled with embarrassment. "I'm really sorry if I said or did anything hurtful." She handed me the towel, her cheeks reddening. "She also told me that you all forgive me."

I wiped the water from my face and caught her in a contemplative stare. "You were pretty rough on us," I said solemnly. "Especially Gabe. You kept gazing at him with a dopey smile on your face and calling him Captain Cuddles."

"Whaaat?"

The look of sheer horror on her face sent me into fits of laughter.

"That's not funny!" she shrilled, swatting at my arm.

"All right. Would you prefer I told you what you

called me, instead?"

"No!"

"Suit yourself," I shrugged. "It was magical though," I said with a dreamy sigh. "A moment I'll always treasure."

It was wonderful to see her laugh, to watch the feelings of guilt melting away, even if they were being replaced by the urge to throttle me instead.

"Okay, you're dry enough," she said, grabbing the towel. "Come into the living room. What did you have to tell me?"

I followed her, barefoot, across the polished boards. I looked at the floral lounge suite and then at my damp clothes and decided to remain standing. Silver rain lashed the window panes, rattling them in their frames. The world outside was a squalling mess of white. "I've just come from another Council meeting. Garrick was there."

"Garrick Leif?" She turned to face me, looking incredibly ill at ease. All the laughter had drained from her face. "Shouldn't they be working out how Earth animals are materialising on Panacea instead of questioning a boy who's been seriously ill?" she snapped.

I was becoming used to her unruly outbursts and had decided on a new way of handling them. I raised my voice. "Do you want to hear what I've driven through a hurricane to tell you, or not?" I snapped back and the fire went out of her immediately.

She bit her lip and gave me a chastened look.

"Yes, sorry. Go on."

"Garrick is extraordinary," I told her. "He has a new and powerful Gift." I paused to gauge her reaction to my news. There was not even a flicker of surprise. "He has the ability to pierce the veil between worlds and Travel to Earth," I said, sounding like one of Earth's TV reporters. She didn't so much as blink because I was telling her things she already knew and was capable of herself.

Her expression was guarded. "Do you know why he has this Gift?" she asked, confused. "I mean, what would be the point of a fifteen year old kid going to Earth?"

"It's beautiful, actually," I smiled. "He's attempting to rescue endangered animals."

"Animals?" she gaped at me, stunned. Her wide eyes blinked slowly as she dropped onto the sofa, her lips parting in surprise.

"He's admitted to the bees, Houdini, all of them. It was him all along. He's teleported hundreds of animals to Panacea in an attempt to save them."

"This is absurd," she whispered, staring blankly at a pile of her mum's cookbooks stacked on the coffee table. "But why?" She was looking at me imploringly as though she thought I'd magically have the answer. "Why in The Source's name would he be granted the ability to bring animals to Panacea? It doesn't make any sense." Her eyes were darting about the room as she processed. She was shaking her head back and forth, her expression hard.

"Lilly, what is it? Are you all right?" The sound of

my voice made her head snap up. She took a deliberate, practiced breath and smoothed her expression but I could still see the confusion in her eyes.

She looked as though she were about to choke. A sheen of sweat was dampening her hairline and she was turning grey, like she might throw up. "But he can't!" she blurted.

I considered her with raised brows.

She fumbled with a tassel on the couch cushion. "I only meant that it's dangerous," she blustered, trying to protect what she knew.

"And how would you know that?" I asked slowly, wondering if she would finally tell me the truth. Then I realised Lilly had no idea that her great-grandfather's secret had been outed at The Council meeting. I could relieve her of the burden of keeping his secret, right here, right now. "Elder Tunes was at the meeting. He's been away on spiritual retreat, seeking counsel, and The Source instructed him that the time was right to reveal your family secret."

She looked up and gasped. It must have been such a heavy burden for her to keep Grayson's secret all this time.

"He told us about your great-grandfather and how he discovered a way to breach the veil and travel to Earth *and* bring your great-grandmother here. The whole Council knows, including your dad, so I guess that means you don't have to keep it a secret anymore."

She collapsed back into the sofa cushions and closed her eyes in relief. "Thank The Source, I'm so sick and tired of secrets," she wailed. "If I'd been allowed to tell you, Chris, I would have. That's what I've been trying to decipher in Grayson's journal. Hidden in those pages, is his method for breaching the veil."

"Elder Tunes told me as much, or at least he suspected that's what might be in there."

"A few days ago I found the answer to why Garrick's energy field was torn. Breaching the veil, having contact with the lower vibration of Earth, it creates damage."

"And Petra discovered that the animals' energy fields were torn too and that's why they're dying. The higher vibration of Panacea is incompatible with their bodies."

"That's horrible! So all of Garrick's efforts were wasted? He ended up dooming the animals instead of saving them?"

I nodded, "And that's not all, Elder Melladon thinks that by allowing Earth's energy to leak through the veil, it's affected the balance of our world. He believes that these weather anomalies are the result." I waved an arm at the raging storm outside.

"The weather?" Her eyebrows shot up in alarm. "I hadn't thought of that, but I suppose it makes sense."

"The only thing left that doesn't make any sense," I caught her eye and held her in my gaze, "is why *your* energy field is torn, Lilly."

She met me with silence. It didn't matter how hard she tried to mask her feelings, I knew her. I could read every twitch of her lips and the way her shoulders were braced. There was a trace of pleading in her eyes, begging me to forgive her but there was nothing to forgive and no reason for her to keep her Gift a secret anymore. I turned away to allow her some breathing room. She probably felt just as frightened as Garrick had when he'd finally told the truth. I walked to the window and watched the whitewash consume the trees and the range beyond. I could barely see where the sky ended and the mountain peaks began.

A soft hum sounded behind me – Lilly's uniter. I turned to see her reach for it on the coffee table, her face stricken. Her eyes met mine for the briefest moment and they were filled with tears. My heart leapt and I hurried to her side. Her hand was shaking as she looked into the screen. "Dad?" she struggled. "What's wrong?"

Jon's face was red and his eyes glazed. I put my arm around Lilly's shoulder and braced her against me.

"Lilly. I'm so sorry, my little flower." Tears rolled down his face. "It's your mum." His voice cracked and his kind face contorted with pain. He was shaking his head and fighting to get the words out. "She's gone, sweetheart. She's gone."

Lilly was rigid against me, shaking like a leaf. "What happened?" I asked. I was fighting back tears of my own.

"She called me from the coast. It happened so fast I didn't understand what was going on. She said Lilly and I had made her happier than any Soul had a right to be and then I saw the wave loom up and wash her away."

"What wave?" Lilly shrieked. Her body convulsed with every sob like she were being electrocuted.

"The storm caused a tidal surge and three villages along the coast have been wiped out. Hundreds are dead."

"How do you know?" she wailed angrily. "There could be survivors!"

"I'm so sorry, honey," he shook his head. "I saw what came for her. I watched it happen. No-one could have survived that, and," he lay his hand over his heart, "I can feel that she's gone."

"No!" Lilly screamed.

I took the uniter from her shaking hand before she dropped it and pulled her to my chest. Her pain ripped through me like steel claws. Tears spilled down my cheeks as her body bucked with every gut-wrenching sob. "I'm so sorry, Jon. Dawn was my second mum. I loved her. May her Soul light a new world."

"Thank you, Christian." He wiped away another surge of tears and swallowed hard. "May her Soul light a new world. Can you stay with Lilly until I make it home?"

"Of course. Whatever you need. Where are you?"

"I know it's hopeless but I'm on the coast, or as close as the flood waters will allow me to get. I Travelled here to see for myself. I had to be sure."

I nodded.

"I'm in a coffee shop on Spicer's Ridge. I can see everything from here. The devastation is horrific."

Lilly jerked away from my chest and snatched the uniter. "Show me," she demanded.

Jon blanched. "Sweetheart, no, that's not a good idea."

"Please, Dad. I need to see."

He nodded once and made his way to the cafe window. The rain had eased to a steady downpour but it was still hard to see clearly through the fogged glass and from such a distance. The sea had been held back by the mountains but not before engulfing entire villages that had nested at their feet. I let out a gasp as the scene before me became sickeningly familiar. *Evangeline's prophecy: the aftermath of a natural disaster and a white memorial candle wreathed with white lilies and jasmine.*

It wasn't Lilly's memorial I had seen. It was Dawn's.

Lilly shuddered and turned away, burying her face in my chest. She had needed to see. It was the only way she could accept that her mother was gone.

"I'm coming home, sweetheart. I'll be there in ten minutes."

"I'll stay with her, Jon. See you soon." The uniter screen went blank.

"She was buying ingredients to make me a welcome home dinner." Lilly's voice was thin as wire. "I bet she was going to make sea scallops... my favourite... she would have driven to the coast to get the freshest and the best. It was supposed to be a surprise."

I gripped her shoulders and turned her body to face me. I reached out with the tip of my finger and lifted her chin, making her look at me. "Because she loves you, Lilly."

Her eyes were haunted pools as she shook her head in slow motion. "You mean she *loved* me. She's dead."

I choked back my tears and drew her close. She wasn't crying anymore. She'd gone into a cold state of shock. "That doesn't mean that the way you felt about each other is gone." I smoothed her hair back from her face. "Death doesn't erase love. When love is real, nothing can."

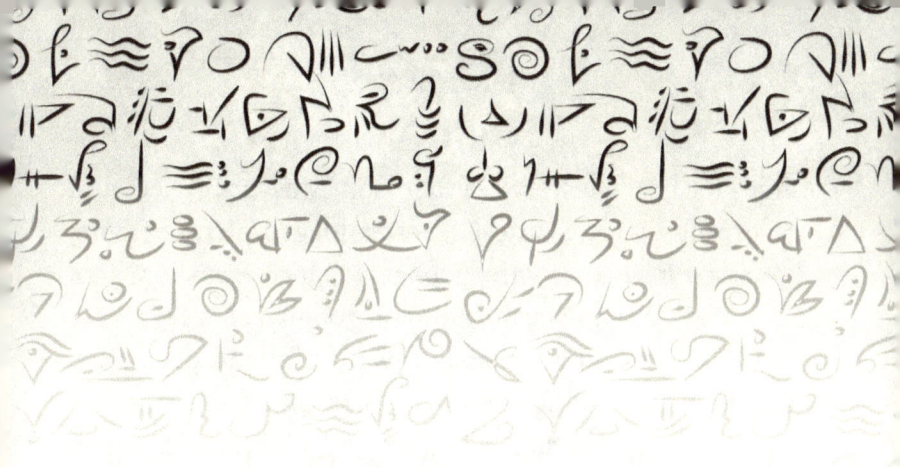

TWENTY-SEVEN

Lilly

The acrid stench of rot assaulted my nose and turned my stomach. Everywhere dead fish and seaweed lay wasting and baking, tangled with the remnants of people's homes and shattered lives. I picked my way through the mud and mangled tree branches. Lodged in the dead limbs were shredded clothes, pieces of smashed furniture and broken toys making them look like a macabre version of Earth's Christmas trees. Kilometres of the eastern coast had been devastated. All that remained was a rubbish heap of death and broken memories.

The sea beyond churned and crushed everything it had swallowed and unceremoniously spat the leftovers onto the shore. The waves looked like moving mountains of rubble. Stoic faces ghosted past me picking through the ruins of their lives.

An elderly woman clutched a wailing, frightened

child to her chest while her son was crumpled and mourning over a shattered, water-logged picture frame. I guessed it was his wife; probably ripped from him in a heartbeat with no warning and no goodbye. My legs were weak as I walked mindlessly toward him and placed my hands on his shaking shoulders. A radiant face smiled up at us from the frame, her golden eyes alight. She touched her fingers to her apricot lips and blew a kiss.

"I'm so very sorry," I whispered.

He didn't look at me. He just reached up to place his hand on mine. "Thank you... thank you," was all he said.

There was bile rising in my throat. He wouldn't be thanking me if he could look into my heart. It wasn't swelling with compassion, it was being strangled by guilt.

Right before the tidal wave erased so many lives, I had been with Jay. I had ignored Sky's warning and shut her out of my life. I had arrogantly ignored my great-grandfather's warning and had gone to Earth anyway. I was selfish and pig-headed and now I was almost certain that my final trip had caused the storm. The death of all of these people was my fault. My mother was dead because of me.

I stumbled and was sick into some flattened bushes. I clutched a leaning section of a tin roof to steady myself. It was speared deep in the mud, a bent mermaid weather vane pointing uselessly to the silver sun.

What Christian had shared with me made perfect

sense. I'd been backtracking in my head through all the visits I'd made to Earth and trying to remember if they coincided with abnormal weather. Not every visit caused a disruption but I knew I was definitely responsible for the snow. That was the night I'd brought Jay to my bedroom. The flooding rains all those weeks ago happened after I pierced the veil for the very first time. The heatwave I could blame on Garrick and the appearance of a grown elephant parading through town. And this, I looked at the carnage all around me, this was the price of being lost in the feeling of Jay's body pressed to mine. Guilt knifed through me. I couldn't reconcile how love could somehow be the cause of such acute suffering. Yet, here it was, everywhere I looked... pain and rot and death.

People moved solemnly through the debris. Already the clean up crews had amassed several piles of rubble to be hauled away. I was grateful my mum's body hadn't been uncovered in this horrible place. I prayed she had been carried out to sea, far away from here. I couldn't bear to think of her lost and buried in all this sadness. Most of the bodies had not been recovered so The Council had arranged a memorial. It was being held the day after tomorrow in the Butterfly Gardens and I didn't know how I was going to face it.

Sky had left me fifteen messages in the last two days. I couldn't bring myself to pick up my uniter. I just wanted to disappear. I was doing everything I could to take care of my dad and give him time to grieve mum's loss before I told him the truth. I was desperate to tell him that I'd caused the storm but I knew how selfish that would be. Even in my broken state, at least I recognised that the need to unburden myself would be too much for him at the moment.

I tripped on a broken window frame and fell to one knee in the stinking mud. My hands plunged wrist deep into brown ooze and I felt a slice across my left palm. I didn't have the energy to cry out. A young couple wearing galoshes and grim faces rushed to help me up. I snatched my arm away from the kind faced man. I didn't deserve their concern. I muttered a thank you and stumbled away, wiping mud and blood on my leaf green shirt.

I wandered back to the safety of the paved road, which had been mostly cleared, and headed for the beach. Out to sea, the gusting wind gouged tracks on the water's surface. It writhed like the skin of a giant serpent; its scales like chips of dull slate. The beach was stained with mud and littered with wreckage.

Christian's words had been playing over and over in my mind. Now that I knew I wasn't the only one who could Travel to Earth I was questioning everything I'd clung to so fiercely. I'd held fast to my belief that Jay and I were meant to find each other for a reason. I thought I knew what that reason was - that I was to help him ascend to Panacea, that he was my great love, bound to me across time and space, destined to rejoin me and release the karma of past hurts. I'd even flattered myself that The One Source had set me this difficult task because I was equal to the challenge. But I wasn't unique and I wasn't special.

Garrick Leif had the same ability as me. I baulked at my own arrogance as helpless tears slid down my cheeks, washing away my conceit and my hope along with it. Was there any truth at all to what I'd believed? The truth, THE TRUTH! I wasn't even sure what that meant anymore... or what mine was. I felt completely lost.

I stared at the churning water and the remains of countless lives being dumped onto the shoreline. I hadn't asked for any of this. I had only ever tried to do what I thought was right... to go where I felt The Source was guiding me to go. How could everything I had believed be so disastrously wrong? I sank onto the salted trunk of an uprooted tree and sobbed.

This so-called *Gift* that Garrick and I shared had brought nothing but misery and destruction. It had turned me into someone I barely recognised. It had killed my mum and all of these people, and it had nearly killed me. I wanted no part of it anymore. I wasn't fit to wield this power or wise enough to be trusted with the manuscript's secrets. I had failed.

I turned my streaming eyes to the metallic sky and cried through gritted teeth, "This isn't a Gift, it's a curse!" My body trembled with grief and rage. It burned with the frustration of not knowing why Jay and I had been thrown together, or why my great-grandfather's manuscript had been handed to me, or why I had an ability that did nothing but hurt people. "Tell me why!" I screamed. The wind blew cold on my tears, drying them to a sticky web on my skin. The grey metal sky stared back, silent and unmoved. I spat a vow at the silver sun that I would never touch the manuscript again, my voice hard and my breathing ragged.

My heart squeezed in my chest. The only thing I was sure of was that I loved Jay. I had given myself to him body and Soul and now I was going to fail him too. I had given him my whole heart only to find that it was slowly killing me and tearing down my world. Yes, I loved Jay, but Garrick was proof that my ability to breach the veil and Travel to Earth, or bring Jay here, wasn't the result of our love for each other. The Source had not rearranged the laws of the universe so we could be reunited in love, as I'd foolishly believed. There wasn't any such thing as being fated to be together; fate was a fickle muse!

I was done dabbling in things I didn't understand. The human-like emotions that had continued to plague me were good for one thing. The unwavering light of my go-lite optimism had been extinguished and I could see my path with the clarity of cold steel. I had finally learned when to give up and let go. I knew what I had to do.

I cradled my gashed hand to my chest. I placed the other against cool, rough bark. I closed my eyes and breathed away the destruction that surrounded me. I breathed in the waiting stillness. My heart felt black; as empty as the void that rose up and enveloped me in endless silence. I floated slowly through the dark, wishing I could stay cradled in her softness and not wanting to face what I had to do.

As I drifted, it occurred to me that even this was dangerous. I stopped moving and hung nervously in empty ether. What if I was pulled through the veil at the very sight of him? What if I couldn't control my cursed power? I still didn't know exactly how it worked, only that the magnetic connection between Jay and I was so strong I could find him anywhere. I hadn't once practiced holding myself back from him and just observing through the veil as I once had as a Soul Guardian. I'd been more interested in flinging myself through to wherever he was and giving no thought to the consequences. I didn't even understand the mechanics of this cursed Gift and how it drew us together. I didn't understand what the bizarre beam of light in my heart meant or why the manuscript 'sang'. How could I hope to control something I didn't understand?

I drifted in circles, pushing my exhausted brain to come up with a plan. I remembered what it had felt like to see him through the veil before I'd mindlessly reached out and placed my hand over his heart. Tears brimmed in my eyes. The last thing I wanted was to say goodbye but I refused to engage with this ruinous power ever again and risk hurting anyone else I loved, including Jay. So goodbye was my only option. There could be no future for us and I needed to tell him that so he could move on with his life. And with that thought, my decision was made. I couldn't turn back now. I had to speak with him, risk be damned.

I felt into the space where my heart beat steadily and moved forward through the velvet void. I pictured Jay's face and within seconds a window wavered open before me. His tawny hair was mussed and crusted with salt. He lounged on his battered surfboard, his feet burrowed in white sand. My heart swelled and I choked back tears. I hesitated, hoping I wouldn't be overwhelmed and carried through the veil. I looked to my heart and found it beating faster but mercifully devoid of the strange beam of light. I stalled a moment more, to be completely certain that I wasn't going to be spontaneously sucked to Earth, and drifted forward. I hovered in front of the Earth window. It shone with the bright light of midday sun, a lone, shimmering circle in a sea of endless black. "Jay?"

His brown shoulders jumped at the sound of my voice and one side of his mouth tugged up in a relieved smile. His clear green eyes searched the empty sand and swept over the foaming waves, desperate for a glimpse of me.

"Close your eyes, Jay."

He obeyed. His gold lashes dipped and his smile bloomed with love as our eyes met. I felt his heart surge toward me, pulsing with want, and I threw up my hands in fear. "Stop, we can't."

The light drained from his eyes as he focussed on my tear stained cheeks and flat expression. "Lilly?" he swallowed. "What's wrong?"

"It's my mum," my voice cracked. "She died."

Shock and sadness carved lines into his olive skin. "Oh my God. Lilly, I'm so sorry."

"A hurricane caused a tidal wave that wiped out the seaside villages... and... and my mother..." A strangled sob wrenched up my throat. I hung my head, guilt, shame and grief tearing at my insides, as burning tears tracked down my cheeks. "She was there when it hit." I was choking on my own words.

Jay's eyes were wide, filling with unshed tears. "My beautiful girl, that's awful. Oh God, I wish I could hold you right now. I'm so sorry." His hands were clenching in fists, copper muscle straining in his arms. "I feel completely useless," he frowned, "when all I want is to be there for you."

I hung my head and a gigantic tear rolled off my cheekbone. It drifted languorously for a moment before disappearing into infinite black. "You can't."

"I know," he said hoarsely, "and it breaks my heart."

I stared at the green waves rolling rhythmically behind him, gulls wheeling overhead, and the pristine, gold sand stretching for miles. It was a stark contrast to the wreck of a beach at home. "I didn't know that Travelling to Earth was tipping our whole world off balance and messing with the weather. The storm hit right after I'd been with you at the water hole and now my mother is... gone. It's all my fault."

"What? No. I'm sure that can't be true."

"It is true. I've found out that I'm not the only person that can breach the veil. The Elders are saying that our powers are the emergence of a new *Gift*." I ground out the last word, hating the taste of it on my tongue. "It means that everything I believed about us wasn't true." It came out more harshly than I'd wanted and Jay stiffened. I was angry but I wasn't angry at him. He was yet another innocent victim of my stupidity and overzealous optimism.

"What do you mean, it wasn't true?"

"I love you Jay, with every piece of my heart." I did, and it felt like those pieces were about to be blown apart and swallowed by the blackness all around me. "But there isn't a future for us." I had to be honest and there was no way to soften the blow, even though I desperately wished there was.

He reeled back in shock, his face going slack. "What are you saying? I don't understand."

"Hundreds are dead, including my mother. This power that I have is dangerous... to you, to me, to everyone!"

Pain twisted his beautiful mouth and he squeezed his eyes shut. "I don't believe this."

"I'm so sorry, but I was wrong. This isn't just about you and me. There's a teenage boy who's been rescuing Earth animals and bringing them to Panacea with the same pointless power. And guess what? They're all dying because they don't belong here," I choked out a cynical laugh. "And he has go-lite deaths on his hands too, all because of this destructive power that has no good use!" I was breathing hard. Wild anger leaping under my skin. "I don't know how I'm ever going to forgive myself for what I've done. I still have to tell my father that I was responsible for Mum's death. How am I supposed to do that, Jay? How?"

Both of Jay's hands were pressed to his stricken face, his tear filled eyes trembled between his splayed fingers. He wiped away the tears and steadied himself. "Lilly, I'm so sorry about your mum," he shook his head, "but you can't blame yourself. You didn't know. *We* didn't know. And your dad, I don't know him but I know that he loves you, Lilly. He isn't going to blame you for this. Look, I can see how much you're hurting, so I understand that you want to give up, but I'm begging you not to. Don't give up on us. Not after everything we've been through."

He was trying so hard to control it, but his desperation clawed at my heart. "I know I promised you I would wait, and I would have. I would have waited for as long as it took because I love you that much. But that was before I knew the damage our love was causing, to us and to everyone else. Jay, I can't keep deciphering my great-grandad's manuscript and messing with a power this deadly just to find a way for us to have a happy ending. Every time the veil is breached, energy leaks through from Earth and who knows what destruction it will cause next? So in five, or ten, or twenty years when you're ready to ascend to Panacea, and you have to come through the veil, are you really prepared to sacrifice other people's lives just to be with me?"

His expression was vacant except for the pain in his eyes. The unwelcome reality was sinking in. He looked broken... again. He was wearing the same tortured look as when I'd first met him and my stomach dropped. I wanted to scream. Everything I had done had been for nothing. His heart had nearly mended and I'd just broken it all over again. "I can't tell you how sorry I am for sweeping you up in my naivety and convincing you that it was possible for us. I wanted it so badly, I still do, but I have to let you go."

He was blinking back tears and I wanted nothing more than to be able to hurl myself through the veil and crush him to me. To crush his sorrow. To wrap myself around him and never let him go. Then I remembered, I could do something even better.

I conjured every ounce of love I had for him and sent a wave of glittering energy through the veil. It encircled him in a gold mist and returned some of the life I had taken away. "I need you to understand that it was never my intention to leave you, Jay," I said softly. "I didn't make the promise lightly and even though we can't be together, I'll love you for the rest of this life and all my lives to come. I believe that we'll meet again," I smiled through my tears. "This just wasn't the right time for us after all."

He sat on his surfboard, stunned. He was completely still apart from the heavy heave of his chest.

When he eventually spoke, his voice was full of angry passion. "I want to say that I wouldn't care what I had to do to be with you, but you're right. Of course you're right; you always are," he laughed. "I understand why, but that doesn't mean we can't be friends. We can still talk to one another though the veil, can't we?"

I squeezed my eyes shut. This was absolute torture. How many blows would I have to deliver before he lost his will to keep on fighting? I released a heavy sigh, steeling myself to crush his last bit of hope. "You need to move on with your life, Jay, and so do I."

After what Jay had lived through, he was doggedly loyal. If I was always there, hovering in the fringes of his mind, he would never build a new life and I wasn't sure I could either. I knew I was doing us both a kindness, so why did it feel like cruelty?

"What? Never see you again? So you expect me to just forget about you? To pretend none of this ever happened?"

"We won't ever forget. Not even death made us do that. There'll be other lives and one of them will be the right time for us," I blinked away tears. "It's the only thing I believe in anymore."

"So, what? This is it?" he shrugged hopelessly. "There's nothing I can say or do to change your mind?"

"I'm sorry."

He stared deep into my eyes and the longing I saw there broke me in two. He tore his eyes open and stood, kicking at sand and staggered away to the water's edge. "But I love you, Lilly." He said it to the sea; he would no longer be able to see me with his gaze fixed on the ocean.

"And I love you. I'm so sorry, Jay." My heart broke as he continued to stare out at the roaring waves, his eyes like glass. I waited for it to sink in, all the while fighting back tears.

"Thank you." His voice was a flat whisper. "Thank you for all the ways that you've saved me, for everything you've done. You'll always have my heart."

I prayed he would close his eyes and look at me one last time, but he didn't and there was nothing else to say. I took a last, lingering look at his tousled blonde hair twisting on the breeze and his fathomless, sea green eyes. I blew him a kiss, retreated from his window and drifted backwards through the blackness, watching him fade. A jagged sob ripped up my throat as the the bright circle of light wavered, and then he was gone.

My eyes opened on a broken world. Mud and blood crusted my injured hand and it throbbed with a fiery pain. My heart twisted in the presence of the loss all around me and it broke for the absence of him. I would never see Jay again.

The sky had turned from silver to soot as the masked sun dipped lower. I sat frozen, unable to comprehend the mess of emotion raging inside me. If I wasn't so exhausted and drained of every last drop of energy, I would have screamed and pounded my fists on the tree trunk where I sat. I would have wept uncontrollably until the dark of night hid my guilt and pain. Instead, I was frozen. The devastating loss of my mother, of Jay, of myself and the life I'd once loved was screaming through me but I couldn't move. I couldn't speak. It even hurt to breathe.

Fear rose in a violent wave. I'd already lost so much of myself and I was terrified I was going to disappear entirely. The salty air felt like razor blades pushing in and out of my lungs. My heart was thumping irregularly against my ribs. "No," I shuddered. "I'm not going to disappear."

I fought against the panic attack and dug deep inside, searching for any last shred of my go-lite nature to cling to. I looked to my heart bursting with fear, where once there had only been love and compassion. I looked to my mind, that used to be still and focussed, now tormented by pain and grief. My energy field, still tattered here and there, was no longer a vibrant thing. It was as weak and dull as this sun's insipid light.

I was a complete wreck.

The full realisation of how far I'd sunk settled over me. My friends had raised warnings when they saw me going down and I hadn't listened. The truth was, I'd been lying on the ocean floor for a while. A despairing sob escaped me. *Please*, I begged The Source, *make me whole again, show me the way. Restore my light.*

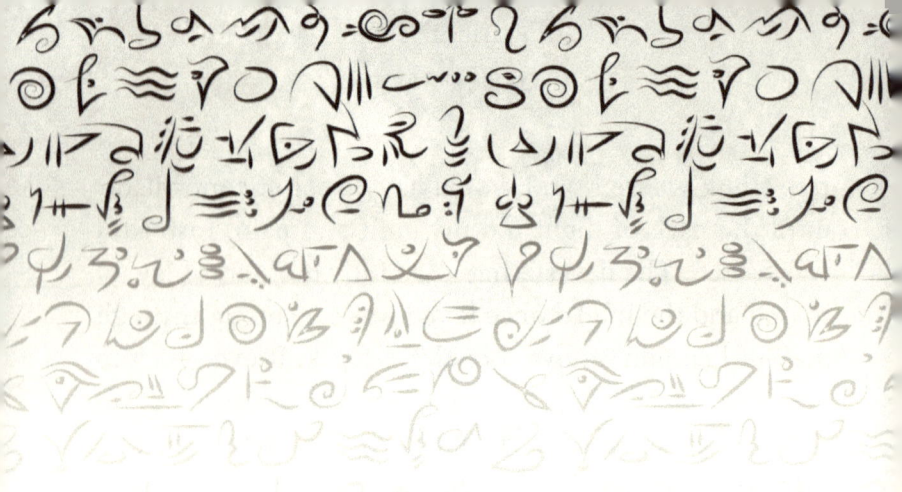

TWENTY-EIGHT

Lilly

A cord of white had unspooled through the streets of
Citrine. Thousands were dressed in the colour of the Soul,
winding in slow procession to The Butterfly Gardens to
farewell the dead. My father walked silently beside me; his
back straight, his face clear and blank, while my eyes were
raw and swollen from endless tears. I kept glancing at him
through the dark curtain of my hair, longing to feel like a
go-lite again. It wouldn't make the loss of my mother hurt
any less, but I would be able to bear the hurt with grace
instead of it eating me alive.

I could hear the swell of another *journey song*
travelling down the procession line.

"Shed the body, shed the mind,
and freedom fly you home.
Oh, shining Soul, less flesh and bone;
a piece of the Divine."

I tripped on a loose cobblestone as we approached the bridge. A broad palm caught me from behind and held me steady: *Christian.* Under normal circumstances he'd be teasing me for it - telling me there was no need to throw myself off a bridge because, 'of course he'd marry me.' There was no hint of humour when I turned to thank him. My mother was gone, my life had been torn apart and I saw the shadows of my grief mirrored in his grey eyes. I turned hastily away, unable to face the pain I saw there. He slipped his warm hand from my waist and fell back into step with his parents.

They'd arrived from Avani yesterday to say farewell to my mother. Despite the distance between my mum and Iris, they had remained the dearest of friends through years of separation. In my relatively short life, I'd managed to alienate my two closest friends with my misguided quest. I'd severed my friendship with Sky and I'd kept so many secrets from Christian that it didn't even feel like we were friends anymore, not the way we used to be.

"Are you okay, honey?" My dad reached for my hand.

"Sure, Dad. I'm fine." The truth was, I was feeling quite faint. I was walking among the countless people whose lives I had ruined and my mind was producing guilt much faster than I could battle it. The only thing forcing me to keep it together was my father.

We started up the gentle slope of the bridge. It

curved over the emerald waters of Ponderence River like a lover's arm. The sky above had been scrubbed clean by the raging storm and it outlined the candy coloured buildings in chilly blue. Flags of white silk fluttered in open windows, dancing this way and that; a tribute to the dead and a reminder that change is the only constant in life.

On the other side of the bridge, tree lined avenues led to the garden's iconic wrought iron gates. The butterfly's black filigree wings stood open in dark welcome. The towns people filed through in a ribbon of white, the *journey song* swelling brightly from their lips in a chorus of love and solidarity. Wisteria blooms of violet and blue hung heavy from the arbor, hugging us in their creamed vanilla scent. The mosaicked path to the garden's centre was lined on either side with slender, silver poles, their white flags surrendering to the will of the wind.

My father squeezed my hand as we approached the golden canopy the Projectors had created over the gathering crowd. It floated above us, a gauzy web of golden droplets that dripped peace and light onto everyone below. It was breathtaking – like a shimmering beaded chandelier. I looked up as a golden droplet fell in slow motion onto my forehead and dissolved to mist around me. Thank The Source for the Projectors. Maybe I could get through this after all.

The three Grand Masters stood before us, decked in their splendid white robes. At their feet was a small city of unlit candles standing in an uneven cluster in the deep, green grass. The crowd shuffled to form a ring around them. Three hundred and forty-seven candles for three hundred and forty-seven Souls; extinguished to mark their passing. *So many.*

The last chorus of the *journey song* subsided and Grand Master Trill stepped forward. "We gather to bid farewell to our friends and loved ones and offer our blessings and well wishes for their next lives. We thank them for the love and joy they have brought to us and we let them go with love."

The crowd responded as one. Their voices strong and sure. "We let them go with love."

"We thank them for the challenges and lessons they came to us to teach and for the part they played in helping us grow. We let them go with gratitude."

"We let them go with gratitude."

"We send to them our love and wishes for their highest and best, that they may travel swiftly back to The Source, to the heart of all creation and be made anew." Grand Master Trill's eyes danced with light and possibility.

Be made anew? I was still trying to accept that my mother was gone from this life, I hadn't even begun to consider what her next would look like. Would I see her again? And would I know her if I did? Would I pass a child on the street one day and be filled with an all-consuming pull of recognition that draws me nearer, that tells me not to walk on by? When I look into that child's eyes will I know her?

A small sob broke through my barrier and my dad moved to put his arm around me. I should have been looking after him. This was, after all, my fault. Another droplet of gold fell from the canopy above and exploded around us in a golden mist. "Do you think we'll ever see her again?"

My father's smile was sad but his eyes were filled with a ferocious, unwavering love, "Source willing, my little flower. But if she's destined to ascend to the next world, you and I have some catching up to do."

"Do you think she'll be reborn on Utopia?"

"If she is, I pray The Source bless her and keep her."

I felt numb. The world kept turning around me while I remained still, locked in my grief as surely as a body frozen beneath the ice.

Grand Master Trill was offering the final blessing. "May The Source grant them the courage to walk through their new lives with grace, carrying with them the wisdom gathered from the old. Should they return to us, let us welcome them with open arms, and if it is their destiny to rise and leave Panacea behind, may their Souls light a new world."

"May their Souls light a new world."

Flourishing notes from a harpairre rolled through the air. A young girl sat astride the glistening blue instrument, her fingers flying over the strings.

Grand Master Mont straightened his robes and opened his arms to the assembly. "Would a representative from each family please come forward to bear the flame."

An elderly gentleman stooped to retrieve a candle from the ground. The Grand Masters embraced him in turn, murmuring words of comfort. As he faced the crowd the Elementals ignited his candle to signify the beginning of a new life. He shielded the flame with a wrinkled hand while tears lit his eyes. One by one, people came forward and flames sprang to life.

"Will you do the honour, my little flower?"

"No, Dad. It should be you," I shook my head.

He nodded once and kissed my cheek.

We walked in a reverent line, nursing our white candles against the breeze, out the garden's gates and down the long avenue to the river's edge. Chris and his parents followed behind us. At the water's edge were hundreds of tiny bamboo rafts, adorned with fresh flowers, carrying coloured glass lanterns to house our candles. Chris silently took my hand as I negotiated my way down the slippery bank. It was warm around my cold, clammy fingers. I gave him a grateful smile when we reached the bottom and he turned to let go and make his way back up the bank.

"Chris," I tightened my grip, "please stay."

He squeezed my hand and turned compassionate eyes on my father. He was squatted by the emerald water. He'd chosen a raft with clusters of wild jasmine and peace lilies wreathing a rosy red lantern. I smiled at his choice.

"It reminds me of her. She was pure and graceful – an endless source of peace to me." There was so much love in his voice. "And she was passionate, always in love with life. Her heart shone through everything she did."

Tears spilled down my cheeks and I went to his side, wrapping my arms around him and holding tight. "She was beautiful," I cried into his shoulder.

"She really was," Chris echoed.

"She had the most perfect name. My darling, Dawn." He laughed through his tears. "She was my sun, never failing to rise." He clutched the candle close to his chest.

"Oh, Dad." I stroked his cheek. "I know how much you miss her. I do too."

The smile he turned on me was dazzling. Full of comfort and warmth, even now. I had always thought of my father as pure sunshine. I had never realised that he'd had a sun all of his own.

He lowered the candle into the lantern – lovingly, carefully – and closed the door. The red glass glowed, like something vital, alive. The white flame burnt steadily inside. I started at it, entranced. It reminded me of how my heart had glowed, lit from within, when that brilliant beam of light was about to surge forth. I still had no idea what it meant. I sighed and felt my heart flutter in my chest. Whatever it had been, it didn't matter now. I was done tinkering with that destructive power.

Together, my dad and I gave the raft a gentle push away from the bank. We stood and watched as the green current drew it upstream to join the others. Hundreds of coloured lanterns winking in the afternoon light, glowing with the love we felt for those we had lost. I couldn't remember the river ever looking so beautiful. The fragile rafts teetered and drifted as they balanced their precious flames. Spiralling trails of petals fell in their wake, swirling in the eddying waters. They glided in ever-changing patterns, coming together in one moment and drifting apart the next, urged on by the current in an unpredictable, mesmerising dance. *Just like life,* I thought.

Chris found me sitting in the doorway of our hollowed out tree, the skirt of my white memorial dress covered in dead leaves and dirt. I'd ripped off my shoes half way across the back yard and thrown them in the direction of the creek. The calm conversation around my mother's table, serving the Palladens tea from her favourite tea service, had become more than I could bear. Chris had had the good sense to leave me be for twenty minutes or so before he came after me. My polite smiles might have convinced his parents that I just needed some air but he knew me better.

He stopped ten paces away from me, his hands jammed into the pockets of his white trousers. "Coming or going?"

"What?"

He jerked his chin at the hollow tree behind me and the dark doorway we had fancied led to other worlds. "Have you just come back from somewhere or are you deciding where to go? Be warned: if you tell me you've been to chocolate land without me I might start to question our friendship."

"Don't you already?" I mumbled, too low for him to hear.

"So," he quirked a brow, "coming or going?"

"I don't think there's any place real or imaginary that would let me escape from how I feel right now." I'd already decided that after Chris' parents had left I would tell my father the truth. I was sure that after Garrick's confession, my father, Chris and the whole Council already knew I must possess the same Gift. I felt sick with nerves and tortured by guilt but he deserved to hear the facts from my own lips. He needed to know that I had caused Mum's death.

I tossed aside the stick I'd snapped into a million pieces and looked up into Chris' kind, grey eyes. Christian – faithful, stoic, Christian – I would need to confess what he already knew. He had come to my house and told me everything he'd discovered at The Council meeting. He had invited me to open up to him right before my Dad called with the awful news. If it hadn't been for my mother's death I was sure I'd have been brought before The Council for questioning by now. I wondered how far my grace period of mourning would extend?

I looked at Chris and braced myself to admit my big secret. His eyes were soft as mist, his face even softer; it didn't bear a single line of thought or worry. A lick of his raven black hair danced forward in the breeze and tickled at his brow. The dusky sunlight limned his silhouette in gold. He was beautiful, standing there: relaxed, sure and gloriously open. He was everything that I was not, a painful reminder of all I had lost. "I'm a sorry excuse for a go-lite these days," I spat a derisive laugh.

"You're energy field is still healing. You can't treat yourself so harshly when you're still unwell."

"If I'm unwell it's because I deserve it. This is all my fault." Wretched tears brimmed in my eyes until Chris' soft face was a blur. I bent my head and wiped them away on my filthy skirt. When I looked up, he was sitting in the dirt beside me, his expression open and neutral. I could hardly stand to meet his gaze and I wanted to shrink back from the love I knew he would always have for me, no matter what. I didn't deserve it. I didn't deserve *him*, or my parents, or Sky, or any of the people I had hurt with my reckless decision making and arrogant stupidity. Without them, I had nothing else to lose. "Aren't you going to ask me *why* it's all my fault?"

"No," he said simply, his calm grating against my impatience, "if you want to tell me, you will."

"How very noble of you," I frowned. "Christian Palladen; protector of the misguided and hopeless."

"Is that how you feel? Misguided and hopeless?"

I suddenly found his eternal patience maddening. "It's not what I feel, it's what I am. I've never been as balanced and wise as you, or sharp and strong like Sky; I ruin everything I touch. I'm a complete failure. The Source gave me a mission and I've not only failed, I've caused death and destruction. Hundreds of people are dead because of me! My... my mother... I killed her!" The words scraped up my throat like I was coughing up razor blades. My chest was heaving.

I could feel Chris wrapping an energetic blanket of calm around my shoulders while he remained quiet and contained. I wanted to pull it over my head, crawl inside the tree hollow and lay in there forever. Instead, I buried my face in my hands. I had the sensation again that my grief and shame were consuming me, towering over the girl I once was and blotting out my connection to the light.

The thought filled me with violent rage. I was so sick and tired of feeling like a human, of letting my emotions dictate and control who I was.

I would not let this pain be bigger than me!

I would not let myself disappear!

I tore my hands away from my face and met Christian's patient gaze with blazing defiance. "I have the same Gift as Garrick!" I blurted.

I saw a look of relief bloom on his face and watched as clouds cleared from his eyes. There. No more secrets. Now he'd heard it confirmed that I could transport beings from Earth and pierce the veil to cross into their world at will. I watched him, looking for any signs of hurt or betrayal and found none. I wanted him to be angry at me; as angry as I was at myself.

Finally, he spoke. "And you think that using your power caused the tidal wave?" he asked carefully.

"I know it did because I was with Jay right before the storm hit."

He frowned at me in confusion. "So what?" he shook his head. "What does your boyfriend have to do with any of this?"

"He has everything to do with it because I was with him... *on Earth.*"

He sucked in a gasp. "Are you telling me that you somehow managed to transport Jay to Earth with you?"

I took a deep breath and slowly shook my head. "No, Christian. That's not what I'm saying."

He stared at me through narrowed eyes. "Then how did you..." A wave of shock and understanding washed over him. His jaw went slack and he closed his eyes, tipping his face skyward. "Your boyfriend is human," he breathed. "Which is why none of us have met him and why he wasn't here supporting you today. And your energy field is torn because you've been going to Earth to see him." He opened his eyes and turned to me. "Oh, Lilly."

I had expected judgement - although I had no idea why - maybe because I wanted to be judged and held accountable for everything I'd done. I hadn't expected the concern and empathy pouring out of Chris and pricking fresh tears in my eyes. I forced down my pain and guilt and glared at him. The only strength I had left inside me was broiling anger and if that's what it took to get through this, I would use it. "Don't look at me like that," I seethed. "I'm the last person to deserve your pity."

He immediately smoothed his expression to placid neutrality and leaned back against the tree trunk.

Self hatred was radiating from my pores. "And you don't have to worry about me hurting anyone else. When you told me about Garrick and I understood what had been happening, and then my Mum..., I broke up with Jay. It's finished. It was stupid of me to think... plain naive... reckless... completely stupid."

Chris was silent, his breathing even. I could hear the occasional trickle of water from a nearby bend in the creek. A cold breeze had picked up as dusk approached and started turning the world to gold. It blew into the hollow tree like a flute, stirring an eerie note.

When I couldn't stand his calm silence any longer I jumped to my feet. "I thought you were supposed to be some kind of Soul Guardian superstar," I taunted. "Aren't you going to say anything to me? Don't you have any wisdom or comfort to offer a person who caused the death of their mother and hundreds of other people?"

I was practically yelling at him and he wasn't even ruffled. His grey eyes held me fast. "You aren't ready to be offered comfort. You want someone to be angry at and to sit through your anger with you."

The look he gave me was so gentle and kind that I felt my anger melting at the edges. I couldn't let that happen. "Fine!" I spat. "Then what would you say to me if I *was* ready?"

"I'd say you can't know for certain that the tidal wave was triggered by your trip to Earth."

"You can't be certain that it wasn't. So how do I live with that? How can I ever forgive myself?"

He laced his fingers together and looked me dead in the eyes. "I would tell you that there's nothing to forgive because you're not that powerful." His low, velvet voice, so soothing; like the peaceful rhythm of a metronome, was at complete odds with what he was saying.

"Nothing to forgive?" I exploded. "How can you say that?"

"We are instruments, Lilly, all of us. We don't decide who lives and who dies, and dying isn't anyone's fault. It was time for those Souls to leave this life and go on to a new one. Will we miss them? Yes. Do we wish we could have held them back? No. Because we know – I know that you still know – that they aren't gone; they've just stepped ahead of us to become something more."

I closed my eyes and breathed in the smell of the trees. Christian's words cradled my breaking heart, giving me pause, caressing the memory of an unshakeable faith in The Source's plan for us all. "To rise higher, to live brighter," I whispered. The rage drained from my body and my face fell flat. I could feel a faint softness unfurling in my chest as Chris rose to his feet and took hold of my hands. It was a mere wisp of what it felt like to be a go-lite, but it was there. I cried out in sweet elation, scrambling to hold onto that feeling, trying to cling to the memory of who I had been. A small safe space had opened in my chest. It was soft and warm and fragile as an eggshell and I could feel it was already beginning to crack. I panicked and lunged to hold it together but my grasping only made it shatter.

Despair came crashing through me, and with it, my descent back into negativity. I tore my hands away from Chris and started for the creek. I needed space. Tears were streaming down my face and I didn't even know when they'd started. "I want to be alone, Christian. Please just go."

"Your mum loves you, Lilly, so much."

I stopped short, my heart twisting in my chest and I began to sob. "Just go," I yelled at him over my shoulder. "Please!"

Source save me, I wasn't strong enough to feel this pain. If I let it all out I would drown in it. I swiped angrily at my face and made myself stop crying. *I will not disappear.*

I didn't turn as Chris walked away. I drew on my anger and wore it like armour. Right now, I couldn't afford to let anything in or allow anything out. It was the only way I could manage to hold myself together. *I will not let this pain be bigger than me.*

I knew how nasty I had been to Chris... and Sky. I'd even been wondering if I had been harsh when I broke up with Jay. I honestly didn't know anymore. The only thing I knew was that I was sick of hurting people. Without the benefit of my go-lite nature, I was next to useless. I needed a way to cope with the endless onslaught of guilt and pain. If I hardened myself to these wretched, overwhelming emotions and didn't allow them through, I could at least keep functioning. I just needed to hold on until my energy field was completely healed and pray that once it had, I'd be back to normal. I was desperate to feel like a go-lite again.

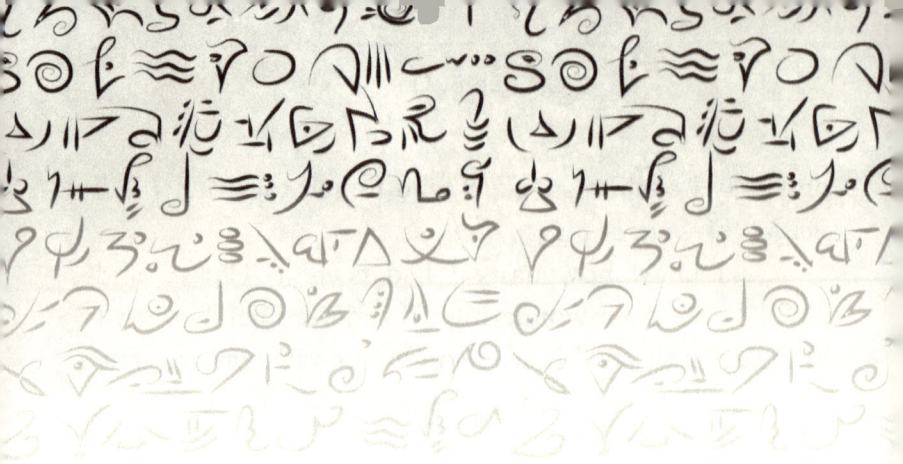

TWENTY-NINE

Lilly

Weeks passed and I barely left the house, except to sit at the bank of the creek and spend hours watching dragonflies. And of course, my father made sure I attended all of my healing appointments at healaxis. Healer Cray said I was getting better. The tears in my energy field were completely healed, so why did my emotions still feel more human than go-lite? I wasn't the out-of-control mess that I had been but I still didn't feel like myself either.

My uniter was overflowing with messages from Chris and Sky. I had ignored them all. There it went again, humming insistently from my night stand. I dragged myself off the bed, plucked it up, and didn't so much as look at it before I hurled it out the open window. It skidded to a stop by the lavendulum bush at the edge of my mother's herb garden. "Lilly isn't here!" I yelled after it.

My dad made frequent offers to Syphon away my bad moods and every time I refused. It had begun as a sad form of self-punishment but now my refusals were purely for scientific reasons. I was keeping a close eye on my reactions and feelings, looking for proof that I was getting better, but so far my observations had been disappointing to say the least. I had not improved as I should have and in order to prevent myself from going to pieces over it, I'd adopted a new strategy to cope. Self ridicule, I had discovered, was highly preferable to crying about my behaviour. It was also fun. "Eleven fifty a.m," I reported out loud to no-one but myself, "adverse emotional reaction: Lilly Broken Brain violently rejects messages of support and kindness from stupidly perfect friends. Result? Threw her uniter *and* their stupid kindness out the window with dramatic gusto. Emotional state post event?" A grim, satisfied smirk twisted my lips, which was answer enough. My rebellious outburst would make me feel happy for a short while, at least.

My unfailingly supportive father had made no move to protest my methods. He didn't make well-timed suggestions for me to call my friends or ask when I planned on returning to my studies at magistrument. He gave me the space that I needed and I repaid him by keeping the house spotlessly clean and preparing all of our meals.

The day after my mum's memorial I'd pulled myself together long enough to tell him the entire, shameful truth about my power and the destruction it had wrought. I told him of my efforts to decipher Grayson's manuscript, and finally, about Jay.

"You've always been extraordinary," he'd said after listening silently to my lengthy confession. "Your mother knew it too." His hazel eyes had glistened, brimming with love as he'd pulled me into a warm embrace.

"But Dad," I'd objected, "I think I caused it. I used my power to visit Jay and then the tidal wave hit. Mum is gone because of me." I could barely speak around the lump in my throat. I'd thought it would choke me.

"No, my little flower," my father's face bloomed with compassion. "Your mother is gone because it was time for her to move on. There isn't any reason to assign fault or blame because there's nothing wrong in it. It's funny," he'd mused, his hazel eyes glittering, "life begins in much the same way for all of us but there are countless ways it can end. Who are we to judge that one manner of leaving a life is better than another? Would you miss her any less if she'd died in her bed at eighty?"

I shook my head miserably.

"You've been given a powerful Gift, Lilly. You can't blame *it* or yourself for your mother's death or anyone else's."

A part of me still did, though. My father and Christian could spout go-lite wisdom at me until I was wrinkled and grey, it didn't change the fact that I'd vowed to never use my baneful *Gift* again, or go near Great-grandfather's manuscript, and I absolutely never would.

As though the pernicious thing could hear my thoughts, a single, high-pitched note drilled down the hallway and through my bedroom door. "For pity's sake, leave me be!" It had been getting worse. Its piercing tone woke me night after night until I'd eventually banished it to the study, burying it back under the pile of books it had come from.

I'd begun to imagine the manuscript as a sentient being, with thoughts and intentions and a will of iron. I'd never understood why it sometimes chose to hum and sing and I had zero interest in finding out now, but boy, it was persistent! It's call had started out as a soothing hum that built to a sweet angelic note. It was enchanting and alluring, but also easy to ignore. As the days and weeks passed while I wallowed and lamented how far I'd fallen, it was as though it had grown impatient with me, demanding that I open its dusty cover and give it my undivided attention. I, of course, had continued to refuse. I wasn't going to be bullied by a wilful, whining book and I wanted nothing more to do with it. Half the reason I spent hours idling by the creek was to escape its piercing, persistent calls. Clearly I needed to do a better job of burying it, if only to spare a distant, future relative the same grief it had brought to me, or at the very least, save them from hearing damage.

I marched down the hall and flung open the study door. Some papers stirred on my father's desk and the ringing note abruptly ceased. "Are you kidding me?" I growled. I loomed furiously in the doorway, my eyes shooting daggers at the teetering stack of books shoved into the far corner. "You wanted me? Well, I'm here. Happy now?"

I went over and started dismantling the stack. "Eleven fifty-nine a.m. – driven crazy by a whining book, Lilly Broken Brain embarks on a quest to rid her world of its evil." I'd hidden it close to the bottom of the stack and I could see its worn leather binding, thin as paper, poking out from under a heavy volume with a red and gold spine. I reached for it, my hands started tingling before I even touched it. I slid it free and the familiar smell of deep, herbal green wafted through the room, overpowering the lingering scent of my father's aftershave and the wall of old books bulging from the shelves. I tucked it under my arm and made a beeline for the garden.

I pushed open the door of the rickety garden shed, wiping away cobwebs and sending spiders skittering up into the rafters. Squinting into the dim, cramped space, I scanned the shelves. My mum's gardening tools and gloves were arranged neatly next to an odd assortment of flowerpots, cans of paint and rusted tools. A chest with layers of peeling pink paint was stowed under the work bench - my old toy chest. I opened the lid and found what I was looking for. My dad had given me the metal lockbox when I was five or so to store my prized rocks and shells. I measured the journal against it. Yes, it would do nicely. I searched the dim, dusty corners of the shed. There was only one more thing I needed to make this ordeal end – a shovel.

I marched out into the sunlight, armed and determined. I was going to bury this burden and put the whole mess behind me and I was going to make sure I buried it deep, where it could never hurt anyone again. I speared the shovel into the ground so hard that it jarred my arms and rattled my teeth. I drove my foot down on the blade and heaved up piles of crumbling, ochre earth. Then I did it again... and again... and again until my muscles were trembling and sweat ran into my eyes. "This ends now!" I promised the manuscript laying inert behind me. I blew messy strands of dark hair from my eyes and could feel a hard, victorious smile twisting my lips. "I won't let you cause any more ruin in my life. So you can sing and whine all you want but no one is going to hear you! Not ever again!"

"Lilly?"

I froze.

"What in The Source's name are you doing?"

I turned, breathless, the shovel dangling from my aching arm. My father was examining me as though I'd finally lost my mind – maybe I had – and next to him, *Source preserve me,* was Elder Tunes. He was standing with his hands tucked into the pockets of his mulberry waistcoat, grinning broadly. The white wisps of hair on top of his head were barely level with my dad's shoulder, yet he took up the space of a giant. My father stared at the lockbox lying open on the ground with the manuscript stuffed inside. I was covered in dirt and panting with effort as he raked me with an astonished look. In that moment I was very much wishing I'd dug a larger hole so I could quietly slip into it and disappear. There was a moment of uneasy silence, punctuated by the twitter of birds.

"How wonderful!" Elder Tunes declared in a fit of argent enthusiasm. "A perfectly splendid day to dig a hole." He cheerfully surveyed the rippling blue sky and chuckled quietly to himself.

Now it was my turn to stare. I opened my mouth, "I..." and closed it again. *Was he serious?*

My father, too, was staring at him in confusion.

Elder Tunes seemed unperturbed. "What buried treasure are we hoping to find?" A look of quiet mischief flashed in his glacial blue eyes then stilled when he saw the manuscript lying in the box next to the hole. "Ah, I see."

"I'm not sure that I do," my dad plucked the book from its makeshift coffin and brushed a few clumps of dirt from the cover. "This was my grandfather's, Lilly. If you no longer want it, we could donate it to the historical archives at Ophanim Dome."

"Oh." A shameful blush coloured my face. I was so intent on getting rid of it that I hadn't stopped to think of the journal's importance to my father. It was a part of our family history.

"Elder Tunes and I have just come from a Council meeting. He asked if he could pay you a visit," my father explained, trying to will a coherent response from me. I was tongue tied with embarrassment and couldn't think of a single thing to say.

Elder Tunes kept grinning and rocked back and forth on his heels. "I was so sorry to hear that you'd been unwell, my dear. Your father tells me your energetic field is quite back to normal now. I'm so very glad to hear it."

I nodded dumbly at him and he turned to my dad.

"Elder Flights, would you mind terribly if I took another look at your grandfather's book? Such a wondrous mind," he bubbled. "And could I bother you for a glass of cool water? I'm feeling rather parched." He ran his chubby hand over his bald patch, smoothing wisps of snowy white hair.

"Of course," my father handed over the manuscript, smiled and disappeared up the back steps into the house.

I felt ridiculous, standing there covered in dirt and hanging onto the shovel like it was my only friend.

"By all means, carry on if you wish," he urged placidly, "I've no desire to stop you. I've always found digging to be a marvellous way to clarify the mind."

"You mean you don't care if I bury it?" I said aghast.

"I care a great deal, but truths cannot be unearthed unless one digs for them first and it seems, this is the perfect day for digging." He wasn't taking in the splendour of our surroundings this time, he was looking at me, and I knew that what he saw was anguish and torment.

I straightened my spine and levelled my gaze. "Elder Tunes, I do not care about digging up *truths* or secrets or risking my life on misguided missions anymore. That book has brought nothing but misery and I want it gone from my life." I jabbed a finger at the repulsive article held against the fine weave of his mulberry waistcoat.

His clear eyes examined me closely and I was certain they missed nothing. They seemed to drink in my entire being. "As you will," he nodded sagely after a time. "It is not for me to decide, and in any case, I am not in full possession of the facts."

"What do you mean?"

"Well, I wonder, what might have spurred you to do away with the book in such a dramatic fashion?" He gave me a ponderous look and then considered the manuscript held lightly in his hands. The dark, worn leather seemed to drink in the sunlight, taking on a ruddy hue. He balanced its weight on his palm and smoothed his other hand over the dilapidated cover. My own fingers tingled, as though they yearned to touch the pages. His eyes fixed on it with burning curiosity and I could feel a hum building in the air.

"Please, Elder Tunes, don't."

But he was already peeling back the cover.

"Stop. I beg you. Just leave it be."

The hum built to a sustained, liquid note. *No!* I cursed the manuscript, *Never again!* I gritted my teeth as the sound tried to insinuate its way into my energy field, pressing at the very edges of me. The shovel left my hand and fell to the lawn, although I didn't hear it hit the ground.

"Whatever is the matter, Child?" Elder Tunes took a concerned step toward me, his bushy, white eyebrows knitted with confusion. It was clear he couldn't hear it – the persistent note that was climbing higher, setting my teeth on edge and pressing down on my body.

"Please, get it away," I panted. My eyes were riveted to the manuscript laying open in Elder Tunes' hands, its pages fluttering in the breeze.

The sound was growing louder, more intense. I felt like I was being squeezed, as though I were sinking to the bottom of the ocean, the pressure forcing the air from my lungs and slowly crushing my bones.

My dad appeared at the foot of the steps, a water glass in hand. He took in my panicked expression and ran for me, the glass tumbling into the grass. "Sweetheart, what's happening?" His face was imploring, his hazel eyes alight with fear, darting over my body, searching for the source of my panic.

I clamped my hands over my ringing ears. "Make it stop!" I pleaded. It was shrill, piercing, like a spike had been shoved into one ear and pushed out through the other. I couldn't stand it anymore. I couldn't make it stop and I couldn't keep it out.

My vision blurred as the wave of sound built to

an unbearable crescendo and blasted through my energy field, sending a shock wave through my body. I reeled from the force of it and my father caught me roughly in his arms. My head lolled against his chest and when I looked up I saw his stricken face through hazy vision. I watched helplessly as his lips formed rapid, urgent questions, none of which I could hear. It all sounded like muffled gibberish.

Whatever was happening to me, it wasn't over, not yet. I'd barely caught my breath when I felt something changing. Instead of pressure bearing down on me from without, now it was building within. *Oh, no. Source help me.* I felt like I was being turned inside out. I tried to keep my eyes open and focus on my dad. I still couldn't speak. Tears were blurring his eyes as he cradled my head in the crook of his arm.

My skin prickled, but not just the tingling in my hands and fingertips that happened when I was close to the manuscript, now every inch of my skin felt electrified. Suddenly, I felt like I was burning. My heart was beating furiously in my chest like it had sprouted enormous, fiery wings. *Whump... whump... whump.* A blazing heat fanned from my heart, the higher and faster it flew. My blood was molten, throbbing through my veins and igniting my body in a map of liquid fire.

My eyes fluttered closed. My father was shaking me but I didn't have breath to speak or the ability to make my tongue form words. My knees buckled and I slipped from his arms, my knees crashing into the dirt. I desperately wanted to lay down, to feel stable ground underneath me, but the pressure building inside wouldn't allow it. It surged and swelled, pushing my body to remain upright, rigid even, as though I had been a deflated balloon and was now being pumped full. Kneeling in the dirt, held up by invisible strings, I felt myself expanding more and more until I thought I would burst.

I was petrified but I was also angry. I had not chosen whatever it was that was taking over my body without my permission. Hadn't I given enough? Hadn't I lost enough already?

All I could hear was the booming of my heart as it pumped violently in my chest, battering against my ribs. I needed to see what was happening to it so I forced down my fear and dared to engage my inner sight. I held back my tears and my terror as I took a shaking breath and I looked.

It was glowing a fiery, ruby red and there, coiled at its centre, was a filament of white light, fine as angels hair. It stretched and moved, stirring with each jarring heartbeat and I shuddered in fear at the sight of it. *No!* I screamed in my mind. *I want nothing to do with any of this!*

The light didn't listen.

It reared back and struck at my heart's wall with viperous speed, sending a fissure across its surface like a crack in overheated glass. Blinding white seeped through as though my heart was bleeding silver. A needle point of light snaked through the crack, and without warning, expanded to the width of my wrist. I cried out in alarm and watched in helpless horror as I realised what was about to happen.

I found my voice. "I don't want this!" I screamed, but the light's will was stronger. My anger and defiance immediately shrivelled in my chest, overruled by the inviolable power that was determined to emerge. I felt as though I was being torn apart as my broken heart sounded a ground shaking boom. The fist of light punched through my ribcage and out of my chest, and raced forth in a blinding flash. My eyes flew wide and the air whooshed from my lungs.

For a few weighted seconds, the world ceased to be while I was rendered blind and deaf. And then... there was an all-consuming stillness. The chaos was over and peace had taken its place. I felt suspended in it – weightless as a rainbow hanging in the sky. Miraculously, I was still on my knees, gasping in ragged breaths. I squinted against the harsh light and could just make out silhouettes of my father and Elder Tunes shrinking back and shielding their eyes.

For a moment I thought the sky had fallen down and that we were standing in a nebula of stars. I blinked through the sparkling glare and dropped my eyes to my chest. A thick beam of brilliant silver light was emanating from my heart and arcing up to the heavens. I traced its path past the tall treetops, curving up over peaks of the mountain range and disappearing through the clouds to mingle with sunlight. I stared at it in shock and awe. As my eyes adjusted, I could see that it moved subtly and glowed with a powder fine dust that twinkled like distant stars.

"Lilly!" My dad was beside me, his hand hesitant on my shoulder. "Great Source above! Are you all right?"

I nodded at the sky, unable to take my eyes off the softly shifting silver beam. "I tried to make it stop and I couldn't," I blinked; stupefied.

My heart was beating a steady, healthy rhythm. The unbearable, piercing whine from the manuscript had mercifully cut off at some point. My body was no longer a source of billowing heat and liquid fire, but there was a stream of shocking silver flaring from my heart and streaking across the sky like the glittering tail of a comet!

Elder Tunes shuffled forward and smiled at me with shining eyes. He regarded me with the same tenderness that you might a baby bird and he looked... *proud*. "It wouldn't have mattered how hard you tried to hold it back, my dear. You can't stop your destiny. The Source has blessed you with a powerful Gift. You could no sooner stop using it than stop the ocean tide. It is a part of you." He reached a wondering hand toward the silver stream and passed his fingertips through shifting starlight. "It's truly beautiful," he marvelled. "Like a silver cord."

"But I don't want this power," I told him with

wide, blinking eyes. "I'm a Healer. I want to save lives, not destroy them, and from what I've seen of this so-called *Gift,* it does nothing but cause harm." I eyed it warily. Now that it had been switched on, I had no idea how to turn it off.

Elder Tunes waved a dismissive arm. "A pen can cause harm if I use it incorrectly. We must learn to respect the instruments given to us. I believe, that with patience and the proper guidance, the purpose of your Gift will be revealed. It has been given to you for a reason."

"Did you know this would happen?" I glanced at the stream still spilling from my chest.

Elder Tunes shook his head. "I felt strongly guided to see the manuscript. I had no idea what I would find, or indeed, that it would lead us here. I know now that I've been placed here to help you." He held the manuscript between us like a peace offering and his eyes filled with such love and compassion that it moved me to tears. "After all you've been through, it may seem as though you've tried your very best and failed, but you haven't even scratched the surface of what's possible, not yet. We must dig more holes, Miss Flights," he sparkled with excitement and conviction, "just as we have this afternoon! The Source has a task for us, and you can protest all you like, my dear," he grinned at the glittering silver cord pouring from my heart, "but it appears, that now, the time is right and you are finally ready to begin."

DID YOU LIKE THIS BOOK?

YOU CAN MAKE

A BIG

DIFFERENCE.

An author's success or failure rests in the hands of the reader. That's right! It all comes down to how many people show the love. Most people don't know that authors are 100% dependent on ratings for their work to be validated by retailers and allowed to show up in search results. Here's why: there are currently over 7 million books on Amazon alone and a book needs a minimum of 20 ratings to be included in search results – which may not sound like many, but trust me, for indie authors that's a real struggle to obtain when on average, only 1 in every 100 readers leaves a star rating. The more ratings and reviews your book has, the more visible it is, and the more people can discover your work. So if you'd like to support the authors you love, and make sure they're still around to keep writing amazing stories, take a few minutes to leave them a star rating or an honest review. Never underestimate the power of those tiny gold stars!!! So go forth! Spread the love! And let your favourite authors know you're rooting for them.

Gabriel x
www.gabriellea-author.com

GET THE FIRST BOOK FOR FREE

Visit www.gabriellea-author.com to receive your **FREE** copy of *The Guardian's Soul*, book zero in *The Lost Souls series*, plus your very own full colour illustrated copy of The Soul Guardian's Code, plus a replica of the original monograph indexing all known go-lite powers. Get everything you need to dive into Lilly's world and discover what happened 15 years ago when memories of Jay and Lilly's previous life together were still fresh in her mind... that is, until a powerful spell changed everything.

www.ingramcontent.com/pod-product-compliance
Lightning Source LLC
Chambersburg PA
CBHW030647120726
47905CB00001B/89